AN AWARD—WINNING LITERARY CAREER

From the start of her writing career, Joyce Carol Oates has earned high literary awards, among them a Guggenheim Fellowship, the Richard and Hinda Rosenthal Foundation Award of the National Institute of Arts and Letters and, in 1975, the Lotos Club Award of Merit. For her novel *Them* she won the National Book Award in 1970. Her novel *Do With Me What You Will* was a major selection of the Literary Guild of America and *The Assassins* and *Childwold* were both Featured Alternates of that book club.

Ms. Oates was a First Prize winner of the O. Henry Awards and her work has been included for many years in the *O. Henry Prize Stories*. In connection with these awards, she was selected for a Special Award for Continuing Achievement.

Ms. Oates is Professor of English at the University of Windsor.

THE SEDUCTION
&
OTHER STORIES

Joyce Carol Oates

FAWCETT CREST • NEW YORK

THE SEDUCTION & OTHER STORIES

THIS BOOK CONTAINS THE COMPLETE TEXT OF THE
ORIGINAL HARDCOVER EDTION

Published by Fawcett Crest Books, a unit of CBS Publica-
tions, the Consumer Publishing division of CBS Inc.

Copyright © 1965, 1966, 1968, 1970, 1971, 1972, 1973, 1974,
1975 by Joyce Carol Oates

ISBN: 0-449-24284-6

Printed in the United States of America

First Fawcett Crest Printing: April 1980

10   9   8   7   6   5   4   3   2   1

Grateful acknowledgement is made to the following magazines, which first printed these stories (usually in somewhat different form): *Triquarterly*, "An American Adventure" and "Notes on Contributors" (Winter 1971); *The Kenyon Review*, "Gifts" (Fall 1966); *The Antioch Review*, "Splendid Architecture" (Fall 1968); *The South Carolina Quarterly*, "On the Gulf" (Fall 1974); *Playgirl*, "Getting and Spending" (February–March 1973); *The Southern Review*, "The Seduction" (published under the title "Help....") (Summer 1974); *The Partisan Review*, "Passions and Meditations" (Vol. XL, no. 3, 1973); *Redbook*, "6.27 P.M." (December 1971); *The Virginia Quarterly Review*, "Out of Place" (Summer 1968); *The Carolina Quarterly*, "Double Tragedy Strikes Tennessee Hill Family" (Winter 1972); *The Quarterly Review of Literature*, "The Stone House" (Vol. XIII, no. 3/4, 1965).

"The Dreaming Woman" was published (under the title "Cupid and Psyche") in a limited edition by George Bixby and the Albondocani Press in 1970. "Year of Wonders" first appeared in a collection of stories *Where Are You Going, Where Have You Been?* published by Fawcett in 1974.

—for John Martin

Necessity is a veil of God.
—Simone Weil

CONTENTS

An
American
Adventure

Waking, I am overcome with a sense of dread. My wife is sleeping beside me but her face will not stay permanent—it dissolves back into its elements, into dots. I look away from her; I am not equal to this marriage. I am not equal to the person I am supposed to be.

Once upon a time I was more name than face. Someone said my name: I answered at once. Now the face has blotted out the name, my name turned out to be only accidental, only a sound, and the face something I can rely upon—in any mirror I see the same face, the same face, and it never dissolves into dots. It is permanent. It is a narrow, kindly, suspicious face, the hairline beginning to recede (though I am only twenty-seven years old), the teeth still excellent.

My face.

My name: when someone says my name now I answer reluctantly, to be polite. It is like waking up in the morning, hearing my name called. I am filled with dread at the sound of it because it is a lie; not exactly a lie, but not the truth. It is not really me and has nothing to do with me, that sound.

My wife says my name now. She whispers it, moving toward me. I embrace her out of politeness, out of the habit of another man—the man who married her, the man I sometimes recall. She is not quite awake and has no idea who is embracing her. She whispers my name; but it is no absolute claim upon me. She falls asleep again, dreaming.

My head aches. I need to jump out of bed. The room is too hot, too stuffy. I need to get out of this room and walk outside, fast. We have lived in this apartment for too long. Our landlady's beige print wallpaper, our landlady's soiled white curtains—at night I can hear our landlady's furniture sneering at us, soft hissing laughs. Since my operation I don't sleep well. My face has grown narrower. But I am a young man, still, statistically, and in two years I'll be done with graduate school and well into my "career," which is waiting patiently for me.

When did I first meet my wife? Did I ever meet her for the first time? Three years now we've lived together in this apartment, slept together, sat with our elbows on the rickety kitchen table, and she can fall back into her primal elements as easily as the toast used to jump up out of the toaster, before rust or crumbs slowed it down; with skin and tissue and bone broken down into their elements, she would be indistinguishable from any other woman.

I imagine things broken down into their elements, everything except my own face, which is cursed with immortality. But everything else can be broken down, stuck into a test tube and tested.

Since my operation—

While I was in the hospital—

I begin many sentences that way, too many. Even letters home: *While I was in the hospital I had time to catch up on my reading. I read the book you sent and enjoyed it.* My "reading" is something I should always "catch up on"; it is like my career, awaiting me mysteriously, perhaps at an intersection of this city. I write letters like this to my mother, who sends me books about the American past, particularly about Abraham Lincoln. She admires Lincoln very much and perhaps in her mind I am confused with him. She owns a very expensive antique highboy, a piece of furniture worth thousands of dollars, that is perhaps also confused in her mind with Lincoln . . . or perhaps it is only in my

10

mind that it is confused with Lincoln.

Anyway, since my operation—

To a friend of mine, my closest friend, I am always saying solemnly: *Since my operation I've thought—you know—more about life.* My best friend lives alone, has no soiled white curtains to stir him awake, no wife whose hair is always drying, loose and damp about her shoulders, or so violently clean it sparkles with electricity. He does not love anyone. He does not love. No one loves him and no one is going to: he hasn't my good teeth. He stands outside the peripheries of "love" and looks in wistfully, with his greenish-gray teeth *his* family didn't spend money on, and envies me. Of my operation he says shyly, "You were very lucky," and either avoids my eyes or stares directly into them, frank and man-to-man.

I "almost died" but that's misleading: you either die or you don't die, nothing else. I didn't die.

I slide out of bed and leave my wife, who is still sleeping. There are gentle hollows about her eyes. A tender stream of saliva in the corner of her mouth; lipstick faint and cracked from yesterday, on those lips. She is a very pretty young woman and if you were to see her somewhere—walking on the street, getting on a bus—you would stare at her with interest, supposing her lover or her husband to be a fortunate man, as I once did. Now that I am her lover and her husband I know better. I know everything.

I get dressed quickly. The shakes are almost on me; I had better get out and on my way to school. The buildings are unlocked early. I can get in early and wait for everyone to catch up with me. No time for breakfast; when I eat I want to test all my food, I want to stuff it into test tubes and run tests on it, to see if it will turn a violent poisonous yellow. So it's better not to eat. I dress myself as skillfully as I did as a child and am on my way out, down the five flights of stairs, on my elastic legs. The stairs go on forever. Other graduate students live in this building, aging like me, with

11

soft bluish circles under their eyes, and soft, pale, speechless wives they once stared at on the street or on buses, not knowing any better. Back and forth we run from the university's unheated buildings, up and down many flights of creaking stairs, our backbones as well as our legs elastic and energetic and still youthful, though we are all breaking down. We carry armloads of books and notebooks with our names inked in them, in case they should get lost. Some of us even carry small metal boxes with five-by-eight cards in them, inked in with bibliographical items and abbreviations and information in code, our names inked carefully on grimy adhesive tape stuck to the outside of the boxes, in case they should get lost. My name is

A name can get lost. A face can never get lost. Even without mirrors you still have a face, but the name can get mislaid and that's that. What was named in me died in City Hospital and what lived on has no name, isn't married or filed anywhere, hasn't yet settled into the bottom of its test tube.

Outside. April? Yes, it looks like April once again. The air swerves from warm to cold here; we are near a lake. A few weeks ago it was unmistakably winter and I was safe in the hospital, dying, looking out at a patch of sky that never changed much. It was an eternal patch of sky. When my wife came to visit me everything broke up into chattering fragments; my best friend made too many nervous jokes, his breath was stale and unused; my mother and aunt took American Airlines all the way out here to seize my hands and stare at me. *How did it happen? How?* There is poison seeping around in my bloodstream yet; they couldn't have drained it all out. An infection. Something went wrong, very suddenly. "They"—I mean my ordinary little doctor, a Korean—couldn't explain everything, couldn't explain life. Try telling that to my mother. My mother's high-toned skin glowed with indignation and her eyes jumped around to find an object: who was to blame?

Across the street, in front of the drugstore, some

hoodlums are standing around. Every day. Even this early. They are black boys, young and loud and careless with their stares; they make shrieking jokes in what seems to be another language. They stand around the corner as if on duty, waiting for something to happen. Or perhaps they are waiting for a bus. I remember each one of them—each familiar face, each familiar jacket with its unzipped zipper— When I returned from dying they did not seem to remember me, and yet I remember them.

I remember everything about this neighborhood, fondly. And with dread. The hoodlums—the mothers and the babies—the boarded-up stores. We've lived in this neighborhood for three years but that's not it—I walk this way five mornings a week but that's not it either. My heart pounds faster, my fingers begin to worry the edge of my notebook. What worries me is that there is a world beyond the world I see that is simultaneous with it. Yes. I am crossing the wide, dirty, wintry street, not as fast as I did before my operation but fast enough, youthfully enough, and I have the feeling that there is another world simultaneous with this one—its dimensions precisely matched with ours, its outlines absorbed in ours.

Why not?

The only difference is that there, in that world, nothing is human. There are no rules or laws or chemical "truths." In the hospital I had plenty of time to think and I did not think of my young wife or of love, neither of which I now believe in, nor of my important career "waiting" somewhere for me, nor did I think of my best friend and his loneliness or of Abraham Lincoln and his problems, and not even of my father, who as a matter of fact died in a hospital some eight, nine years ago, a much better hospital than the one I was in, of a malady considered less fatal than the one I had. No. In my bed I thought of this neighborhood, as if it were the entire world. I thought of this ugly neighborhood. My fate. My mind swam through the dense winter air, re-creating the steps I took five days a week: trying to remember what the world looked like, lingering on signs, store fronts, windows, stretches of sidewalk. A stretch of fence fluttering with old posters. RINGLING BROTHERS CIRCUS JULY 10,11,12.

And that boarded-up Esso station across the street: sometimes I could visualize it sharply, sometimes only hazily. A few Negro children are playing there this morning. In my dreams there were no people, only things. That world might have been bombed clean of people, aired out with one of those extravagant nuclear devices that destroy only flesh and leave objects sanitary and ready for acquisition. It was a hard, vivid world. This ordinary world is flimsy because people are always cluttering it up, hurrying from one X to another X, supposing they have places to get to. Like myself, hurrying to school. We make the world appear insubstantial, a crust. But in my dreams everything was calm and still; no brats to catch the eye and disfigure the background. There was only the faint odor or memory of people, their sofas out on porches all winter or curtains hung limply in windows. And this block of houses—this I always remembered perfectly. I don't know why. Every morning in the hospital I took this route, noiseless and invisible, in a world emptied of people and therefore permanent. The street had no name. The houses belonged to no one. They have always been with me; they are inescapably *real*, and one house in particular—I am approaching it now. My heart begins to pound absurdly because I am approaching it. I think that I could turn off, cut through an alley, but my feet hurry me onward.... My head aches, I need something...I need someone to run up to me and seize my hands and say my name. Save me! Pronounce my name! No, I don't want that. I don't want anything they can give me—I want to get away from them. I want to walk past that house.

In the hospital I took this route dreamily and lazily, on my way to school. And I would see this big apart-

14

ment building here—I'm passing it now—with its grimy brick front and the ends of curtains poking out of windows. In my dreams it was a perfect graveyard, empty. And the next house, a smaller one with asbestos siding. Vacant on the second floor, I think. A stubby lawn where kids have been digging and no grass will grow. And the next house— Already I am staring at it. The dread of this morning rises in me; now I know what I fear. This is the house I never got past.... It's a little better than most of the houses on the block, I know that. I would argue that. Something about its style, the big homey veranda in front of the doors on either side, one leading to the upstairs, a separate flat—the other door, on the right, is *my* door, leading to the first floor apartment. That is my door. In the front window are curtains that are yellow, a mustard yellow. Eh, what a color! The house is stained with soot but the dirt could be cleaned off. How much would that cost? A gray frame house; the veranda is awful, an eyesore; if the house were washed it would stick out on this block and the other houses would look terrible.... In my dreams I floated up to this house like a man in a Chagall painting, my feet lifting airily from the ground, by magic. I turned up the walk and ascended the stairs, as if coming home. I was at peace. Everything was right. And I would try the door and open it, quietly, with no one watching, and then I would be in a dark vestibule which would become lighter, just for me, by magic; there'd be stained glass above the inner door, maybe, I don't know why. Old-fashioned, vulgar, cheap stained glass, someone's idea of beauty. And a woman's umbrella would be out there, leaning in the corner—smelling of rain, of must. A smell of— maybe—clothes in closets, hung away damp, and food in airless cupboards. And I would turn the knob on the inner door and—

The door is opening as I walk by! It is actually opening. A black woman steps out onto the porch. She is wearing a bright blue coat, it is too new, too bright. I

15

try not to stare at her but my eyes ache and I give in: she is a young woman with a light, handsome face. She descends the steps and turns the other way, hurrying. Probably she is going to catch a bus. She has not noticed me. I might be invisible, standing here, just as invisible as I was when I made the trip from my hospital bed.

I stand out on the sidewalk, paralyzed. What is there about this house, what secret lies in it for me? Obviously it has no secret for anyone else; its tenants, white or black, merely use it and would never dream about it, never. It is a big, clumsy ugly box to them, nothing more. It should belong to me. I am the only person who really sees it. And so I stand here in my trench coat, my shoulders not so straight as they were in my youth but rounded a little with the perplexities of life, the need to stare, to think, to worry, to test.... A sense of absolute certainty rises in me: this is my home.

Ah, if I hurry toward the university I will come back to my senses! With each block I will become normal, hurried, petulant, real! The landscape will be alive with hurrying figures—students—girls and young men and some not so young, some crossing the street, some walking in clumps, some alone, some on bicycles dodging traffic. No one will recognize me, but still I will come back to my senses, to my real self; and if it happens that someone recognizes me, I will smile and return their greeting. I make a conscious effort to smile. "We spent all that money straightening your teeth and now you don't smile," my mother used to complain when I still lived at home, a teenager trapped at home. I learned that if I smiled at the right moment I would have friends, even girls; this worked. It was an effort for me to select the right moment, to unspring my smile just at the right moment, but I learned. And so I made friends, won girls, even won a wife. Now I smile but not always at the right moment... a little ahead of time, occasionally a little too late. My problem is that I am always distracted from what is humanly crucial by this other misty, unhuman world, which peeks out

16

from behind the solid world and makes its demands upon me: *this is your true home,* it insists. It is as cunning and irresistible as the young girls, the sophomores in my laboratory sections who compete in their wooing of me, trying to get passing grades. Sometimes I think of what a relief it would be to give in to them, to give them anything they want, to X them out as human beings and forget them! What relief to give in to the promises of that other world, which is as impersonal and silent and precise as the chemical formulas that have made up my life for so long—

I am still standing here, on the sidewalk. The black woman is gone; she won't be back. I am alone. Already I can smell the vestibule and feel that inner door knob—cold and a little damp, with a metallic odor— and once inside the house I would be in a kind of living room or parlor, with a worn, shabby rug, the furniture is cheap—bright blue sofa, maybe—and farther back there is the kitchen with the linoleum worn out in front of the sink and the stove. This is all clear. Then off to the side there is a bedroom—a bedspread with a flower print, maybe. Something chintzy and bright. A clock ticking somewhere. It is quiet, peaceful. I lie on the bed and I am home

...It is raining. When did it start raining? I am damp anyway from perspiring. Here I stand, and now something rigid begins to move up my spine. It moves up to my jaw. It is like a column of mercury, or lead! My gaze falls away from the door and I see that between the house and the one next door is nothing but a narrow walk. Not a driveway or a fence, only a walk. I go to this walk and turn up in it, casually...yes, casually...though everything is rigid in me and my heart is hammering like mad. Be calm. Calm. No one is watching.

And so I find myself between the two houses. All is silent. No one around. The windows are gritty on both sides, and the basement windows are opaque with filth. I hadn't thought about the house having a basement.

All that to imagine, an entire basement! My mind boggles at the thought of it. I walk on . . . keep going to the back yard . . . no hurry. The back yards are barren. Identical. Four houses press in upon one another back here—no, five houses—their back yards all come together, marked off by rickety fences.

It is the center of the world. I have been here before: a priest, an actor in a ceremony.

I put out my hand and touch the doorknob of the back door. I turn it—it's locked. I knock on the door and there is silence. *Be calm.* Then, with my fist, I tap at the glass until it breaks. The glass falls at once, making almost no sound; my hand is not even scratched; I am safe. Everything is silent. The five houses are silent, no one moves in them, no one is staring at me and memorizing my features. . . . And none of this is surprising, because in my dreams I have been here already without incident.

Now I am inside, in a kitchen. Something is making a noise—the refrigerator. It is too loud, like breathing gone wrong. There are dishes in the sink, there is an odor of food. Maybe spoiled milk. The walls have been painted green many years ago and in the sink and on the table are dishes with clots of food still on them. Why is the food still on them? The stove is dirty, there is food spilled over and burnt on it. My heart is still pounding hard. Something is wrong. The whirring of the refrigerator makes me nervous: it is like a lazy, threatening animal. When I pass the table I have to lean against it, and I see there a streak of blood—bright blood—who has been here before me?

Off from the kitchen is a closet without a door: junk piled high in it. Then a living room. Something is wrong . . . the living room does not look familiar. . . . There is a bed in it, a sofa bed. I would never have imagined that. Sheets and blankets lie on the floor. An ashtray of black plastic with cigarette butts in it, some of them spilled over onto the floor . . . beer cans . . . Coke bottles. . . . A television set with a Coke bottle on it. On the wall, a mirror with an ornate gilt frame, a five-and-ten store mirror, in which I can almost see myself. *Better stand back out of sight.* My head reels. Am I in the wrong house after all? This house does not have the right smell. Something is wrong. My hand stings and I notice that it is bleeding, after all, from a long scratch across the knuckles.

A small bathroom—more of that green paint. It's like a green sky, pressing in. The bathroom is very dirty. Hairs in the sink, scum, rings of dirt; better not look any further. Then the bedroom and more green walls, an odor that is musty and green and unaired. There is the odor of food in here too. The shades are drawn crookedly, this cramped little room is sinister and secretive. What has happened in this room? Have the people who live here changed this room? There are clothes scattered on the floor, hung over the back of a chair—a woman's white slip, a woman's yellow sweater. A closet without a door: inside a jumble of clothes. A man's shirt and a pair of dark green trousers are hanging in there. A shiny pink robe lies across the bed, on top of the jumble of sheets and the twisted blanket. The evidence of life is everywhere but it is diminished and sordid, as if all these items were the relics of dead people, tracks they've left behind on their way to die. And there is that strange musty odor too, which was the odor of the hospital I was in and the odor of my body, though it was washed often.

On a cheap dresser there are bottles of cosmetics and perfume. I pick up one of the bottles—"Moonlight"—and unscrew the cap. A bright, shrill smell. It reminds me of no women I have known. The top of the dresser is dirty, flecked with powder. And hairs—dark, curly, kinky hairs. Of course. Hairs everywhere. My heart is pounding helplessly. I open the drawers—more clothes, underclothes. Men's socks. I pull them out and let them fall to the floor. Something is rising in me, my heart seems to be rising, trying to force its way up into my throat. I am bitter with disappointment. What is this

19

place, what has happened here? Is this house no special house after all? Have I broken into the wrong house? I throw things on the floor without bothering to look at them. One of the drawers falls out onto my foot. . . .

My face is burning. Heavily, I sit on the edge of the bed. What to do? What has happened to me? I lie back onto the pillow, adjusting it beneath my head. I lie there motionless. There is nothing. Everything is silent. And now it occurs to me that I have at last entered the other world: I have passed over into that secret world. And what is it, really? I am in it, lying on a bed in it, and yet I don't know what it is. This house is my entrance into that other world, which has been hidden for so long behind all familiar odors and shapes—and in this world nothing is familiar, nothing is safe. I think to myself: *Now your world is vast, your horizons are flattened out forever. There are no horizons. You can never leave this world because there are no horizons, no boundaries, no end to it.*

I lie there quietly, at peace.

Something wakes me—I am lying on my back, the bedclothes beneath me, my head still carefully on the pillow. A room with green walls! I know at once where I am. And then I hear a sound again: a door closing. My heart continues to beat as it must have while I slept, slow and ponderous, cunning. The outer door is closed now and someone is at the second door, putting a key in the lock. I can imagine the woman in the blue coat. I can imagine her seeing me, her eyes leaping over here to me. . . . She will take off her coat, staring at me, and there will be something beautiful about her strong hands and fingers.

The door is opening to the living room. I sit up. The woman is coming—she walks heavily. She must be walking on her heels, tired or angry. I go to the closet and stand inside, hunched over, in the dark . . . from here I can see into the kitchen but there is nothing there . . . then a shadowy image of the woman moves against my eye. Should I call out to her, should I announce myself? But it is someone else, not that woman—it is someone else. She does not look toward me. She is a high school girl with books cradled in her arms, and on top of the books a big soiled paper bag with gym sneakers stuffed into it. She lets all this fall onto the kitchen table.

She stands there, alone. She is a short black girl with slight legs, dressed in a bright green raincoat; there is something very delicate about her neck and the way she holds her head, standing there alone, wearily. I have the idea that she has come home from school too early—maybe walked out of school. Her profile is thoughtful. She is a pretty girl. She reminds me of my wife. She begins to unbutton her coat, button after button, her fingers precise and weary....

"Oh, damn it," she whispers.

She puts a finger onto the kitchen table as if testing something. I can't see what is wrong. Then she wipes the table with the flat of her hand...wiping up my blood?...but this doesn't make snese. And yet, unaccountably, she seems to accept that blood and to want to get rid of it, quickly.... She takes off the raincoat and lets it fall onto the table. She is wearing a red sweater and a tight, short skirt of black wool; her stockings are dark and textured, into diamond shapes. *Grab her. Now.* I should jump out and grab her, I should put my hand over her mouth.... A pang of sexual desire strikes me, I have not felt anything like this in my life....

The girl snaps on a radio and there is music at once. She goes to the refrigerator and opens the door and leans on it, sighing. The refrigerator's yellowish light shows how snub-nosed she is, how perplexed and lonely. The whirring of the machine. The beating of my heart. *You could grab her. You must grab her. But quickly, quickly....*

Then it occurs to me that she is as lonely as I; she is not at home here, either, not in this house; the two of us are isolated in this strange house, which means nothing to us, which we cannot own. . . . These thoughts do not arise in me in such order, with such clarity. No. I feel them, I feel the certainty of. . . . What is that sound? She is humming. Humming along with the music. *You must act quickly, you must. . . .*

She has taken something out of the refrigerator; she sets it on the table. "What did I . . . ? Oh damn it," she mutters, as if she has just thought of something. She leaves the kitchen, goes into the bathroom, closes the door. I am alone, trembling. I am alone.

And now: I am ready to leave.

Through the kitchen, silently. Out the back door. So easy, so easy! The pane is still smashed—glass on the floor—but no one knows. She didn't see it. Magically, I am outside; I am alone, outside the house now. The radio accompanies me partway. Ah, alone, alone. Why don't I feel joy at this escape, why is a sensation of loss rising in me? My hands are trembling. Something went wrong, I am alone, baffled, sick with excitement that cannot discharge itself. . . . In that other world there are strangers just as there are in this world. I almost touched her, but I drew back. An embrace was required, not an assault; I drew back, I could not touch her, I was alone in the house and she was alone in the house, and yet. . . .

Crossing a street near the chemistry building: and someone shouts at me. "Ronald!"

Automatically I look around. It is my friend—my best friend—hurrying toward me. Strange, he must have recognized me at once.

"Ronald, wait. Didn't you hear me calling you? What's wrong?"

Is my face correct, is it my old face? Will he see anything in it?—any secret? Or is a veil, a film, a cautious terrified membrane protecting me once again? Ah, my cut hand—the blood! But he won't notice.

I manage to smile, unspringing my sad smile. He says something in reply. His words are spiced with my

22

name, *my name*, so that I can't mistake him or myself: I am back in my own world, I am a white man, I am named, finite, safe. The sexual tension drains out of me, as it must. The adventure is not concluded: it drains out of me. My heart slows to its dull, ponderous beat, even my sweat is drying, everything slows down to become opaque and permanent once again.

Richard was seven when his father left home. The event froze something permanently into his face, so that he squinted unnecessarily as if fearful that some detail, some tiny hieroglyphic might get by him. His brothers were eleven and thirteen, his sister sixteen or so, already grown up and remote; his mother was a pale, vague, weeping woman, with gray-brown hair fallen loose on her shoulders. When she embraced Richard he saw it, twisting his head silently away, while his mother murmured something about "your father." "Your father, he—" There was an old piano in the front room which Richard was to find out years later was called an upright, and after his father left his mother played the piano often, bent painstakingly over the keys, striking those that stuck with a violence none of her children liked to see. On top of the piano was a long shawl or scarf made of brilliant material, a souvenir of the American Southwest. Richard did not think much about his mother since he understood the flinching, embarrassed shame of the rooms she passed through and did not want to take that shame on himself. While he was in the army and, later, in college for a year, he was able to think of his mother only as the woman who had embraced him too often, calling him "Richard" and never "Dick" so that he had grown up with no other name but Richard—that complacent, rigorous name one could never say gently. Or, if he thought of her further, he remembered the loose untidy hair on her shoulders, and he remembered her sitting at the piano, leafing through old music books impatiently as if she thought she might really find a piece she had never seen before, a nice surprise, while on either side of the piano the ends of the scarf hung down in scarlet and gold fringes.

Of his father he never thought at all. Because his mother had talked of nothing else, Richard and his brothers and sisters stopped thinking about him entirely.

One summer afternoon, twenty-eight years after his father had left, Richard turned into his driveway and noticed that his daughter was not out on the porch waiting for him. She was only five, a child with dark blond hair just like Richard's, and with his stern suspicious features; always she waited for him to come home from work and would run out to greet him. Without her there, Richard was able to notice that his house was a little dirty. All houses in this sub-division were small "ranch" houses, with brick on their fronts only, and a single picture window, and shutters in either bright green or bright pink. The shutters on his house were bright green. The streets had not yet been paved, the broad, sloping ditches on either side filled up dangerously with water after every rain, all up and down the straight road the uniform houses faced one another, and for the first time since they had come here to live Richard felt dissatisfied, as if a change had taken place in the neighborhood.

When he entered the house his son Timmy came running into the kitchen and cried, "There's a man here! Mommy's talking to a man!" Richard did not even put down the newspaper, but went through to the living room. And there indeed was a man, an old man, sitting on the sofa. Richard's wife, Alice, came to him at once, her face queer and pinched. She looked as if she had been crying. "Do you see who's here? Do you recognize him?" she said.

Richard's heart was pounding violently and absurdly. He had recognized the old man at once. But what frightened him was not the sudden appearance of this improbable, lost father, but the terrible change that had taken place in him. Richard tried to remember the man who had left home that day, whom they had all mourned as if mourning a death: a strong, loud man beginning to get fat, with an angular face and a hard jaw, thick dark hair. Richard remembered also his tobacco-stained fingers and the odor of tobacco about him, but most of all his voice, and his look. . . . But now there sat on the sofa an old man with the thin brittle look of the elderly, whose attention and love are divided between the outside world and the inner world of pulsating, waning organs. Richard stared at this man. His father was smiling shyly, as if he knew he had no place here, was not welcome. His smile was guilty, nervous. If his gaze wavered it was because he must have felt Richard's shock—what have you done to yourself? How can you be so old? His daughter Gerry was pulling at his coat sleeve. Richard glanced at her, startled. "Gerry, come away," said Alice. His wife stood by the doorway, watching Richard, as if she had unveiled to him a priceless treasure and was jealous of his interest.

Richard entered the room slowly. Because the old man was still sitting, dressed in a slovenly, outlandish brown suit with a crumpled shirt and no necktie, Richard had the confused, fleeting idea that he was the visitor and not his father. "Hello," Richard said. "Hello," said his father. The guilty smile spread further, stretched itself tentatively. So it had happened at last, Richard thought. He had come back. They had waited so long, and his mother had heard so many rumors, kindly, cruel rumors, but only now. . . . In the first instant of his shock he found himself thinking of strange things. What did this mean, did it mean that he, too, would change into an old man? Had his father come to tell him this? Or to tell him something else? "I knew I should of written, and not been such a bad

27

surprise," his father said humbly. There he sat, on the sofa that was so familiar as to be invisible, surrounded by the slick, economical furniture Richard and his wife had bought several years ago, in a delirium of happiness: the lamp with the flaring lampshade, lemon-yellow, and the glass-top coffee table stained with something—one of the children's spilled drinks—and the easy chair that matched the sofa, big and flashy and worn out, now, its wood scuffed and nicked. The television set in the corner was turned off; Richard saw this with regret, for it meant that something profound and irreparable had indeed happened.

During dinner Richard was able to examine his father closely, and when their eyes met each laughed self-consciously and looked away. Alice was nervous and eager, touching her hair with her long fingers. The children were shy. Richard saw that everything was slow about his father now, where once his manner had been thoughtless and urgent; hurrying in the house, opening drawers, running down cellar to look for something, his boots leaving mud on the floor. Now he ate his dinner carefully and solemnly. His manner, his lowered gaze, seemed to acknowledge the fact that he had no right to be here, he understood, yes, he did not expect to be welcomed. He expected nothing from them. He was not like another father might be, whining and self-pitying in his old age. On their way to the kitchen for dinner his father had alarmed Richard by taking his arm, in a lurching gesture that was almost a caricature of old age, and saying in an emphatic whisper: "I told her already I have some money. I have it saved. It's with me right now." Richard had nodded quickly, embarrassed. "I have it saved. Not much, but enough to take care of me." He nodded back over his shoulder, at the khaki-colored canvas bag on the floor by the sofa; evidently the money was in there, magical, splendid money that would make all the difference to his son.... "Yes, yes," Richard said, his face burning.

The children were quieter at dinner, that was a change. They watched their new grandfather. He was really not very different from their other grandfather— was that what they were thinking? That old man was not so nervous as this one, and he was fat, but he too had the frequent bewildered stare that suggested he had glanced ahead into something he had not wanted to see; that was why his eyes leapt so meticulously about the room, trying to attach him to it. "And what about your health?" Richard said. He leaned forward as if he was afraid he would not hear. "Good. Doing good," his father said, unconvincingly. "And you said you were on that bus three days?" Alice said. "Yes, three days. Couldn't have a seat to myself, either," he said. Richard saw that his father had a strange inno- cent look, as if the years had worn out the tension created by knowledge. The innumerable wrinkles that outlined his eyes and crossed his forehead and cheeks and sagged about his throat were just the opposite of tension, and the shifting acquiescent mouth that seemed to offer its ignorance, hopefully, was the op- posite of the brutal impatience Richard had remem- bered in it. As a younger man he had been abrupt and whimsical, always looking for something, asking ques- tions, throwing things on the floor to look through clos- ets, drawers, shelves. Now he had stopped looking. He asked no questions, he did not pry. His eyes were nar- row and watery; there was something sleek about them, something artificial. He was like a doll of an old man, covered with skin cleverly aged. His transfor- mation into this doll surprised no one except Richard, who would think of it for the rest of his life; it did not surprise the old man himself, having come upon him more slowly than any disease. It did not surprise the children, who thought only of old and young and noth- ing in between, but who really did not think at all.

"Yes, that's what I had in mind," Richard's father was saying. He was answering Alice but really speaking to Richard. "I had it in mind for a long time. Five years or so. I said, if I could save up enough to keep me, then I could come up for a visit. Stay for a while— you know, like they do. Just for a while. Then I could find some nice little place in the city, close enough for visiting, but it would have to be clean. I said, I want to see those two little grandchildren before I die." He ended breathlessly. Richard stared at the old man's fingers, as if expecting them to betray his words. What did it mean to say "before I die" and feel the event of dying so close, so real? Or could it never mean anything more than it did in conversation? Richard felt a pang of fear—maybe the old man was dying right now. His final trick had been to visit his death upon them. But everything about him seemed to say that there were no longer any complexities in him. If he was old, he was clean; his suit might be frayed, but it was clean. He had no smell about him. He did not even smell of tobacco. And he would not talk much, he had his own money, he knew his place. He had just come for a visit.

"How did you know we had children?" Richard said.

"I knew," he said gravely. "I got ways."

Richard wanted to smile to show he recognized this as a lie, but a trivial one. "What about Sonny and Bob? And Mary? What have you heard about them?"

"Some things," the old man said vaguely. "Off and on. It's been some years. . . ."

"You know Sonny's in Texas?"

"I did hear, yes. I heard something like that."

Richard waited for him to ask about the other children, but he did not. "Well," Richard said, "how did you happen to find me?"

"Well, like I said, I know lots of things. I keep up old ties—you know? Back in the neighborhood."

"Who?"

"Nobody you remember."

"But who?"

"Well—Steve that had the drug store. Steve, the one with . . . down at the drugstore."

"The drugstore?"

"The drugstore...."

Richard pressed his fingers against his eyes. As if to spite him, a memory did appear of a drugstore. But not on their block; three blocks away. Almost beyond the boundary of his childhood world. "I didn't know any Steve," Richard said slowly. But then he could not remember what they were talking about.

"Three days on the bus must have made you exhausted," Alice said. "Did you have to sit up, all the way?"

"I can sleep anywhere," he said. "I'm not fussy. I don't cause a fuss."

"Was it a bus with green windows?" Timmy said.

"Yes, one of them," said Richard's father.

"A bus with an upstairs in the back?" said Timmy.

"Yes."

"Is that kind more expensive than the other?" Timmy asked.

"I don't know, I think so," Alice said vaguely.

They had stopped eating. Richard felt a little nauseous.

"What kinds of things do you have in the bag?" Timmy said, sitting up.

"Can I look?" said Gerry.

"I got some gifts, I meant to tell you," Richard's father said. "For the children. I thought I'd pick up some gifts, you know—"

"For me?" said Gerry.

"For you both. I knew all about you," he said. His voice had a declamatory ring to it, now faded and worn; it was not at all the voice Richard remembered. That voice had been impatient and slurred. "That's why I wanted to come, to see them," he said to Richard. "And you too, and your wife. I could rest easier then. I ... got to thinking about certain things, the last five years or so...."

"I suppose so," Richard said.

The children were excited; Richard could feel their

31

excitement shoot off away from him. They wanted to leave the table. "Can I look in the bag?" Timmy said.

"You stay right here," said Alice. "Sit still."

"Why can't I look? He said he brought some—"

"It has a lock on it." Richard's father took the key out of his pocket, smiling. "Can you use a key, Timmy?"

"Sure."

"You didn't really buy them things, did you?" said Alice. "That wasn't necessary. They have so many things—"

"It was nothing. I was happy to do it," he said.

"But how did you know about the children?" Richard said.

"He explained that," Alice said sharply. "What's wrong?"

The children ran to the valise. Timmy squatted over it and fitted the key in the lock. "He has a key for his bicycle lock," Alice said to Richard's father, as if explaining something.

"Just how old is the boy?"

"He's ten. Gerry's five."

"They are very beautiful children," Richard's father said.

"Oh, they're not," Alice said, pleased. "They're. . . . They make a lot of trouble."

"Your home seems to be a happy one."

"Yes, it is," Alice said foolishly. Richard resented his father and tried to think of the years he must have spent in hardship, in exile, those years of abandonment everyone felt to be a crime against his wife and yet a crime slightly tinged with humor—because it was a funny situation, a situation out of a cartoon. He had not even given Richard's mother the dignity of noble suffering. Richard had grown up having to learn that people don't really do such things. Men don't really abandon their families. His father's remarks about his children made Richard's heart beat faster with bitterness, for these were *his* children, his own children, and he was not going to abandon them. He was afraid his words would break from him and accuse the old man—that innocent, gentle old man—shout at him, injure him. If only he were more like he had been, if only he did not seem to be another person! For what sweetness could there be in injuring a stranger?

"Some families are happy," Richard said.

"Yes," his father said, nodding.

Richard pushed his chair back from the table. He was trembling. He saw Alice watching him and felt suddenly that she was on his father's side; that was because she did not understand. He had never explained to her what his childhood had really been like . . . he had been too cold, he had always been too cold. And then emotion, welling up in him suddenly, had the appearance of being contrived.

"So you plan on staying here a while," Richard said, his eyes half-closed.

"I'd like that very much," his father said softly. "I been hoping that for five—"

"All right, good. Good."

"If I won't be no bother," his father said. Richard remembered this habit of his father's—this childish insistence upon saying the last word. He had always done that, Richard remembered. He remembered arguments between his father and mother; his father had always had the last word, shouting it as he slammed the door: "Go to hell!" Richard looked slyly at him now as if daring him to speak that way. "I told you about that money I got saved," his father said, clearing his throat. "I want to make it clear. You and your wife, I don't want to be no trouble for you. I just thought, maybe a nice visit, after so many years . . . when a man gets my age, he. . . ."

"Just how old are you?" Richard said.

"How old?"

"How old? How old? How old are you?"

"Now, that's. . . . I don't seem to know," he said, smiling as if in a daze. "I mean, when you're alone you don't celebrate birthdays, do you? You don't pay attention to them, don't you know, then after a while you forget. I might be . . . going on seventy."

"You look pretty good for seventy," Richard said.

"Well, these last few years I been taking better care. I got to thinking about some things. Don't drink no more, you know."

"You don't drink?"

"No. Gave it up. I gave it up cold."

"You never drink?"

"It's bad for you, don't you know, it's bad on the heart and the stomach. I seen some pretty sick men in my time. I said, I wasn't going to end up like them. . . ."

In the living room the children had discovered their presents. Timmy had a sword made of stiff cardboard, painted gold and red. Gerry had a bag of candy. The bag was made of orange net and the candies were wrapped in tinfoil, so that they looked like rich spoils pulled out of the sea. The little girl leaned against the chair arm and ate the candies, one by one, soiling her dress with chocolate and saliva. Timmy made tentative thrusts with the sword. "I've never seen a toy like that," Alice said.

"Got it at a special store," Richard's father said.

Richard looked at the gifts suspiciously. There was something wrong with them. The candy was a poor gift—Gerry's teeth were already bad. The sword was strange, not really a toy; Richard had the idea that it had been taken from a display of something, a movie perhaps. Its back was plain gray cardboard with staples criss-crossing it.

That night Richard's father slept on the sofa in the living room. Richard lay awake for hours. He could feel the old man's presence as if it were an extension of himself, just as, when there was only one other person in the house with him, he could feel that other person—usually Timmy—intruding somehow, secretive and disturbing. Richard's coldness was the result only of his hatred of complexity, it meant nothing else. He knew that he was not really cold, not icy and remote as his wife sometimes thought him.... There had been too many nuances in the childhood he had escaped, too many rumors and dangers, and he felt a sullen bitterness now that complexity had been introduced again in his life. He hated all things he could not control, relationships and events he could not plan the way he planned their budget for the month, giving his wife only the amount of money she needed. Nothing had terrified him so as the impending birth of their children, not even the memory of his hateful, selfish father—for he had felt their souls as alien to him, strangers who could not help challenging him, coming as they did from separate worlds. After their births he had felt differently, for they had been only infants, not really strangers, no real challenge to his life. He felt that he had taken them to himself and created them.

When he came home from work the next day the old man was in the living room, watching television with the children. His suit coat was off; he wore a plaid wool shirt that looked festive; black suspenders creased the shirt and gave him an alert, efficient look. Richard, who had been thinking about his father all day, stared at him now as if he were disappointed—so much emotion, so much confused hatred, and only this harmless man sitting and smiling at a child's television program. "Here's the newspaper," Richard said to him.

In the kitchen Alice said, "He wasn't any trouble at all. He even helped me with the dishes. I wonder if... if he's well, though; sometimes he seems.... I think he's had some terrible experiences."

"Why do you say that?"

"I don't know. The way he... speaks so softly, so that you have to bow your head to hear him. He spends most of his time with the children, though. Gerry didn't even want to go out to the park with Timmy."

"Sure he's had some terrible experiences," Richard said. "We all have. Why shouldn't he? Is he any different? Probably was in prison for a few years."

"Oh, Richard!"

"What? You don't know what he used to be like. Let's forget about it, the hell with it. But you don't know anything about him and I do."

"Children can't always remember—"

"This one can," Richard said.

In the living room the old man sat reading the paper now, squinting. The light was bad there but he did not dare to move; they were to notice that. His humility, his meekness. A harmless creature. The candies were all eaten and the tinfoil wrappers scattered about, and the sword was already bent. Richard felt disgust for his fears of the night before.

After dinner Richard's father told the children a story about a hurricane in the south. "We were trapped up on the roof for a day and a night," he said. "There was dead cows floating by and they'd get caught on the edge of the barn, and then in the morning the birds come after them. Dirty things! Birds are dirty things! They got bugs, don't you know. . . ." The children were fascinated. Richard, guarding himself against anything that came from his father, listened but did not especially believe. Lying and exaggerating had been part of his father's old life, he thought; at least that was what his mother had told him. Richard could not really remember. The old man who was now gesturing and flicking his eyes from face to face melodramatically was blotting out what little memory Richard had had of his father, his real father. The old man continued: "There was all kinds of bugs and spiders going around, too. They weren't afraid of each other or of people. They'd be in pieces of thicket and junk that came floating by—branches with weeds and underbrush tangled around them, you know. It was gray weather, the sky all white and gray. Everything looked funny. And snakes! My God, them snakes! They were crawling all over, or else resting and—"

"I don't like them," Gerry said.

"—they were all sizes. Lots of kinds I never saw before. And a lot of dead ones too. After that I never thought much of a river, no matter how pretty it looks.

There's nothing nice to it, or to woods or anything. Nothing nice about water. Even water that comes out of a faucet, it—"

"Maybe that's enough of that," Richard said.

"What?" said his father, startled. He stared at Richard as if he could not quite recall him.

"Why don't you tell them about something else, now?" Richard said.

"Just telling them about the big storm."

"Yes, but don't scare them."

"I ain't scared!" said Timmy.

"Me neither," said Gerry.

"No hurricane like that is going to come up here, not this far," Richard's father said. "Don't you worry about it."

"What were you doing in the south?" Richard said.

"Work. Work, of course. Had some connections so I thought I'd go down for a winter. Winters take too much out of you." In his wool shirt—a cheerful blue and yellow plaid—he looked like any grandfather glimpsed through a front window, with that small swelling paunch Richard had not noticed the day before. His white hair, those gentle, spreading brown spots on his hands and face, his fragile manner: anonymous characteristics of age. He would make up for his past by surprising no one, now, he seemed to say. If a past could be wiped away he would do it, if only through the sheer boredom of his words, his long pointless stories. Since his own children had been abandoned by him without much thought, he would give love to these children, who did not need it. . . . "Then they came for us in a boat," he went on, "a nice boat, a motorboat. It had the state flag on it. The state troopers had some poles and nets, to pull people in, don't you know, that had drownded. They had a whole big hillside full of them. Then the people that had got out came back to identify them, when the water went down. I said, I wouldn't ever go back there again if God would just get me out of it . . ."

"What kind of work did you do there?" Richard said.

He did not like the strange glittering look in his daughter's eyes. Was she frightened or just listening closely? She was too much like Richard not to hear every word.

"Outdoor work, with my hands," his father said. He spoke in a slightly different voice to Richard. It was a polite, attentive voice, but it had none of the passion of a moment before. "I always ask for work outdoors. Good for you."

"I didn't know you worked outside."

"Always ask for it, yes. A long time ago. . . . When I was younger, I had a job that never took up my energy. That was the trouble. It never taxed me none, and a man needs to be taxed. He needs to be standing on tiptoe."

Richard saw his father's hands clasp each other. He was silent for a moment, remembering his father's complaints about his job—factory work—because it was too tiring. It was bad for the heart and for the eyes, his father had said.

"Outside is the best work for a man. I'm not saying nothing about money," the old man went on. Timmy was trying to push a loose staple back in the cardboard sword. "I mean, if you want money bad enough to stay put all your life, that's all right. A man has only got one life to work with."

"What do you mean by that?"

"In one of them jobs you look up, there's a ceiling. Look down, a floor, anywhere else—a wall, all of them walls no matter where they are. I saw that right off. Now, a man wants to stand up tall and he can't when he's all boxed in some building all his life."

"I don't feel that way," Richard said coldly.

"Different kinds of people want different things," his father said. "Me, now, I never wanted anything else but quiet. I wanted some quiet and some work that would tax me like I ought to be. How else can a man know how strong he is? I wanted to look up and see the sky and not some wall. And I didn't always want to see the same sky either."

"Were you working on a farm down there?"

"Something like that, that's right. I just wanted some quiet."

Richard's hands were trembling. The old bastard had wanted some quiet!

"It wasn't quiet enough for you at home, huh?"

"What?"

"Not quiet enough at home?"

"Well, now," he said vaguely, as if rolling a piece of food about on his tongue that he could not identify, "there was that . . . that thing in the front room."

"What?"

"That thing she had, I ain't got the name right on the tip of my tongue. . . . The piano, that's what it was. That thing. I never did like noise like that all cooped up in a room."

"But who played the piano?"

"It was one of them things. Either you take to it or not. Me myself, I never had much time for music. It takes a certain kind."

"But she didn't play the piano much," Richard said. "Not until you left. I know that. I know it."

His father smiled foolishly at him.

"I know that. I'm sure of it," Richard said, his heart pounding.

They were quiet. Then Timmy jumped up as if he had been waiting for this. "Can we play that game again?" he said. "Just you and me?"

"Maybe your father would like to play with us."

"He don't like to," Timmy said.

"No, no thanks," said Richard.

"I want to," Gerry said.

"Well, you can't! You're too little!"

"I want to!" She slapped her brother's arm. Timmy swung the sword around and hit her with its flat front side, not hard. When she began to cry Timmy watched his father nervously and said that she could play. "She loses the pieces and knocks the board over, but nobody cares. Let the baby have her way!"

The game came out of a green oblong box with pictures of airplanes on its cover. Richard watched them over his newspaper, as if he had nothing better to do. They took turns shaking the dice, Timmy with a tense arrogance Richard had not really noticed in him before, the old man with a playful smile. Red, blue, and green soldiers were marching around the board. Tiny brown fortifications appeared here and there. When Richard glanced up again he saw his son's face turn ugly, really ugly. He threw the dice down. "I'm not going to play no more!"

"What's the matter?" Richard said sharply.

"I don't want to play."

"Here, take your turn again," Richard's father said.

"I don't have to play if I don't want to."

While his grandfather urged him to take the dice again, Timmy sat by the coffee table with his little backbone hunched and rigid. He made invisible lines on the rug with his fingernail.

"Here, take this fort," Richard's father said. He pushed the brown building on another square. "What about that?"

"I got a bad start," Timmy said.

"You take that fort. You take it."

"Should I take it?"

"You take it," said Richard's father, smiling.

The game continued. After a while Richard went out to the kitchen. His wife had finished everything, was alone, stood leaning back against the damp counter and smoking. "Is that game they're playing my father's?" Richard said. "No, it's Timmy's," said Alice. Richard thought of saying something further, but he did not know what to say. In the other room the dice were thrown down again; Timmy made a sharp hissing sound of delight. "My father is a lot of work for you, isn't he?" Richard said. "No," said Alice. "He keeps them quiet. He's all right." "I don't suppose he said anything to you about how long he was staying here," Richard said. His wife did not answer; she looked tired.

"What does he do around here all day?" said Richard. She flicked ashes in the sink. "He tells them stories. He doesn't talk to me much, really. He doesn't seem to notice me." "He was always like that," said Richard. "He never talked to women. . . . I mean, he never took them seriously." "Then he went out for a walk somewhere, he was gone about an hour. He carried that bag along with him," Alice said. "But he is a nuisance to you," said Richard. "I said no, not at all," Alice said, closing her eyes. "He's your father." "My father!" Richard said contemptuously. "Please don't talk like that," said Alice. "I don't like that. He's your father. You have no choice about him." "No?" said Richard. "No. Legally, even. You have no choice. He came to see you before he died and here he is," Alice said. "What if he never dies?" Richard said. He could not let her words be the final ones; he had to say something that would make her look up at him.

That night Richard had the idea that the old man was walking around. He lay still, listening. If I could only be free of this, he thought. His father had been in the house only two days but it seemed like much longer. . . . He heard a moan. He thought it was a moan. Silence. Richard lay very still and listened while his wife slept. He thought that his father knew he was listening, knew even the way he was lying in bed, not daring to move. Still silence, then the sound of someone lowering himself onto the sofa. Richard lay awake for several hours.

In the days that followed Richard kept waiting for something to happen. His father took his place at the dinner table a few minutes ahead of time, now. He was meek and polite to Richard and his wife, but talked most of the time to the children. If Richard tried to divert his storytelling into the truth, it was impossible to distinguish between the two. One night he told a story about a lost child pursued by dogs and Richard understood that the child was the old man, himself; though moved by the fragmentary story he had had to tell his father to stop, Gerry had been frightened. She had woken up several times one night, whimpering; like Richard she believed too passionately, her intelligent little features retained the imprint of memories others easily forgot. Richard tried to undercut his father's influence with the children by asking repeatedly, "Did that really happen? When was it?"

"Ten, fifteen years ago," his father would say vaguely.

"Did it get in the newspapers?"

"I don't know that. Sure, probably, they write up everything, don't they? I wouldn't know."

About a fire at a circus he said: "That got written up in all the newspapers. It was real big news." He stared at Richard as if his gaze were confused and challenged by the opaque muscular disbelief of this man who was his son. It was the children he loved; they listened to him and believed him and above all knew him as no one else but the old man who had come to visit. Richard thought wildly that he hated this father more than he had hated the other. "Remember that circus I took you to?" he said. Richard's heart began to pound at once, as if he were being challenged. "Took you three boys to it, remember?"

"I guess not."

"*She* didn't want you to go, said if a fire caught in the tent we'd all be killed. Had a big fight, don't you know. But we went anyway and had a good time and that was that. You remember, huh?"

"No," said Richard.

"Had to argue for half an hour. She never wanted me to spend money on you. Nothing for you or the kids or me, even, even if I did work every goddam day. The money had to go in the bank. Everything saved up. But we went over to the circus anyway and had a good time."

"I don't remember that," said Richard.

"You were real little."

Richard felt a dull pain behind his eyes. "I don't

remember it," he said.

"And that whatchamacallit in the front room—with that orange thing on it—the piano. I never could stand a piano. Up and down, bang, bang, thump, one, two, three. I like a jukebox, now, I don't say nothing against different kinds of songs, don't you know, but I got sick of that. A man just wants some quiet."

That was the evening Alice discovered that Timmy's dime bank had been slit open. It was made of cardboard, given out by Richard's bank, with advertising on its sides. Timmy lay in bed with the covers pulled up to his chin, his face innocent and guarded. "It's my money, I could break open the bank if I wanted to," he said. "There was over ten dollars in there. What did you do with it?" said Alice. Richard could hear the alarm in her voice: she too felt she was losing control, losing direction of something, but did not understand it. "Tell your mother what you did with the money," Richard said. His son's face infuriated him; it reminded him of his father's face. "I could break it open if I wanted to," Timmy said. Richard began shaking him. Blood rushed to his head as if joyously freed. "God damn it, tell the truth!" said Richard. "I'm sick of all the lying around here!" Timmy began to cry. "I hid it," he said. "Why the hell did you do that?" said Richard. He had not released the boy. "I wanted to count it," he said. "Why?" said Richard. "Because I wanted to," said Timmy. Richard shook him again. He felt violence rising in him like light rushing in a musty, stale room. "I broke it with a knife and hid the dimes out in the garage," Timmy sobbed. But when Richard and Alice went out to the garage to look they found nothing. Richard could not tell if the old paint cans and brushes had been moved around or not.

"Did my father go out for a walk today?" Richard said. "Why do you ask that?" said Alice. "I'm just asking. Did he?" said Richard. Alice brushed hair back from her face. "I'm so tired with this," she said. "Did he go out or not?" said Richard. "Yes, he went out," said Alice. "Why don't you ask him about it?" They were standing in a dull halo of yellow light. Insects flitted about them. Richard felt the same confused impatience and violence for his wife that he had felt earlier for his son and had felt all along for his father. But he could say nothing about it.

The next day when Richard returned from work—it was just past noon, on Saturday—Gerry was out on the porch. But it wasn't her father she was waiting for. "Grandpa and Timmy went for a walk, they wouldn't let me come," she said. Richard picked her up and pressed his face against her smooth skin. "That wasn't nice," Richard said. She was still for a moment, then struggled to be let down. "Maybe they walk too fast for you," he said. He opened the door but she refused to come in. "Is that Gerry there?" said Alice. "Is she out on the porch by herself? They were supposed to take her with them. . . ." Alice moved out of Richard's embrace, distracted. "Did they go without her? Are they really gone?" On the porch the child waited. The wind blew her dark blond hair and must have made even more rigid her suspicious little features, as she stared out and down the road at nothing.

In a few minutes Timmy came home. "Grandpa's coming," he said. "He don't feel too well." The boy was pale and nervous. Richard hurried out to his father, who was walking slowly along the edge of the ditch. The old man's steps were gentle, as if he were walking on some hard, sharp substance. "Just a little tired," he said. His lips were bloodless. The wind whipped about them in raw warm gusts. Richard put his arm around his father and helped him walk; seen from one of the nearby houses they would have appeared very close, their steps the same steps, they stared at the ground as if they believed it might somehow betray them. Richard was numb with fear. When his father flinched as if struck Richard flinched also, his heart hammering. What he did came to him as if through a fog, suggested by someone other than himself, the behavior of strangers, the impersonality of strangers brought together temporarily to complete an action.

They put him in their own bedroom. He wanted to lie on top of the bed, not in it. "I'm just tired," he said sullenly. Richard sat by the bed and watched his father's stern face. Except for his father's irregular breathing and for the sound of children playing somewhere outside, everything was still. It would have been easy for Richard to ask his father a question—any one of the questions he had wanted to ask for twenty-eight years—but for some reason he could think of nothing to say. He waited. His father's toes twitched inside his dirty socks. "Wouldn't mind a cover over me," he said finally. Richard spread a quilt over him. "The doctor will be here soon," he said. His father shook his head sharply. "Never was to a doctor yet that knew anything," he said. "A doctor told me once I wouldn't live six months, and that was a long goddam time ago. It was a friend of mine. No. . . ." He looked angry and perplexed. "Yes, a friend of mine. He told him he wouldn't have six months to live, but he did. He kept right on. I don't know what happened to him. . . ."

"Lie still," said Richard.

"I'm all right," said his father. He patted the quilt, looking for something. He even tried to sit up. "Got my bag?"

"What?"

"Bag. Locked up."

"You want it in here?"

Richard brought the valise in; it was heavy. His father's eyes took it in but seemed then to be staring at nothing. "Father? Is something wrong?" said Richard.

"They had my stuff in there, in my locker. I mean, I left it there," his father said angrily. "They had me mixed up with somebody else. After the fire, then, they said it was a cigarette, but I never had one. I don't. I gave that up and drinking too. But I got the bag out anyway. I fooled them."

"The bag's right here," said Richard.

"They knew they couldn't keep it. Couldn't prove anything. I'd go to the police, a citizen has equal rights. . . ."

The old man's eyes were suspicious as the eyes of animals in pain. "You were gone such a long time," Richard whispered. His heart began to pound cruelly. The old man muttered something about ". . . those bastards . . ." but Richard could not understand. Something about a fire. "Where was this?" Richard asked.

"A padlock won't do no good if they want to get in. No lock will do no good," the old man said.

Richard asked nothing more and sat down beside his dying father. The old man's hands moved as if enlivened by pain, the dirty nails scraping against the quilt. His father had not come to tell him anything. Richard might wait forever, sitting here and listening to the old man's words, but he would never find out anything he did not already know. Sitting close to him as he was, with his head bent attentively to hear the secrets that would never be whispered, Richard had the look of one falling helplessly into a trance—he wanted yet did not want—he dreaded, yet desired—he would cry—he would not cry—would not surrender to tears—*why, why* should he mourn this man? He hated him! He would not mourn!

Pasts do not entwine: they do not make a single past. Relationships do not spiral upward to a climax. He knew this, he had always known. It was not a new discovery! . . . Years can not be eradicated, sins can not be forgiven and dare not be forgiven, old memories are often no more than discarded junk, scrap paper, things no one should bother to decipher. He knew, he knew. He had always known. Yet he wanted to cry, he wanted to mourn, he wanted— He did not want—

"Why did you do this to me?" he whispered.

At the end the old man was unconscious. Heavily - drugged, impassive. He did not resemble the father

46

who had abandoned Richard: that father, so far as Richard knew, never did return.

When they left the hospital the air was clear and sunny. A hard, healthy wind. The old man's illness and his death were going to be expensive, of course. Everything was expensive. Yet it gave Richard a spiteful sense of satisfaction to realize that his father, having gifted them with his last days, would now gift them with his death and with its cost—how like him that was, how like the father he remembered!

"Why did he do it? Why did he come back?... The old bastard!" Richard said. But Alice had not heard him; she was walking quickly, her head bowed against the wind, her hair whipping back. The wind swept upon them as if from a great distance, harsh, jocular, erratic, propelling scraps of leaves and dirt.

Getting
and
Spending

I met him one cold June morning, in Maine. I was living in the top half of a dilapidated old house on the ocean, back a narrow, rocky road. But it was his wife I saw first—the woman who was his wife at that time, 1961— broad-faced, broad-bodied, with a bronze, tarnished ponytail, standing in the muddy driveway. I had been lying in bed, not sleeping, not exactly awake, and I heard a car drive up and a car door slam, and I rose from my bed with my heart pounding, telling myself that it was nothing important, that no one knew where I was. It could be nothing important. When I looked down there was only a young woman standing there, helplessly. She wore blue jeans and a baggy shirt and she was smiling in confusion, as if to ward off evil. She glanced up at me and her smile faded. I stared down at her.

Then I heard the door being unlocked downstairs. I heard men's voices: the real estate agent was showing someone the first floor of the house. I drew back from the window, angry and embarrassed at being seen. I wanted to press my hands against my ears to drown out the exuberant conversation from downstairs—two men talking briskly, their voices climbing over one another. It was not possible to guess which one of them was the salesman.

It was ten in the morning. I didn't know which day it was—maybe a Tuesday, a day in the middle of the week. Shivering, touseled, sour-mouthed, I stood in the woollen slacks and sweater in which I had been sleeping, and listened to the voices rise through the floor. It was an uncarpeted floor, warped. I stared at it. Now the woman had joined them, entering the kitchen downstairs. I don't deserve this, I thought wildly. Not people here. Not so close.

At that time I was in hiding from other people. I had thought I could be free of them and of the thought of them. If I lived with people—with my family—I would come to hate them; therefore I had had to leave, to escape. I had left college in March of that year. At college and at home the air was jangling and complex and had to be interpreted constantly; I wanted emptiness, silence, nothing.

". . . somebody upstairs?"

A man's voice: lifting suddenly, as if directed toward me.

After a few minutes they went out again and I heard them climb the stairs on the outside of the house. The real estate agent was leading them upstairs, to knock on my door, and there was nothing I could do to stop them. *These people don't matter. They can't hurt me.* For weeks I had been instructing myself in the indifference of all things; yet that morning I felt almost panicked.

He was to tell me, later, that he had thought I might be a little crazy. But not dangerous. Interesting, maybe, if only I had been more attractive. "Your hair," he was to say, with a quizzical, apologetic little grimace, "you hadn't washed it for a long time, huh?"

I let them in. The real estate agent was the same man who had rented this half of the house to me. He introduced me to the woman I had seen outside, who smiled nervously at me, and a short, boisterous man in his mid-thirties. "Good morning," he said, staring at me, "I hope we didn't disturb you . . . ? It looks as if we might be neighbors and I wouldn't want things to get off to an awkward start."

He was no more than five feet seven, rotund in the face and torso, with a tense, restless, somehow clumsy manner. His handshake was brisk and boyish.

"Very private out here, isn't it? Is the water ever warm enough for you to swim? Where are you from?"

"Vermont...." I said slowly.

"We're from California. We've just driven across the continent. Are you here for the whole summer? Alone?"

"Yes...."

He kept asking me questions and I heard my hollow, unused voice try to answer them. I felt heavy and inert beside this man, who was much heavier than I, and even my voice could not keep up with his. I had not caught his name. He was a stranger and yet he was pressing an abrupt, terrible intimacy upon me. His face was merry and forcible, round-cheeked, yet somehow the cheeks were hard, muscular. I had never met anyone so sure of himself.

"What I want is peace," he said. "I think I can find it here."

You were in an old pair of slacks and a sweater, looking as if you'd slept in them, he was to say, years later. *Sleeping beauty! Did we wake you up, knocking on the door of that dump?*

I would protest, laughing. Laughing angrily. But he wouldn't listen. The next time we met he was to claim that he had walked in to discover me in bed that morning—a skinny, frightened girl, nineteen years old, big-eyed with wonder at Roger Craft walking into her bedroom.

"Yes, this will suit my wife and me just fine," he was saying. He screwed his face up into a grimace that was a kind of smile, directed toward his wife but not exactly communicating with her; she looked groggy, exhausted. They had evidently been driving for several days. "What do you say, Barbara? Can you work in that kitchen? Do you think the boys will like it here? I know this young woman will make an ideal upstairs neighbor—quiet and genteel, from Vermont—a lovely girl, isn't she? This is going to suit us all just fine."

We were friends from the very beginning, he was to claim. Without bothering to glance at me to see if this might be true.

They moved in that afternoon: not just him and his wife, but two young boys and an older woman, whom I had thought at first to be his wife's mother but who turned out to be his. They unpacked a U-Haul trailer, Roger calling out orders cheerfully, all of them carrying things up the little wooden steps and into the kitchen downstairs, while I walked out along the beach, alone, my hands thrust in the pockets of my slacks. I told myself that they would leave me alone. They were probably good, kind, simple people; they were not complex, like the people I knew. They would let me alone.

When I returned he was waiting for me, out on the beach. He had changed into a clean, tight-fitting T-shirt and khaki shorts. "Come to dinner, will you?" he said. "It's no trouble. We should get to know each other, right? You don't happen to know me, I suppose ... ?"

I stared at him. His smile was wavering and yet expectant. His eyes were narrowed a little, as if tensed against disappointment.

"Should I know you?" I asked.

"Obviously not; no," he laughed.

He insisted that I come to meet his family. "It's no trouble for her to set another place, I assure you," he said. "I'd like you to meet my people ... my sons especially."

His wife was working at the stove, but did not seem surprised to see me. His mother, who was frizzy-haired and muscular, and who had changed into shapeless over-sized Bermuda shorts, shook hands with me as her son had. "Pleased to meet you," she said. The boys were Johnny and Bob, three years old and five years old, extremely thin, small-chested children, with dark, lank hair like their father's. Roger picked the younger boy up in his arms. He seemed obviously proud of his household. I wanted to get away from them but I sat,

52

in an unresisting stupor, and let his wife set a place at their crowded table for me.

Perspiring, with that same vague, confused smile, she dished us all servings of a tuna casserole. I saw that she was a pretty young woman, though too heavy and messy, rather distracted, probably in her late twenties. She seemed never to look directly at anyone, not even at her children: there was something clumsily evasive about her. The ponytail had loosened and strands of hair lay untidily about her face.

Throughout this first dinner Roger kept talking at all of us—at his sons, giving them orders to sit still, to eat, to stop squabbling with each other, at his wife, complimenting her briskly on the food and asking for more, commanding her to open a large box of potato chips, which he set on the table. His behavior toward his mother was courtly and yet a little abusive, as if there were some long-standing argument between them. "Oh, you're going to like it here; going to love it here," he said cajolingly. He talked at me, sitting directly across from me and leaning forward, his elbows on the metal-topped, tarnished table. "I'm a loner, like you. I have the California tan and the California mock-heartiness, but I'm really a loner. In spite of what you see—this accumulated life, this household. . . . So you haven't heard of me? Roger Craft? You will." He ate in sudden spurts, almost angrily, then put down his fork; sat musing, frowning, as if he were alone. I began to feel uneasy. Once he cuffed Johnny on the side of the head, to make him sit still, and the sudden violent gesture cost him nothing—he hardly glanced at the boy, hardly exerted himself. "At the table we sit like civilized human beings," he said; but without seeming to address the boy.

He pushed his chair away abruptly and went to rummage through a box of books. "Here, a gift for you," he said. It was *Soul Glutton,* with a dull red cover like dried blood. I turned the book over, strangely moved. His photograph on the back cover: *Roger Craft.* He did exist.... A full-faced man with deep, cunning dark eyes, a tense smile. Not a handsome man. I felt him watching me eagerly as I studied the book, as if he were, himself, newly discovering it through me; his manner was so intimate, so aggressive, not exactly unpleasant... somehow *original*. "You're like someone who begins in the corner of an observer's eye, then takes over the entire landscape," I was to tell him bitterly. But that was years later.

That evening he spoke of this novel and of the people who had helped him and the people who had "tried to destroy him," a longer list of names, all strangers to me. "I'm going to alter this world and its complacency. I can't let it alone," he said seriously. He did not really talk with me; he didn't give me time to reply, and seemed not to expect me to reply. Occasionally one of his sons would approach him or squabble with each other, as if yearning for his attention or daring him to punish them. He slapped Johnny again, hard, and said in disgust, "What the hell? What is this?... Okay, cry. Be a baby in front of our guest and cry."

"Why did you do that?" his wife said, exasperated.

"Discipline," Roger said, without glancing at her.

He went on to talk about the critics' reviews of his novel, but I couldn't pay attention because of Johnny's crying. "... said it was too demanding for the era, imagine! The bastard!" His wife was clearing the table, brushing hair back out of her face, perspiring, luminous in the face and almost beautiful—but vague, exhausted. She did not once look at me, one woman to another woman. She did not make contact with me though I sought this contact, out of my uneasiness with her husband. He kept arguing with me, with my silence. He raised his dark, thick eyebrows defiantly and humorously, self-mocking and yet serious: "This summer everything is going to come to a head. I feel it. All I need to produce something fine is privacy and peace...."

He glanced over in surprise at his weeping child.

"Hey. Come here," he said. Johnny ran into his arms and he patted the boy's back, grinning at me. My face went hot with the misery of this ugly, crowded little room, I wanted only to escape, to be alone again, to be free. Yet I could not move. "From you, a stranger until today, I expect an absolutely honest opinion. About my novel," he said. His manner was light and cajoling, and yet commanding. Cheerful, but pushing. Crowding. Did his wives each discover themselves backed up against a wall, crowded into madness? Slapping and then caressed, yelled at and then loved? "I expect an opinion as pure and virginal as your face," he told me. "In me everything is wild and muddy, but I demand sobriety in other people, from women especially, and from my sons...."

I don't deserve this, I thought. Not this man. Not so close.

Yes, we were friends from the very beginning, he said.

Every day they rose early, his family. He got them up early and got the boys out on the beach, shouting orders: "Put that down, Bob! You heard me!" "I'll count to three and you'd better move!" "Get inside—get out of that water and inside or I'll tear you apart!" I would stare out my window at his stocky, energetic figure, hearing those words of his: *I'll tear you apart.* His sons cringed before him, or shouted defiance. I watched them running on the scrubby beach, overcome myself with an inertia that had something to do with the perpetual gray skies of that summer in New England, a disappointing summer up and down the coast. Before the Craft family came I had walked on the beach, thinking my solitary thoughts, not happy but not unhappy, in a kind of vacuum, in a sense without a personality. I did not feel like a daughter, or like a young woman at all. I was free of that. I had brought along with me to this place a few books from college which I had assigned myself to read, thinking that salvation would come to me out of a book. I was certain that salvation was possible, and that it would come out of a book: the book I believed in was Kant's *Critique of Pure Reason*, which I was reading closely and grimly, line by line, in the Modern Library edition. It had been assigned in the philosophy course I was taking that spring, at Bennington. Something had gone wrong with the printing of the edition I had, so that certain pages were not only smudged but the print of one page had offset on the facing page. But I read it anyway. I studied it. The crazy, almost indecipherable printing seemed to me an obstacle I must overcome: like the near-unintelligible prose itself, which promised so much. My head swam with the task before me. I had to get through it; then I would know:

Know what.

Whether anything can be known about life. Anything permanent.

Christ, what a laugh! As if you would really want anything permanent!

The scornful words were Roger's. He would screw up his face and stare out at the ocean, as if my stupidity were an embarrassment.

Before they came I could go outside whenever I liked. Now, the boys were always out there, or Roger's mother—raking the beach with a rake she'd found somewhere, always puffing and frowning, with a cigarette stuck between her lips, wearing her baggy Bermuda shorts and white cotton socks and sandals, and on cold mornings an enormous sporty white sweater with a heavily ribbed neck; or Roger himself would jump up from his typewriter—he had a small, cheap model that slid all over the kitchen table when he typed—and wander out after me, curious about whether I had finished his novel yet.

I don't deserve this, I wept; trying to read that novel of his. It was opaque, argumentative. Scatological. It seemed to be set at Big Sur, but perhaps it was all in the consciousness of a disturbed person in a hospital for the criminally insane, somewhere in the Midwest. The voice was meant to be mad and lyric and very wise,

but through it I could hear only Roger's voice, whee-
dling and crowding, asking me his perpetual questions
about my family (did they have money?—he sensed
that they did, and wanted to know more) and college
(he hadn't gone to college, had rejected *all that crap,*
yet he was reluctantly curious about what was taught
there—what kind of man is a professor?—what kind
of a self-conscious phony would make his living ped-
dling other men's ideas?) and my private life ("There
isn't any such thing as private life," he teased, "it's all
written in your face—your whole bleak pure history,
your uninteresting virginity"). I felt that I couldn't continue reading Kant until I had finished *Soul Glutton,*
but I couldn't finish it; couldn't get through the first
long chapter. While I tried to read I could hear him
yelling at his sons, bossing them around. Why did he
yell so much? I pressed my hands against my ears,
hating him. *Get in that house or I'll tear you apart!*

After the first few days I began to think that he
might be crazy.

Yet inertia kept me there, helpless. I felt bleary-
eyed and older than Roger himself, or his mother; the
skin around my eyes had dried out. He was thirty years
old, according to the dust jacket of his book. I had
thought he was older—the aggressive thrust of his
torso, his swarthy face, gave him a cockiness that usually grew with time. He wore everyone out except his
mother. The two of them were similar in build; they
walked on the beach like rivals, with their athletic,
cocky strides. They were not very friendly, yet the
mother always defended him if his wife objected to his
treatment of the boys. "Kids will walk all over you if
you let them, believe me," she would say. And to the
boys she would say, "Your father won't like that."
Sometimes she abbreviated this to "Father won't like
that," as if, despite his youth, Roger Craft were somehow everyone's father and could not be escaped....

But I tried to escape him. That voice of his, that
perpetual yelling; the inaudible ironic whine he used

on his wife, bullying her into submission. I walked out along the beach for miles, walking fast, until I came to a built-up strip of cheap cottages and a small town, where families like the Crafts rented for the summer—big families, disorderly and cheerful—and where the pebbly beach was strewn with napkins and wrappers and half-eaten buns, and the clothes-lines hung heavily with sheets and colorful striped towels. Many children played here. Many adults lay stretched out on their beach towels, in sunglasses and bathing suits that were not quite right for this climate, not Maine in mid-June. They always glanced up at me, stared at me. Open, curious, friendly. Seeing me so often, some of them cast out experimental lines, as if fishing, with questioning smiles and greetings; but I slipped through.

I couldn't sleep well at night, sometimes hearing voices from below, or waiting to hear them. Sometimes Roger typed until two or three in the morning. He pushed his chair back from the table, got up, made coffee, banged things on the stove . . . and I lay awake listening to each step, counting *one, two, three;* one, the rapid-fire clatter of his typing as he came triumphantly to the end of something; two, the immediate jerking of his chair backwards; three, the banging of a pan on the stove. . . . I couldn't sleep because I kept hearing his voice, his threats, I kept hearing the boys' startled, shrill cries of fear or pain, or the infrequent, sudden explosion of his wife's anger. I walked out for miles to get away from them and from the jumpy, frightening nervousness that made sleep impossible in my room and made the room itself now impossible. I walked to town each day though I felt drugged with exhaustion; I remember approaching the town's small police station, and asking myself if I should mention to someone, just casually, that a man down the beach was always striking his children, and that he got very angry at them, murderously angry, and I thought . . . I was afraid that. . . .

What business is it of yours? I asked myself.

Not my business.

But Johnny's screaming is hysterical sometimes.

How often? Very often?

Every day ... at least every day....

But he wasn't injured. Not that you know of. And there is his mother, even his grandmother, to protect him. It isn't your business.

I tried to control my growing uneasiness by telling myself that I was not yet free, that my melancholy would vanish when other people truly had no power over me. It was my own fault, my weakness.

You could talk to his wife, I told myself. Could ask whether she thought the boys might be in danger....

No, it isn't your business.

One day when I was coming back from my walk, shivering in my sweater and slacks and a raincoat, I saw Roger and his boys approaching me. Roger greeted me happily: "Good news in my life, I've been awarded a grant! Nice surprise after the rotten time I've been having with chapter nine.... Look." And he showed me the letter. He stood close to me, so that I could smell liquor on his breath: at one in the afternoon. I couldn't concentrate on the letter but saw that the award was for fifteen hundred dollars. "It's about time I'm getting some recognition," he said.

I congratulated him.

He turned and began walking toward the cottage with me, in excellent spirits. The boys clamored about going to town. "How come we're going back? We don't want to go back *home!*" they cried. Roger seemed not to hear them, telling me about the committee that had given him this award. He knew all about them, their private lives, the "deals" they had made with one another and with the Establishment, in order to get ahead. He, Roger Craft, wasn't going to compromise with anyone. Not even to get more awards like this. Didn't I believe him? I had better believe him.

Luke Moodie, the playwright, had tried to get intimate with him once: but he had rejected that bastard.

He hated homosexuals. Hated their ingrown, hysterical lives, their freakishness. He believed in nature, in the Natural. "They can't reproduce themselves, so they're not natural. It has nothing to do with morality. I don't give a damn about that," he said. "Do you?"

I didn't know how to answer this. But he didn't wait for a reply.

"Moodie is a fascinating personality, always doped-up, extravagant and doomed," he said with relish, "but I wasn't having any.... I don't believe in any of that. It isn't for me. I believe in marriage, in families... I read that we've inherited certain instincts from the apes, such as the fidelity of a woman to a man, the natural bond of the family, and I believe that our strength comes from that, from our natural instincts.... What do you think?"

But at this point Johnny's whining got to him, and he seized the child and began shaking him. "Shut up! I said shut up! Do you want me to rip you in pieces?"

He struck him on the face, three swift wild blows, and let the boy wrench himself away. "Don't do that, don't hurt him...." I said. But no one heard me. Both boys were crying now. They ran back toward the house; Roger watched them, breathing hard. "You might hurt Johnny sometime," I said faintly, "you might... he might...."

He did not seem to hear me. He said, abstractly, philosophically, "Yes, there are very few sources of strength available for us today. Everything is freaked-out, sterile. We have to reaffirm our healthiest instincts. That's what my writing is about. Have you finished my novel yet?"

"Not yet, but...."

He walked me home, forcing a brisk pace. Bullying. Crowding. *Don't touch me!* I wanted to scream, when he tapped my arm to make a point. He was proprietary, even paternal with me. And yet flirtatious in a jocular way: as if I expected this of him. He was talking about his family now. "I didn't get much from my family, especially not from my father. He was weak, he drank too much. He was nothing. I would rather have my sons die than experience that kind of vacuity. You have to do so much to overcome it. . . . It's like creating your own unique mythology, creating your own God the Father. Do you follow me?"

"Yes. I think so. I don't know."

"My novel is about the terrible task of overcoming all that's weak and sterile in a culture, about making oneself anew. . . . It's about time I've been given some recognition. I've been wondering why they've ignored me. . . ."

His sons had stopped, waiting for us. Pretending not to see their father, but waiting for him, and then marching along in the surf, keeping pace with us. Johnny was still sobbing. Roger did not seem to notice them; he was no longer angry. He talked enthusiastically the rest of the way home, until we came in sight of that ugly, weathered house which I now hated, and we saw his wife dragging something out to the road— a garbage can—and his mother sitting on the beach, almost in the surf, in her short-legged canvas chair, with a blanket over her legs so that only the white tips of her socks showed. I hated that chair of hers, which was always left on the beach; it looked dwarfed, deformed, crippled. As if the sight of his wife and mother irritated him, Roger halted. He turned to me with an impatient grin, he took my arm and said, "I think you understand me. *You*. Because I'm so happy—I feel so strong—no one is equal to me, not *her*, not Barbara— that poor cow— You understand, don't you? You sense what I feel?" There were tears in his eyes. "To live in a world in which no woman is equal to you—"

I drew away from him, frightened.

"Or are you a coward, just like the rest of them?" he laughed.

I ran back to the house, ran up the rickety stairs.

61

I could hear him laughing at me.

The rest of that day I spent packing, planning my escape, wiping tears of anger and frustration out of my eyes. My heart pounded with rage. How had this happened, this man forcing me out?—making me run again, when I had thought I was free? I hated him.

I saw him knock one of the boys down on the beach, and I thought: If he kills them, then he will be arrested.

But the boy scrambled to his feet and ran away. Safe.

Roger returned to the house, began typing. I waited for dark. I waited to escape. Something was going to happen out here, on this lonely stretch of beach, but I was going to escape before it happened.

Or are you a coward, just like the rest of them?

In the end I drove away with only a few things, not wanting to come back for more. I threw two suitcases in the back seat of my car and drove away. Free. Free of him. I kept hearing his angry voice, addressing his sons: *I'm going to rip you in pieces.*

But that was only talk. He didn't mean it.

It wasn't your business.

His family wasn't your business.

It wasn't your business, was it?

Back home I told no one about Roger Craft. I threw away *Soul Glutton.* I thought from time to time of that house out on the beach, and my things still upstairs; I thought of him snooping around, his face twisted up into that jocular grimace. *Are you a coward, like the rest of them?*

It wasn't until September that I drove back, to find the house empty. I went upstairs and unlocked my door and there, slid beneath the door, was a note with a single morose question: *Why did you leave me?*

Because I might have broken. Suddenly. Because beneath my defiance I might have yearned to surrender, like Johnny and Bob; might have broken suddenly, wanting his love.

A coward like the rest of them. . . .

After that I began to hear his name and to notice reviews of his books. For a while, when I lived in New York, I knew some people who were acquaintances of his—and very proud they were, to go to the same parties Roger Craft did—and I always asked about him, reluctantly. I asked about his wife and they wondered who I meant. And his sons? Oh, the sons were evidently fine; he was proud of his boys and carried their snapshots around with him. This was in 1964, when I lived near Columbia, worked as an editorial assistant at a woman's fashion magazine, and took courses at night; I had given up the idea of living a solitary life, with so much time for thinking, because thinking seemed to make me uneasy. Why had I imagined I wanted anything permanent to believe? I believed now in keeping busy, in knowing people. I liked the thunderous sound of women's heels on New York streets; I liked to ease along with that crowd of fierce, hurrying, independent women, so well-groomed and beautifully, indifferently dressed.

One humid spring day I saw Roger Craft on Third Avenue, walking with a young girl. She was extremely young-looking, though probably she was in her twenties; dressed like a teenager, in a leather-fringed skirt and vest, with a lacy, near-transparent white blouse, and leather boots; her jagged, doped-up laugh carried across the street, where I had crossed in order to avoid them. *He* had not noticed me. He was a little heavier than before, though he carried his weight well, like an athlete; he wore ordinary clothes, even a necktie, and was carrying an armload of books. While the girl chattered he kept nodding, nodding, his swarthy, clever face gone abstract. I had seen photographs of him in a number of magazines by this time and wondered if he was famous. To me he was famous and always had been: that first day, that first morning, he had walked into my life with the assurance of a man who is not an ordinary man, and whom ordinary dislike will not discourage.

From across the street I watched him and his girl, striding away. They had the innocent exuberance of young soldiers, marching through a conquered town.

A few days later I read of the sale of his new novel to a well-known film producer; the novel had not even been published yet. But when I saw the people who were "friends" of his, they were noisy with sorrow for his bad luck. "It's been kept out of the newspapers, thank God," they said. "One of his sons died—it was an accident, but it sounds bad—Roger had been drinking and he went out to visit his wife on Long Island, and somehow one of the boys fell out of the car."

"Fell out of the car?" I said. I was stunned. "Which one of them?"

They didn't know: the youngest one, maybe.

"Johnny? Johnny's dead?"

"That might have been his name," they told me. They weren't sure.

"But how did he fall out of the car? What happened?"

"Roger said he was telling the boy to sit still, to behave himself, but somehow the boy got the door open and fell out. Roger was driving about sixty miles an hour...."

They shook their heads over it. Roger was wild with grief, he'd been drinking for a week, no one could talk to him, and on and on, they were sure this would be the end of his career if he didn't straighten out...on and on they went, in their verbose sorrow. I wanted to ask them angrily if anyone cared about the child's death.

Then I remembered the day I had almost gone to the police. But I hadn't gone. I had been afraid. Of the police, of the fuss, but mostly of Roger: how angry he would have been!

It hadn't been my business, I told myself.

I bought a copy of his new novel and read it in one evening, fascinated. I could hear his voice shouting through all the characters' voices, a symphony of Roger Craft arguing with himself. The novel was called *Routine* and it was about an air force pilot. It was much more readable than *Soul Glutton,* much more dramatic, plotted like a suspense novel; very slim, hardly two hundred pages, so that I figured, feverishly, and bitterly, that he would make over one thousand dollars a page, just on the movie sale. Maybe that would console him for the loss of Johnny?—but I had no right to think such thoughts.

The next day I threw the novel out and did not think about it or him any longer.

3

In 1966 my husband and I spent the summer in England, and when we returned by steamship in September I discovered that Roger was on board. Now that I was married—to a young professor of English—I felt less vulnerable to him, even fearless of him. I wanted to meet him again in order to confront the childish, frightened girl I had been, five years before; I was ashamed of that self. Reading Kant up in Maine, looking for salvation in a book! Terrified of Roger Craft's touch! My face burned with shame, remembering those awful weeks and my own helplessness. I wanted to meet him again and exorcise all my memories.

When we were going on board the ship, at Southampton, I heard someone arguing with the officials at Customs, something about a receipt: a man kept demanding to see the baggage steward. They told him the steward was in his office, but the man demanded that he come down: *he* wasn't going to leave his luggage on the dock. I turned around to see who was causing all this trouble. It was a shock to see him: he looked much older, fat and haggard, sickish. His skin was dark and yet pale, glowing with a kind of fierce, maniacal pallor. His voice had a false ring to it, each word articulated deliberately, self-consciously, in a kind of British accent, as if he wanted to keep his words from slurring together. He looked drunk.

"That's Roger Craft," I told my husband.

As we walked on I stared back at him, fascinated. I did hate him, yes. Yet I was shocked at the change in him.

At one time he had been a handsome man, almost. An attractive man. It was a pity that that man had disappeared. . . . I should have felt satisfaction and even delight, but I didn't. I felt instead an absurd sorrow, as if someone close to me had died.

I had thought he was sailing alone, but that evening we saw him in one of the lounges, with a very old woman. His mother! Then I felt that I had to meet him again, to put something right. I was not vulnerable to him now. My husband did not understand and was reluctant to approach Roger, who sat sprawled at one of the lounge's small, squat, ridiculously undersized tables, with his mother beside him and yet turned slightly away, so that she was looking in another direction. They had the appearance of strangers who are seated together but are not aware of each other.

"I just want to say hello to him," I said. It was strange, the excitement I felt. My husband sensed it and seemed to resent it. "I'll only talk with him a minute. . . ."

We moved into Roger's vision and I felt the grab of his eyes at us, his consideration of my husband, his dismissal of him, and then his concentration on me. At first he saw me only as a young woman and my face flamed at his rudeness. Then his eyes narrowed and that old, familiar grimace of his appeared, as he recognized me and yet could not quite place me. But he got to his feet, jumping up. Such agility surprised me, because he looked scruffy and ill; but I put out my hand to his extended hand, smiling a greeting, supplying my name as he groped for it—

"Yes, of course, did you think I had forgotten you?" he asked. "Impossible!"

I introduced him to my husband. He half-bowed from his clumsy waist and shook hands. "Mother," he said sharply, "We have company. Mother. An old friend of ours and her husband, Mother. Say hello."

His mother turned just a little to stare up at us. She looked peevish, thinner in the face than I had remembered. Yet her clothes were still masculine and sporty, gray flannel slacks and a box-like blazer and thick-soled leather shoes with complicated laces. It flashed through my mind, strangely, that Roger would have to help his mother lace up those shoes.

He insisted that we pull up two chairs to join them. He wanted to buy us a drink "to celebrate your wedding." He had already been drinking a while, and he seemed pleased at the prospect of more drinking; his mother nursed along a single drink, something colorless with a limp slice of lemon floating in it. It wasn't clear to me whether she remembered me or not. "We've been sick, Mother and me both," Roger said with a sigh. "You wouldn't believe our combined medical history. Don't let Mother's behavior dismay you—she can't hear every word you say, but she's still sharp, razor-sharp. Butcher-knife-sharp," he said vaguely and cheerfully.

He asked what I had done since that night I fled him, but though he screwed up his face to show that he was listening closely I had the feeling that he was waiting for me to finish with my life, so that he could tell me about his. He asked one or two more questions, perfunctory questions about my husband's work, then slipped into a long energetic monologue about himself. While he talked a four-piece band began playing in one corner of the lounge, and a few people got up to dance, swaying with the ship's occasional lurches, everyone giddy with excitement and a kind of blank, moronic alarm. Roger noticed none of this. He was blowsy, soiled, in a sports jacket and a shirt without a tie and white trousers that were too tight and too short for him. His tongue seemed too large for his mouth, somehow. Its tip kept showing as he talked. Even in the dim, pink glow of the cocktail lounge his eyes looked bloodshot, nearly blind; he was like an eagle in his vigilance, though, glancing from me to my husband and back again, jealous of our attention. "My life is a comic opera," he said, "but I haven't had any hand in writing it. That must be one definition of hell."

He wore a brief, thin goatee, fringed with gray or perhaps with stains of some kind—food or nicotine. His hair was thin at the crown, but rather long and scruffy at the back. He smoked constantly, coughed and cleared his throat constantly. Smoking was a new habit of his, evidently. In this setting his voice was too robust, sometimes breaking in a high, angry-sounding rattle of a laugh, that drew the attention of other passengers. He insisted on buying us another round of drinks. "Yes, my health has been a continual problem, but I've kept it out of the newspapers. There've been enough rumors as it is," he said. "Life is such a strain, such a risk. . . . Actually I've been sicker than Mother, but I haven't wanted to worry her. I've got a house in Malibu Beach now; the problem is how to get to it. I don't fly. I would never fly. I'm too neurotic to get very high off the ground. You remember my wife, my first wife Barbara . . . ? She's back in Seattle, where her people are from. She never remarried. Bob is living with her and she got an injunction against me, to forbid me visiting him, in an effort to destroy me. She spends her time drinking ale. She's a mess, spread-bellied and ugly. You did meet her, didn't you? Or was it Francine you knew?"

The waiter came with our drinks and Roger argued

with him over the change. He didn't seem to understand British currency, though he had evidently spent a year in England. He had won another grant, he explained: for travelling, for the broadening of a writer's experience. He made a downward gesture, toward his ham-like thighs, and laughed. His mother snickered. "Yes, I have broadened handsomely," he said. "Well. After *Routine* everything collapsed. I tried to do the screenplay, I lived in a motel in Beverly Hills for three months, but they didn't like anything I did, not anything. They are very cold, intelligent sons of bitches out there, not hopped-up and crazy as the clichés suggest, just businessmen, and I couldn't do business with them. They paid me twenty-five thousand dollars to get rid of me. And Johnny was dead by then, you know," he said slowly. "He died in a tragic accident. A stupid accident. It wasn't my fault and yet I keep blaming myself. . . . You heard about it, didn't you? Johnny's death? And then money flowed in all directions, a lot of it to *her*, I mean Francine, but also to Barbara, to shut her up. She was a hysterical woman. So was Francine, but in another way. I know you never met Francine but she was very beautiful . . . is very beautiful. . . . And taxes. Jesus, the taxes! I owe back taxes even now. I've been broke for years. I support my mother, who needs all kinds of medical treatment, and of course my son Johnny . . . I mean Bob . . . Bobby . . . who is going to an excellent private school out West. Those are two deductions, but still my taxes are fantastic. The other year I made $350,000—I think—or $550,000—in one fiscal year—and they taxed the hell out of me. It was a disaster. . . . I'm very famous, yet no one knows my face. Like right here. In this bar or on the ship. They don't appear to know me. They snubbed me in England. You wouldn't believe the incredible jealousy of people, not just writers—I could understand and even sympathize with that, because a talent like mine is alarming to ordinary writers—but other people, wishing the worst for me but always ready

69

to borrow money and to drink my whisky. When the lawyers got through with me I was wrung dry. I didn't have enough energy to hang myself. What did me in was Johnny dying like that, in that stupid accident, and her moving out West with Bob. She said I couldn't see him again. A woman knows how to destroy a man. My second wife wouldn't have any children, so I kicked her out. . . . You know, a man without children isn't a man. He doesn't have a soul. He isn't defined . . . isn't defined. . . . He's *undefined*. Do you understand?"

Roger took my hand drunkenly and tried to pull me toward him. "You're looking good, better than I remember," he said. "Marriage must agree with you. It agreed with me too, I was never happier, it's natural and healthy to be married and to be faithful to one person. . . . Don't think ill of me. I've become gross, dealing with gross people. Life is too cannibalistic. . . . Let me give you my blessing."

I tried to pull back, but he took my head between his hands and kissed my forehead, the top of my forehead at the hairline.

"You belong to a good, clean period of my life," he said, his eyes filling with tears.

When we managed to get away my husband was angry, at Roger Craft and at me. He was a very tall, intense young man, thirty years old, who wore a suit and a tie every day of the ship's crossing, while most of the passengers degenerated gradually, wandering the ship's several floors and staring listlessly and groggily at one another, fighitng sea-sickness. The voyage was monotonous, the ocean choppy and dark, reflecting no sky. Small irritations were exaggerated: my husband kept making remarks about Roger Craft, about how he had kissed me, how I had allowed him to kiss me. "That wasn't like you. That wasn't worthy of you," he said. We stumbled up stairs and down stairs, answering the calls for breakfast and lunch and dinner, the two of us bound together by our marriage and yet perplexed by intimacy. Five days on the ship exaggerated everything, especially intimacy. To please him I avoided Roger. I avoided even the sight of him—he was usually in the lounge, with or without his mother, waiting for someone to join him. I stood outside once and listened in fascination as he complained loudly to one of the stewards about the ship: his stateroom was too small, the lavatories stank, the English food stank— "pressed ox tongue, fried liver, kidney, meat pies filled with who knows what crap!"—the constant vibrations of the ship's engines were driving him mad, loosening his spinal cord, the faucets spat out hot water but cold water came in a trickle, there were teenaged kids in the stateroom next to his, banging against the wall and giggling all night long, until he wanted to rush out and kill someone, and he hated the decks, the closed-in decks, where old people lay bundled in their chairs like dying patients in a nursing home, it was obscene and he wouldn't bear it. He ended by weeping just as the four-piece band began, as it did every day at this time, with a swaying, sentimental version of "Stardust." I didn't tell my husband what I had overheard.

On the fourth day out there was a rumor that someone had collapsed at the first sitting of lunch. A man, we heard. An old man. Then it was a woman, someone swore, an old woman. I saw Roger wandering the ship, alone, in his same soiled white clothes, and I wondered if it had been his mother. He looked groggy, stricken. He was carrying a loose-leaf notebook and turning the pages as he walked, stumbling, catching hold of a wall as the ship dipped and lurched, and then righting himself and walking on. The ocean swell was strong that day and many passengers were sick, including my husband. I was alone with nothing to do: I couldn't read, couldn't concentrate.

I followed Roger out to the deserted deck. He propped himself against the rail and wrote in his notebook, his head lowered against the wind, his face twisted into a grimace. He was a short, dumpy, sick-looking man, with a stained goatee and stained clothes, yet there

71

was something about him that fascinated me. I wanted to ask him a question but I didn't know what the question was. About power, about the power some personalities have, and others don't? About his talent?—it may have left him, his career might be finished, but he had had talent once. Or did I want to ask him about life and death, about the way he had brought a child to life and then taken life from him?

He straightened as if aware of someone watching him. He turned to look at me.

"Good morning! Come here! Come look at the ocean with me!"

I came forward to stand beside him, half a head taller than he. My hair blew in the wind. I was an attractive young woman, and he was a woozy, aging man, and yet I felt a strange pride in standing beside him. He was Roger Craft, after all. He was a famous man even if no one here recognized him.

He was taking notes for a new novel, he explained. He showed me a page of his notebook as if he suspected I did not believe him, but I could make out only scrawled lines. I smiled and nodded. Yes, I believed him. "It's going to be a mammoth novel. If I can only get straightened out. . . ." he said morosely. "You believe in me, don't you? You always have, haven't you? I need only one person to believe in me, the loyalty of one person. . . ."

In the bright, harsh ocean air his eyes were very bloodshot. It alarmed me to look at him, to stand so close to him. I wondered if he had been crying, if something had happened to his mother; but I was afraid to ask. I thought of that last day on the beach, when he had struck Johnny and I had said, so faintly, "You might hurt Johnny sometime. . . ." I had been afraid of him then and I was afraid of him now.

"I remember how we met," he said suddenly, "you were in an old pair of slacks and a sweater, looking as if you'd slept in them. . . . Sleeping beauty! Did we wake you up, knocking on the door of that dump? I like to think we did wake you up. I woke you up. You and I were friends from the very beginning, weren't we? You always had faith in me, didn't you? Not like the rest of them. After all, we were lovers once, we meant a great deal to each other once—"

I stared at him.

"—can't deny that, can't lie about that—" he muttered, smiling into my face.

Then he fell silent. His lips still moved and I could smell the liquor on his breath. Now he was not looking at me but through me, musing on something beyond me, his slack face tightening with cunning as if with the memory of pleasure.

"It's the one thing a woman can't lie about," he said confidentially.

I left him there, at the railing.

A rumor went around the ship that someone had died, of a heart attack or a stroke. But no one knew who it was. The ship's officers would not give out any information. We docked the next day and I didn't look around for Roger; I didn't want to see if he was alone, or if his mother was still with him, I didn't want to know anything more about his life.

We were lovers once, he had said. I would never forget those words.

4

In December of 1971 I was assigned to interview Roger Craft. After years of silence he had published a new novel, eight hundred pages long, called *Losses;* it was argued over, acclaimed as a masterpiece and denounced as melodramatic and messy, but it was making money, and again people were talking about him. He keeps coming back, I thought. He won't disappear.

By this time I was thirty years old, now an adult, completed. There was nothing girlish in me. I was the age now that Roger had been when we first met, with one marriage behind me, one disappointment made compact and forgettable. When I was asked to fly to Florida to interview Roger Craft, for a fashion magazine I had done several articles for in the past, I felt only a slight thrill of shame: that man had thought we were lovers!

But it didn't seem to matter. Why should it matter? Nothing was permanent or very important.

With a photographer, I flew down to see him in Palm Beach. His house was enormous, like a fort, with high white walls and palm trees, fronting the ocean. I didn't understand: was he wealthy? Had he been wealthy all along? He was noisy in his greetings, shaking hands and kissing me, a short, busy, fattish man who looked much older than forty. The goatee was a little fuller and cleaner, but he was nearly bald. He embraced me and said happily, "What a good surprise, to see *you*. *You'll* write an intelligent, sympathetic piece, won't you? You'll settle the controversy about me, won't you?"

He brought us around to the pool to meet his new wife, a blond woman younger than I, and his wife's children from a previous marriage, a girl of about five and a boy of about eight. But his big surprise was a baby girl named Claudine: "Isn't she a beauty? What do you think of *that?*" he said. "Be sure to take a picture of her, will you? Make sure Claudine gets in the story."

Like a small, portly king he led us in triumph around his house, inside and out, while his wife trailed behind with a fond, vague smile. She wore tight-fitting silk slacks and a halter made of an expensive scarf and open backless shoes with transparent heels; Roger wore swimming trunks and a yellow sports shirt which was unbuttoned, and he was barefoot, padding silently and heavily and enthusiastically from room to room. "It's beautiful here, isn't it? The ocean, the sun? I've found peace here, I really have. I've been searching for it all my life and I've found it here. I always do my best work by the ocean—you should write that down, explain that to them—because it's infinite, no boundaries. I feel a kinship with that. Do you understand?"

I was a little dazed by his good fortune, staring at the potted plants, the cactus and palm trees and flowers, the huge blocks of decorative glass, the gleaming white Mercedes in the driveway. So many possessions! It was easy to be happy for him, he seemed so simple in his joy. It was easy to share in his pride. We were served luncheon out by the pool, lobster salad with large chunks of ham and chicken and pineapple and nuts, Roger's own creation, and many drinks—he drank liquor thirstily, in gulps. He talked all the while, answering the kind of questions other interviewers had evidently asked, launching into brief, trim, well-modulated paragraphs that covered the various phases of his life. I glanced nervously at the notes I had brought with me, for this interview "in depth"—*Craft's novels are genuinely moving, unforgettable, yet they always fall short of greatness, as if deliberately; as if Craft were reluctant to admit their terrible gravity, masquerading as an ordinary man*—but I was shy of asking him about such things. I didn't want to stop that flow of hearty good spirits, I didn't want to displease him. It was flattering to be teased by Roger Craft: he broke off in the middle of an anecdote about a reception in Washington, which he had snubbed, to speak of the humble beginnings of our friendship—saying that he had walked into my bedroom, waking me up, a frightened girl of nineteen who had retreated to a dump of a house in Maine, with Immanuel Kant, looking for salvation with Immanuel Kant! He laughed, wheezing, and the rest of us joined in. For a dizzy moment I could not remember what had really happened that morning.

"Not that I scorn Kant," he said quickly, "because I don't: I'm renewing my interest in the German Transcendentalists, you can write that down, though I don't take them any more seriously than anyone else. Great men compete, you know, for our serious attention. They *compete.* . . . You were married, weren't you? What happened to that prig of a husband of yours? I never approved of that marriage, I never thought the two of you should marry," he laughed, grabbing my hand. His wife smiled routinely at this, as if he was always testing her, teasing her. Her blond hair had been prepared carefully, stacked and curled around her head. She looked like an actress or a chorus girl. She was prettier than Barbara, but just as silent. The photographer took pictures of her and Roger as they sat at the luncheon table, dozens of quick shots like the blinkings of an eye; I could see the strain in his wife's face, but Roger seemed more energetic than ever, eager to please. The eight-year-old boy, Mike, hung around him, wrestling with him, as he launched into a half-hour recitation of his work habits: "With me it's mainly intuition. You can tell them that. Rational construction comes later, much later. I work from the unconscious. From the instincts. That's the only true source of a man's strength—the instincts." I jotted down notes hurriedly, conscious of the discrepancy between Roger Craft's words and the hearty, insatiable energy he represented. He rubbed his hand playfully over Mike's head, he shifted his weight in his chair, made gestures that seemed to embrace the whole of this perfect world of blue water and blue sky. I noticed ants and other insects crawling about the poolside, feeding on bits of Roger's salad, which he had dropped. A lizard scrambled around the dry, hard, perfect trunk of a plam tree nearby. In the air were sudden flocks of birds, migratory birds from the north, gulls, even pelicans, but something about this part of the world made me uneasy: life was abundant here, but strangely artificial. The flowers were too large, too brightly-colored. The sun was too close to us, for December, its rays too naked. I felt as if I were in a glaring white room, tile-lined, all perfect light and sand and walls, with no way out.

Roger paced around the pool, instructing me to *tell*

them this, explain this, set them straight on this—! "I know you'll do a great job," he said. The little boy tugged at his hand and Roger glanced down at him, with an abstract smile, which then sharpened as the child came into focus. "Hey, kid, show our visitors what you can do, huh? He's like a fish, this kid. I've been giving him diving lessons, maybe you could take a picture of him, huh? His name is Mike and he's eight years old. I'm pretty proud of him. I think he takes after me even if . . . even if he's *by a previous marriage,* as the saying goes," he laughed. He lifted the boy up onto the diving board. The boy did not have a bathing suit on, only a pull-over shirt and cotton shorts. He took a few steps out, then hesitated.

"Roger, it's right after lunch," his wife said suddenly. Her voice was throaty and alarmed, a surprise.

"The hell with that, that's an old-wive's tale, about cramps and all that," Roger said. He set down his drink in order to instruct the boy more carefully. "Come on, Mike. Don't let me down. Maybe you could take a picture of him, huh, at the height of the dive? I'm really proud of this kid."

The boy stared down at the water, a thin, very tanned child, with close-cropped hair bleached almost white by the sun. Roger's wife clattered over to the pool in her clumsy heeled sandals. "Roger, I don't thin—"

"Come on, Mike. Not scared of a little water, are you? Or are you shy? You have to get used to it, performing for other people," Roger said more sharply. We all watched the boy.

"Roger—" said his wife.

"Shut up," Roger said, but almost gently, courteously, an aside not meant for the photographer and me to hear. Then, more clearly, he said: "Life is a constant performance in the face of all kinds of risks—every day you take chances, you perform, you walk out on the diving board and *complete the dive.* That's life. . . . Come on, Mike, we're waiting."

The child backed up, then took several quick steps

forward, his hands pointed up just before his face, as if in an attitude of prayer, and dived off into the air and into the water—a tidy, perfect little dive, without any splashing. Roger applauded vigorously and the rest of us joined in.

"Bravo! Excellent!" Roger cried.

The boy swam to the side of the pool and climbed out, and Roger grabbed him to swing him into the air. He turned his happy gleaming face toward us. "Life is a constant risk, it's cannibalistic but you've got to face it, struggle with it, emerge triumphant. Write that down. It's the secret theme of all my work. Write that down. Tell them that."

Splendid
Architecture

1

That room was his first room away from home. It was in a boarding house not far from the University, and it faced the east. A new shade had been put up above the only window; there were limp white curtains, really no longer white. The walls were no longer white either. There was a narrow bed and a short, scuffed bureau, a desk and a chair and a lamp—the room of an ordinary, anonymous student. He himself was an ordinary, anonymous student. His parents, helping him carry suitcases and grocery store boxes filled with things up from the car, were for some reason humbled by the room, and this annoyed him. He said, "Nice view," meaning to be ironic—there was a parking lot outside. His parents stared toward the window as if they could not see through it. "I guess I'll be all right here. I'll get along," he said weakly. His parents looked very tired. His father looked old. He realized that his irritation with them was a desperate attempt to keep himself from crying; he had to look critically at them, harden himself from them, or he would humiliate himself by crying. They would say to people back home, "Edward is really too young to go away to school...."

"Nice view out here," he said, making his mouth twist into an ironic smile.

He had to work part-time and so he stayed up late at night, studying. That first semester was the worst period of his life though he did not know it. He was a tall, lean boy, with an angular face. He looked as if he had come from the mountains, from some distant improbable land, where the air was somehow colder and thinner. His eyes had a distracted look to them; it was nothing he controlled. Really, he was quite humble. He was like his parents, humble and afraid of being humiliated. He called older men "Sir" and people thought he was from a wealthy family, dressed eccentrically for his own reasons; but really he did not know any better. He called men "Sir" who wore neckties. He was not from the mountains either, and not even from the country, but from a town of twenty thousand people which was downriver from a large Ohio city. Having lived all his life on the periphery of a real city, Edward had the slightly foreign, unfocussed vague air of one who hears distant music but cannot quite make it out. He seemed always to be staring into the distance, waiting.

He was enrolled in the School of Architecture, one of the best schools at the University.

The room became cluttered with projects and with sheets of sketching paper. He liked to doodle in short, swift patches, as if his hands had a life of their own. He liked pencils sharpened with a knife. He did not use ball-point pens, but he sometimes used old-fashioned fountain pens. For ink sketches he used special pens, of course. He loved to draw. Sometimes he found himself drawing sketches of people—and this was strange, for he had no use for people. The human figure was a waste of time because no one could perfect it. Other structures could be perfected, switched about, distorted, stretched, obliterated; but not the human figure. Still, he found himself sometimes drawing pictures of men and women. The women were vague, clothed in long skirts, the men were more precise, with sharp, brittle, intelligent features, arms poised as if to catch hold of something, and their clothes were not old-fashioned but contemporary. Edward's eye must have noticed university styles without his brain knowing anything about it, or approving. He spent some time one evening on a foot-high sketch of a man, with Edward's own face. The man wore a neat, conventional suit. He was handsome despite his lean face. His stance, his straight, confident shoulders, and his intelligent expression showed that he was a man on the brink of a successful life, without fear. He was a man who had descended from some unreal, foreign land, and was about to take his place in the real world. It would be necessary for him to leave everything of his old life behind.

Upstairs there lived a loud Negro boy of about twenty, who was in something called Physical Education. His name was Robinson. He came down to visit Edward in his cramped room and peered at the sketches of buildings and houses taped to the wall, a little suspicious of them. He himself was in Physical Education, which he always pronounced in its entirety, as if the sound pleased him. He also played football. He was friends with Edward because Edward was too weak to say no. Robinson liked to talk about many things, sitting on Edward's bed, smoking, his big hands sometimes clutching at his ankles and giving them a shake. "What's the sense of all them drawings and things?" he said. "That one's sort of nice, that one there—what is it, a church?"

"A model for a drive-in bank."

Robinson looked with more respect at the sketch.

"So you're going to build houses and make lots of money?"

"I'm not interested in money," Edward said.

"Oh hell!" Robinson laughed.

The room became too small. When the Negro boy came in—which was nearly every night—the room shrank perceptibly, like a room in a dream. Edward sat at his drawing board in a kind of daze, looking toward Robinson and listening to the boy's long, drawling, curiously ominous speeches. "Looks like I ain't going to settle down, not yet. I'm in no hurry yet. There's some people right here who'd like to make trouble for me—you know Kilroy?"

"Who?"

"Kilroy. Nelson Kilroy, that bastard."

Edward was nervous and distracted. He said he did not know.

"Sure you know him! Christ, but you're strange—you're weird. You walk around like you're asleep or something. Sure you know him!"

Robinson needled him all the time. It was good-natured but it went on too long. Edward began to draw sketches of Robinson, exaggerating his friend's dark, heavy face. His lips looked bloated. He drew at his desk while Robinson, over on the bed, chatted and smoked and drank the beer that would have gotten them both expelled, had the authorities known. But he kept on drinking it. He sat right on Edward's pillow and thought nothing of it; he sat on the bed without taking off his shoes, which were mud-encrusted sneakers, and he sometimes hunched over in the midst of telling Edward an ugly story, taking hold of his thick ankles and giving them an affectionate squeeze as if to illustrate the point of his story. His laugh was a dark roar. "Never heard of that where you come from, did you, kid? Huh? They don't do things like that there, do they?"

Other boys saw Edward and Robinson together and avoided them both; but one time a boy said, in a curious, flat midwestern drawl: "Don't let that nigger bother you, and don't lend him any money. He smells."

It was true: Robinson did smell.

Edward listened to Robinson's stories and tried to enjoy them, but after a while he did not really hear them. Instead he drew short, deft, nervous sketches of the boy's body, sometimes topping it with a gorilla's head. He did this without thinking about it, as if his hand were working by itself. While Robinson droned on about his family—it was a pathetic, ugly, but monotonous story—Edward found himself sketching memories of his own family, his old home. It was his "old home"; he did not belong there any longer. He sketched a wheel barrow half-buried in snow; he sketched the big barn, which had been struck by lightning and partly burned. He sketched the apple orchard, showing how scrubby the trees were. He sketched the one-room school house he had attended for eight years, eight very long years. As he drew, his lips seemed to swell with bitterness for the ugly life that had been his, and he felt for the first time that his rapidly-moving pen was enough to free him from it. It was enough to free him from anything.

There was a large crack on the ceiling of his room, and a galaxy of smaller, finer cracks everywhere. Edward sketched the cracks of his room idly. "Why don't you come up to my room tonight? I got some beer," Robinson said. He was trying hard to be friends. Something in him cringed at the white boy, even this outlandish awkward white boy who should not have counted much, and he had to make up for the cringing by a slight forward thrust of his neck and shoulders. He was a very tough, solid boy. His face looked as if it were made of muscle, like the rest of him. Edward sketched him into the wall, imprisoned in the bar-like cracks of the wall, his face caught in an expression of anguish and terror that was the real expression of his face, though always kept secret.

"I'm flunking English, there's this bitch of a teacher—" And so Robinson went on with his tales, comand threatening. Edward drew his body lying flat on the ground, arms and legs comically outspread. He drew him dead. A column of ants marched upon him and into his mouth, his nose, his eyes. You could imagine that they were building small cities in his head, in what had been his brain. . . .

One night Robinson said suddenly: "What's that stuff you're always drawing?"

"Homework." Edward showed him a sketch of a model shopping plaza.

"No, what you're doing now. Right now."

Edward looked at it: it was a picture of Robinson,

naked. His body was smooth and grotesquely bulky, like a doll's body, with nothing to it but arms and legs and bulk. It was not a man's body. The toes were enormous, each toe arched out and seizing the earth beneath it.

"Nothing, just junk," Edward said.

He tried to turn the page but Robinson said sharply, "Let's see it." Edward was nervous but there was something cold and deadly about him; he handed the pad wordlessly to Robinson. Robinson grinned and said, "What the hell..." and he shook his head, his teeth slightly bared—like a dog shaking his head, half-serious and half-cringing. "What's this sposed to be?"

"I don't know."

"This some kind of a joke or something? What is it?"

"I don't know."

Robinson handed the drawing pad back in silence. Edward did not look at him. For a while the two boys sat silently; Edward's head ached with the strain in this room, this tiny cluttered room, the strain of that large loud friendless Negro who demanded too much. His room was a precious place in spite of its size and clutter, and his head ached to think that it had been invaded.

After a while Robinson slid off the bed. He muttered something Edward did not try to hear. Turning to leave he bumped into Edward's desk and said, "Jesus Christ," as if he were a sleepwalker and not sure of what he had struck. Edward, breathing quickly and shallowly, looked up to see Robinson staring at him. "You dirty white bastard," the boy said in a caressing voice. He had an open, amazed look; it was almost one of admiration.

When Edward was left alone in the room he felt the room return to him. It was his again. He had bypassed a terrible danger. He thought of this room as a box, an ordinary box-shaped structure, hollow inside. It was reeling through space. Outside the box there were whims of gravity and attraction which were unpredictable; but inside, there were laws that were Edward's, his own laws. It was essential to keep the box closed and protected. There was no room for the agitation of air, or the streaming sunlight from the east that sometimes dazzled his eyes. He was alone in his room and safe.

2

The apartment was in a long low building. There were about twenty separate apartments in it, each with its own front and back doors; the front of the building was dull red brick and the back wood, with peeling paint. Edward hated its ugliness but preferred it to the more exotic and vulgar apartments available. Here, everything was keyed-down and minimal. There were no pretensions. The manager was an old man who walked off-balance, not limping but just tilted; he had a wild face crisscrossed with veins and was probably an alcoholic. No pretensions here.

One long narrow room was a "living room" at one end and a "dining area" at the other. Off this was a small old-fashioned kitchen with a grease-stained ceiling. There was a bathroom and a closet and that was all. Edward, who had a good beginning job now with an architect's firm, and who wore the kind of clothes that made the apartment manager humble, looked around with his usual ironic, bright smile and said to his friends who visited: "This is minimal on purpose." His friends—they were more like acquaintances—nodded their understanding. They were all young and they were all living minimally, "on purpose."

Five or six of them went out together often and visited one another's apartments. Edward was quick to see, covertly, what range and what style their apartments had, comparing them with his own—for though it was purposefully minimal it was his apartment, it belonged to him. It was the outward expression of himself so long as he lived there.

He hung his own paintings up on his walls. With his new job he had not so much time for painting as he had had in school, but there were five paintings he cared for, in a way. Sometimes he liked them and sometimes he wanted to take them down and get rid of them. He was very critical. He kept staring up and down the length of the main room, wondering if it was ugly or in a way attractive. At least it had long, smooth lines. The walls and ceiling were a good shade of white—off-white, oyster—and this very blankness was good. His paintings looked striking against the white walls, particularly the bluish-gray one that put people in mind of a prison scene, or an asylum scene: a dark face seemed to be staring out past bars, or cracks in the very painting itself. That was a strange painting which people liked but which Edward thought might be too melodramatic. At the top of the walls was a wooden border which Edward hated, and which seemed brought to life by the wooden frames of the paintings. This border often caught his eye and irritated him.

Those paintings might have been painted by another person entirely, someone more gentle and preoccupied than Edward. For he looked, now, like a young man in an advertising photograph: he wore good suits, good shoes, and he carried himself well. He was self-conscious about his bearing. Left behind in his ugly university room was that Edward of the distracted, agitated look, the gawky boy with nervous big-knuckled hands. Here was another Edward. It had been quite simple, really, just a matter of his deciding what he wanted to be. He created himself as if he had drawn himself, a bold neat sketch of his future.

He worked very hard at his job. Coming home in the winter he marvelled at the building in which he lived—what an achievement of solid, complacent ugliness! With trees shorn of leaves, the front lawn a muddle of dirty snow, the building revealed itself in its cheap unimaginative squalor. Yet it was solidly built. It was a good building in certain respects, while the new apartment of one of his acquaintances—a showy luxury apartment everyone envied—was just trash, not worth mentioning. The walls of that modern apartment were so thin one could hear anything through them, anything. In Edward's apartment, he could sometimes hear sounds from next door but that was all. It must have been when a closet door was opened on the other side of the wall. But he had only to move quickly away from that spot and he could hear nothing.

On weekends he tried to paint but no ideas came. He stared with a perplexed bitterness at the paintings on his walls, envious of the energy that had gone into them. His apartment was really ugly, seen in the morning. Could he really live in such ugliness? The border at the top of the walls was filthy with dust.... He could not paint, he hadn't any ideas. He sat on the sofa that became a bed at night, staring at the wall. Sometimes he lay and slept, though it was daylight. And sometimes he sat rigid as if hypnotized, listening to sounds from the apartment on the other side of the wall.

It turned out that he could hear through the wall, if he listened closely.

Sounds of thuds, as if overshoes were being dropped. Into a closet. A rustling sound. A man's voice—casual and vague—perhaps flung over his shoulder at an invisible woman. Did the woman live there too? Edward was not certain. He hated nosey people and would not allow himself to peer out the window in the hope of seeing the people next door.

But a man lived there, obviously. Edward often heard his voice. And the man had a television set or a radio, because there was always that steady droning in the background which Edward thought should irritate him but which really did not bother him much. These apartments were only one long room and all tenants slept on sofa-beds. Edward, at night, thought of how the building would look if the walls were suddenly stripped away—in each room a person would be discovered lying motionless under his bedclothes, in approximately the same location and set down row after row as if for a joke.

He was learning things at his job that had not much to do with architecture but a great deal to do with people. He became cynical and lines formed around his mouth, sharp dissatisfied lines. His clothes were more expensive than ever; he bought an expensive coat that prompted one of his acquaintances to say, "Where are you going in that?" Edward kept thinking about that question. It had been just a joke, of course, but still he kept thinking about it.

Alone a great deal, he found himself listening for sounds on the other side of the wall. Silence there made him nervous. He stopped playing records, so that he could listen for those sounds. A man's voice, muffled. The thud of shoes. The constant hum of the television set. Voices, music, a blend of noises. He found himself thinking of the noises of his home, far away. He rarely visited his family. While there, he yearned for this apartment, which belonged to him and to no one else. He had no other home. He lay on his sofa, listening to those sounds. Sometimes he fell asleep waiting for them and, when he woke, a recollection of sounds ran through his mind and he felt tremendously excited. He was able more often now to paint. Or to draw something, to sketch a thought. When he used a pencil he always "drew" things, that is, representations of things. He was honest with a pencil. When he painted, however, the cynical lines in his face deepened and he was a "painter"—he painted not the shapes of real things but the technique he would use were he simple enough to paint "real things." It was technique isolated from any object. He was, of course, no longer simple enough to bother with real things, ordinary objects. He painted explosions of color and arranged them into a private grammar or structure, which was his alone.

He was always alone in the room now. Sometimes

he thought, *I should get married.* It was an abstract thought, like his paintings. There was no content to it. In his business and in any business it was good to be married; it was part of a good image. Edward did have an interest in women. But he found it difficult to know them, just as he found it difficult to know anyone. His acquaintances were drifting away. So he spent time alone, lying on his sofa, thinking, listening for sounds from the other apartment.... He waited for a woman's voice, but when it came he thought perhaps it was from the television set. Did a woman live there? He could go next door and ask them about something. Borrow something. Because of the turnover in apartment tenants he often received mail that wasn't his, and perhaps somehow he could go next door and ask them about it... if they knew who should be getting this mail, or whether it was theirs. But that was nonsense, of course. He did not know that "they" lived there, whether there really was a woman there or not....

He painted swirls of color that were approximations of feeling, but the feelings were always lost. He could not recapture them from the paintings. More and more he thought that he should get married. He knew a few young women but his manner was stilted and abrupt with them, to cover his shyness. He did not know how to get from the chatty daylight level of friendship to the more urgent, intimate friendship of the dark. And there was the peculiar notion, too, risen out of his unconscious mind, that giving any place to a woman would make less room for himself; that he might somehow lose his "place." He had had recurring dreams, since childhood, of being locked out of a building and finding no doors, no way of re-entering. But it was absurd to mix the desire for a woman up with this childish fantasy, and he tried to put it out of his mind.

One night he woke to hear a strange noise next door, a long, low, muffled wailing. It made him tremble violently. He lay awake listening to it, his heartbeat quickening with an immediate, futile sympathy. The wailing was perhaps a woman's wailing. Edward listened. He thought of the two of them, him and that unknown person, lying in bed side by side in apartments that were side by side, both beds probably facing the same window, both bodies stretched out parallel in the dark. It was a strange, haunting picture. The wailing continued and Edward leaned against the wall, listening. Who was crying? What was wrong? He wondered if he should go next door and volunteer his help.

In the morning everything was silent. Edward rose filled with energy and went to work on a large painting in whites and grays. It was to be one of his best paintings. It was a painting that, years later, people who had met Edward were to remember about him, as if it were somehow a substitute for him.

3

This was a colonial house, not a very expensive one. But it was in a good, older neighborhood. Edward approved of the simplicity of the design—the uniform brick, the colonial top painted white, the shutters. Everything conventional. His own home would be built sometime in the future, he was in no hurry.

They lived there for five years. He was married to a young woman who wore her blond hair snipped short. She was a lively, energetic young woman, not exactly pretty but very alert. She admired Edward's talent. The living room had been an ordinary room, with a fireplace at one end, but Edward's imagination had transformed it: the walls were a dull, metallic blue, the ceiling white, and on each wall were those strange, disquieting paintings of his. The hardwood floor was sanded and polished, and Edward had selected an Oriental rug for it. The expense had been considerable but it had been worth it, of course. Everyone was struck by the room, which they supposed would be ordinary, and raved over Edward's talent.

He did his work upstairs, in a room which would have been a child's room had they had any children.

His wife's name was Brenda. She came into his life, introduced by an acquaintance at the office, and passed out of it so unobtrusively that he was to doubt later that he had ever known her. She was a simple, kind person; she admired him greatly. She had, also, wanted to get married. Like him, she had wanted to get married in the abstract, and Edward had married her one spring day. He remembered her, later, as the girl with the short blond hair, polishing the hardwood floor downstairs in that good house he had bought and fixed up. He remembered coming downstairs and seeing her, turned from him, fooling around with a blue-handled mop and a red plastic pail and there, there would arise from the dirty water a plastic disposable mop that was sometimes yellow, sometimes blue, sometimes violet! It was a picture that struck the eye but one which he would never have bothered to paint.

"It's your fault. You never talked to me, never," she wept. He had disengaged himself from her, gradually. She understood. "You never talked to me!" she said. But there was nothing to talk about. At parties, in the homes of the wealthy people he now knew, there were women with whom one never "talked" about anything; there was no need for it. Somehow the air was filled about them, like the sunny jangling air of the sea, with melodies that had no content to them and no need for content. They were not weighed down with thought. Brenda, his Brenda, walked heavily among them and had a good, bright, lively face; she screwed it up often in a comical way he had once liked. But she was too heavy. It had nothing to do with her body. "You don't love me, you don't make love to me," she cried, hating him and fearing the loss of him, and what could he say? He was a tall, critical, successful man. He knew his worth. He had outgrown her just as he had outgrown the house, finally. There is a certain day, in a certain house, when you wake and understand that you must leave the house and go on to the next one. It is time. Hatred has nothing to do with it. There is only the heaviness of time which must be escaped.

4

There was an extraordinary painting on the landing of the front stairs: a muted scene that looked like a foggy landscape at first, but became gradually the shape of a woman, outstretched as if on the ground, vague, gray, uncertain, a yearning shape that made the viewer uneasy—was the anguish of the painting real, or an illusion? Was that the body of a woman, or was it simply a surrealistic exercise?

Edward's house was far from the city, on four acres of expensive land. It was a house few people could describe except to call it "contemporary." The usual glass, unfinished concrete, some use of timber; a giant two-sided fireplace. The ceilings rose for two storeys in some places—and there was a great carved door, bought on his trip to Mexico, that divided the living area from the dining area. The house looked massive and labyrinthian from the outside but, on the inside, was very economical. One stepped from one room immediately into the next. There were no halls. On the concrete walls were Edward's paintings. He had another new painting, an old-fashioned painting that women always liked: it was of a wheel barrow half-covered with snow, an incidental, modest thing, as if glimpsed out of the corner of an eye. It made them nostalgic for the country childhoods they had never had. And the furniture was a surprise; it was mostly French Provincial, very elegant, with golden silks and brocades, and Edward's wife Roberta brought to it certain antiques of her family's—chests, vases, a small writing desk. It seemed almost a trick of the eye, the way the burnished brocade on the sofa caught the burnished wood of the big carved door, and the way the excellent antique Oriental rug smoldered in its rich, deep, gentle colors, as if it had a strange depth that might draw the eye hopelessly down into it.

Many people visited them, Edward's clients and friends from this "city," which was called Fernwood Heights but which was not a city at all. Roberta's children—she had two boys from a previous marriage—went to an excellent school a mile away. The children had their own part of the house, and the adults their own. There was an area in the center which belonged to both of them, a recreation room with panelled walls and a big fireplace and a big round table that could not be damaged. Edward's wife was a short, quick woman with elegant red hair, who was always answering the telephone. She had a busy life which had begun long before Edward had met her, and which he was proud of; but he was also a little jealous. She was not a beautiful woman but her assurance and her clothes were more important than beauty. She was always saying, when people came to photograph their house, "I can't be in the picture, are you serious?" She resented Edward being in any photographs, even though he had designed the house. It was vulgar to be photographed among one's possessions and her family looked down on him for it. It was hard for them to understand that since he had designed the house it was really not a possession, in the sense in which their own homes were possessions.

"This is the beginning, then?" Roberta would say, examining one of his sketches. "How do you fill it in? How do you know how big it is?" He had his own studio now, a room that extended out the back of the house. It was an excellent workshop with a great deal of space for wire and metal and other junk he liked to fool with. He was exhilarated by the thought of the wonderful house he had built and by the presence of this woman, whose questions were, in their very naiveté, symptomatic of her wealth and her indifference. The boys were named Lloyd and Charles and he was proud of them, too, though they were another man's achievements.

Roberta went out to lunch with friends nearly every day. At about four o'clock she often brought them back with her and they went to visit Edward's workshop. Edward, hearing their voices and their high-heeled shoes, felt nervous and yet excited. His wife had a high, admiring voice. She found a great deal to admire. Her friends came into his workshop, admiring everything, and told him to "go on with his work." One of them was usually someone who "painted." Roberta forced this information out, and the women all laughed as if such information were both shameful and delicious. Edward would say, usually, "Do you have much time for it?" because this led on to the next remark, the woman shaking her head from side to side in a quick, amused pretense of embarrassment, saying, "No, it's awful, it's just awful how little *time* I have—" and turning on him her sincere, soulful eyes. These women always meant everything they said, as they said it. They were always sincere and always admiring.

He liked to walk about his house, alone. With everyone gone except the maid it was a museum he had created. There was something glacial, something profound and timeless about it. Strong, hard lines—open spaces rigidly contained—the suggestion of weight and protection, It was a very protective house. Roberta sometimes joked about the concrete walls as "prison walls" but Edward did not think that was funny, nor did he think it was accurate. The walls were the opposite of prison walls. In later years he had stopped having that nightmare of being locked out, because he was so firmly protected. He envisioned this marvelous house as a sort of machine, its parts as ingenious and intricate as a machine, reeling through a universe of chaotic space that was unformed and had no value. The only value was the house itself, which was his. It was lighted, and the space outside it was dark. That kind of space was blackness that fell forever. But the house was his and it belonged to no one but him, and he sensed that its good strong walls were measured against the parallel walls in his mind, which were strong and tall and which kept out, forever, his old terrifying dreams.

There was no beauty and no truth in rubble, whether it came after a house or before a house. "Rubble" was rock, wood, concrete, steel beams, glass. "Rubble" was what Edward used to create his buildings. There was no truth in any material but only in architecture, which created shape out of that material, and this truth belonged to him.

5

The doorbell rang and Edward went quickly to answer it. "Well, hello. Merry Christmas," he said. Charles was brushing his hair up off his forehead, embarrassed. He stood in the doorway holding several presents.

"Merry Christmas," he said. He stepped inside with a slight stooping gesture of the shoulders, an almost imperceptible gesture that seemed to be a sign of shyness. Edward understood that it was no more than a gesture, but was grateful for it; it reminded him of Charles' boyhood. Now he stood, taller than Edward, with his blond hair dampened from the snow but still unruffled, his coat collar turned up, his handsome pigskin gloves stuck in one pocket.

"Was the driving bad?"

"Not too bad. All right."

They walked into the living room from the tiny foyer, Edward indicating the black expanse of window as he said, "It's been snowing all day. Look at it."

"Yes, it has been snowing," Charles said.

Charles was eighteen now. He had a fair, courteous, patient look, and Edward could see that he was carrying the three Christmas presents in a deliberately awkward way, as if there were many more than three presents, so many he could hardly handle them. "I suppose those are for me?" Edward said, smiling. He raised his eyebrows, and Charles, handing him the presents, gave him the faint signal—a mutually embarrassed smile—that allowed him to let his eyebrows relax again. But he could feel the lines in his forehead, which did not relax.

"Thank you. Why don't you take off your coat? I'll make you a drink."

The boy took off his coat so quickly that Edward wondered nervously what it meant—a deliberate attempt not to hesitate? Because Charles was a fine, cool, intelligent boy, as contemptuous of his mother as he ought to have been, but bound to her by ties of tradition and gentlemanly acquiescence; his very coolness was a tribute to her. "I've been drinking sort of, off and on all day," Charles said. "You know. We've been going around to places. . . ."

"Visiting friends?"

"Not with the family. Just some friends of mine from school. . . . So I really don't think I should have anything now, thank you."

"Are you sure?"

"Yes, thank you."

They sat. Edward sighed, then laughed in pinched alarm at this sigh, and smiled across the gleaming surface of the coffee table at his step-son. It seemed very strange, Charles visiting him like this. And yet it should not have been strange, because Charles had been the only one who had come in the past—Lloyd refused, and Roberta, of course, had nothing to say to him any longer. She seemed to be incorporated somehow in this boy, in the handsome, confident set of his head, her very absence clanging in the air about him. He was an easily embarrassed and yet confident boy, who allowed embarrassment as a kind of natural limit to his superiority, a gesture to other people. "Why don't you open your presents?" he said.

"Oh, I think I'll wait until later," Edward said. The presents were wrapped handsomely in silvery paper, tied with silvery bows. "Are you sure you don't want a drink, Charles?"

He saw in Charles' eyes a look of misery which was stifled at once by what must have been an effort of will. "If you don't mind, I'll fix myself one," Edward said. He had been drinking most of the day. It was now about nine o'clock in the evening on Christmas Day, and he had been waiting for a telephone call for many hours the day before and that day he had waited for Charles to arrive since about four. But he forgot his many hours of waiting and was grateful to Charles for having come at all.

"I like what you've done to the apartment," Charles said.

"You haven't seen it for a while, have you?" Edward said. He glanced around at the room. It was painted a light gold. On the walls were three of his better paintings; the others were in other rooms and the rest in storage. Though this apartment—on the twenty-fifth floor of a high-rise apartment building in the city—rented for five hundred dollars a month it was really quite small. The living room was almost large enough to look like a real room, especially since Edward knew certain tricks to make it appear larger, but it was nothing like the space he had been accustomed to. Still, he had understood that when he had leased the apartment. He had no complaints.

"And how is everything at home?" he said carefully.

"Oh, about the same."

"Your mother is well?"

"Roberta's fairly busy. The same sort of thing."

"Did she get away to visit the—those people, those friends in Florida?"

"No, she didn't have time. Something came up."

They fell silent. Edward sipped at his drink. He could see, falling softly in the dark outside the house, indolent snatches of snow. It was very secure, up on the twenty-fifth floor. He really did like the apartment. He found himself smiling faintly, but he did not know why. His face muscles were so weak, so stretched out of shape by the anguish he had suffered, that he sometimes found himself smiling limply for no reason—as if all struggle were over, finished, and why should he hold himself rigid any longer against being hurt? It was over.

He said to Charles, "You're looking very good."

Charles smiled in embarrassment. Edward remembered that this was the sort of remark adults should not make, but he did not know what else to say. It would not work, he saw shrewdly, to question Charles about his mother. All that day he had rehearsed questions, but now, seeing the boy, he understood that it would not work. Charles' sense of decorum was too great. And his objectivity, his indifference—cultivated after his mother's first divorce—in a way made any discussion irrelevant. He was not deeply involved with his mother, and he was "friends" with his step-father. The friendship was based upon a cool, detached respect. The other boy, Lloyd, was the one who loved his mohter, weakly and tearfully, and who therefore could not be "friends" with Edward. But Edward might have been able to talk with Lloyd, arguing and begging and pleading with the boy, while he could say nothing at all to Charles.

"Did she get a Christmas tree up?" Edward said.

"No, there wasn't time. It's the same old thing . . . lots of people in, things going on. I missed not seeing a tree there, by the window. That was a good idea," Charles said. He was trying very hard. But the look of misery showed again. Edward, sipping his drink, understood that he should allow the boy to leave. Minutes were passing, silence lay painfully between them, and he would never be able to ask whether Roberta had "reconsidered" anything. So he might as well let the boy go.

"I suppose you're in a hurry?—you probably have somewhere to go," he said.

"Oh, there's another eggnog party in Aurora Point," Charles said indifferently.

"Some friends from college?"

"Yes . . . no . . . some friends from high school."

They stood. Charles reached for his coat and put it on slowly, as if he were reluctant to leave. He glanced down at his pocket, frowning, to make sure the gloves were still there.

"I'm glad to hear everything is all right at home," Edward said. "Tell them Merry Christmas for me."

"Yes, and I'm supposed to tell you Merry Christmas too. From them," Charles said.

Edward saw him to the door, and when he wandered back into the living room he noticed the presents and thought with a shock that his own presents were still in the apartment. . . . He hurried back to the door and opened it, but Charles was gone already. The carpeted corridor, with its slightly stale odor, was empty. Edward lingered there in the door, thinking. He had bought presents for them the day before yesterday, and he had had them wrapped in the store. And now they were left behind, in his bedroom, and what had been the point of buying them, then? He did not know if Charles had missed the presents and that was why he had acted so strangely, or whether Charles had not thought of them either, hadn't had a thought of them at all.

He snapped off the living room lights and watched the snow fall. This apartment was an extraordinary thing: he lived so high in the air now, so privately, that he had the illusion of living in a kind of desert. Other tenants in the building were hardly more than muffled sounds. Edward sometimes woke at night, alarmed, from the dream of being locked out in space and having no way in, no key, not even any door, and no one to call to. The apartments seemed very remote from one another, though the building would look like an intricate insects' nest if stripped of its walls.

He was to have another apartment after this, a smaller one. This was several years later when the five hundred dollars a month was impossible; the new apartment was much more reasonable. It was farther out, in an area of apartment buildings and residential houses now given over to rooms and flats. It had old-fashioned wood panelling, and three box-like rooms, walls coated and coated with layers of wallpaper, a fireplace which was built into the wall but into no chimney; a fake fireplace. Edward had laughed shrilly at that.

6

He was not certain of the dimensions of this new room, but he recognized the white walls and the window. He was fascinated by the window. At night the space in this small room expanded and he felt a kind of terror, because it was empty space into which one might fall forever; but in the morning he saw that the walls were there, very firm and solid, and the window was just an ordinary window.

He slept much of the time. There was sometimes a sharp, jarring pain in his body, but he was able to sleep in spite of it. The nurse injected a hot fluid into his thigh. He slept. Sometimes he heard someone talking but could not awaken and answer politely.

"How long has he been like that? Is he like that all the time?"

"Mother, he'll hear you."

"Isn't he under sedation?"

"Yes, of course, Mother."

"Frank has too large a practice, I'm not pleased with

what he's doing. He's such a social climber...."

"He's doing the best he can."

"Of course they have such wonderful drugs now, but still.... You'd think they could save him. It's terrible, like this."

"Mother...."

"But he looks so thin, the poor man. It's awful. He could have been a great artist, you know.... Why isn't Frank here today?"

These voices were not quite believable: people stood at a distance, behind a kind of veil, no longer significant. They had hurt him in the past—had hurt him very much. But no more. He could not believe in them now, as he believed in himself, in pain, in the flickering of light across his eyelids, for which he was grateful. ... When he woke the room was empty. He studied its dimensions, trying to estimate them. A small room, with a cheap aluminum-framed window. An overhead light, not burning. Or was it? ... The doctor spoke to him. The doctor's name was Frank but Edward kept forgetting. They had once been friends or perhaps they still were. Legends died slowly. Perhaps he should lie, shouldn't hurt anyone's feelings ... some memory of a swimming pool, a fine cloudless summer day ... Frank's swimming pool, or Edward's? Who was Edward, and who was Frank? Why did people ask so many questions? He had no interest in questions or answers. His lips felt ungainly, as if swollen out of shape.

A great artist. Someone had said that of him. Yes, yes, he remembered ... *a great artist ... artist ... art.* These words seemed to mean something, seemed to be tugging at his soul. He thought of space hacked and straightened by lines, and by solid walls; he thought of sunny, wind-agitated space scooped up in his hand. He had done that. But not well enough: not well enough. He had not been a great artist, he had not even been an artist.... Something had gone wrong. Too many people, voices, a constant commotion, a hypnotic din whose meaninglessness had been veiled from him all his life. He had not been a great artist. Not an artist. He had not....

Space was breaking in upon him, through the window of this cramped room. A rectangle of glaring impatient light, eager to get into his brain. There it would burst. He was terrified of floating off into that sunny emptiness but he wanted it just the same. He didn't want the voices, no longer wanted even the art, he thought, "I want—" but there were no more words. Light filled him as if it were now giving him a shape of his own, his final perfected structure.

When she woke, groggily, she might have been anywhere. In a motel room anywhere. She knew it was a
motel room because of the size of the bed—king-sized,
enormous. She was alone in the bed. She found it very
hard to wake up. She was trying to shout at herself,
a tiny shouting angry voice, something about the Gulf
of Mexico and those scarlet blossoms she'd seen and the
sandpipers, yes, dear God, and pelicans and gulls and
robins and a white clear clean glowing glaring sun just
like the sand, earth and sky and earth white-glowing,
so beautiful you would want to step into it arms outstretched, if only you can get out of bed, you lazy bitch.

Later, she discovered a gas jet on—the left rear
burner of the stove. She had rented a motel room with
an "efficiency kitchen." She had heated some water the
evening before, fairly early in the evening, and she'd
gone to bed early, exhausted from the long day, to bed
early, sanely, at eleven o'clock, and all night the gas
had seeped into the room faintly and not aggressively
and not lethally. That was why she had slept so late!

She felt relieved, to know she wasn't naturally lazy.
I'm not a bitch after all, she thought.

Aren't you a bitch? she thought, when she saw the
Gulf. *Shouldn't you be punished?* But the palm trees
and the wide white beach were harmless. The flowering
tree with its nameless scarlet blossoms: enough to sear
one's eyes. The wind from the west came in constantly,
constantly across the Gulf—high in the trees, the palm
trees and the pine trees both, rattling and mysterious,

103

a sound that reminded her of her girlhood: wind blowing through the elms outside her bedroom, constantly, so wildly in bad weather that she had had nightmares. Weren't such noises, heard throughout life, from a language people didn't know? —Finally her father had had part of the elm removed, the diseased part; the city had done it for him, for a minimal fee. He had resisted for some time, until a neighbor got an injunction against him. After that she had nightmares occasionally, but not because of the tree.

A bad dream is punishment enough, she told herself sanely. There was a certain luxury to all this—the faces of the other guests, the tanned arms and legs, the expensive bathing suits and beach equipment and the bare feet in January—yes, a luxury, and luxuriously she thought that the gas jet had been enough for one day.

You have such a strange sense of humor, someone told her.

Walking stiff-legged, like a convalescent.

Walking this way she had the shadow of an old woman: good. If it fell across a man's path he might not notice. Might draw back, shivering in the hot expensive white sun. Good. *There might be bleeding, why not?—a little blood never hurt a woman.* She had laughed hard, to show that she had a sense of humor. It was one thing to make jokes—everyone she knew made jokes, even Judge Hartley—for some reason she was thinking about him—had dreamt of him?—but quite another thing to appreciate the jokes of others, to actually listen, patiently, without interrupting or yawning, and then to laugh at the required time. That was courtesy; the basis of social life; the basis of civilization.

What about Judge Hartley?
She had been a fifteen-year-old runaway, detained

in the House of Correction, until her mother got there from Cincinnati to insist that the abortion go through—the girl had run away from it, back in Cincinnati. She was a minor. She didn't know her own mind. Judge Hartley, the youngest judge in the county, might have sent a Legal Aid man to the girl, since she didn't want the abortion; but it wasn't his case, he hadn't better get involved, he'd be standing for election a year from this November.... He had not gotten involved.

But she wasn't a fifteen-year-old runaway, she had not been fifteen years old for a long time. No, wait. *You have such a strange sense of humor,* someone told her uneasily, sitting beside her on the plane. He had been very courteous: had offered her the window-seat. No thank you, really. No. No thank you. Well, all right. Thank you. *I don't want to resist as long as we're fully clothed.* Somehow, he had misunderstood. He was a youngish man to be retired—unless the white-gray-yellowish hair confused her and she had supposed it was blond—his suit was casual, sporty, like the clothes her husband forced himself to wear at the office and at court. She studied his hands, covertly. No, they didn't look old. They looked like hands that might reasonably grab and paw and tear, if you resisted, but up here thousands of feet above America, with that constant hum and vibration and sense of *maybe it will crash, we'll all die together!*—why, nothing would happen, not that. He asked her where she was going and she said, without pausing to lie, *Aurora Key.* A heroine in a story or in a television play might have hesitated, thinking that someone was listening, a friend of her husband's, a spy, or that this man—a gentlemanly stranger who appreciated her sense of humor though he didn't really laugh very much—would somehow telephone back to Cleveland and tell them *Aurora Key.* She forgot to hesitate, and spoke as naturally as if she were lying.

The runaway's name was Barbara. Her own name was something different.

The second day there, she felt stronger. She dressed like everyone else and put on sunglasses and walked out, waiting for a seepage of blood, almost listening for it. What a queer sensation, like a trickling of a stream somewhere in the mountains, in the distance!—which you must hear before you can feel! The sky was clear, exactly like the over-exposed blue sky in the advertisement back home, in the travel agent's at the shopping plaza. She had stepped into the poster and stepped out here, proof of magic... except, as she walked, she saw how filmy clouds gray and thick at the core were gathering, converging, now that she could not change her mind and cross out the check and her name and rip it in two, stammering that she'd made a mistake, another mistake. Still, she kept the sunglasses on. They had white plastic frames and made her skin look healthier, by contrast; in a day or two she would be tanned like everyone else, like the pretty grinning girls in the travel posters. She would be transformed into an advertisement for Aurora Key. Someone might take her picture, on a whim; and, years later, many years later, someone back home would discover it. *Isn't this...?* No. *It looks just like....* No.

Everyone was out walking, in spite of the gathering clouds. There was a defiance to the human world, down here, a refusal to see the future shaping up. It was just after New Year's; a tremendous effort, to get the old year past!—and the new year, the expanse of an entire year, was too much to consider. It verged upon the absurd, the limits of what a human imagination could bear... so the men wore white trousers or shorts, and handsome sports shirts, though they looked a little awkward, pale from winter in the North, now strolling along a beach somewhere and wondering what they were doing. On the beach, they walked with their heads bowed, against the wind. It kept coming. Not many wives there, on the beach, they were strolling through the town... yes, now everyone was strolling through the town, relieved to get out of the wind, grateful for the boulevard of shops. There were three arcades she counted, and one palm-tree-lined courtyard, boutiques all around it. Women with wind-blown hair studied wigs in the show-windows. The wigs were set firmly on stylized heads, pastel colors, with no more than a hint of eyes nose or mouth, and stumps for necks. Beneath the wigs, these heads were nicely bald: there would be no problem about the scalp.

A secret from him, from everyone: tiny white flakes from her head, sometimes, when she scratched it. And then beneath her fingernails. She remembered staring at her fingernails once, at the horrible white grit beneath them ... thinking *Am I like this, after all? Am I so human?* ... while forty miles away her husband was asking her precise, urgent questions, across the tangled expressways of a city and outlying townships, their entire marriage reduced to a man's voice over a telephone and a woman staring at her fingernails, distracted, not remembering why she had telephoned home or why she had thought anything so important.... "I don't want to go through with it after all," she said, then she said, "No, I just called to talk to you ... or to someone.... I don't know why I called, I'm sorry." She heard him speaking at the other end. When he paused and it seemed she must reply, she said, "I'll hang up now, I'm sorry," and she did hang up, and she was sorry.

At the very center of Aurora Key was a circular park. Eight streets led to it and then around it, one-way traffic, moving cautiously and awkwardly, because most of the drivers were from out-of-state; it was difficult to drive anywhere in Aurora Key because of so many pedestrians and drivers backing their cars into parking places. Yet few people used their horns: it must have been the holiday look of the place, the great court palms everywhere, the enormous pink-and-scarlet blossoms, the bushes with white and yellow flowers. They had paid for this, they had paid to come here.

There was a value here almost spiritual—because they had paid for it; they could believe in it. Up North, in their own cities, nothing was valuable in the public world, one might drive faster, sound his horn more frequently. Here, an oasis of expense and beauty and sun, not to be violated.

No one stayed here for longer than a week or two.

She would not stay longer than that; but she had nowhere else to go. She couldn't think of anywhere else to go. Walking out on the second day she seemed almost to know the entire town—it was very small—and the only thing that interested her in the town was the park, which no one else bothered with. It was difficult to get over there, because of the continuous traffic. A station wagon packed with a family from Ohio nearly ran her down—but she got across, running awkwardly, like an old woman. *Don't hurt me, don't hurt me again,* but she was safe in the park and no one would hurt her.

No one else was here. The park was quite small and, she could see, really served as a kind of traffic device. Around it, ceaselessly, cars moved in a slow counter-clockwise blur, no more than ten miles an hour; Aurora Key was crowded at this time of year. *Where will you go, if you leave him?* her mother's voice had asked her, calmly. Not her mother: only her mother's voice. Sandra had lost touch of her mother. They telephoned back and forth, Shaker Heights to Chicago, Chicago to Shaker Heights, her mother's throaty sweet-gruff voice and Sandra's sixteen-year-old voice, which she had never dared outgrow, and asked each other various questions, waited for various answers, but Sandra had had no answer to that particular question. At the time, only a week or ten days before, she had not even heard of Aurora Key.

Her parents had often gone to Miami Beach or Bermuda or the Barbados, since for some reason the western coast of Florida had not been popular. Sandra was not sure where she was: the travel agent had showed her a map, running his finger along the coast, a manicured forefinger that moved in rhythm with his enthusiastic voice. He recommended Aurora Key. He said it was lovely. He said it was not crowded, like Miami Beach; and there was a good class of people there, not like Key West—which was all right in its own way, picturesque, of course, but populated with fishermen and unemployed blacks and, he'd heard, with drifting aimless living-off-the-land young people as well, who took drugs and might be dangerous. Sandra had smiled to show she was listening and that she was not disturbed by his intonation, *young people*, as if he were referring to a class of human beings she might know nothing about.

... the morning after the day of the operation, she had looked at herself in the bathroom mirror and had to admit that it wasn't a young face, really. But that was encouraging. Her husband had married her for her face, so now he might have no objection to letting her go.

Evidently there had been a storm the day before. There were puddles everywhere in the park, small shallow ponds that had not yet drained away. Sandra noticed birds bathing in them. Robins, were they? Robins. Now she noticed them in the palm trees, and descending from the sky ... and, in the puddles, shaking and ruffling their feathers. She forgot about the motel room, which she hated, and the gas jet, and someone shouting at her—*Leave, then! Leave!*—and stared at the birds. There were no benches in the park so she couldn't sit down. Probably the Chamber of Commerce in the town did not want to encourage young people to gather in the park ... so she stood beside one of the enormous trees, watching the birds, and trying to fix her mind onto thoughts that made sense. She was not like the runaway girl, captured by police and brought home again, a minor, to be ordered about by other people; she had acted of her own free will, it had been her decision, ultimately. So she had had the operation. But: it was fascinating, the way the birds bathed themselves, then flew up into the trees, while others descended, reeling, in a commotion of wings. Sandra was not hiding behind a palm tree, just standing beside it. There was no need to hide. No one in Aurora Key knew her; but it was a good idea to be unobtrusive just the same.

Her mind slipped away from the birds, and away from Aurora Key. She forced herself to remember the map of Florida: the man's forefinger, caressing the seacoast. Miles and miles of clean white sand. The Gulf of Mexico. Privacy. Luxury.... The palm trees were very tall. They seemed to her unnaturally tall, for trees. They resembled concrete poles, except for their great, brittle leaves, which made a dry rustling noise. She stared up at them, until her neck ached. She did not know if she liked them or feared them. What relationship could anyone have, to trees?... to birds?... to his own body? It was nature, unknowable. It could not be possessed. Yet there was the compulsion to analyze, to weigh, to compare, to wonder, to judge... in the end it came to nothing, it did not matter. The robins continued to bathe, noisily, and the leaves of trees rustled in the wind, forever. These particular trees looked so peculiar to her because they were not multi-branched, like the trees of the North, but columnar, and smooth as human skin, tall, uniform, trees of sleep, of nightmare, which one might grasp at helplessly....

Long before her marriage she had had a vague, unarticulated fear of confusing night-thoughts with day-thoughts. Dreams expanding into daylight. Private thoughts, public utterances. Her husband had consoled her, one night when they came home late from a party, both rather drunk, but cheerfully and amiably drunk: everyone was afraid of that sort of thing, he said, and so what the hell did it matter?

A dread shared by the entire species cannot matter: it is no more than nature, in the mind.

Leaving the park she was almost hit by someone driving a white Mercedes-Benz. A gray-haired old man, or perhaps an old woman. The driver tapped his horn, a series of short light scolding honks. *Look what you nearly made me do, nearly made me run you over!*

In disguise as a young woman who might look like a tourist, in white cotton-and-rayon slacks and a lime-green jersey blouse, in white-rimmed sun glasses, her leather sandals scuffing on the sidewalk, she made her way through the stream of pedestrians, back toward the Seacliff Inn. She took a wrong turn, wandered a few blocks out of her way, noticed that the Gulf was in another direction, and went that way, walking quickly . . . costumed for the role of a young woman like herself, exactly like herself. She had long, thick, rather ostentatious black hair, which her mother had always prized and envied—her mother's hair was ordinary, in spite of all the rinses and dyes—and she had coiled it around her head in two braids, so that she would not resemble her Northern self. No one was following her, no one was hunting her; she knew that. Deirdre Ferris, the wife of a Cleveland manufacturer, only a few years older than Sandra, had left her husband and flown to a private club in Southern California, but her husband had had her traced . . . detectives, an international detective agency, the real thing, the hilarious deathly melodramatic routine itself! . . . but Sandra was reasonably sure that no one was following her. Unless her husband borrowed money from his father. Unless he was so angry that he wanted her back, in order to shout at her. Unless he had talked to her mother in person, not over the telephone, and had forced her to tell the truth. . . .

Sandra doubted it. Her husband was too proud. He wouldn't want anyone to know that his wife had left him, and if he stayed away from the house—if he took a room in a downtown hotel, near his office—in a short while he might forget she had gone. Then, when her money ran out and she called him, it would be a pleasant surprise; he could forgive her, welcome her back, arrange for a seat on a plane.... Sandra had gotten the idea for the braids from one of the Spanish-speaking maids at the motel. But she hadn't the woman's bright, confidential vitality. The braids made her head ache.

No one appeared to notice her, on the street. But she couldn't be sure.

What day was this?

...the sky had changed, while she stared at it. She wanted to get back to the room to change her clothes; she was afraid of soiling the white slacks. Why had she worn white...? Walking in the direction of the Gulf she seemed to step in and out of pockets of air, chilly gusty wintry air, not promised by the travel agent, and overhead ridges of dark clouds appeared. Other tourists were hurrying. Women who had come out unwisely dressed—in sleeveless or short-sleeved dresses—were hugging themselves. It was January, after all. Wasn't it January? Winter? But on the broad sidewalks men were ringing bells. They wore vests of red and green, and cardboard hats that spoke of "Holidays for the Handicapped of Aurora Co.," so Sandra wasn't sure if Christmas had come and gone, and when a burly suntanned man blocked her way and rang a bell in her face, she laughed and fished in her purse for some money, yes, just a minute, yes yes, a quarter?...not enough?...a fifty-cent piece?....She gave him a dollar. He thanked her warmly. In exchange she received a crepe-paper flower of some kind, perhaps a rose, to stick through her buttonhole.

"Not alone, are you?" the man asked.

"Why do you say that?" Sandra laughed.

"I saw you yesterday, didn't I? Alone?"

"Not me," Sandra said. "My husband is at the motel."

She laughed and walked away. At the Seacliff Inn her husband would be waiting, perhaps having a drink in the cocktail lounge...distracted and oddly, prematurely tired, like the other men down here, removed too abruptly from winter in the North. She would glance in the darkened lounge, locate him, and go to him. . . . He would inquire about the flower. She would laugh. With both hands she would clutch at the heavy aching braids around her head.

The expensive boutiques, the antique and silver jewelry shops, the art galleries . . . the leather shops . . . the small, smart Hallmark Card shop . . . the French restaurant, the Spanish restaurant. . . . All these reminded her of something she had been forgetting: something about money. She had taken several hundred dollars from the checking account, but had left quite a bit in, out of fear; not consideration for Anthony, not even out of caution, but simply out of fear. Money. Everyone required money. After a while, without money, you couldn't even shampoo your hair . . . and an ugly rank animal smell would take over your body. Sandra shied away from thinking of it, because it meant that they would win, in the North; she would be defeated. And the clots of blood, the huge endless sticky bloodclot, would have been for nothing, just nature, just protein-and-water, draining out of one body and into something else, to be flushed away. . . . She found herself staring in a shop window. She was staring through tinsel-and-cotton-batting snowflakes, at dresses with long skirts and sequinned tops. What did it cost, what had it always cost, this kind of wealth? Fake-lovely stylized faces, mannequins with high-piled hair that consisted of dozens of tiny, glinting silver ornaments, white plaster faces partly hidden by black velvet masks . . . in all this, Sandra's own floating reflection, the sunglasses showing mute exaggerated astonishment. Her body seemed to fade away, below the neck, lost in an elegant clutter of silver and gold jewelry arranged on a kind of Christmas tree, a skeletal tree-shape . . . and someone's familiar voice sounded near her, in a familiar mock-whining drawl, "*Why* are you walking so fast?" Sandra glanced around and saw a couple she knew—the man a friend of Anthony's, the woman only a peripheral acquaintance of Sandra's. They were passing behind her, arguing. The man was in his early forties, self-conscious in his new sports-clothes and sandals, the woman aggressively stylish in a pink-and-white pants outfit. Sandra felt faint, with dread of their noticing her. Yet she could not turn away. The man was an older partner in her husband's law firm; her husband was not yet a partner. The man did glance at Sandra, but seemed not to see her. His wife reached out to tug his bare arm. "*Why* are you in such a hurry?"

She had not been recognized.

It was the last time she would come so close to being captured, she thought. Another last time had been during her stop-over in Dallas, sitting on the edge of a bed in a Holiday Inn near the airport, trying to do something about her fingernails. They were all broken, cracked. It was mysterious, but she would not bother about the mystery. Where all the people had been going on the plane with her, the plane from Cleveland, the man with the gray-blond hair and the courteous manner that had not alarmed her, all that was mysterious too but she would not bother about it. Someone had told her once—her mother, perhaps—that you asked questions until the age of thirty, thirty-three, and after that you never asked questions. She might have asked the doctor about the broken fingernails and her dried-out scalp but she had forgotten. On an impulse she took off her shoes and stockings and inspected her toenails, but they were cut so short, she couldn't tell if they might be cracked or not. She felt dizzy, looking at them for the last time. How perfect the body was, with all its near-invisible blemishes and scars and creases, a perfectly-kept secret . . . a complicated substance that could be released and drained away, into nothing. A galaxy. A universe.

She had forgotten the couple's last name. Hurrying

back to the Seacliff Inn she forgot about having seen them. She would have forgotten the name of the motel itself, except for the key, which she had in her purse; she took it out to examine it. Seacliff Inn. But it puzzled her—there was no cliff, only the beach. Crossing a vacant, partly-wooded lot to the motel, she paused beside a cactus plant that had grown enormous, and someone said to her: "Are you lost?"

A man was approaching her on the path.

"You're not lost, are you?" he said smiling. He was very friendly.

"I'm not lost," Sandra said.

He saw the key, the maroon oval disc it was attached to; he said, "We're in the same motel."

"I'm not lost, I was just going there," Sandra said.

The man seemed to be waiting for her. He was not very tall—only an inch or so taller than Sandra, and she was wearing sandals. He might have been thirty-five years old. But when she looked at him again she saw the deep indentations in his face, which meant that he was smiling and thinking at the same time, and it seemed to her he might have been fifty years old. His hair was as black as hers—so thick, so glossy! Perhaps it was dyed hair. She could not understand why he waited there, a few feet away.

"Are you going back to the motel?" he said finally.

"No," Sandra said. "No, don't wait for me, no, I'm all right."

His smile slackened. He wore a red-and-white striped shirt, the stripes vertical, too bright. His trousers were made of a coarse, oatmeal-colored fabric, with a wide pale leather belt that fitted them perfectly; he wore sandals and white socks. Sandra felt the slow sickening rush of blood into her face. She wanted him to go away, she could not bear to walk with him, or with anyone. But he was waiting for her, politely, bullyingly. He could see the craziness in her face.

"Look what you're stepping on," he said.

"What?" she cried.

She looked down—the path was made of tiny white shells, ground fine, scintillating in the dull light, almost glowing, with their own reflected light. From somewhere, the sun had emerged again; a white, chilly illumination spread up from the earth.

"A million little animals," the man laughed.

Sandra tried to laugh.

"They don't mind, though," he said. "They consider it an honor."

"I didn't hear you, exactly," Sandra said. "I've been taking some prescription pills and they make me miss connections, parts of sentences. I have to leave now. I can walk by myself."

"You walk in a strange way, I was watching you," the man said. "Sort of stiffly . . . isn't it? I was watching you, back on the boulevard."

She could hear a foreign accent in his voice, but could not place it.

"Are you following me?" she asked lightly.

"Oh no," he said. "Never."

"Have you been hired to follow me?"

". . . been what?"

"Hired."

"Hired?"

And he stared at her so openly, with so perplexed an expression, that she knew he must be a stranger.

"Don't follow me," Sandra said. She began to cry. "I don't want to go back home. I can't go back home. Just don't follow me . . . let me alone."

"How come you are crying?" the man asked.

"Because I'm not going back home," she said.

In her motel room she took another of the pain-killer pills, a big yellow citrus-flavored pill, because of the trembling and a vague knotty pain in her loins. So much had been sucked out of her, vacuum-sucked, she knew it would be too difficult to keep the rest of it from being drawn out as well; *this is the last time, she promised herself, the last pill.*

She was awakened by a knock on the door.

A timid knock, yet with a certain stubborn force behind it.

She lay motionless, atop the unmade bed, listening, not frightened so much as numb, at peace, as if she were only a dead body and not responsible for opening her door to anyone.

I don't have to let anyone crawl in with me, in any bed at all, she thought.

The gas jet had not been left on. So she woke to a regular morning, a regular day, sunny as advertised. She dressed quickly, excitedly. People had been complaining about the weather—a hurricane fifty miles south of Aurora Key, in Naples—wind that tore at your hair—so it was important to get up and dressed, to take advantage of the expensive sunshine.

Wisely, she did not wear white—she had another attractive outfit, blue slacks and a yellow smock-like blouse, which might make people think she was pregnant if the wind got into it and belled it out, so they would let her alone. She did want to be let alone; it was not the way Anthony believed—*you draw away, but you really want me to pursue you; you had this neurotic fear of becoming pregnant, yet you became pregnant*— Her error had been in marrying too intelligent a man. He listened to her, but he retained his own private thoughts. He loved her, so he said, discounting her as she cried or shouted or laughed, but fixing his attention upon a ghostly transparent woman who inhabited her body, giving its true value to that body: Sandra Voorhees, its name was.

She had registered here as Sandra O'Connell, taking the name from a girl she had admired in school, many years ago.

Her eagerness to get out onto the beach gave her hope: it was encouraging, since a few mornings ago she had hardly been able to get up. So she hurried out, blinking into the white sunshine, afraid that some new sensation would take hold of her and slow her down, beginning with her legs and working upward. But momentum helped her. She maneuvered herself along the broad flagstone paths, beneath the towering palm trees—or perhaps they were poles made of concrete, the sunshine was so bright she couldn't be sure—around the beds of gaily-colored flowers and the chemical-blue pool, where children screamed and shouted, and she found herself in a kind of dead-end—a ramp at the rear of the building, where a laundry truck was parked. Black men were heaving immense white bundles and when they happened to notice her, she felt herself go blank, stammering blank. She walked away. She steeled herself to go through the motel itself, through the main corridor and the foyer, where boys in red uniforms were pushing carts of luggage merrily around, and new arrivals were walking slowly and smiling and a man with a New York accent was saying something about the congestion in the air, the sky was filled with airplanes and nowhere to land, but he was no one Sandra dreaded. The coffee shop made her realize that she had forgotten to eat again. The reason for renting an efficiency room, with its own little kitchen, was to save money; to keep to herself, to be private. But she kept forgetting to buy food. Through a glass partition she saw a pale, annoyed young father lifting a sandwich to his mouth—seated at a table with two squirming children and a woman whose back was to Sandra—and she could almost taste the meat, a hamburger juicy-red on the inside and slightly burnt on the outside, though she must have imagined the man's trembling hands—her trembling, not his. Did people eat because they were hungry, or was it habit?—duty? Protein dutifully turned itself into protein, and got up and walked out onto the beach, in plenty of time to enjoy the sunshine.

Yes, it was sunny. It was a beautiful day. The wind had died down—that disappointed her, for some reason. She seemed to recall a storm somewhere. A plane bound for Atlanta had been forced to fly all the way to Dallas—was that the storm she remembered? No, it must have been another, a more recent storm. Today was a clear, bright, slightly chilly day, though a few people were swimming or wading in the surf. Sandra shuddered, seeing them. Several boys and girls in their late teens or early twenties were strolling along, barefoot in the surf, eating Danish pastry provided by the motel—they wore jeans cut off at the knees, and gray sweatshirts with a university's insignia on them. Complaining about something. Bombing raids, was that the subject again? "...*Zap*, you're annihilated," one of the boys laughed thickly, snapping his fingers, and he happened to notice Sandra; there was a moment of acute embarrassment. Sandra hobbled by. She hoped they would take pity on her. But no, no pity, a girl's giggle and a boy's muttered words were mixed in with the surf, and she didn't look back at them but thought of how lovely it would be, annihilation, deafness and muteness and immobility given a permanent sanction, almost a divinity.

She shaded her eyes and looked up, at the terraces of the motels that faced the Gulf, and thought, panicked, that she had been walking in the wrong direction. Ten minutes wasted. She was walking toward the more congested area, where the big multi-floored Holiday Inn and Ramada Inn and Travelodge were located, and what she wanted was isolation—She paused, not knowing what to do. An aching sensation in the pit of her stomach should have drawn more of her attention, but the outside world was so lively here, so many children running around, so many warmly-dressed older people strolling through the sand, arms linked together, why some other stretch of the beach, why not this stretch? Why one place and not another? Why one body and not another? She happened to notice a girl she'd seen the other day, on the sidewalk in front of an ice cream parlor, and now the girl was lying in a two-piece bathing suit, deeply and elegantly tanned, frowning into a paperback novel. Except now she was not alone: beside her sat a large-boned, fleshy young man with a rather peevish expression, a handsome boy, his eyes moving around restlessly. They even moved onto Sandra, then past her; then back onto her, then past her again, rejecting her. She was a few years too old for him, after all. Also too pale, haggard, peaked-looking; he could probably sense the hysteria. He wouldn't like that sort of behavior. Sandra felt a keen rush of sympathy for the girl, who was pretty, yes, but not pretty enough to keep him.

He seemed to inspire her, releasing her from something—what was it, what had it been? The indifferent movement of his gaze, onto her, up and down her slender body, and then away from her—yes, that was a gift, that kind of indifference. She walked along through rough patches of sunlight that moved with her, but in jagged, unrhythmic plunges, occasionally interrupted by other people's shadows, and she could not even remember why she felt so encouraged, so free. By now she had walked a mile or more from her motel. She was leaving the motel area. Along this stretch of beach there were fewer people—a public parking lot, where campers and trailers and Volkswagen buses were parked—and the palm trees and wild cactus looked shaggier, unkempt. A trash can filled with refuse had tipped over; beer cans spilled onto the sand. Dogs were running freely. The waves were thunderous, the air was not hospitable, children ran shouting through the surf and one of them nearly collided with Sandra, not noticing her, and avoiding her at the last moment but still not seeming to notice her, as if his vision simply excluded her, with so much else to see. An immense woman in overalls prowled hunched-over, carrying a child's sand-pail, looking for something in the sand—shells? crabs?—and a fat, soft, pale boy yelled for her to notice what he had found—*Hey Ma! Ma!*—holding a partly torn starfish between two fingers. Then he dropped it in a patch of seaweed.

Fewer people here. The waves were louder. Spray was blown against her face. Clouds were thickening again but she could walk forever. How good it was, how healthy, to exercise her legs!—to feel her heartbeat working to keep pace with her! She would show it, her body. She would determine what it would and would not do. She shivered with the cold, but it was good, good to shiver, good to walk so freely out along the beach, now that the coastline was so wild—all pines and scrubby, twisted little trees, no more palms. Her legs were a little weak, the backs of the knees oddly weak, so she sat down suddenly. Wet sand. Quite cold. Everywhere around her sand mixed with tiny white shells. *Look what you're sitting on!* someone had joked. She could not remember the correct reply. She had noticed up ahead a kind of cove, rocky and noisy and wild, and it occurred to her that a person in good health could swim from this side to the other; that was a challenge. But she felt sleepy, perhaps from the pill, or from the ceaseless wind. It seemed to be blowing right into her head. It did no good to duck her head, or to turn aside . . . the wind blew into her head anyway, curling and darting around her.

. . . no one knew where she was.

A two-passenger plane passed overhead, probably from the airport at Naples. Droning engine. Then the waves again, the surf, the wind. She noticed a half-dozen birds—sandpipers?—scurrying along the edge of the beach, their absurd little legs carrying them so quickly, and in perfect rhythm—it struck her, uncomfortably, that the birds knew one another's thoughts, they never hesitated, but moved together as if an invisible film or envelope joined them. How could it be?—not six or eight separate birds, but one thing, one creature, magical and autonomous and unfaltering.

The thought alarmed her. She got to her feet. The last time she had tried to swim any distance had been years ago . . . years ago . . . in high school, so many years ago. She was now twenty-nine years old. Swimming, gasping, kicking, arm-over-arm, the sharp smell and taste of the chlorinated water, the amplified shouts and laughter, all that made her feel rocky, too old, too exposed. There had been a connective tissue back there, perhaps, even there—and in her family, certainly—like the sandpipers she hadn't been alone, but she had not known it, and in that way she had been alone, deceived.

She stumbled down through the rocks, toward the cove.

"Are you lost?" someone cried.

She looked around: the man who had spoken to her the other day, the dark-haired man with the accent. He was dressed for the beach today, in sporty plaid shorts and a pull-over shirt of white terry-cloth; jammed onto his head was a white hat that gave him a nautical look. He scrambled down the incline to her. She had an impression of hairy calves and thighs, hairs black and thick and wiry. She stared at him. Her feet were wet from the surf and she had sunk a fraction of an inch into the wet sand, so it was explicable that he should seem so much taller than he had the day before. He was saying something about the undertow here, riptides, rocks, and his accent was softer—he might have been a southerner. But the noise from the Gulf confused them both.

"There's nobody around here," he said. "Are you lost?"

"I was alone," she said.

"I saw you climb down here, the way you moved, I thought it was an older woman," the man said, talking loudly into the wind, "I thought maybe . . . maybe you'd need help getting back up. Are you from one of the hotels?"

He was very tanned and watchful.

"You know where I'm from," Sandra said.

"What? I can't hear you."

"You know," Sandra said bitterly.

. . . You dreaded getting pregnant and yet you wanted it; you wanted the abortion too, the experience of it. And

122

so you had it. And then you wanted the experience of regretting it. . . . But she had screamed for him to shut up. She had screamed, screamed.

"I'll wait up here just to watch you," the man grinned. "I'm not going to let you alone for five minutes. . . . You know what?"

Sandra cupped her ear. "What?"

"I give myself credit for saving a girl's life, a few months ago," he said. He leaned toward Sandra. His hair stuck out in thick, dark tufts, around the bottom of the hat; his eyes were a pale gray-green, bulging mildly, as if he had something to tell her she must not refuse. She stared at him, not knowing what they were talking about. "Hitch-hiking on the road through the Everglades, a girl from Florida State, a college girl, and I stopped to give her a ride . . . and the next day's paper had headlines about some guy cruising around looking for girls, girls alone hitch-hiking and helpless, that he would drag back into a field and mutilate. . . . So I saved her from that, maybe. Have you been reading the papers?"

Sandra could not follow all this. She noticed the man's mouth—unusually dark, grape-colored lips, something bruised and gentle and attractive about them. When he smiled his face creased in several places; he must have been in his mid-thirties, though his manner was paternal, declarative. Sandra told him that she was fine; she was on her way back to the motel now.

"Which direction is the town, do you remember?" he asked shrewdly.

"I can find my way back," Sandra said. "I'm not bleeding now."

He couldn't hear her well, because of the waves. He smiled uncertainly. He said that his camper was parked in some trees by the road—would she like a ride back to Aurora Key?—that was the name of this town, wasn't it? These little resort towns in the keys and along the coast were all so new, he said, new since

World War II, some of them only two or three years old—it was hard to keep them straight—but she looked a little shaky, so maybe he should drive her back. "It's only a five-minute walk," Sandra said. But he told her no, no, it was longer than that; she was nearly two miles from town. Sandra hesitated. His easy, amiable drawl and his slightly protruding eyes were too real to have been invented. He told her that he was on his way back to Key West, from Tampa, that he'd been up there on business and was anxious now to get home.

He helped her up the incline. She discovered that she was quite weak.

"You like to walk so far from town, alone?" he asked.

"Things happen when you're alone that never happen any other way," Sandra said.

He said something about hurricane warnings along the west coast of the state, but what the hell?—you had to take chances. Sandra agreed. They walked with difficulty through the sand, toward the groves of trees where his camper was parked. Farther down the beach, a man was jogging; a few boys were running in the surf. The sun had disappeared but the entire sky, the layers of cloud, were now glowing a pale lemon-white. He asked her again if she was alone and what she was doing, and she considered telling him about her mother . . . a story she had never told anyone, not even her husband: how, at the age of forty-eight, her mother had discovered a small hard lump in one of her breasts, had imagined it was cancer and that she hadn't long to live . . . and in a rush of joy had made plans to . . . had made plans . . . had hoped to . . . had wanted at last to. . . . How fiercely happy that woman had been, imagining herself doomed, and free! . . . but finally she turned herself in, she had the biopsy, was declared fortunate, *one of the fortunate* . . . and so she had been returned to her life again, to exactly her old life, unchanged. Gradually she forgot it all. Even the operation. All that remained was the sad disfigured left-hand side of her body, which Sandra had actually seen, once. . . . All the rest of it was forgotten, especially the fierce joy of those days of freedom. Believing herself doomed she had known what freedom was. Then she had forgotten it. Sandra remembered, however.

Or would she forget, too? Was that nature, such forgetfulness?

"I've always wanted to go to Key West," Sandra said. This was a lie, but she spoke with such enthusiasm that it sounded like the truth. She repeated the words: they were transformed into the truth. "It's the farthest tip of the continent, I mean the nation, isn't it, and I've always wanted to—it would be very kind of you—How far is it to Key West? It isn't very far, is it?"

"That depends upon what you mean by far," the man said.

He promised to wait for her while she checked out. When she paid the bill her hands were trembling. "How far is it to Key West?" she asked the desk clerk.

A bluish-gray cloud of exhaust rose from the camper, idling out there in the motel parking lot. It was a medium-sized camper, painted white, though flecked with rust on the bumper and fenders; it looked incongruous, alongside the lower, sleeker, more expensive automobiles. When the man in the white hat saw Sandra struggling with her luggage, he jumped out of the cab to help her. "It's very nice of you," she said eagerly. "It's very kind of you. I can pay you, if you want—I mean I—I'd be happy to—"

"Don't talk about that," the man said, with an embarrassed laugh. Then he said. "We'll see about that; there's no hurry."

The
Seduction

He heard the telephone ring.

No.

He heard his wife answer it, on the extension in the kitchen. Three short steps, he could count them, could almost see his wife's brisk eager step—*Hello?*

He was in the living room at the time. Thursday evening's newspaper lay at his feet, scattered pages, used-up, the three-color advertisements too bright for comfort. *Muscular automobiles for today's young challengers.* Yellow, brown-green, and blue. A clever advertisement. In the kitchen his wife's voice lifted, a not-quite-familiar voice. Surprise? Alarm? In the full-page advertisement a young couple—very young—the girl with a heart-breaking heart-shaped face and long hair, the boy curly-haired, lithe and grinning into space, not much older than Douglas's own son—on a beach, a sunset beach, a sportscar behind them and not even needing to hold hands because it was evident that—an easiness, litheness, indifference in love as in any muscular activity—melodic and mocking—what mercy might you expect from either of them? In the kitchen Douglas's wife was now speaking loudly, loud enough for him to hear if he chose.

"What is this, a joke? Who is this? What do you want?"

Douglas bent to gather the papers together. Gather them up neatly, neatly. His wife would not like this

127

mess. As he bent over his face grew heavy; blood rushed into it. Awkward. He could feel flesh gathering on him as he bent, thickening, a mysterious heaviness he did not quite acknowledge. But when he stood up straight it all vanished. He had the appearance of a slender, trim man, almost a young man, though he was forty-three. Not a graceful maneuver, stooping to pick up the paper. Fortunately no one could see him.

His wife's voice: "I'm going to notify the police—"

She slammed down the receiver. Douglas, the papers under his arm, went toward the kitchen, the papers held tight under his arm, the nerves and blood vessels in his armpit holding them tight, tight, and his wife appeared in the doorway. "What's wrong?" Douglas asked, surprised.

"It was—on the telephone—some girls on the phone, I could hear them giggling— Doug, some girls, they must be teenaged girls, they called and asked *if my husband was here*—it must be some new high school game they play, with nothing else to do but—"

"They asked for *me?* For *me?*"

"The little bitches, I've heard of this kind of thing! If they call again I'm going to notify the police!"

"Maybe they only wanted to talk to Hal. It was probably for Hal," Douglas said.

"No, it was for you, they asked for my *husband*," Connie said angrily. "They had the nerve to put it that way, in those words, they asked for my husband Douglas—the little bitches! I suppose it could be some friends of Hal's, though, from school. I don't know. I'm so angry, my heart is beating so hard. . . ."

"It seems like a harmless thing," Douglas said. He touched her arm, gently. But she drew away without seeming to notice; she was very warm, very upset. "I'm sure they won't call again, Connie. Why don't you forget about it? I'm sure they won't call again."

"You remember how those girls in Denby harassed a woman, they kept telephoning and taunting her about her husband—"

"What girls?"

"Oh, don't you remember?—Edith was telling us Saturday night?" Connie said impatiently. She took the newspaper from Douglas, as if for something to do. Her color was ruddy, flushed, healthy as if she'd been out in a brisk wind; Douglas felt the palpitation of excitement in her, and knew that, excited as she was, she would not really notice anything about him. He must only listen, sympathize. He must listen. Must not drift away, walk away, run away. Must only remain where she could see him in order to speak to him. "—it turned out to be three very young girls, twelve and thirteen years old, they were terrorizing this woman just for a joke, because her husband was in the army—in Vietnam, in fact—and they kept calling and pretending to be from Western Union, with a telegram, asking her if she'd like it read or whether the shock would be too much— Oh, it was sickening. Edith told us all about it, don't you remember?"

"Yes, I remember now."

"Well, it was sickening. That was in Denby but it's probably something going on here too. Those girls in Hal's class, they look just like sluts—they seem to look worse every year—"

The telephone rang again.

Connie turned at once. Furious, triumphant, she snatched the receiver up before Douglas could even move. "Hello?" she said sharply.

But it was not an enemy. It was a friend. "Oh Esther! Hello!" Douglas' wife turned slightly from him, her voice rising warmly, intimately. A friend, evidently. *Hello!* It was not an enemy, not hers and not his.

There were three people, and they all lived in a house together. Two were adults. One was tense and springy and athletic. His eyes occasionally shifted out of focus, as his thinking shifted: out of focus, out of reach. Douglas, watching his son when his son was not aware of him, loving him, wondering, fearing, saw how the soul of Hal had achieved a sizable body in so brief a span of time—only fifteen years? fifteen years? Now the boy was five feet ten inches tall; perhaps taller.

It would be hard to measure the boy's height, when the boy was so lithe and uneasy and stoop-shouldered and absent.

Hal was *his*, and Hal was a *son*.

The first room he'd had, the ceiling had been papered over with small planes and rockets and shapes like birds. Douglas had picked out the design. That was in a house long since forgotten, in another part of the country. Now, if Douglas poked his head into Hal's room, just to say hello or ask how things were, or to peek in when he knew Hal wasn't around, his eye was besieged by posters, the walls covered over with posters, advertising rock bands or people's faces, bare faces, mysterious and unnamed. Like a zoo, Douglas thought in irritation, how could the boy live in a zoo? a zoo of ugly faces? He half-wanted to tear all the posters down. But of course he would never tear them down and would never even mention, as his wife did, how much they annoyed him. Let Connie complain: she liked to complain. Douglas loved his son too much to bother him.

Once at supper Hal had been day-dreaming, the lower part of his face mechanical with the activity of eating, vague eating, slow chewing of food over and over...and Connie had said sharply, "What on earth is wrong with you? Sit up, sit straight! I can't stand the way you're sitting! Are you doing this just to drive me crazy?"

Hal had looked at her, amazed.

"What's wrong with you?" Connie had asked.

"I was.... I was thinking about something," he said. He had been too surprised even to be sullen. His expression was frank, clear, as if he'd been awakened out of an intimate dream.

"Oh, thinking? What were you thinking about?" Connie asked. She tried to make a joke of it; the edge of her voice must have startled her.

Hal frowned. Douglas liked it that his son's skin was not blemished, not inflamed and outraged by the grape-colored, bruise-shaded acne other boys his age suffered. He, Douglas, had had a fairly successful boyhood; he'd been rather handsome, like Hal, though not as tall. Not quite as handsome, maybe. But that part of his life, that very important segment of his life, had certainly been successful. Hal glanced up at him as if he were aware of Douglas' train of thought. He frowned again. "I was thinking . . . about thinking."

"What?"

". . . thinking about thinking. About. . . ."

The boy paused. He was *the boy*. Douglas smiled, waiting for what he would say next, prepared to encourage the boy, to smile sympathetically, to offset the rather edgy, combative tone of his wife's voice.

"About how it comes to the mind, thinking, thinking about things . . . about words. . . ." Hal said slowly. "How I didn't always do it. I mean, it didn't happen to me, the words didn't come to me. I was wondering where I was, then. . . ."

Connie looked uneasily at Doug. And so he said, quickly, "What do you mean? I don't understand."

"I was wondering where I was, then. Before I could think. I mean, at some time in my life . . . or in this world . . . when I wasn't around to think, before I was born or something. I don't know," he said cheerfully. His mood had altered abruptly: now he was boyish and amused with himself. He was being *cute*. "I guess I was daydreaming."

So the incident passed. *I guess I was daydreaming.* Doug would have imagined his son's daydreams differently; he remembered being that age, that tormented age, fifteen or sixteen or even seventeen years old. . . . He remembered his own boyhood in Des Moines, the closet-sized room in the attic, the way he had lain on his bed and dreamed, let his brain run wild with dreams, fantasies, galloping thunderous massive shapes that seemed to spring out of the corners of the room, leaping viciously into the familiar room. . . . And did he have them now? Oh yes. Altered, grown-up, in different costumes . . . but the same, exactly the same.

He would have imagined his son's daydreams differently.

One Saturday morning when no one was home Doug went in Hal's room and for some reason approached the bed. He wanted to lie down there, on his back, and see what his son might see, in the ceiling. But he hesitated. No. Maybe not. So he squatted by the side of the bed, awkwardly, and craned his neck to look up. Disappointment: the ceiling was blank, monotonous. But after a moment he saw a faint pattern of cracks, and one dark gray, dirt-thickened strand of cobweb, which did not float free of the ceiling but seemed to be fixed to it. A white painted-over white ceiling. You must use your imagination. In this room, beneath this ceiling, the boy had achieved a grown-up body . . . very quickly, involuntarily. Only fifteen years old. And yet it did not seem, in fact *it could not be,* that Douglas and Connie had been married so long! Douglas felt a rush of words like shouts, protests, little cries of *Who said so? . . . Who is so interested? . . . Who is telling such lies?*

His thighs and knees and calves ached. A sharp awkward pain. Not to be borne. . . . But out of the ceiling's corner emerged a hesitant shape, only the shadow of a shape, it looked like a head, a human head. . . . Douglas blinked and the shape vanished. Only a trick of the light. A shadowy unclear corner of the room. He waited, his breath a little labored now because of the effort of squatting like this, but nothing happened. In the old days, as a boy, he had imagined horsemen, horses, swords, darting shapes galloping across the top of the walls, around the room in a hectic chase, feverish, triumphant. And then automobiles: racing back and forth, a hypnotic nearly-audible sound of their motors, murmuring, buzzing, roaring in his ears. And then of course the girls, the human shapes that were girls, so many girls . . . girls. . . .

Ashamed, Douglas straightened. His legs did ache; he drew in his breath sharply. He was sensitive to pain, fearful and ashamed of his fear, knowing he exaggerated everything and yet unable to push through it, to get to the other side of it as he supposed other people did. Connie had had a complicated bladder problem a few years ago, had had to go to a specialist who inserted a long needle. . . . But no, he would not think of that now, he felt dizzy and sickened just to think of it.

He left Hal's room, in a hurry.

Yes, he would have imagined—invented—other daydreams for that son of his. He had to conclude that the boy was lying.

The cars sprang out of the room's corners, and one grew big enough to fit me. And then I fell asleep for a few years. The dream got big. The car was going up a steep incline, very steep, almost straight up, and I was afraid it would tip over backwards. I was so afraid. I started to cry, I was afraid it would tip over. . . . I couldn't steer right. The steering wheel came loose, I couldn't make it work, oh can't handle it, can't steer. . . .

Oh help me.

"Help me, can you help me with this?—I can't see what I'm doing—"

Douglas went over to his wife, who was poking blindly, nervously, trying to fasten the clasp of a string of pearls. He had no trouble with it. Standing there, close behind her, he could smell the familiar warmth of her body, the tender flesh of the back of her neck. When her fingers brushed against his they were cold—she was quite nervous. She was saying, "I hope it isn't too crowded. I hope it isn't all people we don't know."

"We don't have to stay long," Douglas said. "Mr. Jaeger only wanted me to put in an appearance . . . he thought someone should go, and he's too busy as usual. . . . You look very nice in that."

"Do I?" Connie said critically. "I don't know. Do I really?"

The reception was held at the large, furniture-cluttered home of the president of the local university, on a fine May afternoon. Graduation ceremonies had taken place that morning and the university had conferred honorary doctorates on two celebrated strangers— one of them a black woman who was evidently on a Federal Commission or Committee, concerned either with equal rights for all citizens, or with the scandal of the "battered child syndrome," or maybe both; Douglas had had time only to glance through the newspaper article on her, since that morning had been unusually rushed for him. He had forgotten her name temporarily. The other celebrity was Kenneth Lederer, an expert in the new field of "electronics-communications"; it was a coincidence, but Lederer's new book was first on the list of the nation's non-fiction best sellers, and Douglas had made a mental note to buy it and *read it* very soon. Lederer was evidently a perplexing but very important man.

The reception was too large, too many people had been invited. Douglas always went eagerly to such events, even when he only represented Mr. Jaeger and the firm, but his enthusiasm was usually dulled at once, by the sheer confusion of the first few minutes. . . . Though he had lived in this city for nearly nine years now, he still didn't know very many people. At large parties he had to fight a sensation of dismay, almost of panic, and force himself to smile and shake hands; but once the process began it was easy enough. You smiled, you shook hands. Douglas had a kind of talent for it, and his face was genial, robust, unstartling. At the correct moment you looked into the face opposite yours: you smiled and shook hands.

He liked people. Sometimes it worried him that there were so many people, even in this small city. Obviously he wouldn't have time to meet them all and they wouldn't have time to meet him. What missed connections?—missed handshakes?

The president of the university was a small, white-haired man in his sixties, an ex-champion golfer, an ex-lawyer, who had been Dean of the Law School before being named as president. He knew Mr. Jaeger, but not Douglas; he asked after Mr. Jaeger, listened closely but with a peculiar cloudy expression to what Douglas had to say—a few murmured remarks—and then spoke rapidly and impersonally about Belva Hull's contribution to humanity (Belva Hull was evidently the black woman) and about the crucial importance of the Battered Child Drive, apparently a local campaign. Douglas did public relations work for Jaeger Homes, and he wondered if perhaps the president of the university had mistaken him for a newspaper reporter. But it did not seem to matter; he smiled and nodded, the crowd grew noisier, and after a few minutes the president shook hands with him enthusiastically and excused himself. "Be sure to mix and meet everyone! Be sure to meet Belva Hull and get her to talk with you *personally*," he said, backing away.

Relieved, Douglas noticed his wife standing by herself, and went to get her. They smiled together nervously. Douglas asked if she would like another drink?—but the sherry was very sweet, rather sickening, and she said no. "I don't see anyone I know," Connie whispered. Douglas sipped his drink and looked around the room. It was a privilege to be here, he knew, even if the invitation had been for Mr. Jaeger. His gaze leapt about the room, undirected, hopeful. Surely in this crowd a friendly face might appear! He noticed several very elderly men, and supposed them university professors, probably retired from teaching; something about the elderly made him uneasy, jumpy. Trembling hands. Pity; pitiful. A very old man walked through the crowd, supported by a middle-aged woman who must have been his daughter. Douglas looked away.

Connie located friends of theirs, a couple they sa often. So they maneuvered their way over to them. Relief. A bright exchange of smiles. Obviously their friends had also been uncomfortable. . . . Now all four were lively, elated. Douglas heard himself laughing. "Did you attend the graduation ceremonies?—we didn't," Connie said. The other couple had not attended them either. Their name was Rowe, Edith and Bob. The Rowes. Douglas sipped his drink happily and looked around the room. Safe. He liked the Rowes. He would not have to listen too closely to the conversation, since Bob was rather quiet and Edith and Connie would do most of the talking.

"... she's evidently very intelligent, I was reading that she's on the President's advisory committee or something like that," Edith was saying. "Isn't she dark, though? I mean—she's very striking, very handsome, you wouldn't be able to tell her age at all. But evidently, I was reading, she's very accomplished and has been teaching at Harvard, I think, for a long time, a sociologist. ... Did you get introduced to her? We didn't. I'm sort of afraid of her, she looks so. ..."

"I wonder why Lederer is wearing that scarf?" Connie said. "He's so short! It looked in the paper as if he was a taller man, at least I got that impression ... of course he was standing next to Mr. Tate and *he's* so short. ... Doug and I just got shuffled along in here, as soon as we came in. It's so crowded and this sherry is so sweet, isn't it? I'm so glad you two are here—when did you get here? We were a little late getting started because—"

Lederer was being introduced to one of the mayor's assistants by the president of the university; Douglas stood only a few yards away and observed these successful, well-dressed men, not envying them, well perhaps envying them a little, but noting how short Lederer was in spite of his fame, and how uneasy he appeared. Probably he had never heard of this city and the university before today; probably it was all a blur to him, one page of a book he was trying to write but only half-writing, since other people were writing it along with him. *Daydreaming. I must have been daydreaming.* Lederer's face shone with the effort of being

136

equal to all this attention. He looked squashed-down and bulky in spite of his youthful gold-buttoned nautical jacket. Edith's voice insinuated its way into Douglas' consciousness: she was talking about Lederer, in a low voice. "His face seems to be pitted when you get closer to him. Isn't it...? Or is that the light? We haven't read his book yet, have you? *The Permanent Crisis,* I think that's the title, I read a review of it somewhere and it seemed.... I want to read it as soon as possible. It's about television in a democracy, or something like that, or what television or movies do to kids...."

The elderly professor was being introduced now to Lederer, and Douglas was reminded suddenly of his father. It had nothing to do with the old man's appearance, nothing to do with the taste of cheap sherry in Douglas's mouth, so he looked away...a little shaken, somehow nervous, queer. He noticed a boy of about nineteen coming through the wide-arched doorway, and he forgot about Lederer and the other men. He half-consciously joined in a burst of laughter—Bob had made a witty remark—but really he was not paying attention. The boy was dressed in a white outfit, like a servant; he was carrying a tray of drinks. He walked shyly into the cheerful noisy room of adults. Rather shaggy hair, but at least it was clean. A college student, no doubt. Slightly downcast expression, perhaps fearful of bumping into someone with the tray.... And someone did step backward, almost colliding with him. A woman in a fringed red dress, with a half-dozen strands of glass beads looped around her neck. The boy drew back. Safe. Douglas was glad that an accident hadn't happened, it would be embarrassing, a sudden noise and broken glass....

The boy offered drinks to people. He was taller than Douglas, but too thin. Why were they all so thin? He passed near Douglas and offered drinks to a couple Douglas remembered from PTA years ago, though he didn't know their name. The boy moved into the other room and Douglas drifted away from his wife and the Rowes, in order to watch him. In this room, a dining room, a long table had been set up and two other young people—one of them a black girl—were arranging plates and silverware. Douglas stood idly in the doorway. The three of them were really not attractive; the girl's face was sullen, purplish-black. But there was something very attractive about them. The way they moved, awkwardly and yet somehow in a rhythm, hesitantly, setting things down, dressed in their servile white outfits...hired for the occasion and probably a little embarrassed....

The woman in the red fringed dress came into the dining room and spoke to one of them, maybe she was Mrs. Tate, the president's wife?...or maybe she was just a guest, looking for another drink. She did take a glass from the boy's tray and thanked him and turned to leave. Douglas saw how the three college students exchanged glances, amused and mocking, the three of them looking toward one another at precisely the same moment, the same instant; they shared the same expression.

It was a miracle, that swiftness, that exchange of looks!

Douglas backed away, hoping they would not notice him. He returned to Connie and the Rowes. His eyelids burned slightly, as if he'd been here a long time and the smoke from cigarettes and the airlessness of the room were becoming oppressive.

Sunday.
Connie is talking to him about Frances, or Constance—a woman-friend of hers. Instance. *Instant-remover: removes all stains except....* She will be hostess for her bridge group on Wednesday. Bridge would be an interesting word, Douglas thinks, dazed behind his attentive smile, if only it weren't misused. He is half-waiting for Hal to come downstairs, no he is fully waiting for Hal, *waiting for Hal,* who came home after two

o'clock in the morning when Saturday had turned into Sunday. Douglas had waited up for him, so that Connie could go to bed and forget about it all. And then Douglas had deliberately gone to sleep in the recreation room, so that he need not confront his son, because three people had to live together in this house and why . . . why should he make their living-together so difficult . . . ?

A thumping overhead that means Hal is in the bathroom. Douglas waits, listening to his wife and to a lawnmower next door. His eye is drawn to the telephone nearby, peach-colored plastic, on one of the kitchen counters. Very modern, clean. Will it ring? Behind it is a simulated-pinewood panel, and the colors do not quite match. The peach-toned plastic is one thing, the pinewood another. All this is like a poem, a structure made of words, and Douglas is aware of "Hal," a word, a word he must often say to himself, now on his way downstairs.

"Excuse me," Douglas says to his wife, getting up.

He confronts Hal in the front hall. Hal's fawn-colored hair is damp. "Hal," he says, "where are you going?—are you skipping breakfast?"

"Yeah, I'm not hungry, I'm going out for a while," Hal says.

Douglas himself is dressed for a calm secular Sunday. He knows he is trim, casual, sporty; a coincidence, his trousers are made of the same pale blue synthetic material as his son's. He looks Hal fully in the face and smiles. He would like to shake hands, almost—there is that impulse, to show that there are no secrets, nothing harmful between them, no confusion. ". . . are you going?"

"Over to Ralph's."

"Is that John DeFree's son, the one who—"

"Yeah. Ralph DeFree, yeah."

"The one who—"

"Yeah."

The boy is already at the door, has opened it. Back

and forth between them leap sparks of knowledge, sheer knowledge that is bodiless as electricity. *He knows,* Douglas thinks calmly to himself, *he knows.* But still he must think again: *Does he know . . . ?*

". . . we hardly see you any more, your mother and I, your mother was complaining that you're in and out of the house before she has a chance to talk to you, she has a number of things for you to do, and, well, she isn't very happy about all this. . . ." His voice has taken on Connie's whine, but he knows enough to stop; to adjust his expression. He looks fully, openly, into his son's face. Not like his own father, who would never admit anything, hadn't any time for Douglas, had not even existed around the house except as a presence. Douglas is not his father's son. . . . Hal mumbles an apology, an excuse, swinging his head one way and then another, but he certainly intends to escape and Douglas cannot grab him and make him stay.

". . . be back later, then."

"When, later?"

"Oh later this afternoon. Later," Hal says.

"All right, but. . . ."

But goodbye.

Douglas watches his son walk out to the street. A tall yearning boy, too thin like all the boys his age. Yearning, greedy, restless; absent. He doesn't look back at Douglas. Maybe that is love, maybe that was love?—not looking fully into Douglas' face? He hadn't met his father's startled stare that evening a few weeks ago, when they blundered together on several square yards of dirty sidewalk, a mathematical improbability in an infinite universe, but it had happened—what bad luck—what crazy bad hellish luck—but of course it could have been explained if—

But Hal had turned away as if he hadn't seen, hadn't noticed anyone, he had walked quickly away, had denied his father, had disappeared. Douglas remembers all this with a chill, incredulous terror, as if it had taken place in a movie seen long ago. So now he calls out after his son's retreating back: "—Have a good time!"

Douglas stayed away from the Flood St. drugstore, he stayed away from the U.S. Burger drive-in restaurant, though one Friday, around eight-thirty, he drove by to see if. . . . Connie was beside him; they were going to someone's home for the evening. It was quite natural for him to take the Boulevard. But he couldn't see who might be there, the cars were all alike, of course he couldn't make out any of the girls at this distance.

Another day, on an impulse, he looked through an aged photograph album that had come to him when his mother had died, along with a household of old, useless furnishings, most of which had been sold or given away to the Salvation Army long ago. Douglas had not bothered with the snapshots at the time, partly because it had been a very busy, hectic, feverish time in his life— the funeral, the quarrel with Blue Cross and Blue Shield over his mother's hospital bills, his own congested work-week—and partly because he had not wanted to look at them, dreading what he might see. Now he felt more optimistic.

. . . But the first snapshot he saw, opening the album at random, was one of himself as a boy!. . . and yet it was not the "self," the Doug he remembered, but another boy entirely. He stared at the picture. It had been taken at the beach, and there he stood: so skinny that his ribs showed, his damp bathing trunks clung to his thighs, his hair was streaming water and his face was the face of a quite ordinary, homely, not-quite-intelligent boy. He had been maybe fourteen, fifteen, when the picture had been taken. Disappointed, Doug pushed it aside. Many of the snapshots were loose in the album. Some were warped, discolored. It was a surprise to notice how many of them hadn't turned out well—too much sunshine, over-exposures, or under-exposures; or double-exposures; or just inexpert, crude picture-taking, the intrusion of blurred figures in the foreground,

141

tree limbs or unidentifiable objects, awkward poses, squinting faces, hair blowing absurdly off to one side. . . . Another snapshot of Doug, taken when he was a little older, was a close-up that showed vividly the eruptions and blemishes of his skin, particularly on his forehead; and his hair had been cut so very short, shaved up the back of his head, so that he looked skinny, starved, pop-eyed, gawky, ugly . . . and even his smile was clumsy, far too strained and self-conscious. . . .

Doug stared at these snapshots, at first in disbelief, then with a mounting disgust. He felt as if he had been betrayed. Who was this boy, this common homely boy from the country, what did it mean, why should he pay any attention to that face?—why should he acknowledge it?

He thought of his own son, and of how Hal would be contemptuous of *this* son. Hal's friends would laugh at him. And of course the girls would laugh at him . . . the girls were cruel, quick to laugh, to giggle . . . they could not be fooled. . . . Douglas gathered up all the snapshots of himself, quickly, not lingering over any of them, and stuffed them in one of the garbage cans in the garage. He made sure they were stuffed far enough down so that if Connie came out here and lifted the lid, the snapshots couldn't be seen.

Why should he acknowledge that ugly boy? He didn't have to acknowledge anything from the past.

"What is your name?"
"What is yours?"
"I asked you first."
"Who wants to know?"
"Where do you live?"
". . . do you live?"
"You tell me!"
"*You* tell me!"
"*You!*"

"You're out late, aren't you?"
"It isn't late."

"Maybe your watch stopped. Let me see."

"It doesn't work right."

"It's a pretty watch—why doesn't it work right?"

"You can't see it."

"I can see it. It's light enough."

"I can't see what time it is."

"... like a new watch?"

"*I* can't see right. I don't feel right."

"Would you like a new watch?... a new watch?"

"I don't give a damn what time it is."

"What time is it? What time do you have to be...."

"I don't have to be anything anywhere. I don't give a damn."

"How old are you?"

"What's your name?"

"Who wants to know?"

"What's your name, tell me, seriously, just your first name, what's your name?"

"What's yours?"

"You tell me!"

"*You* tell me!"

Long afterward, in his own bed, he would feel his heartbeat still racing. He would hear the panting laughter, the giggles, the rise and fall of voices, a mysterious language he couldn't quite understand. *You tell me! Who wants to know?* All that had been a race, and now, in his own bed, beside his wife, he knew that the race was still going on but he was not in it, he was trying to sleep, *trying to get some sleep,* his brain was raw and terrible, his eyeballs burned. Drifting into sleep he felt as if he were being nudged into the earth, someone's hand at the back of his neck urging his face down into the earth, into dirt, so that he would have to suck for air through the loose particles of dirt, burrowing, his eyes and eyebrows and nose and mouth filled with it, nostrils stuffed and aching, yearning, screaming for air.... Behind all this, encased in his skull, his brain screamed for air!... for air! *O help me.*

Suddenly a crowd of witnesses: passers-by attracted

by the commotion, secretaries at the office in mini-skirts and chunky platform shoes, his long-dead father with a wig of white, white hair...someone with a box-camera, trying to center him in the lens as if it were a rifle's sight...*Help me, help*...his son Hal staring, staring, never closing his frightened eyes....The ceiling lifted: more faces, peering grinning frowns, contemptuous smirks, pencil-drawn cherubic eyebrows lifted and arched and mocking, the inside cover of one of his boyhood prayer books with an army of angels in fake-silk pearl-smooth gowns and white sexless sneering faces girlish blond, all girls, all blond, and so lovely so delicate so fragile and cruel, a blond sneering beauty that astonished his soul: *Who is he? What is he? Look at him! Listen to his heart!—listen! That man is going to have a heart attack!*

He woke, terrified.

He got out of bed. Stumbled to the door. Connie called out at once: "Doug, what is it? Doug? Are you sick?"

"...sick."

"What is it? Is it your stomach again?"

He made it to the bathroom. Did not turn on the light. His wife was still calling after him, he heard her voice but not the words, and with his eyes shut tight he whispered: "...my stomach, just my stomach. Just my stomach."

She was right outside the door. "...Doug...?"

"Leave me alone, go back to sleep. I'm all right. It's just my stomach."

But I love you!
O you want to eat me!...want to gobble me up!
Yes, but....
Yes, yes! I have dreams about mouths like yours, lips like yours! I'm not kidding! I don't lie! I gave up lying, uh, last year—gave it up—I thought what the hell, why should I lie? Why should I? I don't give a damn about what people think, why should I lie?

144

*That's very interesting.... *

O what are you doing, why are you doing that? I can't stand that!

*But I love you.... *
*But I don't love you.... *
But I love you.

He listened to the phone ringing at the other end and half-hoped no one would answer. An old wish of his, a half-hoping for failure, for missed connections! But his wife did pick up the phone, on the second ring. "Yes? Hello? Doug?" she said quickly.

"He isn't—?"

"No, he isn't here, of course he isn't, I thought maybe—then you didn't find him?"

"Not yet. I just thought I'd—"

"Where are you calling from?"

"A filling station on MacKenzie."

"Well, I—I hope— I hope you—"

"I'll call back in an hour if I don't find him, just to check," Doug said hollowly. He had already been cruising around the city, checking parks, drugstores, restaurants, peering anxiously at the faces of boys on the street.... "I think it will be all right, honey. I mean I'm sure it will be. This isn't the first time that...."

"But it's the first time he said...."

"Yes but honey, honey," Doug said, closing his eyes, "he didn't mean it, he was just upset, honey, you should realize... I mean I try to... I try to realize, to remember, what it was like to be that age... myself... I try to sympathize with him.... I know it's a shock, all that rage in him, I know it was a shock to you, the language he used, and... well, he didn't mean it, I'm sure, it's just that when boys are that age they find life very difficult, tumultuous...."

He heard her begin to cry. He hated, feared, could not bear the sound of adult women crying. So he tried to talk over her weeping, as if not hearing it, not acknowledging it: "... whatever he said to you he didn't really mean, try to remember that, he didn't really mean it, it was just his rage speaking, his wildness, and . . . and anyway . . . anyway if it comes right down to it, I would rather he had yelled at me than what he did, just to ignore me as if I weren't there. . . . Connie? Are you listening?"

"Yes. I'm all right."

"Are you all right? Because I should hang up now. . . ."

"I'm all right. I'm fine."

"To ignore me the way he did. . . . I . . . I think that's more terrible than, than . . . than the other . . . than what he said to you. . . ."

"I'm all right," his wife said.

After hanging up he sat for a while inside the telephone booth, thinking. It was strange that his thoughts were not crowded and savage; really, he felt hollow, almost lethargic, as if he had been through all this before. In a sense it was true because one winter day Hal had "run away" after a quarrel, and Doug had gone out to search for him; but he had located Hal almost immediately, at a friend's house. This time it was different. Yet it was familiar to him, this situation inside a telephone booth, the vague awareness of someone watching him . . . his own reflection in the transparent plastic window of the door.

He went back to his car, double-parked on the street. Motor running. The signs of emergency, theatrical excitement. But he felt dowdy, middle-aged, not equal to the role he must play. *I've come to bring you home!— to forgive you for what you said!—to love you!*

He drove slowly along MacKenzie until he came to the shopping mall, where he turned in and drove through the parking lot, slowly, slowly, looking for a crowd of boys though he half-knew Hal was surely alone this time. Some high school girls were washing cars—$1 CAR WASH—dressed in blue jeans and oversized, baggy, sexless blouses, their clothes damp, one girl squealing as a hose was accidentally turned on her—Doug noticed how wild she looked, her eyes shut tight and her hair spinning around her face as she turned away— The owner of the car, a man his age, was standing nearby and watching, self-consciously, twirling his car keys. $1 CAR WASH McK'ZIE HIGH. It wasn't Hal's high school; so there would be no point in stopping to talk to those girls.

Though probably Hal knew them: probably he knew all the girls.

Doug circled the shopping mall several times. He saw a boy Hal's size, walking with his mother and carrying a package of groceries ... an odd coincidence, but the woman resembled Connie too. But of course it wasn't Hal: too young anyway.

He drove past the car wash again, saw that five or six cars were lined up, waiting to be washed ... the girl with the wet clothes was now squeezing out a sponge, bent over, her hair drooping around her face ... rather muscular, athletic-looking, but in spite of that a pretty girl. ... Doug scanned the crowd, the milling people, caught and released the faces one by one, felt that something terrible was going to happen and that his own role, his own words, would not be equal to it.

He called Connie back in forty-five minutes. No luck. And then he drove out toward the airport, on a hunch; saw two boys hitch-hiking, slowed down but didn't stop since neither of them was Hal; regretted slowing down, because the boys had thought he was going to stop and. ... One boy flashed an obscene gesture at him, swiftly and mechanically. Doug drove on, pretending he hadn't seen.

At the airport he relaxed for a while in the cocktail lounge. He had a martini, felt somewhat better, had another. ... Sat there thinking, contemplating, yet aware strangely of himself as *thinking, contemplating,* somehow apart from himself as if sitting a few yards away. In fact, someone was sitting a few yards away. Watching him? Contemplating him? Guiltily he glanced in that direction and saw a man in a businessman's suit, neatly dressed, a stranger ... who was not watching Doug at all, but staring into his own glass. A martini also. Doug looked away before the man noticed him.

He drove back to the MacKenzie area, through the shopping mall again, but the girls' car wash was gone. Only a few puddles on the pavement; no one around. On a hunch he drove to a drive-in restaurant nearby, where beer and ale were served, and cruised through the parking lot. . . . He didn't see Hal. He parked and a car hop came immediately over to him; a girl he didn't know, evidently she was new here? . . . or hadn't he happened to notice her before? . . . . She looked very young, a blonde with an astonishingly delicate face and body, her legs a little bowed. Or were they? Doug didn't want to stare. When she approached him, smiling and squinting—the overhead lights were glaring—he was relieved to see how pretty she was. It depressed him when girls were not pretty. It was all right if women, adult women, were not pretty because . . . because it did not matter so much with them, especially if they were married. . . . But girls Hal's age, girls like the car-hop, really ought to be pretty. Otherwise Doug felt depressed.

He ordered a bottle of beer. No, nothing to eat. No food.

When she brought him the beer, rather ceremoniously on a tray, he was able to get her to talk for a few minutes. Asked her if she knew Hal, his son; his son Hal; described him. . . . "Actually he was supposed to meet me here," Doug said. With a wave of his hand he indicated the parking lot, which was now fairly crowded. Teenagers were cruising through it. The girl frowned and tried to think; she was very pretty, standing there in her tight white shorts, her silky pink blouse tucked in tight, frowning and pretending to think. . . . She told Doug that she didn't guess she knew his son, off-hand.

"You don't? He knows all the girls," Doug said. He laughed and shook his head, as if not quite approving. The girl was glancing back at the restaurant, so Doug thought he'd better order another beer; he didn't want to take up her time and not spend much money. He knew these girls didn't make much. So he handed her a dollar bill and told her to keep the change when she returned, again with the tray and the bottle of beer perched on it, as if she were serving someone very important. He liked that. He appreciated that. Before she could turn to leave he said, "Maybe you've met my son but didn't know his name. For all I know he uses different names! I can't quite keep track of him myself."

"Well, uh, I don't think I know him, offhand," the girl said. Doug noticed that she was chewing gum. Another car pulled up and she had to leave, backing away with a sweet little smile for him and a nod, to show that she didn't especially want to go wait on these new people, but it was her job. Doug half-expected her to return to him, but she didn't. After a while he finished both beers and considered driving home, but the thought depressed and angered him, there was something unfair about it—who was making him do these things?—who was torturing him like this? He hadn't eaten since noon and he felt a little rocky. But anyway he flicked his car lights to get the girl back and when she came—not in any hurry, either, damn it—he stared resentfully at her pale, slightly bowed legs—who did she think she was?—a little slut like that?—when she came, smiling, he ordered another bottle of beer, *Another of the same*, and this made her ask if he didn't want something to eat too, so he said no, Jesus no, he'd had enough to eat in his lifetime and that was the trouble with women, they always wanted to feed you, didn't they?—but the girl couldn't quite follow this. She might have been a little stupid or hard of hearing, but at least she was pretty. Doug decided to tell her this. When she came back with the beer he told her that she was very pretty. Her white-blond hair, her delicate features—so pretty! He insisted that she was, though she hadn't denied it. He paid for the beer with a five-dollar bill and told her to keep the change.

"I don't want all that change," the girl said nervously.

"What? Huh? What do you mean?"

"I don't want it," she said.

She counted out dollar bills and change for him, and Doug resented it, her pretense, and wouldn't take it from her. So she had to leave it on the tray. He laughed at this. "Oh, who are you kidding? Who are you kidding, honey?" he said. "I know all about you . . . I know all about this dump. . . . My son tells me all about girls like you, who are you kidding? Wait—" She walked away. He drank the beer, silently, sullenly. Some of his good humor had gone and he felt now rather chilled. He felt a little sick. But he didn't want to drive away and give that girl the satisfaction of. . . . Who did she think she was, anyway? He was positive he'd seen her somewhere before. She reminded him of a girl named Trish. She probably knew him but was pretending not to. It was so confusing. . . .

He didn't want to leave without telling her something. He wanted to apologize for upsetting her, or maybe he wanted to whisper something in her ear: *Who are you kidding, you little bitch?* But when he got out of his car he felt immediately dizzy. God, he felt dizzy. He waited until the buzzing in his ears went away, then walked shakily over to the restaurant. It was circular, with windows all around. Lights glared from all sides. A sign said NO LOITERING. His little waitress was inside and he was going to tell her a few things, he wasn't going to drive meekly home and forget about being insulted, but when he got inside he felt suddenly very sick. He shut his eyes tight.

"Mister, are you—?"

He stumbled against a table. He felt blood sink from his head, he felt a horrible nauseous faintness. Someone was holding him by the arm—a boy—and asking him if he was all right, would he like to sit down?— but Doug pulled away from him. That was a mistake: the exertion was a mistake.

He leaned over a table and began to vomit.

When the first spasm passed he turned, blindly, and stumbled back outside. All he needed was fresh air, he needed to be alone.... The boy followed him. Doug didn't know if this boy was someone he should have known, a friend of Hal's, or a waiter here, or a stranger... he didn't know what the hell was going on... he felt so terribly sick, it was all turning out wrong, many mistakes had been made but it was too confusing to backtrack and remember them, he was only human, he hadn't eaten since noon but he was vomiting stuff that seemed solid, along with all the beer, and some of it was on the front of his shirt.... He got halfway to his car when another spasm wracked him, and he bent over helplessly, helplessly. The boy caught up with him.

"Maybe if you—"

"I'm all right," Doug said angrily.

He stumbled to his car. The door was open; good. He climbed inside, very dizzy. Someone was close behind him. He could hear the little waitress' voice and another voice, a boy's, and they were discussing him as if he weren't even present, insulting him when he was too sick to defend himself. "The keys are in the ignition," the girl said. "We can drive him home. I bet his wife would like that. Should we drive him home?" The boy said something that must have been amusing, because the girl giggled. She said, "Oh no, I don't mind, I told you I'm going to be a nurse. I had my first half-year at St. Mary's, nothing disgusts me now. Hey look, just get his wallet or something and look up his address, and we can drive him home, it's the only way he's going to get home."

The boy leaned in. He said to Doug: "Mister, I'll drive you home. Move over. You can tell me where you live, okay?"

"I'll drive myself," Doug said weakly.

"No, it's okay, mister, I don't mind," the boy said. Doug wanted to look around at him, to see if he was a friend or an enemy, but the effort was too much. He slid over and the boy climbed in. The girl climbed in the back seat, giggling. She told the boy again that she was going to be a nurse—the boy's name was Eddie—who were these people?—where had they come from so suddenly? Did they know him? Doug managed to sit up and clear his head slightly, but still it was too much of an effort to argue with them.

The boy switched on the ignition as if the car were his.

"Now wait—" Doug protested.

"I'll get you home," the boy said, "don't worry about it, just relax—tell me where you live and relax, okay?—okay, mister? Just relax."

"But I—"

"Oh just lay back and relax and don't worry!" the girl said cheerfully. "It's no trouble for us!"

"I'm perfectly capable of—"

"Just lay back, you're going to be all right," the girl said.

"I'm perfectly capable of driving my own car—"

He must not have spoken clearly enough, since they didn't seem to hear him. The boy was already backing the car around, aiming it toward the street; all Doug had to do was indicate which direction he should turn in, that would be enough for the moment, since he felt a little shaky and the exertion even of arguing might make him sick again. So he indicated which direction the boy should turn in. The boy said, "Great! Thanks!"

He lay back. He relaxed.

Passions
and
Meditations

6 October

Dear Keith Lurie:
Let me say at once that I have never written a letter
like this before—but this is not simply a letter of admiration. I have a double purpose. First, just to thank
you for your exciting, unforgettable work—parts of
"American Cosmos" will show the way forward to
young American composers, after the sterile cul-de-sac
of so much of contemporary music—it is quite as icon-
oclastic, and as rich, as Ives!—and, second, I am putting
together a detailed study of American culture, tentatively titled *Passions and Meditations: Eight Young
Artists,* and I wonder if I might interview you. I realize
that your schedule is a crowded one and that, perhaps,
you receive many requests for interviews. But I hope
you will find time for me. My knowledge of music may
only be that of a devoted layman, but my appreciation
is limitless!

I found your speech last Friday at the Academy not
only brilliant but inspiring. (I managed to get a ticket
for the program through an old professor of mine at
City College—Morris Gruber, whom perhaps you remember? You took a course in European history from
him in 1961, and received a grade of A—naturally!—
he looked up your grades in his grade-book for that
year, which he still has. Professor Gruber is another

fan of yours and asks to be remembered to you.) I agree with your remarks about freshness and innovation, but I'm afraid I must question your statement that "there is no tradition, only memory." Perhaps I failed to grasp your meaning, but it seems to me that much of the experimentation of recent years—Baxterhouse's* "Symphony for Silence," for example, and all of the electronic pieces—are simply admissions of defeat. We don't need more experimentation or apologists for it!

My admiration for your work is immense, and I hope to bring your name to a wider public. Of course you are quite famous among those of us who follow closely all new developments in the arts, but the average American—unfortunately—has yet to hear of you. Could we get together next week for a few hours of conversation? My number is 945-0095 and I will be waiting hopefully for your call.

Sincerely,
Roberta Bright

*I just realized that Ezra Baxterhouse is a friend of yours—I hope you won't take offense at this remark!

11 October

Dear Keith Lurie:
I am writing to inquire whether you can set aside an hour or two for an interview (tape-recorded, if this is agreeable to you). I am working on a detailed critical study of your work. Please contact me at 945-0095, any day after 5:30.

Perhaps I should introduce myself: I am a young woman (26), a serious student of contemporary culture, born and educated in New York, whose quiet and even monastic life allows her an objectivity sadly lacking in many of our "professional" critics and reviewers (I wrote an angry, devastating letter in reply to Donald

154

Sullivan's ignorant and cruel dismissal of your work, in the *New York Times* last month, but I am still waiting for the letter to be published). I think our meeting might be enjoyed on both sides, and I promise not to ask you any embarrassing questions!

(I did write you a similar letter on October 6, but I understand that you might have been out of town, or could find no time in your busy schedule to call me.)

Sincerely,
Roberta Bright

21 October

Dear Mr. Lurie:

Having waited hopefully but futilely for your reply, I would like to explain myself a little more. I am not—repeat, *not*—an ordinary seeker after the talented and illustrious. As I said at the outset of our correspondence, I have never before written a "fan" letter (and hardly anticipate doing so again); indeed, my desire to talk with you is purely professional. As I am at this moment working on a lengthy analytical study of your work, it can hardly be said that my appeals to you have been mere "fan" mail (I detest that ugly term). Perhaps you have misunderstood.

Is it possible that you are so deluged with awards (the recent Academy grant was richly deserved—but why did they wait so long to give it to you?) and invitations and congratulations and offers of various types (beyond my ability even to imagine, I suppose) that you cannot recognize a legitimate inquiry when it arrives? Or is your mail scanned by a secretary, who has only a superficial concern for your career and a limited awareness of what might truly advance it? It is something of a tragedy, I have always believed, that sensitive, dedicated people with much in common can be separated, perhaps forever, by middle parties with no clear grasp of what they are doing.

Please let me hear from you—I will be home all weekend, awaiting your call.

Very sincerely yours,
Roberta Bright

26 October

Dear Mr. Lurie:

Why didn't you call?

I am very disappointed but I guess I understand.

Let me explain further: it isn't just your work I admire, but you yourself, the personality I sense behind that rigid, careful face of yours. It is not a handsome face, but strong, powerful, commanding—it speaks of a titanic soul. Have you read Edgeware's biography of Beethoven? There are uncanny similarities between you and that great, unhappy man.

Enclosed is a pen-and-ink drawing based on one of your photographs. I thought it might amuse or interest you, and I would appreciate it very much if you would autograph it and return it in the enclosed stamped envelope. My drawing abilities leave much to be desired, I'm afraid, but the picture does you justice, I think (though even the photograph doesn't convey the moody power of your eyes).

Thank you!

Gratefully,
Roberta Bright

1 November

Keith Lurie:

No need to pretend you've been out of town. Or to imagine that I think so. I happen to have seen you in person three times during the past week—merely sitting in the park across from your apartment building,

156

without being especially on the alert for you. I spent some profitable hours in that park, quite peaceful, even rather content, turning over and over in my mind the folly and cruelty of human relationships.

Perhaps you don't believe that I actually saw you (in your Olympian detachment!)—but I can enumerate the occasions.

1. Wed. 5:30 P.M. Left a taxi, entered your building. Wearing a dark trench coat, shoes of fawn-colored suede (or some other soft material), carrying a brown leather briefcase and a small brown bag (liquor?—groceries?). I wondered if I should approach you; I lost my nerve, of course. The taxi driver was waiting to make a U-turn, so on a sudden impulse (I sometimes do things like this, amazing myself—but then, life is not logical) I ran over to him and got into the cab. I had him drive me home, though I could hardly afford it! The driver was quite a pleasant fellow. I asked him if he had recognized you—no—didn't even know the name "Keith Lurie"—guessed you might be a prize-fighter or a football player (!)—so I set him straight. I explained that he had just driven home one of America's (the world's?) finest composers, who, at the incredible age of 32, has such unlimited promise that we may anticipate another Stravinsky in our midst. I hardly mean to flatter or to embarrass you—but this happens to be true.

2. Thurs. 10:45 A.M. Leaving your apartment, in a hurry, wearing a bright rust-colored tweed outfit, vest and all (English-made? possibly bought on your trip to London last spring?), carrying that same briefcase, which I imagine is stuffed with material you are working on. Your hair was damp (from a shower?—I try to visualize you doing such ordinary, mundane things!) and you wore sun-glasses with wide black frames. Are they prescription lenses? I noticed at the Academy that you wore blue-tinted glasses, though it was evening. I wear glasses myself; my eyes are fairly good, even after years of abusing them through over-work, but occasionally my left eyeball seems to tug, the muscles

pull oddly. No pain, but it's a frightening sensation.

3. Friday. 11:30 A.M. Again, descending the steps quickly (there are twelve steps, an even dozen), as if you were late for an appointment. I was waiting out on the sidewalk, unobtrusively and patiently. I had been imagining you for some time—seeing your image there, approaching the glass doors of your building—how disappointed I was when other men appeared, middle-aged, ugly, without your special radiance! Then at eleven-thirty you finally appeared, hurrying, in a dark green corduroy jacket, a yellow and white striped shirt and an elegant dotted tie, passing so close to me that the dots of your necktie danced in my eyes, making me dizzy. I could smell your shaving lotion, we were so close! It was fresh, green, the odor of trees and meadows. Your trousers were dark brown, your shoe-boots dark leather, ah, what grace even in the way you hurried, saying good morning to the doorman (a very fine old man, who I've chatted with) and glancing at me, almost smiling, I think, though you were obviously late for wherever you were going and I was a total stranger to you. Yet—did you recognize something in my face?—my expression? I was stunned at our sudden closeness though I had been waiting for two hours, somehow it all happened so quickly—you came and went so quickly. I stood there like a fool, unable to speak. After you had gotten in the cab I came awake and wanted to lean in the window and say, "Mr. Lurie—may I share this taxi with you?" Would you have minded? What would you have said?

I walked 25 blocks home.

Disgusted at my own meekness, my fear. Back to my non-doorman-manned dump, climbed up to the fifth floor, let myself in, stood in my tiny bathroom for half an hour, staring at my face—Why? Why? Some are born to beauty and power (like you—even your thinning hair won't make you appear weak), some are born to—well, not ugliness, not monstrosity—but to neutrality, weakness, nullity, nothing. Why?

In the universe there are stars in which all nuclear fuel is burned up, all energy dissipated into space, stars that then turn in upon themselves, becoming dense to infinity, crushing in upon themselves.... Helplessly, forever, they turn in upon themselves until they are points in space. No light can come out of them: the light is dragged back into them by their powerful gravity. They have collapsed to points, to the point of a pencil, they are dead, more than dead, black holes in which everything stops. I am one of those black holes. A point of consciousness condensed in upon itself. The black holes are all dead and cannot communicate with other black holes. Why? Certain bodies of energy continue to live and to give off light. They are propelled through the universe as if alive. Why? Why are some of us dead and others alive, why am I a point of silence and neutrality and you a being of light, always in a hurry, always with a destination? Why is the world put together this way?

I stand grinning into my six-by-eight inch mirror, accepting my fate. What else can I do? All my life I have *accepted*. The world is divided into those who accept, and those who act and live and stride forward and brush past others. If I slashed open an artery in honor of you ("this is my Body and my Blood, etc.") would you take notice? If I told you that I would perform this act at noon, Sunday, November 14, would you try to stop me? Would you at least be aware of the clock on that day, watching as noon approached?

Would you give a damn?

You won't telephone me or reply to my letters. You won't pay attention to me. These declarations of love— so frank, sincere, undisguised—these mean nothing to you. Couldn't take five seconds to autograph that drawing of you, though I worked on it for days, discarding a dozen attempts. I enclosed a stamped, self-addressed envelope but you must have thrown everything away. You or your secretary, who stands between us.

Men like you are arrogant bastards. Beneath the

melody of your music (which is often derivative) is the heavy dull throb of Ego, Ego, selfish Ego.

R. Bright

9 November

Dear Keith:

I have the power to enter the back doors of lives. A hole in space, a black hole, is invisible. I can let myself in the door of your apartment (eighth floor, but *not* facing the park, is it? very expensive and yet antiquated and drafty, isn't it?) and wander through the rooms, wherever I want to go. I have to imagine the carpeting in the hall: probably new, thick, bought when you moved in a year ago. Dark green, maybe. Dark brown. The rug on my floor is from Woolworth's, straggly and "modern," hunter green. I don't compare the two of us, you with your family's money and me with nothing (my father taught high school in Queens but died when I was a child), you with your "prodigious talent" and me with nothing. I don't compare your bedroom—with those high, elegant windows and drapes, the expensive furniture—and this room of mine, one single room, a bed I don't bother to make up. In your bedroom I would walk on tip-toe, as if in a sacred place. I would go to the closet and open the door, gently, and thrust my face into it, to breathe the odor of your clothes, seize one of your jackets and press my hot face against it. *You,* you are present in my hands and my head, a proud prisoner in my imagination. *You.* You cannot escape.

You refuse to answer my letters. Why?

Ought I to have typed them? But typing is so formal and impersonal, so bleak. If you read my handwriting you are already close to me—almost intimate with me.

Or do you sense how your silence teases me, inspires me? The building in which I live smells of sewage, and overhead someone is walking heavily, back and forth, a television set is blaring, children are yelling, and yet I feel fierce tonight, strangely omnipotent. I don't know why. I think I am transported out of my own life by the contemplation of you. Let that bastard walk upstairs, making my ceiling and walls vibrate, let the children yell, I am free of them tonight. I am free because of you.

This is my theory: by reading my letters, by scanning this line as you are, quickly, impatiently, perhaps nervously (because you don't know what I might say next, do you?), even by ripping open the envelope which I have so carefully and lovingly sealed, you have opened the back door of your life to me.

You pretend not to see the shadowy figure that has slipped in through the door. You pretend there is no one there. Upon your bed I will lie, submissive as an animal laid upon an altar, with my eyes lightly closed, waiting for you to return ... I am not a match for you, pound for pound. But I could be equal to you. Don't doubt me. You may pretend that you have not allowed me in the back door of your life, but never doubt me. That would be a mistake.

(next morning)

... I want to tell you about something that happened seven years ago, in London. I never told anyone about this. I was travelling alone during the summer, without much money, and I spent a week in a small hotel near Russell Square. I brought back to that hotel with me a young man with your build and face—that lanky Lincoln-like type, so American and artless, and almost homely but not quite—and he stayed the night willingly, but in the morning began asking me for money. Started talking in a loud voice. I panicked, was nearly sick with the shame and the suspense and I whispered, "Please don't, please," I begged him to leave. Gave him money but he wanted more ... and how he grinned at me, pitiless at my terror, an American kid in his twenties who'd been bumming around Europe for a year, living off people like me, helpless with our love.... Ah, how I did love him, and wept when he left!

Yes, you resemble him, though you're older than he was and less striking. Your skin looks a little rough—acne scars? I don't mind. I like your hair, though it's thinning. I like your clothes. I would dress myself up as your twin if I had the money—how unfortunate we all can't have rich parents, a member of the board of A.T. & T. for a father! But my own clothes are nothing to be ashamed of, I want to reassure you. They are decent and tasteful enough. I emerge from my ugly little room like a butterfly from a cocoon . . . bright with hope, my eyes shining with the prospect of another day, so many empty hours that might be filled, like magic, with bursts of joy. . . . Yet the days pass, Keith, the years pass, and nothing happens. I await redemption. The touch of some god's fingers against mine—ah, I would accept a minor deity, like Keith Lurie!—yet the transformation doesn't come. Should I wait for you in the darkened hall of your building, on my knees? A devoted, submissive lover, on my knees?

I will make the first move. Don't doubt me. My body tingles and stiffens at the thought.

Last night I wandered through the alley behind your building, completely content. Unseen. Armed only with a flashlight, so that I could look into the overflowing garbage bins in the hope—I have no false pride, Keith!—of discovering something that might have belonged to you. Papers, debris, garbage that did not really smell unpleasant; yet I found nothing that was yours, uniquely yours.

Will you help me?

Yours,
R. Bright

R.B. desires meeting with K.L.
Much to be explained & enjoyed.
    —The Village Voice

Dear Keith:
Enclosed is a little ad I ran the other day—probably you missed it.

Have I described myself yet? Eyes dark brown, lustrous. A boy's eyes, even at my age (you'll have to guess at the age—just add a few dour years to your own). Not a young woman, no. Not young. Not a woman. Anything else you care to know?

Run and I will pursue you. I know all about you: the black holes of the universe drag everything into them, their gravity is so great, so deathly, everything is sucked into them and dies. Is absorbed. You are inside me, in my head. You will find it comfortable there so long as you don't resist. After all you are my possession, *mine*. You belong to all who know your music and read about you but especially to me because I have claimed you; my love makes me omnipotent.

... You looked right at me the other day, on the street. I half-think you recognized me. I was the man in the dull-brown coat, hatless, with the pale forehead, the eyes cringing and begging behind my glasses. Since your marriage ended a few months ago you must notice more people around you, people like me. Or was I the man in the blue suit who stepped aside so that you could go into a mid-town restaurant? He shot you a quick, keen, hot smile which you pretended not to see. You were with a woman, a negligible creature, bony-faced and laughing too shrilly.... Or was I the figure lean as a boy, in black trousers and a black turtleneck sweater, with my hair combed down onto my forehead in a fan-like bang, following you slowly, weightlessly, along the street, following you into that drugstore on 59th Street, waiting for you to make your purchase (a carton of cigarettes)? I happen to know that your oldest brother, Carl, died at the age of forty-one from lung cancer, yet you can't seem to stop smoking. You are addicted, aren't you? Perhaps you wish for death? Smoking = Death.

I have never smoked. It's a disgusting, weak habit.

I surround you, I possess you. You have never possessed yourself the way I possess you. How can you escape? Do you think you can knock someone like me aside, if you found me kneeling mutely in your corridor? How? You need me to worship you, my love is more pure than any you have known, I will lift my voice in hosannahs: *Genius! Beloved!* When you die I will kneel beside your grave, or one like it. When you're dying I will hang around the hospital, overhearing the whispered conversations of your friends—if you have any friends left by then—sniffing the odor of your suffering. How I will cherish it—*your suffering.* Can you guess? I will imagine your death before you do; I will live it for you, shuddering at it, alive with the delicious sensation of it, Keith Lurie's death—his death imagined and cherished *before it even takes place.* And then afterward—ah, yes, many times!—many times afterward, indeed! Can you guess what ecstasy this is, the healthy wholesome worship of a great man, by a devoted believer? Can you guess?

I have resisted vulgarity. Consciously. I have resisted what is called The Obscene. But to give a name to myself, I must be reckless and risk losing you—or gaining you? (And after all, Keith Lurie, you aren't very important and you know it: die tomorrow and nobody will miss you, a "minor American composer with promise" in small headlines in the *New York Times!* You know this!) I will define myself: I am your disciple, your single believer, your *fan.*

We are united. A point of flaming rushing light, a "star" (and what an obscene word that is!) and his mate, a black hole, oh a very articulate and courteous black hole, but black nevertheless, a *hole* nevertheless, a speaking breathing chewing worshipping hole nevertheless . . . a fan. Your death won't delight you, but it will delight me because it will be your death. I will be waiting. And I will remember. Can you guess how very specialized fans are, how very loyal? How much more deep a hole can be, more permanent and dependable than any star?

Other people will forget you. Your wife and your children will forget you. But your fans will remember ... I will remember ... forever and ever. I will live and relive your death. Will it be agony, or peaceful? Will it be well-publicized, or one of the smaller obituaries, one of many? I will cherish every morsel of news, every scrap of gossip. Have faith in me. Of your fans (and you probably haven't many, since you are rather minor; you can't afford to be choosy) I will remember you best, so have faith. And give a sign. In fact, for your own good give a sign. As soon as possible. At this point in my life *I need you, my dear, as much as you need me.* So for your own good, give a sign.

Faithfully,
R. Bright

7:30 a.m. Squinting in the bathroom mirror. Her eyebrows are growing out coarsely—shouldn't have shaved them—a mistake. She steams her face and plucks her eyebrows. That looks better. A thin, arching curve. She pats pink moisturizer on her face, rubs it into her skin in small deft circles, mechanically, hurrying. Hears Bobby fretting at the table. "Hey Bobby, you finish that cereal yet? Eat that cereal, it's good for you," she calls over her shoulder. She can hear the tinkle of his spoon against the bowl: but is he eating it or not? Her face, seen so close, is enormous like a balloon. After the pink moisturizer comes the liquid make-up—expensive stuff, eight dollars for the medium-sized bottle—which she rubs into her skin quickly, with upward strokes, up toward the outsides of her cheeks—and then her lips outlined with a lipliner, and then her lipstick, then rouge—very lightly on her cheekbones—and then the eye make-up which will take ten minutes—"Hey Bobby, you're eating that stuff, aren't you? You better eat it all down," she cries. The kid had bad dreams last night and who can blame him, with a father like his? Glenda strokes mascara on her eyelashes, swift upward strokes, frowning into the mirror. Already she is chewing gum—no cigarette this morning—and her jaws are moving constantly, agreeably, as she appraises her face and her high-puffed pink-blond hair, hair like cotton candy. She looks all right.

8:00 a.m. Lets Bobby off at the nursery school. His collar is wrinkled—a mass of wrinkles that look baked solid, how'd she manage that?—"You be good now, y'hear?" she says, and Bobby swings his short legs across the car seat, manages to get the car door open without any help from her. He looks back at her and says, "Is Daddy coming back tonight?" and Glenda feels her face go sour. "I sure as hell hope not," she says with a shudder. Bobby doesn't let on whether this is the answer he wanted or not.

8:15 a.m. Fifteen minutes late. She struggles into the pink uniform—tight around the hips—and snaps on the radio. Coral is fussing around at the counter up front and yells back to Glenda, "Who's this supposed to be at eleven? Looks like "W" something—" "That's Mrs. Wieden," Glenda yells up front, plugging in the hot plate—she's dying for some coffee—and glancing at herself in the mirror. The mirror runs the entire length of the shop, so Glenda has to parade around in front of it all day long. Always strutting in front of mirrors, her mother used to scold—Glenda pauses, thinking of her mother. Gray-faced and sour, the old woman, but not a bad old gal—except she wouldn't do anything for Glenda's wedding, and she paid out a lot for Glenda's kid sister—but she had it rough on that farm, a few acres in Texas, down in the southeast corner. Glenda is staring at herself in the mirror and her gaze becomes vague, watery.

8:30 a.m. Roxanne is doing her first customer, but Glenda's first customer—a regular named Babs—hasn't showed up yet, so Glenda answers the telephone when it rings. "Hello, Coral Hardee's," she says, but there is no one at the other end—must have been a wrong number. She hangs up. Coral, who is going over some bills, looks over at her. "Nobody there?" she says suspiciously. "Must of hung up when I answered," Glenda says. Glenda inspects her fingernails—it's been almost a week since she did them—thick gold lacquer, very attractive, worth the extra dollar. The telephone rings again and she answers it and this time it's her eight o'clock customer, Babs, with an excuse Glenda doesn't believe for one minute. But she says, "Sure, okay, Babs, I'll put you down for eleven-thirty. Sure." She hangs up. Coral says, "That one is always late." Glenda grunts in agreement. She tears the wrapper off a stick of peppermint gum and pops the gum in her mouth, wishing she could smoke a cigarette instead, after the rotten night she had . . . four or five hours of sleep, maybe less, ruined by the kid's nightmares . . . then the kid has to go and ask, "Is Daddy coming back tonight?" Jesus Christ.

10:15 a.m. A woman with a northern accent, her hair practically down to her hips, looking at Coral with big blue innocent eyes and asking if it costs more for long hair. "Afraid so, honey," Coral says. The bitch blinks as if she'd never heard of such a thing and Glenda holds her breath, hoping she'll walk out, but she decides to have her hair done anyway. Just Glenda's luck to be free for the next twenty minutes. So she spends ten minutes washing that haystack (inky black hair, probably dyed with a do-it-yourself kit) and ten minutes setting it up, using the biggest rollers in the place, and the woman is watching her in the mirror all the time, sharp-eyed as a lynx, trying to make small talk. Glenda notices a big diamond on her finger. "Are you from Miami?" she asks Glenda. "No, Port Arthur in Texas," says Glenda with a business-like smile. "I'm from Chicago," the woman says, in that harsh whiny accent Glenda can't stand, "and I want to tell you that my husband and I just love it down here . . . everybody is so friendly down here. . . ." The woman chatters and Glenda nods, barely listening. When she had long hair herself, long wavy blond hair, she sure as hell didn't go to a beauty parlor to have it done; she'd have been sitting under the drier all day. She washed it herself and let it dry loose, running around barefoot, and at five o'clock on the dot she'd stop whatever she was doing and get fixed up for Guy, brushing her hair until

169

it gleamed, putting on fresh make-up, checking herself from every angle. Guy liked her in slacks best. Her white slacks. She'd stand sideways and pose, assessing herself in the mirror critically—a nice trim waist, broad hips, a big bosom—she was all right. They had lived in Pensacola then. "You married, honey?" the woman with the black hair says, as Glenda packs her away for a nice two-hour session under the drier. "Was," Glenda says with a fast, tight smile, to shut her up.

11:35 a.m. Babs finally shows up, wearing a red play-suit, a girl blobbing all over—you'd think she would be ashamed to walk on the street like that, half a mile from any beach. She calls out hello to Coral and Rox-anne, has to be friendly to everybody. Glenda is a little put out this morning and deliberately keeps still for the first few minutes, as she brushes out Babs' hair—the set is still stiff from last week, sticky with hair-spray—and Babs winces. Glenda begins washing, no-tices that the spray is hot, but Babs doesn't complain—probably embarrassed for coming late. Glenda says, grudgingly, "How're you this week?" She gets Babs all toweled up and leads her over to the counter, to her chair. A big orange plastic container of hair rollers and pins is on the counter; it says "Glenda" in nail polish on its side. In the next chair Roxanne—with a new red wig, looking good—is toiling with a little old lady who drifted in from the street; in the other chair Coral her-self is doing an old customer, Sally Tuohy, an ex-dancer at one of the clubs, the two of them chatting loudly and smoking so that Glenda's eyes water. She would give anything for a cigarette, herself. But she won't give in, she absolutely will not give in. . . . "You heard from him lately?" Babs asks. Glenda, winding a strand of blond hair around a pink roller, wonders who Babs is talking about—then she remembers that she was telling Babs about a new friend of hers, Ronnie Strong, the race-track man . . . or was it her other, fading friend W.J. Hecht, the mystery man? She doesn't think it was Guy;

170

she doesn't talk about Guy if she can help it. So she says with a little grin, "Can't complain."

12:25 p.m. A guy in baggy shorts and sunglasses leads an elderly woman in—says to Coral, "Can you make her beautiful? Make her beautiful, okay? I'll be back in two hours." Thank God Roxanne is free, so Roxanne gets stuck with this dilly; the poor old woman is so feeble she can hardly walk. Glenda and Roxanne and Coral all glance at each other in the mirror—at the same instant—all thinking the same thing, what hell it is to be old, doddering like that, especially in Miami. Glenda goes across the street to get some sandwiches and coffee for them. When she strides in the restaurant people glance at her. Men glance at her. For some reason this makes her nervous today—maybe because she has been thinking of Guy so often. She dreads running into him. Maybe seeing him in a place like this. He'd be sitting at the counter and waiting, waiting. . . . Guy with his cowboy hat and his denim work-clothes, walking sort of bow-legged, showing off to her or anybody who would watch. Guy with his bleached-out hair and face, looking weathered at the age of thirty-one—reddened skin, a boil on the side of his neck, his looks ruined from too much sun and too much alcohol. Jesus, she thinks in amazement, she was married to that man for six years. . . . She feels a kind of kick in the belly—the memory of a kick from when she was carrying the baby—and the men's eyes up and down the counter make her shiver, they are the same eyes, Guy's eyes, always the same. "Hey, Pink Princess," one of the men whispers, referring to the "Pink Princess" stitching on Glenda's collar, but Glenda ignores him. Her uniform is too tight. Should lose a few pounds, or buy another uniform. "Hey, Pink Princess, are you snooty?" the man says, but Glenda pays no attention to him. She waits nervously for the sandwiches and the coffee. She has always liked men to look at her, but today she feels different . . . today everything seems different. . . .

171

1:15 a.m. Shelley, the part-time girl, who is a hat-check girl also at one of the clubs, hurries in to pay back the ten dollars she owes Glenda; she is all perfume and clattering heels. Glenda likes Shelley even though the kid is pretty stupid. She's twenty-three and Glenda is a few years older, she's a few decades wiser, but Shelley won't listen to her advice. It's always hurry, hurry, hurry with her. Shelley got out of her marriage without any kids, no threats, no crazy telephone calls, no spying...now she's heading into trouble with a married man, but do you think she'll listen to Glenda? Glenda feels irritated with Shelley's excitement. The girl is always in a hurry, a sweaty erotic daze, her perfect lips curled up into a mindless, pleased smile....Her eyes catch onto Glenda's in the mirror and she whispers, "Murray says he saw Guy the other night. Is he back in town? Is he bothering you again?" Glenda's heart begins to pound. "No," she says, "No. I got an injunction against him." "Yeah, well, Murray says he's back in town, says to tell you," Shelley says, on her way out. Her white skirt is so short it looks like a slip, nothing more, straining tight against her thighs. Glenda stands staring after her, holding the ten-dollar bill in her fingers.

2:05 p.m. The telephone rings. Glenda is in the middle of brushing out a customer and Coral is out and so Roxanne finally dashes up to the desk at about the tenth ring. Glenda's nerves are on edge. She pauses in her brushing of this woman's hair, her rather square chin contemplative, stern, hoping the telephone isn't...isn't for her....But Roxanne yells, "Hey Glenda, for you!" So Glenda hurries up front, just knowing that it is Mrs. Foss at the nursery, that sorry old bat, with some bad news, or maybe W.J. with some far-out story about why he hadn't called her for two weeks, as if she gave a damn....But when she picks up the receiver the line is dead. Not even a dial tone. "Hello? Hello?" she said sharply. "Hello?" She slams the receiver down, since Coral isn't in. Roxanne, lighting a cigarette, asks her what it was—Glenda shakes her head, nothing, no one—Roxanne says whoever it was was a man, and asked for Glenda in person. "Well, that could be anyone, couldn't it," she says sharply, and goes back to her customer. She hates Roxanne always snooping into her business.

2:15 p.m. One of her regular customers, Mrs. Foster, is being teased and brushed and sprayed. The poor old gal is withered on the bottom and puffed out on the top, her hair a bright burnished red, glowing from the tint—you'd swear she was a kid until she turned around and you saw her face. She always gives Glenda a dollar tip. Coral is back, chatting over the telephone with someone. So the telephone can't ring. Glenda stops herself from thinking of that call—the dead line—stops herself from thinking of Guy, because it never does any good to think about him. That's over. Gone. He has enough sense to leave her alone, since that night in the parking lot when he tried to beat up a boy friend of hers and the police carted him off—he never was stupid—he's got enough sense to leave her alone.

3:05 p.m. Cute little Bonnie from the insurance place down the block comes in for a shampoo and set; Glenda likes her, approves of her petite figure, no more than a size 5—Glenda is a size 12 now, going on 13, she's going to have to lose a few pounds. She approves of Bonnie's long pink fingernails and her golden tan. She's cute, all right, but most of it is make-up ... some of it gets on Glenda's fingers when she washes Bonnie's hair. Bonnie is getting married next month. "Ma wants to have three hundred people, isn't that wild?" Bonnie laughs. "How many'd you have to yours?" "Oh, not more than a hundred," says Glenda, adding a few people, and reluctant to think again about that hot Texas afternoon, getting drunk and squabbling all during the reception with one another and with Guy—not wanting to think about the hotel in Houston that stank of insecticide, and the bed with its musty covers and mattress. No, she doesn't want to think about that Saturday, or about how it all ran down to a day last July, also a Saturday, with Guy screaming at her that he was going to kill her. Washing Bonnie's hair, briskly, she rubs a row of very small pimples just at Bonnie's hair-line, and the pimples begin to bleed, just thin trickles of blood mixed in with the water . . . and while Bonnie is chattering about her wedding gown Glenda is trying to blot the blood with a towel. She leads Bonnie over to the chair, sees that the bleeding seems to have stopped, it looks O.K., tosses away the stained towel, then sprays Bonnie's hair with the bluish hair-set mixture. She puts two rows of pink rollers on Bonnie's head, a back row of green rollers, and pins down the back hair carefully. Sprays it all. The spray stinks—almost chokes Bonnie. God-awful stuff. Glenda reaches down, grunting, to fish out a pair of ear-protectors. They are made of flesh-pink plastic. She fastens them over Bonnie's reddened ears, puts a hair-net over the whole business and draws it tight. Fixed up like this, Bonnie looks small and trivial; her face looks pasty. "There you are," Glenda says, leading Bonnie over to the hair-drier where Angel Laverne is all set to come out.

3:30 p.m. Angel Laverne strolls with Glenda up to the front desk to make next week's appointment. Angel always asks for Glenda. She is a dancer at the Cutless Club and much admired by everyone, for her long trim legs and her expensive clothes. "It looks great," Angel says, admiring her high-stacked orange hair, with the row of stiff curls across the front. It is an open secret that Angel had silicone injected into her breasts and that the operation was a marvelous success; Angel sucks in her breath, glances at herself in the mirror approvingly. Once in a while she tells Glenda, seriously, that Glenda should try out at the club—"you'd make a great dancer," she tells Glenda—and Glenda laughs in embarrassment, not mentioning the fact that she tried out for something like that back in Houston, but with no luck, and she was younger and better-looking then. Angel thanks her again and says goodbye. Glenda goes to the book to see who's next but someone starts shouting—an old biddy under the hair-drier—"Glenda, Glenda, what time is it?" She has a hoarse, froggy voice; her double chins tremble. Glenda tells her the time, though she knows the old girl won't be able to hear—why the hell do they always try to talk under the hair-drier? So Glenda strides over and holds out her arm so that the woman can see her wristwatch. "Oh. Three-thirty," she says stupidly, as if she thought it might be some other time. Glenda feels sorry for her, the old dame is a widow and probably hasn't anywhere to get to; this town is filled with widows. It occurs to Glenda that Coral Hardee's Pink Princess Salon is like the backstage of a theater—the audience is men, made up only of men, who know what they want to see and who are impatient with anything else. She goes back to check the book. God, is she tired, and it's only three-thirty. . . . Three more customers coming up, one right after the other, and the first one wants a permanent. . . .

4:10 p.m. And the call does come from the nursery: a very unconvincing story about Lynda going home early, having to babysit for a neighbor who's had a baby, or some such lying crap, so could Glenda come pick up Bobby early? "No, I cannot," Glenda says in a soft furious voice. "I'm going to report you to the Better Business Bureau if this keeps on!" On the other end Mrs. Foss stammers, no doubt she's been drinking and the kids have been running wild, no doubt, Glenda is fed up with Mrs. Foss's problems and says firmly: "Look, you know I have a job here and I can't leave early. It's your responsibility to take care of those children until the mothers get there—Mrs. Foss—" Mrs. Foss hangs up. Glenda wonders if she should call back, maybe the old bat is passed out, or whether this means she has won. Scaring her with the Better Business Bureau probably did the trick.

4:45 p.m. "Did you read here about Jackie Kennedy and Onassis, what's-his-name, they spent twenty million dollars in one year?" Glenda's customer, a woman with thinning brown hair, is tapping a movie magazine angrily on the counter.

Roxanne, standing next to Glenda, says, "He can't be such a geek, or else how could he make all that money? Or is the twenty million just the interest, you know, the interest on the stuff they own?"

"Jesus, twenty million," Glenda says, whistling through her teeth, "that's—that's like more than what all of us make in a year, or in our lives—"

She is backcombing her customer's hair energetically.

"What I feel sorry for is the kids, those two little kids—"

"Yeah, those two little kids."

"Caroline, you know, she has a shrine devoted to her father. It's in their New York apartment. What do you think Onassis thinks about that?"

"If he wants to have any opinion on it, let him get himself assassinated. He's only a guest in this country."

"I wouldn't want his nose—"

"Isn't he ugly?"

"Caroline has a whole staff of servants to occupy her mind, and all the allowance money she wants to occupy the rest of her mind," Roxanne says. "Think of all the clothes and stuff she could buy—"

"How Onassis got started," Glenda's customer explains, "he bought some ships from the United States for ten million dollars. Just bought them. The United States gave up some navy ships, I mean fighting ships—"

"Really?"

"They gave them to him, and he went back to Greece—which is incidentally just about the poorest country in Europe—he went to Greece with them—now, ten million dollars' worth of boats, in a country like that—that's why the United States can't get the money back. That's what was behind all that to-do about Onassis not being allowed in the country."

"Which country?"

"*This* country. He was barred, until he married Jackie Kennedy. That was in the newspapers."

"Well, he can't be such a geek if he made all that money. But I wouldn't want to be married to him!"

"If you can prove you're a blood relative of his, he'll pay you $25,000 a year interest-free for life. That's what they say. But he never gives any money to charity, not one dime."

"I wouldn't want to be related to him," Glenda says with a laugh. "You ever see his sister? Her nose? I wouldn't want that family nose, Christ!"

"Yeah, there's a picture of his sister or somebody in one of these magazines, a few months ago, she's all pock-marked and's got eyes sunk ten miles back in her face, all bags and stuff—I wouldn't want to look like that just to be that guy's sister!"

"Me neither!"

5:00 p.m. Coral has to go to the lawyer's—some fuss about a customer who got her eye poked by one of the part-time girls, the girl stuck her little finger in the woman's eye, just an accident, but Coral has bad luck. Glenda takes over. She tries on a red wiglet, remembers when she was a red-head, smirks at herself, exchanges wiglets with Roxanne—they always fool around when Coral is out of the shop—and wonders if maybe she should invest in a red wig. Only forty dollars with her discount. Maybe. Maybe for a change. But seeing herself in the mirror, that striking face—like a billboard, that face—she feels uneasy, because the red hair will make people look at her, men, men will look at her, men will look at her in that certain way, and does she want this to happen? To happen again?

5:10 p.m. Telephone rings. Coral isn't back yet, so Glenda goes to answer it. Begins to perspire even before she picks up the receiver. She approaches the desk, legs working hard, fast, the muscles of her thighs straining against the tight skirt, *she can feel, remember, the football-sized baby inside her,* she picks up the pink plastic receiver breezily....

"Hello!"

No answer.

"I said hello. This is Coral Hardee's. Hello . . .?"

Be calm. Calm.

"Hello . . .?"

She begins to pick at one of her fingernails. The gold polish is chipping. She says suddenly, "Listen, Guy, if this is you you'd better cut it out. I'm going to call the police—" She can see him suddenly: the grimy cowboy hat crooked on his head, his grin that had nothing to do with his eyes, his wise-guy grin, his little-boy wise-guy grin, the way he'd sit with a toothpick in his mouth and stare at her. At first she liked it, but then after they'd been married for a while she could feel him staring at her even while she was in another room, staring through the walls at her. Sometimes he'd joke with her, slapping her rear, *Hey, is all that mine?* he'd say. He liked her best in slacks. Out on the street he got mad if other men looked at her, but he liked her to wear slacks, especially that pair of white knitted slacks. . . . "I'm going to call the police!" she says, hanging up. She is about to cry. Roxanne is watching her, hesitating . . . not knowing if she should say anything or stay out of this . . .

5:15 p.m. The door opens. A man enters.

Glenda stares at him, frowning. He is short, stocky, wearing neat beige trousers and a shirt and, in spite of the 85 degree temperature, a dark green wool sweater, armless, and a large wristwatch. Glenda feels a dull automatic tug in his direction, wondering how his face will change when he sees her. Their faces always change, always; she shivers with excitement, though the man is homely himself—a swarthy face, too small, a very small receding chin, sunglasses with cheap plastic frames, hair that looks a little kinky.

"Hiya, Jere, that you?" says Coral, who has just come in.

He takes off the sunglasses with a grin, and Glenda, shocked, sees that this isn't a man after all, but that woman—"Jere"—who comes into the Salon every two

178

weeks to have her hair cut.

"Hiya, Coral. How's business?"

"Can't complain."

"I can't complain either."

Jere smiles and waves at Glenda and Roxanne, but shyly: she knows they won't smile back.

Ugh.

Glenda glances at the book to see who's stuck with this character—too bad, Roxanne!—Roxanne is down for 5:15. Last customer of the day. Glenda ignores Jere and starts tidying up her things. Feels sorry for poor Roxanne, but thank God it isn't her. Coral, bustling by with an armful of wigs, winks at Glenda and Glenda winks back.

5:30 p.m. Sits with Coral in the back room, smoking. Her first and only cigarette of the day. "Tomorrow I'm giving it up permanently," she tells Coral, "but today I feel kind of nervous. Real jumpy." Coral chain-smokes and drinks coffee all day long. "How come you're jumpy?" she says. "I don't know," Glenda says slowly, "on account of Guy...." "Oh, hell! Is he back in town again?" says Coral. "That I don't know," says Glenda. She hesitates, wanting to tell Coral about the telephone calls. She can't stop shivering. Coral says with a harsh expulsion of breath, "Listen, kid, frankly I never liked his looks. I mean he's nice-looking and all that, he's a handsome guy, but, you know, he *knows* he's handsome, and...." She glances out to see if the last customer is gone. Yes, Jere is gone and Roxanne is gathering up the towels. "And handsome men, when they go to bed with you, you know, they're going to bed with themselves. I read that."

Glenda stares at her. "They *what?*"

"They're doing it to *themselves*. The woman is just a mirror or something. I read it in a psychiatrist's column in the newspaper."

"I don't get it."

"Well, that's what he said. A good-looking man is apt to be a son of a bitch and the woman doesn't count.

179

I mean he wants a good-looking woman himself, I don't mean that, but whichever one it is doesn't count because, you know, he's doing it to him*self* and the woman is the mirror he looks into. I read it. It was real convincing."

Glenda shakes her head, confused. "Yeah, well, Guy's handsome and all that...but....Coral, could you maybe come over to my place with me after work? After I pick up Bobby?"

"What? Why?"

"Oh, we could have supper together and then go to a movie, all three of us, you know, like we did that one time.... I was just thinking...."

"I don't know, Glenda, I got a lot of work to do tonight."

"Bobby ain't no trouble, is he?"

"Bobby is a real sweet kid. Does he still wet the bed?"

"Not so much now."

"How's that what's-her-name, Foss? She any better?"

"Oh, she's all right," Glenda says nervously. "We could send out for some Chinese food or maybe a pizza...."

Coral lights another cigarette and gets to her feet. "The problem is I got to look through the bills and stuff tonight...start making out some refill orders, you know...."

"Bobby ain't no trouble, he sits real still in the movies."

"Oh, Bobby is sweet, he's a sweetheart," Coral says vaguely. "Oh, hey, Roxanne, don't forget that peroxide thing—"

"I put it away," Roxanne calls back.

"Half-full, did you?"

"Yeah, it's half-full."

"Did you put it down for re-order?"

"Okay, I'll do it now," Roxanne says wearily.

"She always lets things go, it never fails," Coral mutters to Glenda.

Glenda has finished her cigarette and is staring at it, at the dry lipstick stains on it.

"So you can't make it tonight, then?" Glenda says.

"Some other time, maybe... okay?" Coral says.

Glenda puts out her cigarette. For some reason the cigarette made her feel cold.

5:50 p.m. Doubleparks by Mrs. Foss's, and what the hell—there comes Bobby running up the street! "What are you doing out by yourself?" Glenda shouts. Bobby climbs in the car; his mouth is stained with something greenish. He looks a little sick. "What happened, did she kick you kids out on the street?" Glenda cries. Bobby says, vaguely, "She said you was sposed to come at five-thirty and you didn't." Glenda has half a mind to leave her car out on the street here and run up to Mrs. Foss's door and pound on it until the old bitch answers.... "Oh, goddam her, goddam everybody," Glenda whispers, so angry she could almost cry, and now somebody is honking his horn behind her.... "You gonna cry now?" Bobby asks scornfully, fearfully.

6:05 p.m. The A & P, very crowded, Glenda has picked a cart with wobbling wheels, just her luck. Bobby is muling and whining and pulling at her. She moves as fast as she can up and down the aisles, her stomach jumpy, she buys a barbecued chicken wrapped in greasy cellophane and some potato chips that Bobby starts to eat right away—probably didn't get any decent lunch—probably got slapped around all day. But Glenda has no time to think about Bobby and Mrs. Foss, she has to get this stupid limping cart over in line, she is perspiring with strain or with worry, something seems to be wrong with her nerves today. If she got married again....

But she isn't going to get married again. No.

But if....

The cashier has pink-blond hair, like Glenda's, ringing up the items one-two-three, very efficient and skillful. Glenda notes approvingly the girl's pierced ears and tiny gold earrings, her large, rather sullen red mouth, her red-polished nails. Men would like her looks. She probably does well with men.

6:15 p.m. Parks crooked at the curb, runs into the drugstore for some sleeping pills—a new brand called *Sleepeez*, might as well try something new—and some laxatives, the usual. She feels a little sick, like rocks in her intestines, her stomach is bad again and has been for the last week; on her way out she remembers that she needs some toothpaste, she'll have to get it tomorrow—hell—and her first customer is due in at eight, that fussy skinny bitch with the "sensitive scalp"....

6:25 p.m. Parks behind her apartment building. Bobby groggy, sniffing; what if he's coming down with another cold? She checks his forehead and it seems very warm. She notices that the garbage men haven't come yet to pick up the enormous piles of junk out behind the apartment building, there was talk of a slow-down this week.... Hell, she is so tired of slow-downs and strikes and demonstrations.... "Bobby, come *on*, carry one of these packages," she says in exasperation, because he is just sitting there, staring. "What are you staring at?" she says. He shakes his head. Nothing. She looks and sees only the back of the building, the dreary back entrance and the stacked boxes and damp, scattered newspapers. There is nothing here. No one there. She lives on the first floor, her apartment is nearby, there is nothing to worry about. "Bobby, come on, please," she says, and this time he rouses himself and starts moving.

Out

of

Place

I have this memory: I am waiting in line for a movie. The line is long, noisy, restless, mostly kids my age (I seem to be about thirteen). The movie must be . . . a Western, I think. I can almost see the posters and I think I see a man with a cowboy hat. Good. I do see this man and I see a horse on the poster, it is all becoming clear. A Western. I am a kid, thirteen, but not like the thirteen-year-olds who pass by the hospital here on their way home from school—they are older than I was at that age, everyone seems older. I am nineteen now, I think. I will be twenty in a few weeks and my mother talks about how I will be home, then, in time for my birthday. That gives her pleasure and so I like to hear her talk about it. But my memory is more important: the movie house, yes, and the kids, and I am one of them. We are all jostling together, moving forward in surges, a bunch of us from St. Ann's Junior High. Other kids are there from Clinton, which is a tough school. We are all in line waiting and no one is out of line. I am there, with them. We shuffle up to the ticket window and buy our tickets (50¢) and go inside, running.

There is something pleasant about this memory, but dwelling upon memories is unhealthy. They tell me that. They are afraid I will remember the explosion, and my friend who died, but I have already forgotten these things. There is no secret about it, of course. Everything is open. We were caught in a land mine explosion and some of us were luckier than others, we weren't killed, that's all. I am very lucky to be alive. I am not being sarcastic but quite truthful, because in the end it is only truth you can stand. In camp, and for a while when we fooled around for so long without ever seeing the enemy, then some of the guys were sarcastic—but that went away. Everything falls away except truth and that is what you hang onto.

The truth is that my right leg is gone and that I have some trouble with my "vision." My eyes.

On sunny days we are wheeled outside, so that we can watch the school children playing across the street. The hospital is very clean and white, and there is a kind of patio or terrace or wide walk around the front and sides, where we can sit. Next door, some distance away, is a school that is evidently a grade school. The children play at certain times—ten-fifteen in the morning, at noon, and two in the afternoon. I don't know if they are always the same children. I have trouble with my "vision," it isn't the way it used to be and yet in a way I can't remember what it used to be like. My glasses are heavy and make red marks on my nose, and sometimes my skin is sore around my ears, but that is the only sign that the glasses are new. In a way nothing is new but has always been with me. That is why I am pleased with certain memories, like the memory of the Western movie. Though I do not remember the movie itself, but only waiting in line to get in the theater.

There is a boy named Ed here, a friend of mine. He was hurt at about the same time I was, though in another place. He is about twenty too. His eyes are as good as ever and he can see things I can't; I sometimes ask him to tell me about the playground and the children there. The playground is surrounded by a high wire fence and the children play inside this fence, on their swings and slides and teeter-totters, making a lot of noise. Their voices are very high and shrill. We don't mind the noise, we like it, but sometimes it reminds me of something—I can almost catch the memory but

184

not quite. Cries and screams by themselves are not bad. I mean the sounds are not bad. But if you open your eyes wide you may have latched onto the wrong memory and might see the wrong things—screams that are not happy screams, etc. There was a boy somewhere who was holding onto the hand of his "buddy." ("Buddy" is a word I would not have used before, I don't know where I got it from exactly.) That boy was crying, because the other boy was dead—but I can't quite remember who they were. The memory comes and goes silently. It is nothing to be upset about. The doctor told us all that it is healthier to think about our problems, not to push them back. He is a neat, clean man dressed in white, a very kind man. Sometimes his face looks creased, there are too many wrinkles in it, and he looks like my father—they are about the same age.

I like the way my father calls him *Dr. Pritchard*. You can tell a man's worth by the way my father speaks to him, I know that sounds egotistical but it's true, and my father trusts Dr. Pritchard. It is different when he speaks to someone he doesn't quite trust, oh, for example, certain priests who look too young, too boyish; he hesitates before he calls them *Father*. He hesitates before he says hello to Father Presson, who comes here to see me and hear my confession and all, and then the words "Father Presson" come out a little forced.

"Look at that big kid, by the slide. See?" Ed says nervously.

I think I see him—a short blur of no-color by the slide. "What is he doing?"

"I don't know. I thought he was. . . . No, I don't know," Ed says.

There is hesitation in Ed's voice too. Sometimes he seems not to know what he is saying, whether he should say it. I can hear the distance in his voice, the distance between the school children over there and us up here on the ledge, in the sun. When the children fight we feel nervous and we don't know what to do. Not that they really fight, not exactly. But sometimes the mood of the playground breaks and a new mood comes upon it. It's hard to explain it. Ed keeps watching for that though he doesn't want to see it.

Ed has a short, muscular body, and skin that always looks tanned. His hair is black, shaved off close, and his eyebrows of course are black and very thick. He looks hunched up in the wheel chair, about to spring off and run away. His legs just lie there, though, and never move. They are both uninjured. His problem is somewhere else, in his spine—it is a mysterious thing, how a bullet strikes in one place and damages another. We have all learned a lot about the body, here. I think I would like to be a doctor. I think that, to be a doctor like Dr. Pritchard, you must have a great reverence for the body and its springs and wires and tubes, I mean, you must understand how they work together, all together. It is a strange thing. When I tried to talk to my parents about this they acted strange. I told them that Ed and I both would like to be doctors, if things got better.

"Yes," my father said slowly, "the study of medicine is—is—"

"Very beneficial," my mother said.

"Yes, beneficial—"

Then they were silent. I said, "I mean if things get better. I know I couldn't get through medical school, the way I am now."

"I wouldn't be too sure of that," my father said. "You know how they keep discovering all these extraordinary things—"

(My father latches onto special words occasionally. Now it is the word "extraordinary." I don't know where he got it from, from a friend probably. He is a vice-president for a company that makes a certain kind of waxed paper and waxed cardboard.)

"But you will get better," my mother said. "You know that."

I am seized with a feeling of happiness. Not because of what my mother said, maybe it's true and maybe not, I don't know, but because of—the fact of doctors, the fact of the body itself which is such a mystery. I can't explain it. I said, groping for my words, "If this hadn't happened then—then—I guess I'd be just the way I was, I mean, I wouldn't know—what it's like to be like this." But that was a stupid thing to say. Mother began crying again, it was embarrassing. With my glasses off, lying back against the pillow, I could pretend that I didn't notice; so I said, speaking in my new voice which is a little too slow and stumbling, "I mean—there are lots of things that are mysteries—like the way the spine hooks up with things—and the brain—and—and by myself I wouldn't know about these things—"

But it's better to talk about other matters. In my room, away from the other patients, the talk brought to me by my parents and relatives and friends is like a gift from the outside, and it has the quality of the spring days that are here now: sunny and fragrant but very delicate. My visitors' words are like rays of sunlight. It might seem that you could grab hold of them and sit up, but you can't, they're nothing, they don't last—they are gifts, that's all, like the other gifts I have. For instance, my mother says: "Betty is back now. She wants to know when she can see you, but I thought that could wait."

"Oh, is she back?"

"She didn't have a very happy time, you know."

"What's she doing now?"

"Oh, nothing, I don't know. She might go to school."

"Where?"

"A community college, nothing much."

"That's nice."

This conversation is about a cousin of mine who married some jerk and ran away to live in Mexico. But the conversation is not really about her. I don't know what it is about. It is "about" the words themselves. When my mother says, "Betty is back now," that means "Betty-is-back-now" is being talked about, not the girl

187

herself. We hardly know the girl herself. Then we move on to talk about Harold Spender, who is a bachelor friend of my father's. Harold Spender has a funny name and Mother likes him for his name. He is always "spending" too much money. I think he has expensive parties or something, I don't know. But "Harold Spender" is another gift, and I think this gift means: "You see, everything is still the same, your cousin is still a dope and Harold Spender is still with us, spending money. Nothing has changed."

Sometimes when they are here, visiting, and Mother chatters on like that, a terrible door opens in my mind and I can't hear her. It is like waking up at night when you don't know it is night. A door opens and though I know Mother is still talking, I can't hear her. This lasts a few seconds, no more. I go into it and come out of it and no one notices. The door opens by itself, silently, and beyond it everything is black and very quiet, just nothing.

But sometimes I am nervous and feel very sharp. That is a peculiar word, sharp. I mean my body tenses and I seem to be sitting forward and my hands grip the arms of the chair, as if I'm about to throw myself out of it and demand something. Demand something! Ed's voice gets like that too. It gets very thin and demanding and sometimes he begins to cry. It's better to turn away from that, from a boy of twenty crying. I don't know why I get nervous. There is no relationship between what my body feels and what is going on outside, and that is what frightens me.

Dr. Pritchard says there is nothing to be frightened about any longer. Nothing.

He is right, of course. I think it will be nice when I am home again and the regular routine begins. My nervousness will go away and there will not be the strange threat of that door, which opens so silently and invites me in. And Father won't take so much time off from work, and Mother will not chatter so. It will be nice to get back into place and decide what I will do, though there is no hurry about that. When I was in high school I fooled around too much. It wasn't because of basketball either, that was just an excuse, I wasted time and so did the other kids. I wore trousers the color of bone that were pretty short and tight, and I fooled around with my hair, nothing greasy but pretty long in front, flipped down onto my forehead. Mr. Palisano, the physics teacher, was also the basketball coach and he always said: "Hey, Furlong, what's your hurry? Just what's your hurry?" He had a teasing singsong voice he used only on kids he liked. He was a tall, skinny man, a very intelligent man. "Just what's your hurry?" he said when I handed in my physics problems half-finished, or made a fool of myself in basketball practice. He was happy when I told him I was going into physics, but when I failed the first course I didn't want to go back and tell him—the hell with it. So I switched into math because I had to take math anyway. And then what happened? I don't remember. I was just a kid then, I fooled around too much. The kids at the school— it was a middle-sized school run by Holy Cross fathers, who also run Notre Dame—just fooled around too much, some of them flunked out. I don't think I flunked out. It gives me a headache to think about it—

To think about the kids in my calculus class, that gives me a headache. I don't know why. I can remember my notebook, and the rows of desks, and the blackboard (though it was green), and the bell striking the hour from outside (though it was always a little off), and I think of it all like a bubble with the people still inside. All the kids and me among them, still in the same room, still there. I like to think of that.

But they aren't still there in that room. Everything has moved on. They have moved on to other rooms and I am out here, at this particular hospital. I wonder if I will be able to catch up with them. If I can read, if my eyes get better, I don't see why not. Father talks about me returning. It's no problem with a wheel chair these days, he says, and there is the business about the artificial "limb," etc. I think it will be nice to get back to books and reading and regular assignments.

I am thinking about high school, about the halls and the stairways. Mr Palisano, and physics class, and the afternoon basketball games. I am thinking about the excitement of those games, which was not quite fear, and about the drive back home, in my car or someone else's. I went out a lot. And one night, coming home from a dance, I saw a car parked and a man fooling around by it so I stopped to help him. "Jesus Christ," he kept saying. He had a flat tire and he was very angry. He kept snuffling and wiping his nose on his shoulder, very angry, saying "Jesus Christ" and other things, other words, not the way the kids said them but in a different way—hard to explain. It made me understand that adults had made up those words, not in play but out of hatred. He was not kidding. The way he said those words frightened me. Fear comes up from the earth, the coldness of the earth, flowing up from your feet up your legs and into your bowels, like the clay of the earth itself, and your heart begins to hammer. . . .

I never told anyone about that night, what a fool I was to stop. What if something had happened to me?

I was ashamed of being such a fool. I always did stupid things, always went out of my way and turned out looking like a fool. Then I'd feel shame and not tell anyone. For instance, I am ashamed about something that happened here in the hospital a few days ago. I think it will be nice when I am home again, back in my room, where these things can't happen. There was myself and Ed and another man, out on the terrace by the side entrance, in the sun, and these kids came along. It was funny because they caught my eye when they drove past in a convertible, and they must have turned into the parking lot and got out. They were visiting someone in the hospital. The girl was carrying a grocery bag that probably had fruit in it or something. She had long dark hair and bangs that fell down to her eyebrows, and she wore sunglasses, and bright blue stretch pants of the kind that have stirrups for the feet to keep them stretched down tight. The boy wore sunglasses too, slacks and a sweater, and sandals without socks. He had the critical, unsurprised look of kids from the big university downtown.

They came up the steps, talking. The girl swung her hair back like a horse, a pony—I mean, the motion reminded me of something like that. She looked over at us and stopped talking, and the boy looked too. They were my age. The girl hesitated but the boy kept on walking fast. He frowned. He seemed embarrassed. The girl came toward me, not quite walking directly toward me, and her mouth moved in an awkward smile. She said, "I know you, don't I? Don't I know you?"

I was very excited. I tried to tell her that with her sunglasses on I couldn't see her well. But when I tried to talk the words came out jumbled. She licked her lips nervously. She said, "Were you in the war? Vietnam?"

I nodded.

She stared at me. It was strange that her face showed nothing, unlike the other faces that are turned toward me all the time. The boy, already at the door, said in an irritated sharp voice: "Come on, we're late." The girl took a vague step backward, the way girls swing slowly away from people—you must have seen them often on sidewalks before ice cream parlors or schools? They stare as if fascinated at one person, while beginning the slow inevitable swing toward another who stands behind them. The boy said, opening the door: "Come on! He deserves it!"

They went inside. And then the shame began, an awful shame. I did not understand this though I thought about it a great deal. Someone came out to help me, a nurse. When I cry most people look away in embarrassment but the nurses show nothing, nothing at all. They boss me around a little. Crying makes me think of someone else crying, a soldier holding another soldier's hand, sitting in some rubble. One soldier is alive and the other dead, the one who is alive is holding the other's hand and crying, like a baby. Like a puppy. A kitten, a baby, something small and helpless, when the crying does no good and is not meant for any good.

I think that my name is Jack Furlong. There was another person named Private Furlong, evidently myself. Now I am back home and I am Jack Furlong again. I can imagine many parts of this city without really seeing them, and what is surprising—and very pleasant—is the way these memories come to me, so unexpected. Lying in bed with no thoughts at all I suddenly find myself thinking of a certain dime store where we hung out, by the comic book racks, many years ago; or I think of a certain playground on the edge of a ravine made by a glacier, many thousands of years ago. I don't know what makes these memories come to me but they exert a kind of tug—on my heart, I suppose. It's very strange. My eyes sometimes fill with tears, but a different kind of tears. I was never good at understanding feelings but now, in the hospital, I have a lot of time for thinking. I think that I am a kind of masterpiece. I mean, a miracle. My body and my brain. It is like a little world inside, or a factory, with everything functioning and the dynamo at the very center—my heart—pumping and pumping with no source of energy behind it. I think about that a lot. What keeps it going? And the eyes. Did you know that the eye is strong, very strong? That the muscles are like steel? Yes. Eyes are very strong, I mean the substance of the eyes is strong. It takes a lot to destroy them.

At last they check me out and bring me home—a happy day. It is good to be back home where everything is peaceful and familiar. When I lived in this house before I did not think about "living" in it, or about the house at all. Now, looking out of my window, I can see the front lawn and the street and the other houses facing us, all ranch houses, and I am aware of being very fortunate. A few kids are outside, racing past on bicycles. It is a spring day, very warm. The houses on the block make a kind of design if you look right. I am tired from all the exertion involved getting me here, and so it is difficult to explain what I mean—a design, a setting. Everything in place. It has not changed and won't change. It is a very pleasant neighborhood, and I think I remember hearing Mother once say that our house had cost $45,000. I had "heard" this remark years ago but never paid any attention to it. Now I keep thinking about it, I don't know why. There is something wonderful about that figure: it means something. Is it secret? It is the very opposite of rubble, yes. There are no screams here, no sudden explosions. Yes, I think that is why it pleases me so. I fall asleep thinking of forty-five thousand dollars.

My birthday. It is a few days later. I have been looking through the books in my room, a history textbook, a calculus textbook, and something called *College Rhetoric*. Those were my books and I can recognize my handwriting in the margins, but I have a hard time reading them now. To get away from the reading I look around—or the door in my mind begins to open slowly, scaring me, and so I wheel myself over to the window to look out. Father has just flown back from Boston. Yes, it is my birthday and I am twenty. We have a wheelchair of our own now, not the hospital's chair but our own. There is a wooden ramp from our side door right into the garage, and when they push me out I have a sudden sensation of panic right in my heart— do they know how to handle me? what if they push me too hard? They are sometimes clumsy and a little rough, accidentally. Whenever Father does something wrong I think at once, not meaning to, *They wouldn't do that at the hospital.*

My uncle and my aunt are coming too. We are going out to Skyway for dinner. This is a big restaurant and motel near the airport. There is the usual trouble getting me in and out of the car, but Father is getting used to it. My uncle Floyd keeps saying, "Well, it's great to have you back. I mean it. It's just great, it's just wonderful to have you back." My aunt is wearing a hat with big droopy yellow flowers on it, a pretty hat. But something about the flowers makes me think of giant leaves in the jungle, coated with dust and sweat, and the way the air tasted—it made your throat and lungs ache, the dust in the air. Grit. Things were flying in the air. Someone was screaming, "Don't leave me!" A lot of them were screaming that. But my father said, "We'd better hurry, our reservations are for six."

Six is early to eat, I know. They are hurrying up the evening because I get tired so fast. My uncle opens the door and my father wheels me inside, all of it done easily. My father says to a man, "Furlong, for five—" This restaurant is familiar. On one side there is a stairway going down, carpeted in blue, and down there are rooms for—oh, banquets and meetings and things. Ahead of us is a cocktail lounge, very dark. Off to the left, down a corridor lined with paintings (they are by local artists, for sale) is the restaurant we are going to, the Grotto Room. But the man is looking through his ledger. My mother says to my aunt, "I bought that watercolor here, you know, the one over the piano." The women talk about something but my uncle stares at my father and the manager, silent. Something is wrong. The manager looks through his book and his face is red and troubled. Finally he looks up and says, "Yes, all right. Down this way." He leads us down to the Grotto Room.

We are seated. The table is covered with a white tablecloth, a glaring white. A waitress is already at Father's elbow. She looks at us, her eyes darting around the table and lingering no longer on me than on anyone else. I know that my glasses are thick and that my face is not pleasant to look at, not the same face as before. But still she does not look at me more than a second, maybe two seconds. Father orders drinks. It is my birthday. He glances over to the side and I see that someone at the next table, some men and women are watching us. A woman in red—I think it is red—does something with her napkin, putting it on the table. Father picks up his menu, which is very large. My mother and aunt chatter about something, my mother hands me a menu. At the next table a man stands. He changes places with the woman, and now her back is to our table. I understand this but pretend to notice nothing, look down at the menu with a pleased, surprised expression, because it is better this way. It is better for everyone.

"What do you think you'll order? Everything looks so tempting," she says.

They were in a hurry and the wounded and the dead were stacked together, brought back together in a truck. But not carried at the end of a nylon cord, from a helicopter, not that. This memory comes to me in a flash, then fades. I was driving the truck, I think. Wasn't I? I was on the truck. I did not hover at the end of a line, in a plastic sack. Those were others—I didn't know them, only saw them from a distance. They screamed: "Don't leave me!"

"Lobster," Father says. He speaks with certainty: he is predicting my choice for dinner. "I bet it's lobster, eh?"

"Lobster."

My mother squeezes my arm, pleased that I have given the right answer. "My choice too," she says. "Always have fish on Fridays...the old customs...I like the old customs, no matter what people say. The Mass in Latin, and...and priests who know what their vocations are.... How do you want your lobster, dear? Broiled?"

"Yes."

"Or this way—here—the Skyway Lobster?" She leans over to help me with the menu, pointing at the words. There is a film, a gauzy panel between me and the words, and I keep waiting for it to disappear. The faces around the table, the voices...the smiling mouths and eyes...I keep glancing up at them, waiting for the veil to be yanked away. *He deserves it. Don't leave me!* In the meantime I think I will have the Skyway Lobster.

"You're sure?"

"Yes."

"My own choice also," my mother says. She looks around the table, in triumph, and the faces smile back at her and at me.

Notes

on

Contributors

BENJAMIN ACKLEY. Author of Zoological Lyrics (Touch Press). Arrested February 10, 1970, in a raid on a Detroit rooming house, held for possession of illegal drugs; a coordinator for the April 15 Moratorium Day March; long-limbed, sandy-haired, freckle-armed, -shouldered, -legged; his head shaved in awe of the martyrdom of Morley Hill, he kneels for two hours each day and chants Morley Hill's prayer *Speed it up, speed it up, speed it up.* His mother, a widow from Livonia, Michigan, has granted interviews to both Detroit papers and has appeared on WWJ-TV as a guest of Jack MacCool, "The Voice of the Seventies." She says, "Bennie was a tool that they used. That's all he was just a tool."

EVANGELINE BART. Married Morley Hill in 1962, divorced Morley Hill in 1963. "The Volkswagen bus was mine, but I let him use it. It needed a new muffler. The windshield wipers kept flying off. He tried to pay me rent for it, he was always trying to give me money— ten-dollar bills in books, you know, those crazy books he was leaving around the house. I sent everything back. He had nothing, not even the kids. They loved him but they have their own friends, you know? Saturdays kids like to play with their own friends. He was always showing up here in Cleveland. My husband didn't mind him but he sort of got underfoot, you know? Lora and Ronnie will miss him."

ROY DEVLIN. Twenty-six years old, an organizer of the Futurists Coalition for Jimmy Querbach (who campaigned for the Michigan House of Representatives but gave up in mid-summer of 1969) and an ex-student of Morley Hill's, who followed Hill from San Francisco to Cleveland to Rochester, New York, to Detroit, Michigan. Wanted for questioning in the Ackley case and in connection with a supply of ammunition and dynamite found in an apartment in Highland Park, Michigan; consequently out of town on May 1, 1970; given to fits of depression, hard hot breathing, fever and chills, headaches, racing heartbeat, a sense of desperation. "Each cell of my being radiates despair," Devlin has written.

WHITNEY FARBER. Ex-student of Morley Hill's, born September 10, 1942, died May 1, 1970, in the parking lot of Recorder's Court, Detroit. Taught in the Composition Clinic of Oakland Community College. His students recall him as "zany but dedicated."

STELLA HANZEK. Notes on Morley Hill: "He is angelic. His skin is translucent. His eyes are apocalyptic, they have seen the corners of the universe and all the tides. I would die for Morley Hill." Died May 1, 1970.

MORLEY HILL. Born June 3, 1933; died May 1, 1970. Survived by his children, Lora and Ronnie Hill.

LIONEL McEVOY. Identified by bridgework. Background confused—a mother in Georgia, a father somewhere in Texas. No fixed address. Arrested August 7, 1968, for camping out on the museum lawn; fined; released. Rode with Morley Hill in the Volkswagen bus from Cleveland to Detroit; evidently a friend of Ackley's. Born in Georgia, 1943 or 1944; died May 1, 1970, in Detroit.

NORMAN PRAEGER. Born 1915, Long Island; was driving his 1970 Buick through Recorder's Court parking lot at about five miles an hour; bald, sunny, flush-faced, talkative, a polka-dot personality; sports commentator for WST radio; survived by a wife and twenty-two grandchildren.

JIMMY QUERBACH. Author of the pamphlet *Why Must We Kill?* Peace candidate in 1969; ex-friend of Morley Hill's; interviewed in New York City, he said recently: "Why is everyone pestering me about Morley Hill? I only met him three or four times. Always a big crowd, always Hill slobbering and crying through a megaphone—he had no heart for politics, he said, and he was right. He had no head for politics either.... Why are people always bugging me about him? He got us beat up by some hoodlums at a Big Boy Hamburger Stand, then when the police came he yelled at them to leave us alone. That innocent slob of a murderer!"

RACHEL RANDALL. In the back of the Volkswagen bus with the box of explosives, the lunch-bag with the tinfoil sandwich wrappers carefully folded for safe-keeping, the kite that belonged to Morley Hill's six-year-old son, the Esso roadmap, the old olive horse-blanket, the three grimy tennis balls, etc. 1968 graduate of Southfield High School, Michigan, a diary of green-inked cascades of love: *Speed it up, speed it up, speed it up....* Blond hair cropped short; a long eager nervous neck; intelligent nostrils; two parallel lines between her youthful eyebrows; shoulders hunched forward in dedication. Recording Secretary of the Futurists.

ABBOTT SMITH. Patrolman who stopped the Volkswagen but not ten minutes before the collision-explosion. "He was driving all over the street and I said to myself, what the hell is that? But when I talked to him he looked so scared I let him go. I could see the sweat on his chest, where his shirt was pulled open. He looked like he was going to cry—a guy of about forty, losing his hair, driving these kids to Kensington Park for a day of hiking, so he said. I should of asked him what the hell he was doing downtown then.... He kept saying *Thank you, officer. Thank you.* He was so scared

I let him off with a warning."

BUDDY TATE. Born 1960. Blinded by shattered glass from the explosion, likes to listen to television in the back bedroom of the Tates' "modest frame home" on Wolverine Street. "He is a brave little boy," Mrs. Tate said in an interview with Alexis Crane of the Women's Page of the *Detroit Free Press*. "Sure, he can't see the Get Well cards personally, but he loves to get them. Every morning I read him the mail. We sure appreciate all the cards and presents and we want to thank everybody so far, but also tell them not to forget Buddy. Out of sight is out of mind, so they say, and I hope people won't just forget him."

HANNAH WIGEL. Teaches sociology at the State University of New York at Buffalo. Met and married Morley Hill when he was an instructor in English at the University of Rochester, in 1967; divorced him in late 1969. Her apartment on Kenmore Avenue is small, clean, bare, ascetic; Miss Wigel herself is small and nervous, her dark hair parted carefully in the center of her head. She has an Oriental look, a dark, deft, submissive, very feminine look about her, though she is from Potsdam, New York. She says of her marriage to Morley Hill: "He was always running from one place to another. He lived at the center of a circus, and it was a moving circus. The people around him changed— the faces got younger—they were all ratty, all loud. I suppose I failed him. Those girls who bothered him, his students and girls who just hung around, they were always saying that he was a saint; well, I don't believe in sainthood....I don't believe in martyrdom....I don't believe it was any accident, his getting blown up. No. I believe he did it on purpose. As soon as I heard about it I believed he had done it on purpose, and whoever happened to be with him didn't matter to him.... He said he loved me, the way he loved his two children, but it had nothing to do with his behavior. I loved him very much but I couldn't take it. All that talk, those months of talk....Sometimes the saliva would fly from his mouth, he would be so excited. . . ."

FRITZ WURDOCK. Instructor at Oakland Community College. Shared a desk with Whitney Farber: Farber had the morning use of the desk, Wurdock the afternoon use, someone else—unrelated to this subject—used it in the early evening. One day in April, 1970, he was approached by Farber, whom he knew slightly, an anxious, long-haired, skinny young man who seemed much younger than twenty-eight, and whose bony feet glowed whitely and angrily through the straps of his sandals, and another man, a stranger to Wurdock. Both were very agitated. Farber kept saying: "You must listen to us. There is a plot to put us all in jail, beginning with Ackley. It is a political arrest, it has nothing to do with drugs. They planted the drugs. The charge is irrelevant. Don't think that you and your family will be spared once they get going . . . just talking to me like this will be enough to get you arrested. . . . They're getting concentration camps ready for all of us." Wurdock was on his way to teach a class but Farber kept touching him, tapping his arm angrily. The stranger, a man of moderate height, faced him eye to eye with a small, kind smile. He was about forty years old. His face was ravaged, very pale, ironic and jaunty; his shirt was pulled open at the neck and he was scratching nervously and absent-mindedly at a rash there. He wore ordinary clothing which was wrinkled, but clean, as if he had thrown it into a washing machine, dried it, and had forgotten about ironing it. He wore shoes and socks. He kept saying quietly, while Farber spoke in a high, hysterical whine, "The end is in sight. The end. We are coming through." Wurdock began to feel a little frightened, so when Farber said, "We're only asking for a hundred dollars from you. For Ackley's defense," he gave in almost at once. Later, he began to remember more about Morley Hill: something about the man's eyes. But he was not certain that he wasn't inventing most of it.

The
Impostors

There she was.

He had been walking blindly across the caked, gritty sand, his eyes narrowed against the chilly breeze from the ocean, and then he happened to look up—his gaze moved upon a girl, drifted up her legs and torso to her head, the halfway averted face that meant nothing to him. And then the face became a profile as he stared, and the profile became fuller as she turned toward him, not yet seeing him. He felt the blow of her face in his body, a sudden sickening blow that left him weak.

There she was, Andrea.

He didn't dare come to an abrupt stop, because that might draw her attention to him. And he did not dare continue walking toward her because in another moment they would be face to face. So, clumsily, his heart racing with a bouncy, sickening sensation he had not felt for years, he continued his pace but turned to one side as if he had meant to head this way all along, a man in a hurry, a stranger. He was often in a hurry. He gave the impression of being in a hurry, when other people might be watching him. *Gerald in a hurry, always hurrying.* That was a sign of his wanting something: his appearing to be in a hurry.

Andrea had not noticed him. He was walking fast in the coarse sand, and he stepped on something sharp but did not bother to pause and brush it off his bare foot. Only a thistle or a sliver of glass or a ring from a pull-top beer can....

Safe. Some distance away, a safe distance away, he turned to look back at her. She had not noticed him at all. Would not expect him to be here, obviously. In his anxiety he hadn't noticed that she was with other people, all strangers to him. But of course she wouldn't be out here alone. Not Andrea. A man was standing close beside her, and two other men and a woman appeared to be talking to them. Their conversation was punctuated with bursts of laughter. Gerald shaded his eyes, staring at them. He was no longer in danger; she wouldn't recognize him at this distance. And there were other people around him now, tourists wading through the scummy surf, children running noisily on either side of him.

No danger.

He wondered if she was staying in Provincetown. Or if she were only out here for the day. She and her friends were probably going to drive back to the city this evening, so there wasn't much danger of his meeting her. He turned and blundered into someone—a large, soft woman in a white pants suit, with greasy suntan lotion on her face—and excused himself, embarrassed. He walked quickly away. He didn't look back.

He had been on his way to a grocery store, so he kept on going. He parked out in the unpaved street, hurried inside; he wanted to stock up enough food so that he wouldn't have to bother going out again for a while. He hated to shop. He hated to leave the house, except to wander down to the beach, alone. So he bought two large bags full of groceries and drove back to the bungalow he rented, seeing no one on the road he recognized. His house was on an unpaved, dead-end road, in a shabby corner of town. Sand blew lifelessly everywhere. Paper napkins, tossed out of car windows by vacationers, were dried and baked into the sand or caught in the complex roots and branches of stunted, ground-hugging bushes, permanent eyesores. Most of these things Gerald no longer saw.

204

Alone in the little house, safely alone, he wondered about Andrea and what she was doing now. And why was her hair so blond? Stark bone-blond hair, unnaturally light. Not her true shade. He recalled her erect, almost exaggerated stature there on the beach, the blunt way in which her tanned bare toes gripped the sand. A sense of exuberance about her. Health. The coy tautness of her backbone, at attention, as she talked with that man. . . .

But he didn't want to carry that vision of her back here with him, into this house. It was a house Andrea knew nothing about: he wanted to keep it clear of her. He rented it every summer—from May until the second week in September—from an old couple, the McNieces, who lived in town. They were probably in their late seventies, timid and suspicious of nearly everyone, even of Gerald, whom they should have begun to trust by now. He was always exceptionally kind to them; he smiled down from his awkward height of six foot four at these stooped old people, listening to their complaints, their bitter, frightened observations about the way Provincetown was degenerating: *filling up with trash,* as they said.

"It isn't too bad," Gerald always protested.

They seemed to want to hear that from him, though they never agreed.

He saw them occasionally in the city, with several young children who must have been their grandchildren. At these times Gerald did not call attention to himself—he didn't want to have to talk to them, not with the children around. Not with children around. Not children, not even the children of strangers. It had been ugly enough, their initial questioning of him— Why aren't you married?—Were you married? And he felt a strange, uncomfortable awe for their very age and their look of being enchanted, *married,* two people under a kind of enchantment he could not understand. They lived in a bungalow more dilapidated than the one they rented out, yet they gave the impression, on the street, of being superior to everyone else. Mr. McNiece was a paunchy stooped old gentleman in drooping trousers, who wore sandals and white cotton socks, and Mrs. McNiece was a shy, disapproving, really sexless old woman, in housedresses that sank far below her knees, her stockings rolled about her ankles—that embarrassed Gerald, horribly. Yet they clearly believed themselves superior to the expensively-dressed tourists who crowded the streets.

At first he had been afraid of them, of Mrs. McNiece especially, thinking she might try to mother him—but there was no need to worry. Gerald was a stranger, from another part of the country; they would never quite trust him. Even his efforts to be cheerful, his uncharacteristic efforts, brought him no closer to them. "This is just what I want," he had said, the first time he'd seen the bungalow, as if wanting to please this impoverished old couple. That had been three years ago, just after the end of his marriage. He hadn't been himself then. He had been quite sick. Perhaps that was why the McNieces didn't seem to trust him.

Since then he had developed the habit of doing things quickly, too quickly. Rushing through, his smile widely fixed, eyes blinking, not want to look too closely. No. No need. He never asked questions. Why ask? He had rented an apartment on Long Island and this cottage outside Provincetown without fuss, not taking the time to really examine them. Anything was good enough. He wanted only a private, nameless, unknown place near the ocean, dismal and scrubby as this part of the beach was. The house didn't matter. He noticed the rotting tarpaper on the roof, the shingles that fell off if pried at with a finger, the roaches, the occasional mice, the rust-flecked water that trickled from the faucets, the toilets that flooded or would not flush at all, the warped linoleum floors, the shanty that was supposed to be a garage but was heaped with debris, the accumulation of decades. . . . None of these things bothered him. He was going to be alone, no wife here, no wife-and-child, no responsibility. One day he investigated the shanty, overturning logs to stare at the beetles and grubs that crawled painfully in the sunlight, too stunned to be afraid. . . . He unfolded ancient yellowed newspapers to read their headlines. . . . He discovered a child's toy, a bear on a wooden block. It was very old, many years old. What had happened to the child who played with this?—an adult now? Who was it? Where did he live, now? Gerald stared at it, turning it over in his hand. Most of its paint was gone but it would still work, its four wheels were still intact.

He left the toy in the shanty, on top of a box; in a place where it might easily be found if someone came to claim it.

Putting groceries away he tried not to think of it, of that, but someone's face flashed to him: the curious slanted eyes, the sunny laughter. Why so blond? He didn't want to think of her. He looked around the kitchen to see what must be done, to distract himself; the stove was dirty, its white enamel stained with splashes of food, sauce, now baked dry. Most of the stains were tomato sauce. And the refrigerator smelled: he should clean that soon. He didn't want to live like this, too lazy to care about insects in the cupboards and in the drawers, he didn't want to live like men did, men who looked like him, men who rented apartments and bungalows without bothering to check them. *Anything is fine with me,* these men say.

It was too early for him to start drinking, but he knew he must do something with his hands. He had quit smoking. The coughing was so bad, it made him ashamed of himself—not that he minded the coughing itself, or the pain—but he minded people looking at him, pitying him. *Don't pity me!* he had wanted to shout. . . . He opened a can of beer, anyway, and wandered through the several small rooms of the cottage. He stared at his work as if he were a stranger. Any good? No good? Embarrassing? Interesting? *Dramatic,* maybe? He didn't know. He really didn't know how to judge himself.

He was a painter; that is, "Fine Arts instructor" at

a Long Island university, a community college until 1970 and now mobilized to expand and to compete. Gerald was the artist-in-residence and one of three instructors in the Fine Arts Department; he had always been amazed at the high, generous salary he received there, an actual, regular, reliable monthly check. His students were enthusiastic and prolific, but not very talented. They were affectionate in spite of their occasional arrogance, and would have appropriated most of Gerald's life if he had allowed them to, if he had hinted at the emptiness in which he lived since the end of his marriage—his miserable little twenty-four-month marriage—but he said nothing about his private life, giving them to imagine he hadn't a private life. He was invulnerable as a wall. Gerald a blank featureless wall. He carried this cautious, almost sinister blankness over into his work, unfortunately; that was one of his problems. Inertia held him back, weighed him down. Though he was always hurrying from place to place, a man in a hurry, yet he carried inside this perpetual inertia and weakness, a dispirited awe of himself: at the age of twenty-seven he had been strong, promising, and lucky—he had been awarded a Guggenheim grant; at the age of thirty-one his career had been finished and he had had to force himself to continue with the outward gestures of a career.

Outward gestures: he looked at the several canvases in the small living room of the cottage, feeling nothing for them. They were faces of a kind, hiding their essential features from him, exposing only their surfaces. He drank beer and eyed the canvases. He didn't know and had never known whether he was any good or not. In his twenties, he had been praised and encouraged by older men, painters themselves who taught painting at universities, and Gerald had believed them at the time; now, he didn't know. He was a teacher himself now and he understood how a teacher praised his good students, eagerly and indiscriminately, wanting only to get rid of them . . . wanting to make them happy, to push them on, to say goodbye. It was a way of getting through life.

The canvases played with flames of oily black and green. His favorite colors. They made him uneasy, irritated him. He thought suddenly of Andrea. Her white-blond hair—her slacks fitting her body tightly. She had always dressed like that. She had always made him uneasy, irritated him, with her firm agile little body, disturbing him the way those colors disturbed him... fascinating him. Andrea had about her the same smudged, slovenly beauty he remembered. How old was she now? Over thirty. Thirty-two, at least. On the beach, acting out a certain girlish, shrill role in front of that man, she had been at her best: always at her best in a man's sight.

Gerald forgot about the canvases and went back to the kitchen for another can of beer. It was going to be hard to get through this day. And then the night. He went out back into the scrubby yard, narrowing his eyes against the wind, which was blowing bits of sand into his face. Next to his cottage was a vacant lot which had been used as a dump for years—posted NO DUMPING—and on the other side a cottage rented this summer by a number of young people, in their late teens and early twenties. Idly, Gerald had counted eight boys and girls in that place. He had not wanted to pay attention to them. He did not especially like children of any age. A few weeks ago the Provincetown police raided that cottage, early in the morning, and in their zeal had even dropped in on Gerald "just to check"—but Gerald didn't resent the kids, he just didn't want to think about them. He was beyond all that. He was maybe fifteen years older than most of them. He had lived through all that, the skirmishes and the delirious adventures and the betrayals, and now the long-haired perpetually laughing girls did not interest him much more than the bare-chested boys in sunglasses who were always scrambling around on expensive motorcycles. If one of them waved to him, out of an excess of good spirits, Gerald would wave back but that was as far as it went. He sensed himself a careful swimmer, an individual swimming cautiously through a debris-swollen body of water, a flood of many currents, many waves, in which others were swimming at differing speeds, unaware of the danger they were in.

His stomach was jumpy. Thinking about *her* made him lose his appetite. If he could channel his agitation into work, into painting, he would be all right. He would have to think about that. Would have to start thinking seriously about that. But he understood with a forlorn certainty that he would not be able to paint, not now.... It was as if Andrea had charged into this rented bungalow, ablaze in her white slacks and her tight, absurd little blue sweater with the armholes cut far up onto her shoulders, like a man's T-shirt, piking and prodding at him, at his canvases, peering at them with her quizzical skeptical smile, saying, "What are all these things supposed to mean? Do you know, yourself?" Staring at him with her smile, her tilted face, those frank blue eyes seizing him and releasing him, indifferently. There was that final, awful indifference to her beneath her energy. The man with her on the beach couldn't know. You saw Andrea at her best, her face flushed with excitement, her body glowing with a kind of juice just beneath the skin, and you could never guess at the deep, fatal indifference of her soul.

He was too restless to work. Of course he was not going to stay home.

He washed his face and the upper part of his body, hurriedly. He was very excited. In the discolored little mirror his face stared back at him, a face defensive in all its features, as if angrily resisting criticism. His hair was short, unfashionably short, because he hated hair around his face, and this made him look leaner, rawer, more abrupt, younger than he really was, his head a little small for his long body. He was always poking out of things, out of his sleeves and trouser legs; since childhood he had been self-conscious of his height.

Andrea had had to stand on her toes. Stretching her body in order to slide her arms around his neck. Stretching against him, her breasts uplifted, taut and young, her neck straining backward....

She had liked roughness. Fooling around. Slowness annoyed her; if Gerald was gentle with her she had felt uneasy. "What's wrong?" she would ask. "Why are you so serious?"

In Andrea's imagination, people always seemed to mean more than they said. She was cheerfully suspicious of them, as she was of his paintings: *What do they mean?* She couldn't believe him when he said that they meant nothing. *What, nothing? Who are you kidding?* He could almost hear her voice, in this tiny bathroom with him, light and darting as the sparrows that flew everywhere out here, living off refuse. That voice forced him outside again to his car. He drove back to town, making himself drive carefully. He wanted to tell the truth to himself because, living alone, a man who had chosen to live alone, he had to be honest with himself. It was the only way a man could live alone without going crazy. No deceit. No lies. In a marriage you had to lie, it was all a tissue of lies like a play in which the two actors wrote their own lines, haphazardly, sometimes angrily, making mistakes they couldn't go back to erase, yes, marriage was based upon lies, but living alone necessitated telling the truth. Yet he didn't want to admit the truth of what he was doing.

He got rid of the car on a side street and joined the idle wandering weekend crowds. Tourists crossing and re-crossing the streets, peering into the windows of shops and boutiques, assessing restaurants, preparing to make that ultimate decision of the evening: *where to have dinner? Where to deposit twenty-five dollars?* Gerald tried not to resent these people. Their worn-out, whining children annoyed him but he tried not to notice them. So much bickering, so much love! There were many children on the street with their parents, dressed for the sea-shore, staring with glazed, exhausted eyes at the shops with their cluttered windows, tugging at their parents' arms, whining, begging for attention, for love, for food. Their energy, even at the end of the day, was amazing.

And there were small hordes of teenagers strolling up and down the street, boys and girls, more of them every weekend this summer: Gerald could understand the McNieces' fear. And couples. Young couples strolling the streets, their arms around each other. Many young men. Gerald was right behind two young men who were modishly dressed in polka-dot trousers and shirts, their sideburns long and curling, the crowns of their heads identically balding, young-old men of the type who came out here every weekend, and when another young man eased by them with a smile Gerald heard one of the men say to his friend, "Who was *she?*"

He didn't hate them either. He didn't hate anyone.

He went into the Green Devil for a drink. Saw no one he knew. The television set was on though no one was watching—coverage of a fire in a hospital on Boston's North Side. Gerald felt that he should shout at the people in this bar, insist that they watch the television screen where the flames were still being shown—now the firetrucks—now firemen—now a shot of a crowd— The news shifted to another subject. Gerald finished his drink. Why was he here? He didn't want to think about it. He was a man who had expected to become famous before the age of thirty; he hadn't made it. Instead, at the age of thirty-one, he had become a divorced man, an ex-father, a near-alcoholic, a near-wreck with stomach troubles and insomnia, the memories of a middle-aged man. After that the years had passed swiftly and soundlessly.

He began to feel restless again. Must get out of here. He left that bar and wandered along . . . in and out of the cruising gangs of young people and young men . . . his eyes jumping everywhere, nervous as roaches, attracted to gift shops, dangling corks and net and pink plastic lobsters and other junk, propped-up reproductions of sentimental art, seascapes and children with enormous bruised eyes, kittens, cocker spaniels, Mexican madonnas—why Mexicans, why up here?—and the usual blatant still lives, huge pots of huge flowers, pink and yellow, and items thought to be connected with the sea, fishermen's thigh-high boots, weathered rowboats, wharves, rotting posts in water illuminated by moonlight. One art gallery featured paintings of the sea, all silver and mist and storm; another gallery displayed a half-dozen reproductions of a portrait of Christ, who seemed to be blessing everyone who passed on the sidewalk, with a small hazy smile, making no critical judgments. Gerald passed by all this, not letting it upset him, in fact forcing his smile to imitate Christ's smile—why criticize, after all? If you judged other people you were like to be judged, yourself. That might be dangerous.

He wandered across the street to the little movie theater, where a long straggly line had already formed for the seven-thirty show; anyone watching Gerald would have believed he intended to see the movie. He studied the posters as if considering it. It was a documentary film of a rock music festival held the year before . . . the festival had taken place on the West Coast and was famous for including a murder, an actual unrehearsed authentic murder, included accidentally in the film footage . . . yes, a murder, Gerald peered at the photograph in the advertisement, evidently of that scene, though it was blurred and a little disappointing. . . .

He seemed to change his mind about seeing the show, and wandered down the block to another bar. Just as he entered the place someone called out his name.

He turned, startled.

A man named Jack. He was not a friend of Gerald's, only an acquaintance; said to be a sculptor. But Gerald had never seen his work. He was a big burly hearty man in his forties. Tonight he was already drunk. He put his arm around Gerald's shoulders and said huskily, "C'mon over here, there's some friends of mine for you to meet. Where the hell you been all summer?"

Gerald tried to resist, feebly. But he could think of no reason not to go with Jack.

And there she was again.

She was standing there, at the bar. She hadn't seen him yet. Gerald was being led right to her, right to the group of people she was with . . . they were milling around at one end of the bar. . . . She was laughing, her shoulders raised girlishly, her head back, eyes closed in a helpless spasm of laughter. Gerald's stomach turned. Then she opened her eyes and saw him and stopped laughing at once.

Did anyone notice?

She stared at him. Jack was saying, "Wantcha to meet some friends of mine—Gerald—this is Gerald—this is Ron and this is—what?—Billy?—and this is my great lovely little doll Andrea, whom I have just met this past hour, and this is—"

Andrea's face seemed to shift, jerk and shift—Gerald had the confused sense of someone straightening a blanket, jerking all the wrinkles out at once. She opened her mouth to say something—stammered hello—put out her hand to Gerald, so that the two of them were forced to touch each other, to actually hold hands, as if in a conspiracy to hide from the others their trembling fingers.

"Andrea, is it? Your name is Andrea?" Gerald said.

"Yes. Your name is Gerald?"

He was dizzy, frightened. His heart raced. He would have to write his lines in this heated, hectic daze, staring helplessly into Andrea's face, hoping she would not break down. Would have to make up his dialogue, his lines, while Andrea made up her own, rapidly, too rapidly. . . . She was shorter than he remembered. Not wearing shoes, that was the reason. Her face looked strained. The laughter had run out of it, the animation remained only in the over-bright glitter of her eyes, and the fluffed-out blond hair around her forehead and in front of her ears. The rest of her hair had been pulled back and tied with a piece of ordinary twine at the nape of her neck. Very neat. Almost severe. Yet there was something voluptuous about it, Gerald thought as he stared at her, the same slovenly indifferent voluptuousness he had remembered.

Everyone was talking loudly. Gerald ordered a drink. He knew he should force himself to look away from Andrea—but she seemed to be insisting that he talk to her. Gerald was vaguely aware of Jack watching the two of them. He stared critically, harshly, at her face—that audacious, rather blunt beauty that not every man would admire—and saw that her eyebrows were too thick. Unfashionable. They would meet across the bridge of her nose, Gerald knew, if she didn't pluck them there.

He ducked to hear what she was asking. "I'm from New York," he said. "What about you?"

"California," she said levelly. "I'm visiting friends in New York." He didn't want to stare at her—not at her breasts in that tight-fitting, almost vulgar little pull-over top, the kind of thing a teenaged girl might wear at the beach. He didn't want to stare at the way her throat rose from the ribbed collar.

He wondered if her palms were stinging with panicky sweat, like his.

"Are you— Are you out here for the day? For the weekend?" Gerald asked.

He tried to smile. He saw himself side-stepping this scene, staring in disbelief at what was happening. *Again. Again.* Andrea was answering his question, earnestly, even leaning forward so that he could hear over the commotion of the bar—was she telling the truth, frowning like that, or was the puckering frown only a way of making her lies convincing? He had never understood.

"We're supposed to stay over at someone's house," Andrea was saying. "Elinor—Elinor Wright or something like that, do you know her? I don't know her. There's a party or something at her house. Why don't you come along? Come with us."

Gerald began shaking his head. He felt suddenly old, beside Andrea's energy. Old. Gaunt. Used-up. Yet it flattered him that she should be speaking to him in that low rapid murmur of hers, almost begging him, while the other men overheard. With a nervous pawing in the air he said, "I can't, sorry. I haven't gotten much done this summer—the summer is shot to hell and I—"

"Please. Come with us," Andrea said.

Her man-to-man frankness, her level murmuring voice. It was almost a parody of frankness. This puzzled men; it had puzzled Gerald for a long time. He knew, now, that it meant nothing to him, it had no power over him, and yet he remained there, as if paralyzed, staring at Andrea's thick eyebrows, which had always seemed to him a sign of confidence—most women would have plucked them thin, into a neat feminine arc. Andrea had always been contemptuous of such things. Not very clean, to tell the truth. Soiled underclothes worn day after day, out of laziness. Little nuggets of food dried between the prongs of forks—the sort of thing you might expect from a man like Gerald himself, a man living alone, but not from a woman. Hairs in the sink. On the bathroom floor. Soapy milky scum ringed around the bathtub after one of her long lazy baths. The smell of her flesh hanging in the steamy air, an intimacy Gerald had been unable to escape....

So he went with them. The five-minute ride in someone's car, wedged beside an open window, gave him time to think. He loathed her, yes. Loathed the glow of her face, the way she kept chattering from the front seat of the car, in her throaty jesting way, dominating the conversation as she teased the driver about something but was really talking to him, to Gerald. He felt that the other men sensed this and that their silence was baffled and resentful.

The house turned out to be a large, barn-like, handsome Cape Cod, one Gerald had admired from the road, imagining quiet, stable, sane lives lived inside it; but tonight it was crowded and noisy. Rock music sounded from a complex stereophonic unit, the music of children, though there were no young people here. Gerald pretended to be examining the enormous stone fireplace. He was very much alone. Jack headed for him, poked him in the ribs, made a growling noise meant to be comic, and said, "Jesus, what is it with you and her? That Andrea? The way she looked at you. . . . Her whole face changed, even her body changed. I saw it."

Gerald tried to laugh this off.

"No, really, I'm not kidding," Jack said. "She's really onto you. Look, right now she's watching us. Look."

Gerald went out into the kitchen in order to avoid her. Someone was standing at the sink, a greenish-gray young man with frizzy hair, his shoulders hunched; a girl stood beside him, patting his arm. Gerald ignored them and went to the refrigerator, looking for a beer. He could handle beer. A woman in a sunsuit of some fluorescent flowered material—she must have been his hostess—came up behind him and started complaining about motorcycles and Hondas out on the road. Did he rent a place up here? Did he notice how bad it was getting?

Gerald tried to pay attention to her, but he kept staring at the doorway, waiting for Andrea to appear. Finally he interrupted the woman to ask, "Do you know that woman, Andrea?"

"Who?"

"The blonde. Her hair is very blond. She's wearing a blue sweater, a little slip-over sweater, and white slacks. . . ."

"Andrea who?" the woman asked sourly.

After a few minutes Gerald excused himself and walked into the noise of the other room, like a blind man. He must trust his instinct. He stood grinning, a can of beer in his hand, looking around in a circle until he came across her flushed, gleaming face, the perfect skin damp with perspiration as she stood there, waiting for him.

They stared at each other. There was a moment—Gerald sighted it like one of those floating dots in his vision—when the two of them might have looked away, turning to other people. But their gaze held. The moment passed. And so, his stomach urging him against this, his bowels sending sharp little darts of pain, he forced his way over to her. She was with a mop-haired man in his fifties, and she interrupted him to touch Gerald's arm as if Gerald might not stop by them otherwise. "You're a painter, you said?" she asked, in a bright breathless ballooning voice, like a young girl unaccustomed to alcohol. "What kind of things do you paint? Do they have any special meaning?"

Her eyes were fearful above her wide smile.

"No special meaning," Gerald said.

"No meaning," Andrea repeated, as if this were important. The man beside her was blank, cold. He did not smile. Andrea had already turned from him; she seemed to have forgotten him, rudely. "Is that on purpose? Is it a comment on something? What do you do with your paintings—do you sell them?"

Do you sell them? It was the same question she had asked years ago, the first evening they had met.

"Not any more," Gerald said.

"But you keep painting? You have faith in your work? Is that it?" Her voice was rapid and unfocussed, her mouth still grinning, smelling of whisky, her eyes blue and frightened. Gerald could not tell if she were pretending or not.

"You have faith in your work?" she insisted, staring at him.

"I have faith in the future, not in my work. Not in myself," Gerald said, trying to avoid her hectic stare. "After all—the future is unavoidable, whether I contribute to it or not—"

"It's so hard to have faith in anything, I mean the way things change," Andrea said rapidly, as if she were

218

not listening to her own words. "People can't remember right now things that happened to them a few years ago, let alone what happened a few years ago in history or in the war—you know—it's all changing so fast—I'm one of the old people now that I used to see at parties like this and sort of feel sorry for—How old would you guess I am?" Andrea said with a smile.

"Twenty-five?" said the mop-haired man.

Andrea paid no attention to him. She was staring at Gerald.

"Thirty-two," he said flatly.

"Thirty-two," she repeated, smiling. "Is that it?"

"That's it," Gerald said.

He could not have walked away from her now. It was too late. The rock music was pushing him toward her, and behind her that part of the room had become distorted, warped as in a curved mirror, bending her toward him. In fact, she seemed to be about to lose her balance and would have fallen toward him if he hadn't put out a hand. Andrea had never learned how to drink. She never got sick, didn't throw it up as Gerald sometimes did; alcohol flowed to her brain and made her beady-eyed, like a life-sized mechanical doll. After a few hours of drinking her skin would go dead-white. No beauty then. Gerald had not noticed this before their marriage, but he had noticed it often enough afterward—his husky-voiced, confident, beautiful wife going suddenly limpid, her breath surprised and foul, hands shaking. He had watched her once, in some rented kitchen of some rented flat, years ago, trying to open a can of something, soup or beans or tuna fish: adjusting the can-opener and then trying to turn it, dropping the can onto the cupboard, picking it up again and adjusting the opener, again trying to turn the handle, dropping the can, with a stifled sob picking it up again. . . .

". . . some fresh air?" Andrea was saying.

They left through the kitchen, which was now crowded. The woman in the fluorescent playsuit seemed about to call out after Gerald, but he pretended not to notice.

"This is better. The night air. Yes, this is better. Thank you," Andrea said.

They walked down to the beach. The waves rolled toward them without effort, quietly, as if waiting for them. "I can breathe now," Andrea said. Gerald kicked off his shoes and walked along the surf. For a while they could think of nothing to say.

Then they both started to speak at once. Andrea laughed and said, "Go on—you talk."

"No, you."

"I was just going to ask how you were. I mean your life."

"The same."

"No better?"

"Maybe a little better," Gerald said.

"Someone told me you were teaching in college. Where is it, on Long Island? Do you have an apartment there?"

"Yes, an apartment in a one-storey building, like a motel. It's all right. The job is all right too."

"And your health?"

"Much better."

"You do look good, Gerald," she said with a rush of warmth. Gerald glanced at her, helplessly. "When I saw you in that bar—oh my God—I thought I might faint, it was such a shock—You looked so—so—"

Gerald dreaded her.

"—so much the way you did. I mean, when we were— you know—when we first met, even. You don't look much older. Just around your eyes, the corners of your eyes—"

They walked along the beach, at the edge of the ocean. Gerald stared down at their pale, ghostly feet.

"I couldn't hide what I felt," Andrea whispered.

"I couldn't hide it either," Gerald said.

Everywhere along the beach, in the cottages and

220

cabins, there were people laughing, a jumble of lights, the odor of food—a complex stench, debris burning, maybe the odor of rotting fish or dumped garbage. The sounds of happy people, intoxicated people, were mixed with the surf in a kind of music. Gerald's mouth kept sliding into a grin, as if in sympathy with this music.

"Are those people friends of yours?" Gerald asked. He was careful to keep his voice detached.

"God, no. I don't even know them. I don't know who they are," Andrea laughed.

He had always disliked that about her—her habit of brushing people aside, friends they had both had, even members of her own family. He had imagined her speaking of him in the same way. *I don't even know him. Don't know who he is.*

"Do you think much about...about it?" Andrea asked.

Gerald had not quite finished his can of beer. But he threw it out into the ocean.

He did not answer her.

After a moment she pressed against him as if by accident, maybe exaggerating her drunkenness. She said, "Do you ever think about me? Ever about me? The way I think about you?"

"I don't know," he muttered.

He wanted to draw back from her, repulsed.

"Gerald, don't make me cry. Not tonight," she said childishly. "This was going to be a happy night. I don't even know those people. They're nothing to me. It's you.... I want to talk to you. Did I tell you I've been living in Los Angeles?"

"No," Gerald said cautiously.

"Don't you want to know?"

"No."

"I live in a nice little efficiency apartment. On the first floor of a building. It's very nice. Don't you want to know? That I didn't get married again, ever? That it's light out there—I mean sunlight—people are

221

friendly and very free and don't ask questions. My father was just out to visit me. He always liked you. I liked you too."

Gerald laughed angrily.

He felt as if a mist were passing over his brain. He could not help the direction in which they were walking. Andrea slipped her arm around his waist, leaning against him. She started to cry. Her thin effortless tears were so familiar, so awful... Gerald could not bear tears, not the tears of his babyish stubborn wife or the tears of his child or of any child. So he said, roughly, "Stop that. You know better."

"Back there, when I saw you... I thought it would kill me...." Andrea whispered.

Yes. He understood.

His mind reeled and he confused her with those students who came to his apartment, sometimes early in the morning, troubled, hysterical, a little drunk or high on pills, drawn to him because of his shabbiness and his courtesy, his air of being as helpless as they, a dignified mess; they wanted to talk about their "work" with him, but really they wanted to talk about their lives, their souls. Sometimes they even pressed against him, like this. The girls. And he held them, abstractedly, with an abstract affection. The boys paced restlessly around his room, talking, their eyes searching the squalor of his belongings as if seeking out his secret, his essential soul. Because somehow he *knew*. He understood, he knew. They could see it in his face.

"Do you ever think about it? About him?" Andrea whispered.

"Yes," Gerald said.

By the time they were at his cottage the night air had cleared his head and Gerald was terrified that he would become sober. So he got out a bottle of whisky for them, for the two of them. They sat at the kitchen table. Andrea said, "We've missed a few anniversaries." Gerald was relieved that she did not ask to see his paintings, that she seemed to have forgotten about them.

It was getting chilly; they eyed each other for warmth, as they had when they first met. Gerald felt the same nervous irritating desire for her that he had always felt and Andrea, as if sensing it, squirmed and turned upon it, a lovely fish on a hook, teasing the hook and the line, working it in her mouth, smiling tensely at him. Gerald felt that he must fight the heavy-headed lethargy that threatened him. *He would take her to bed.* No, he did not want her. He despised her.

She smiled at him. He did not return the smile. Yet she smiled, she seemed to be sinking back into that swaying helpless cunning of hers, knowing that she would win in the end, that he was being forced to her. The two of them forced together, like waves striking the same beach, again and again, helplessly....

She drew one leg up, clumsily, so that the heel of her foot caught on the edge of the chair, her chin pressed against her knee; he saw the long full tight span of her thigh, and his mind dissolved.

"It was your fault," he said.

"No."

"Yes. Your fault."

She licked her lips with a drunken, careful coquettishness. "No. No charges were brought against me."

"Nevertheless...."

"No. It was an accident."

"You were smoking. You fell asleep."

"I was waiting up for you."

"But you fell asleep. You killed him."

His voice had ascended, almost to a shriek. But it must not have sounded outside him. He heard it, he felt it; but Andrea was shaking her head slowly and heavily, like fate. "No. Not me," she murmured. She kept her eyes fixed on his face like a dancer with her eyes fastened to something solid, a permanent horizon. "I was only waiting up for you. I loved you."

"Why did you drink so much?"

"You walked out and I had to wait up for you. You couldn't get away with that—no—not what you said."

Gerald tried to remember what he had said.

"Couldn't let you get away with it," Andrea muttered. "It was unjust. The whole thing. I wanted justice then and I want justice now. . . . Anyway you didn't love him. Or me."

He didn't want to speak, because of the shrieking. That had happened before. He remembered, even if she didn't. But he should say something to stop her—he should say *No. Yes. Yes, I did. No. I didn't, no. Leave me alone. I am only here for the summer.* If he did not speak to her that dull, dark tide would draw him to shore, to her. There were waves that repeated themselves again and again, helplessly. He would have to cry out against them, he would have to resist, to fight. *No! Stop!*

"You didn't love him," she said slowly. "You didn't love me."

They stared at each other. Gerald felt time blacking out, drawing back to nothing. A secret lay between them: it enhanced this woman, made her slack-mouthed face glow. She knew. She knew him very well. She was watching him, hearing the soundless shrieks, knowing him, waiting for him. *You loved me. You loved him and me both. You loved us both. Loved us.*

"I did love you," he said.

"Do you love me now? . . . Try again, now?"

He wanted to cry out against her, against that drunken terrifying voice. But he could not resist. There were waves that threw themselves again and again upon the same stretch of beach, helpless to stop. He couldn't resist. He helped her out of the chair and led her into the bedroom and she lay down on the rumpled bed, muttering something. She was very drunk. He lay beside her. Time had been blacked out and now there was no secret between them, they were free, they were back at the beginning. Nothing had been lost, not yet. Everything was ahead of them. Andrea was asleep or he would have explained it to her. He put his arms around her, shivering; his arms like rubbery coils, oh yes he did love her, he couldn't resist her, this is what people cannot resist, the magic in them and the secrets they learn, together, like the war-headlines of old yellowed newspapers. He did love her but he was too exhausted to turn off the light. The hell with it, the hell with the little insects that kept striking the bulb. Too exhausted. He did love her but was too exhausted. He fell asleep in several rapid stages, slipping backward into sleep as if into dark water.

Year
of
Wonders

Twenty-eight entrances, all equal in size. The "Main Entrance" is no different from the others—a double thermopane door that opens automatically when you approach it. It faces Seaway Avenue and the "A" parking lot. But it is no larger than the twenty-seven other entrances. So the way you choose to enter is just an accident; but it can decide your life.

You can get to *Meiker's Records* equally fast by entering the door by *Merlo's Washer-Driers* and *Jacobi's Shoes,* or by taking the door to the *Grand Mall Twin Theaters,* where the yellow marquee sticks out over the sidewalk. But there is an usher who works there, Tony Grossi, who is eighteen or nineteen, with sideburns and a fast, nasty grin. Sometimes he hangs out in front of the ticket-seller's booth, watching shoppers go by, and sometimes he even sits on one of the bright orange benches, smoking a cigarette. I came in that way with Sandy and Barbara once and he looked at all three of us and made some kind of a face, so that his lips turned out and upward, *You don't make the grade.* . . . Another time, on a Saturday when I was with my mother, I saw him walking along dressed in regular clothes, not in his usher's uniform, down at the other end of the Mall, and he seemed to be sort of staring at me as if he was hypnotized or something . . . but when we got closer to each other I could see that his eyes were going right through me. My mother didn't notice anything at all.

Sometimes we enter right through *Lingard's,* the big department store. But Entrance 8 takes you through Yard Goods, where there are counters and counters of cloth wound around things, and then you have to go through Childrens Togs where little kids are fooling around or crying or bumping into you, and their mothers are mad, and are likely to give you dirty looks. Once we ran into Sandy's sister there!—her married sister, who was dragging her three-year-old and her five-year-old along, and she asked Sandy what the hell Sandy thought she was doing out here?—*Does Ma know about you hanging around?—what are you up to, shoplifting?* Sandy went white, she hated her so and always did, and started to cry while the rest of us just stood there, so embarrassed. *Little brats!* Sandy's sister said, looking at us all.

Most of the time we take the way in right off Lot C. This is the parking lot that goes all the way back to Mercer Boulevard. You can cut through the football field out back of the school and cross Mercer, if you run fast—it's always packed with big trucks heading for the expressway north of town—then through the parking lot, where the cars are parked in rows, some of them sticking out farther than others, or at an angle, some of them parked up right close to the poles as if the women who parked them were afraid somebody might run into the rear-ends of their cars. Then you take Entrance 13, between *Arnold Jewellers & Gifts* and *Ing's Chinese Restaurant. Meiker's* isn't too far away by this entrance, the second shop on the left on the corridor third over, from the fountain at the center of the Mall.

One day in September we took Entrance 21, which is not very interesting, but there was a chance that someone we knew was working down below—there is a loading place, for trucks, and some boys from school work there, helping unload. We didn't see anyone we know. Then I saw Vic Pedroza, helping some man roll a barrel to the very edge of a truck, the two of them working very hard, it looked like, but they didn't glance up at us. One of the girls I was with whistled and we ran inside, giggling, but I don't think anyone heard us. Inside, a few shops down, there was some kind of an artist out in the center of the corridor. There was a flower-bed there, with pots of geraniums and mums arranged inside it, in a circle, and wooden benches that went around it, for people to sit on. The artist had his things set up on one of the benches and was just standing there.

He was looking toward us as if he was waiting for us.

He had an easel set up and some examples of his drawings arranged on the bench, one of them even balanced inside the flowers somehow. There were four or five sketches, in colored chalk, of girls' faces; one of the girls looked like somebody we knew. We felt funny, the way he was looking at us, and I started to giggle, then he smiled at me and said *How'd I like my portrait done?* I was embarrassed but we went over anyway and looked at the sketches, and they were very good, they looked very real. The girls were all very pretty. One of the girls had short puffy red hair, like mine, and a snub nose, and beautiful eyes with long thick lashes. All the eyes in the drawings had a sparkle, done by white crayon or chalk in the center of the eye; that had a very strange effect, it seemed to go right through you as if the girl was alive. The artist was joking with us and teasing us. He was maybe in his twenties?—he was thin, with long hair that was stiff from not being washed, a mixture of platinum blond hair and ordinary blond-brown hair. He didn't have a real beard, only hairs that looked like wires. His mouth was very pink. He was very handsome.

". . . boy friend'r mother'r father'r somebody, huh, to give one to for a present? Christmas, birthday? Okay?"

He seemed to be asking me. "Okay what?" I said.

"Okay for a portrait? Five bucks. Half-an-hour, amazing likeness, your boy friend'r mother'r somebody'll awful happy. Okay?"

I said I didn't have five dollars.

"What? Hell! Everybody's got five dollars!"

He grinned but looked a little mad. He was rubbing his hands together, bending toward me. He was taller than I remembered my father was—he was leaning over and making his lips move, without any sound, as if he was whispering to me. But I couldn't hear anything. Then he said, out loud:

"Three bucks, then—seenashowy'r so pretty— Three bucks, okay? How about it? Y'r girl-friends c'n watch, learn a few tricks athetrade, okay? Okay?"

"I don't have three dollars either," I said.

"Yes she does," Barbara said.

"No I don't."

"She *does.*"

"I don't!"

The artist listened to us and joked and teased, then he did something very strange—he noticed somebody behind us and just pushed us away, not shoving, but just pushing me away so he could get past. There was a woman there with a little boy in one of those strollers you can rent, a woman maybe my mother's age, in an ugly mustard-yellow pants suit that was too tight for her; it turned out she wanted the little boy's picture drawn. The artist forgot all about us and we walked away. When we got to the end of the corridor I looked back, but there were too many shoppers, I couldn't see anything. There are so many decorations and lights going on and off, things get lost, it's worse than at school where the center hall is so long people sort of evaporate when they walk away.

One day in November I was alone. I took the same way in—Entrance 21 by the loading place—but the artist was gone, now they had the regular flowers gone and poinsettias were there instead, in little pots with silvery green wrapping paper around them. I walked down past the dry cleaner's and *Newberry's* where they had some cute hamsters and white mice and things in cages, in the display window, and a big hook-beaked bird with fantastic green feathers that looked dyed, they were so bright, sitting on a perch with his leg chained to the perch; $75 for that bird, it said, and it looked so bright-colored and funny, with yellowish eyes like plastic, that you wondered if it was real.

That was bad luck: a minute later Don Lamont and Mike Koziek came up to me, knocking some people out of the way, and were laughing and yelling like crazy, *Here's Reeny! Reeny from seventh grade!* They were high on something, they were wild and crazy and the other people, the women shoppers, made a wide circle around us and walked by fast. I tried to kid around with them but they weren't listening or couldn't hear me, they were just sort of poking one another and giggling, bent over giggling, saying *ReenyReenyReeny* as if that was a joke, and finally I got away from them and ran away, and ran past people looking at me, because I was crying and probably funny-looking and I went to the Ladies Room in *Lingard's* and was all right.

One day after school a few weeks later, right before Christmas break, we saw some art-things set up near the center fountain—but it was pottery and ceramics, done by the Women's Art League. Some of the women were there, selling things. One of them was somebody who knew me, because she cried out, *Doreen!*—so I had to go over. "How is your mother?" she asked. "I feel so bad about us not keeping in touch.... She still lives in Pine Woods, doesn't she?"

"Yes."

My face got red because my friends were waiting around, behind me, and could hear this. The woman was trying to be friendly. She was saying something about her life being all changed, she even moved to a different apartment, and what was our telephone number again?—because maybe she had the wrong number, every time she called that number nobody ever answered. So I had to tell her our number. She nodded and pretended to remember it, as if that was such an important number, then she said, embarrassed, that she hadn't tried to call since summer because my mother never answered the phone, but maybe she should try again. "Should I try again? Or . . .?"

Her voice trailed off. She looked a lot younger than my mother, so I wondered if she was really a friend of hers. She wore a short green velvet jacket with tiny gold buttons, and a short velvet skirt, and light-green tights that bunched out a little too much at her knees, where she was chunky; it was a strange outfit. Only the shoes—regular small-heeled black shoes—were like something my mother would wear.

"I don't know," I said. I was very warm. I wanted to get away.

My friends were getting restless and I could feel them pulling away from me. I didn't want them to leave. The woman pretended not to notice them or maybe she didn't notice them, she was frowning at me, saying something about my mother trying things like this—she meant the pottery, she picked up a beige conical pot with slashes in it for decoration, like you might make with a fork in pie dough—that life didn't have to come to an end because of some bastard or other— she was speaking very softly but her voice was tight, hard, and her lips were held very hard, and I said *Yes excuse me* and had to get away, and somehow I got away, and my friends and I went shopping all that afternoon, trying on things in *Business Girl Fashions*, where Sue's sister works. I bought a poor-boy sweater marked down to $3.98 from $6.98, a pink-and-red zigzag pattern, but when I got home my mother looked at it and found the unraveling part, under the sleeve, and threw it at me, laughing, saying she was disgusted, but so what? *What else can I expect?* she said.

A few days later I went back, by myself, because I felt bad about something. I didn't know what it was. I felt guilty about something. I didn't bother with *Meiker's* or a new display of animals and birds and things by *Lingard's* but ran down to the center of the Mall, where the Women's Art League had their stand set up. But the woman who had talked to me wasn't there.

I bought my mother a ceramic thing because it was all I could afford—$1.98 for a seal on a rock, lacquered and shining very hard, with whiskers made of some tiny black wires.

In January I was alone, looking through the New Releases, when somebody ran his finger down by back-bone. It turned out to be Mike Philbrick—but I knew he was only kidding around, he didn't mean it. He is in senior high. So I didn't get too excited or anything but just laughed and kept thinking *I don't give a damn, I don't give a damn if he walks away,* so I didn't feel bad when some other girls came in *Meiker's* and he went over to them and started teasing them. I got to the end of the New Releases and that was that.

In February my friends and I came in by the *Grand Mall Twin Theaters,* but the usher wasn't around, but it was bad luck anyway because some kids from DeWitt were fooling around in the lobby. They had bought tickets for the next show and were waiting for the other show to let out, so they were fooling around out in the corridor where the lobby opens into it and they saw us and followed us, saying things to us, *Think you're so good at Mercer, don't you?* They were four boys, in jeans and boots and jackets with bright yellow letters on them—*Wildcats*—and one of the boys grabbed hold of me by the hair and it hurt me so that I screamed, and that made him mad, so he knocked me down and they all ran away. I hit my forehead against the edge of something. But I got up right away and was all right. My head felt sort of numb.

The security guard ran over and was mad at us.

The other girls wanted to go to *Meiker's* but I knew I looked ugly so I went home. The side of my head was numb and prickly. I told my mother I wasn't hungry and went upstairs and thought about myself coming through that entrance—walking through the door when it opened automatically—through *that particular*

233

entrance and what it had done to me. I kept seeing myself there, I wanted to say *No don't!* Then my mother called me for supper, she must have forgotten what I said, and we had supper in the recreation room, where it was sort of cold because in the winter it isn't heated right, it's built over the garage and the garage is very cold, but my mother didn't notice anything strange about my face. Afterward I remembered something Barbara had told me, about somebody she knew in the hospital, who was paralyzed, and the doctor stuck pins in him to see if he was alive, so I pricked a pin against my forehead and cheek and after a while I could feel some sensation, so I was all right.

The next time—a few days later—we went to the Mall, the artist was back, the boy with the long greasy blond hair. He had his things set up like before, but the drawings were different. He had a customer: a girl my age, about thirteen, sitting on the edge of the flower-bed. She had a fat face but nice eyes and was very embarrassed, the way people were standing around, watching. The artist was working fast, with colored chalks. I got behind him so I could see what he was doing—and he was drawing her so fast, the face just came out of nowhere, a light-brown face all shadings and very filmy and delicate and pretty—I felt tears come into my eyes, I didn't know why—just to see how he was drawing her and how the face came out onto the white paper. He looked the same, except now he was wearing a kind of burlap shirt, a baggy pull-over thing, and while he was drawing the girl he didn't pay attention to anyone, but was frowning and muttering to himself. The girl was blushing, with so many people around. Two or three of her girl friends were there, trying to make her laugh, then one of my friends—Sandy—got crowded in too close and knocked against the easel. The artist looked at her, but like he didn't see her. He fixed the easel and kept on drawing: now he was using a pink-orange chalk in his right hand, and was holding a dark brown chalk in his other hand, so that he changed them back and forth, very fast, and was biting his bottom lip and staring at the girl. People were giggling now, I mean kids were giggling. There were some boys from school fooling around. "Go away, let him alone!" somebody said. One of the boys knocked Sandy against the artist, again, and this time the boys laughed and ran away down the hall, and the artist straightened the easel up again and kept on with the drawing. My girl friends got bored and wanted to go away, so I told them I'd meet them at *Meiker's,* so they went away and I watched until he got the drawing finished. It was a pretty drawing but the girl's face was really fatter than that. And her eyes were nicer: younger. I felt strange. I wanted to tell him or even shout *her eyes are too old, wait! don't! don't show it to her!*—but of course I didn't say anything and by now there weren't so many people around to watch, only her girl friends, and they all thought it was very wonderful. The girl herself thought it was wonderful, she said "Oh thank you" and paid him some money, I think it was a five-dollar bill.

He was tired, he drew his arm across his forehead, it was a gesture my father used to make. His face looked older than I thought it was. For some reason I thought of him looking in a mirror and pricking himself with a pin. The girls walked away and I was the only one left. I felt very frightened for some reason. The backs of my knees got cold and wet, and under my arms I could feel that I was wet, out of nowhere. "I don't have any money," I said, "Excuse me," I said, and ran away.

I didn't meet my friends at the record store.

When I got home my mother yelled at me: ... *do you hang out? ... your father'n you joy-riding, laughing at me behind my back?* I stammered and told her I was at the Mall shopping and she said *Liar! Slut!* and I said, I said to her something that flew into my head to help me, I said something I could not have made up so fast, I said that a lady at the Mall was selling pots and vases and ashtrays and that she'd asked about her—

about telephoning—and my mother believed this and calmed down and said she was sorry. As soon as she quieted down she was always all right, she always said she was sorry.

In March one day Sandy and I were alone and trying on slacks in *Princess Ann* where there are the metal tubings and neon lights and amplified records, and Sandy bought something, so the saleslady was nice and asked if we were sisters, we looked alike—we both have long straight brown hair and are the same size—but we said no, we giggled and said no, but afterward I thought about it and started to cry. Sandy wasn't my sister. She went out through *Lingard's* and I went out the other way, because it's closer to Pine Woods where I live, and I was crying, I felt very strange, I wasn't sad but I was crying, I couldn't even see where I was walking but bumped into some damn big-mouth pushing a shopping cart from the *Kwik-Shop,* where she had groceries and a kid piled in, and she told me to look out where I was going.

"Go to hell," I said, and ran out.

It was that spring that the boy in *Meiker's* went crazy or whatever he did. He was Terry Bowman's sister's financé, a boy back from school at the University, working at the record store full-time; they said he was back for Easter vacation but he stayed home, he didn't go back. I don't know much about it. He was wearing a camouflage shirt and a buckskin vest and jeans and we liked him because he didn't mind how long we stayed in the listening booths, but I didn't know him or joke around with him, I was too young for him, he never bothered with me . . . I wasn't able to see what he did, because of the crowd jammed in there. I came over with some girls from school, it was about four-thirty and pretty crowded, and all of a sudden there was this loud funny conversation or argument, and it turned out the boy was arguing with the manager, but he was arguing too loud, in a funny way, and there was a record going full blast—The Ultimate, a new single of theirs—but you could hear him anyway, his voice going higher and higher. I couldn't see very well, I was way in front of the store. Somebody said that he had a gun, he was waving a gun around, but I couldn't see for sure, then the Mall police came—one of them was even on the little motor-scooter they use for patrolling the parking lots—and we had to leave. Terry Bowman is in our grade but she wouldn't talk about it and was mad if anybody asked her about it, but it said in the paper that he had a real gun but without any bullets and that he had threatened to kill the manager, then he had threatened to kill himself, and had pressed the barrel of the gun against his stomach and pulled the trigger, but nothing happened . . . but Terry said the newspapers were lying and were going to be sued. So I don't know what happened. It was very strange, I didn't see him really with any gun and yet I remembered him with a gun and I even heard the click of the trigger when he pulled it, like it really had happened, and I could remember it in my mind.

Then I thought about the way I had entered the Mall—through Entrance 13—and I wondered if that was why, it was bad luck, and I must never take that way in again. . . .

In June, a Thursday afternoon, I came over alone across Mercer Boulevard and through Lot C, and instead of going in through Entrance 13 I went over to 12, which is by a hardware store and *Dean's Flowers,* and inside I saw that artist again. . . . There he was, with his things set up, but no customers. Maybe everyone was used to him by now. He had three sketches propped up on the orange bench, and a fourth one that had fallen over but he didn't notice, and he was standing there, by his easel, looking at women shoppers who walked by, but they didn't bother with him or if they did they just glanced at him and then away. A few of them walked faster, by him. His hair was longer than before but the ends were broken-off, and it was that funny mixture of colors as if it had gotten bleached by the sun unevenly, so that he looked out of balance. His head hung over toward the right, anyway. He had the same little frazzled beard; he kept pulling at the hairs, stroking them, while he waited for somebody to look at him and maybe smile, but nobody did. I stood watching him. I was standing back against the *Fanny Farmer's* window, watching.

After a while he looked over and saw me.

"I don't have five dollars!" I cried. I was very frightened.

He started to smile, then stopped. I wondered if he recognized me: but he didn't seem to. He smiled again. He cupped his mouth and said, I should come over and have my portrait done, I was so pretty, only five dollars and I could give it to my boy friend or my mother or—

"I don't have any money!" I said.

"Three dollars!" he shouted.

He laughed, it was like a joke, just teasing. I laughed. I was going red in the face, I hated that because I could never stop it, but I laughed anyway, and came over by him and pretended to be inspecting the other drawings, like I had never seen them before. He hung over me and was pulling at his beard, saying I was so pretty, my boy friend would love a picture of me—wouldn't he?—only five dollars and it would be treasured forever and ever—

"You said three dollars. You said I could have it for three dollars."

"Did I say that?" he laughed. "Okay. It's a deal. Your portrait for three dollars marked down from five—okay? Okay?"

Then I thought: I would give the drawing to my mother.

I would write *Love, Doreen* on it and give it to her.

The artist hung over me and he smelled of complicated things—something chalkish and dry—and a smell of his hair—and his breath was warm and ticklish. So I said yes. He said something that might have been *Thanks!* but I couldn't quite hear it, then he had me sit on the edge of the flower-bed, now there were pots of mums back again—white mums that had been sprayed partly blue—and he arranged my skirt and had me sit with my hands in my lap and last of all he held my face between his hands, lightly, to adjust it so I would not be unbalanced. "Pretty girl, pretty girl, prettyprettypretty," he murmured, but he was not really looking at me; he stared down into my face and through it, balancing my face, with his two hands on my cheeks.

Then he stepped back to his easel and began to sketch me.

A few people stopped to watch, but I ignored them. My face was hot. It was hot to my hairline and down at the back of my neck, beneath my long hair, but after a while I felt the embarrassment drain away, I sat there with my hands clasped in my lap, calmed-down, quiet, grateful that I had worn such a nice dress to school that day—a nice color, I mean, blue-green that goes well with my eyes. I just sat there and stared back at him, at his face, but I didn't really see him, the way he didn't really see me, we just gazed at each other, we were peaceful, shoppers passed around behind him and glanced at me and there were a few kids, maybe kids I knew, but I didn't bother to look at them. I would write *Love, Doreen* on it; I would give it to my mother.

From a distance I could hear music, piped into the Mall, and voices of people going by, and I could see the stream of people behind him, out of the corner of my eyes I could see more people, but I didn't unfasten my gaze to see who they were; I didn't want to look at them. The artist switched pieces of chalk, from one hand to the other. A few times he paused to draw his arm across his face, as if he were sweating or nervous, but I didn't really see him. I just sat there. I knew a face was being drawn there, on that piece of paper, paper with nothing on it, and that it would be my face: I would sign it *Love, Doreen.*

When he was finished with it he snapped his long hair back and grinned and said, "Complete!" He brought it to show to me; his hand was shaking. I knew he was afraid of something and I was afraid too. "Very pretty! Very pretty girl!" he muttered. I stared at the sketch. *It wasn't me.* I couldn't say anything, I just stared at it, I felt my insides sink . . . it wasn't me, the face wasn't mine, it looked almost like me but it was the wrong face . . . the eyes were wrong. . . . "It's a perfect likeness," the artist said nervously. "Boy, they'll love that at home. That's gotta get framed." He hung over me, he must have been afraid I wouldn't accept it, I could feel how my face was tired-out from being drawn and stared at and now so disappointed, seeing this.

The face in the sketch was a girl's face, but she was older than I am. She had funny angular eyes, farther apart than mine. The hair was exactly the right color, but it seemed to grow up out of the scalp so that you could see it, it didn't look right. It almost looked right, but not exactly right. I don't know. I was blinking fast, afraid I would cry. The artist was scratching his neck, very nervous now, and saying something about a real bargain for only three dollars . . . he knew my parents would like it . . . anybody would like it. . . .

He had made the mouth too red. The upper lip looked swollen. The face was pretty, it was a pretty face, yes, except for the eyes which looked sort of old, and scared, and the outline of the eyes was a dark brown, not like my own eyes, where the lashes were almost blond. But it was sort of nice. I wiped the corners of my eyes with a kleenex and tried to laugh, I was so disappointed but couldn't tell him why, and when I happened to look up at him I saw that he was afraid of what had happened; he couldn't control it now.

"C'n get a nice frame right at *Newberry's*," he said, swallowing.

So I looked at it again and told myself *Yes, that's it, that's me,* and I paid him the three dollars and said

240

how wonderful the drawing was, that he was a very wonderful artist, and he folded the three dollar bills up and put them away, up under the big smock he was wearing. He had heavy blond eyebrows that seemed to grow together, over his nose. He tried to smile; he pulled at the hairs of his beard. He told me to be sure and get a nice frame, a nice frame would make all the difference in the world, and I thanked him again and said it looked just like me, and he said Thanks!—and I should tell my girl friends, he could maybe give them bargains too—

I walked away, looking at the picture, looking at the eyes, and almost bumped into people. I went out by the *Kwik-Shop* and *Doubleday's*. It must have been raining out because there were puddles on the sidewalk and in the parking lot, but thank God the rain had stopped, the drawing wouldn't get wet. I ran across the lot to the road and across that to the street that leads back into where we live and when I got home it was only five-thirty. At first I didn't think she was home. I said, "Mother? Mother?" walking around downstairs and then upstairs, the way I do, and then I heard her say something, and went in the bedroom where she was lying on top of the bed, with the lights out.

She switched the bedside light on.

"What? What happened?" she said. "I've been fighting a cold all day."

Her voice was hoarse. Her head sounded stuffed-up. She stared at me and her eyes were watering. "What time is it?" she said. While she looked for her watch I got a pen from the dressing table and wrote *Love, Doreen,* on the drawing, and showed it to her. She stared at it. Then she took it out of my hands. "Is this for me? Is this a present for me?" she said. She stared at it, then up at me. Her eyes were sore-looking. She had been fighting a cold all week; her face looked tired. "Why, this is a present for me, it's you giving yourself back to me," she said, trying to smile, "but you look just like me...."

241

She looked from the drawing, to me, and back to the drawing again.

I was very nervous, I kept thinking she might get mad or rip it up or laugh at it. Or she might even start to cry: she cried sometimes, so hard and so long. . . . The backs of my knees got wet, my knees were shaking. Like the artist, his hands shaking so you could see them, and he couldn't hide, couldn't stop you from seeing. . . . My mother was staring at the portrait. I was afraid she would laugh or tear it up or cry. Then she looked at me, over the top of the paper, looking from the girl in the drawing to me and back again. Her eyes were blurry, the sharpness I was afraid of was veiled, and she said:

"Thank you, Doreen."

The
Madwoman

Late one afternoon in January, a man and a woman were together in a car parked high above the river, about seven miles north of the city, when someone came running toward them—cutting through the sparse grove of pines they believed shielded them from the highway. They came here often: parked for an hour or so, not far from a drop-off of about a hundred feet. Below, the river flowed choppily to the east, back toward town. On the river-bank were a few junked cars, cast-off sofas and refrigerators, other debris lightly covered with snow. In winter it grew dark early, before five. Then the lights of the radio-television station tower a few miles away would come into view, the woman would notice them, discomforted, aware that it was getting late, thinking that the tower's lights were always there but invisible because of daylight: like stars, always there but invisible because of daylight. She had not yet noticed the tower's lights when the child came running toward their car.

She and Wesley moved apart.

It was a girl of about twelve or thirteen. She would have knocked on Wesley's window except he had already opened the door. "Mister? Mister?" the girl cried. "Could you help me?—I need some help— My mother—" Wesley tried to calm her down: got out to stand beside her, tall and paternal, even touching one of her shoulders. Arlene was not so nervous as she might have expected herself to be. She slid across the seat to see what was wrong. The girl was frightened, out of breath, stammering something about her mother—her mother was sick and needed help—could they help? Her face was small and round and childish, framed by a parka of some synthetic fluorescent-orange material; she had red hair, pale red-blond eyebrows and lashes, extraordinarily fair skin and freckles. She looked ghostly, vulnerable. Wesley tried to make out what was wrong but the girl kept repeating that her mother was sick, awful sick, could they come help?

"If you could just drive me back there, mister—"

So Wesley drove the girl home.

She sat in the back seat and Arlene tried to question her, gently. If it was an emergency, shouldn't they call the hospital?—the sheriff's department? Was there a telephone at the girl's house? But the girl answered these questions in a vague, shallow voice, shaking her head as if none of this mattered—would not even meet Arlene's gaze. It was Wesley she was interested in. "If you could just help me, mister—" she kept repeating. Arlene seemed to remember her from somewhere: Saturday afternoons at the shopping mall just outside town, a girl strolling with other girls her own age, their children's faces subtly disguised by newer, more stylized faces caked and colored and pencilled in above the old, laughing shrilly together, in jeans and boots and jackets like the one the girl was wearing now. Today she wore no make-up. Her eyelashes and eyebrows were thin, nearly colorless. She had hazel-green eyes blurred by tears, set close together; her fingernails had been polished, a bright peach-pink, and she kept picking at her teeth, not quite looking at Arlene.

"I got to get some help—got to get some help—"

She lived down a side-road about a mile away. An old farm, the frame house set well back from the road, a narrow rutted lane, fields on either side gone wild—patches of snow—a few melancholy, broken hollyhocks in the front yard. The outbuildings, including the main barn, were evidently no longer used; their roofs were partly rotted, collapsed. The house itself was not in poor condition, but rather ugly—asphalt siding only on its front—junk piled up on the veranda. No one was around. Arlene looked from side to side—only the empty snowy fields broken by shrubs or tall weeds. It was very quiet.

The girl tried to talk Wesley into going to the door by himself—knocking on the door. If he gave a good hard knock—thumped on the door—

"You'd better come with me," he said.

"Nothing will happen—she'll let you in—" the girl muttered.

But Wesley refused to go to the door alone.

Arlene tried to calm the girl down, tried to catch her eye. But she jumped out of the car and ran up onto the porch and began pounding on the door. "Ma! Hey you! Ma! I got some people! You better open this goddam door—I got some people—some man is here from town!"

She opened the door herself: it looked as if no one was there, in the doorway. She turned back to Wesley, gesturing angrily—indicating that he should join her. So he got out, rather apprehensively. He murmured to Arlene *Oh Christ.*

At first it seemed that no one was home.

The girl led them into a kitchen. It was quite large, with a high ceiling. Things had gone wrong: the wallpaper was rain-smudged, the pipes were exposed and looked rusty, in places the linoleum had worn through and the floor-boards were exposed. The windows must have been poorly fitted, since it was drafty in the room. "Ma! I got some people!" the girl cried. But she hung back. The place smelled stale, stuffy, in spite of the cold.

A woman entered the kitchen—she walked in unhurried, as if nothing were wrong. Disheveled, smelling of liquor: Arlene could smell her across the room.

She was wrapping something around her. She wore a flannel bathrobe, a pale beige with shiny buttons and sash, and over this she was wrapping a shawl or a man's sweater, something large and bulky, of black wool, not very clean. The woman's eyes swung from her daughter to Wesley to Arlene. "... What? What's this noise?" the woman asked. She stopped. She stared at Wesley. He was about to explain when the woman herself interrupted him, asking him who the hell he was and what the hell was going on, him barging in like this. ... Didn't he know there was a law? He began to explain that the girl had told them she needed help, but the girl interrupted him, screaming at her mother—something about the police on their way, the sheriff, people from town—she was going to be arrested and dragged to the hospital and thrown in the ward for crazy people where she belonged.

The woman slapped the girl—so quickly, with so little effort, that Arlene could not quite believe it had happened. The girl began to cry. The woman turned back to Wesley, grinning angrily at him. "Who's crazy? Who's accusing who of what?"

"Your daughter came to our car—"

"Where? What car? Who are you? What the hell's going on?"

The girl took Wesley's arm. "Listen, you know what? She's crazy. I mean she's *crazy*. She wants to kill us all. I get home from school and she's in there laying in bed smoking—started a fire last week like that—told me she didn't give a—"

"Hey, who are you?" the woman asked Wesley. She turned to Arlene, staring. "... some school-teachers? Are you school-teachers, from the school?"

Arlene thought suddenly that it was very funny: she would start to laugh.

It was funny, it was irresistible. The woman was a few years older than Arlene, in her late thirties. She stood hugging herself, in a filthy bathrobe and a sweater, staring pop-eyed at them, exaggerating her surprise. She did not even appear to be drunk. While her daughter wept and spoke of "starting a fire"—"going crazy on purpose"—the woman looked from Wesley to Arlene and back again, like a comedienne, like someone in a movie, obviously enjoying all the confusion. She was strangely attractive, in spite of her grins and grimaces, her hair much lighter than her daughter's, very red, a mess of curls. And she had the red-head's pale, pale complexion, gone sallow now, coarse. What had happened to her hair?—a permanent wave, done at home? It looked awful. Small bouncy sausage-like curls, as if her head were alive. Arlene stared at her. Then gradually she felt sick, sickened: the tiny curls reminded her of worms.

"Your daughter said you need help," Wesley told her. "Is there anything we can do? I'd be happy to—"

"My daughter," the woman said slowly, "is a liar.... She's a little bitch of a liar, aren't you? Bobbi. Bobbi-bitch. Huh, aren't you a liar?... Look at her hiding behind you, what the hell is she so afraid of? What's she been telling you two?"

"She said you were sick and needed help," Wesley said. He spoke in a voice Arlene had heard a few times—level, controlled, kindly. Or perhaps it was the pretense of kindness, the forced pretense, disguising his real terror. He was managing not to step away as the woman advanced, though Arlene knew he must want nothing more than to jump away from her; a sane, practical man, he must want nothing more than to get out of this house. The girl was babbling, weeping. She was in fact hiding behind Wesley, awkwardly, telling him that her mother had been crazy off and on for years, that she was going to burn the house down some night, she'd been threatening to do it and would, she'd wait till very late at night and—and they would all die, would be burned up—

The woman laughed. "What a joke!... Just look at this," she said, opening the sweater suddenly, stretching both her arms out as far as she could and shifting

247

her weight so that her abdomen protruded—it looked as if she might be pregnant, the belly just beginning to swell. It was round and hard and fierce, pushing out through the soiled robe. "If I'm sick now and then who's got a better right, huh? Who's telling tales on who? There's a law against kids informing on their parents, telling lies around town, there's a law against strangers barging in without knocking and without—without a warning or prior notice— Did somebody call the sheriff? Is that son of a bitch really coming?"

"I don't think anybody called the sheriff," Wesley said. He was very confused. His face had gone ruddy in patches. "Your daughter only said...."

"I never tried to burn the house down," the woman said slowly.

She spoke to both Wesley and Arlene now: the three of them adults, reasonable. For several minutes she told th~m a complicated story, with many interruptions and digressions, and though Arlene tried to listen to it, to make sense of the words, she found herself unable to concentrate on the story: the woman's hair, her coarse, clever face, her manner of being both logical and savagely whimsical... her striking eyes, which were larger than her daughter's and far more attractive... a peculiar green that seemed to shift its hue, now bronze, bronze-green, now coppery-green... nearly yellow, now... nearly golden... green-gold, greeny-gold, and again a light lime-green.... Arlene found herself wanting to laugh, it was so absurd. But if she were to laugh, might it not come out as a shriek of terror or rage? The woman held them all captive there in her smelly drafty kitchen, explaining to Wesley, mainly to Wesley, that if it came to people being sick or burning things down, who had a better right than the people who owned them, huh?... Did he think he could barge in on them and boss them around? "... anyway the upstairs is closed off, it's cold as hell up there. Nobody's up there. You think it smells like somebody died up there or in here, well, it's in the cellar... the crawl-space... it isn't anything of ours but maybe a ground-hog or rabbit or something that crawled under and died, the way they do. The goddam things. Here, come in and look at the bedroom. There's nothing to hide. I'll show you the mattress, strip the sheets off it you want me to, sure there's burn-marks but your own mattress probably has them, huh?—and nobody barges in to arrest you. Come in here."

She pulled Wesley along, forced him to accompany her into the other room. Arlene went no farther than the doorway. It was messy, as one might anticipate, the same water-stained wallpaper, clothes and towels lying around, a pile of what must have been dirty laundry partly on a chair and partly on the floor, having slid down. A ginger-striped cat lay on it, watching them. The cat was watchful but unalarmed; it did not move at all.

Wesley said a few more words, and managed to get away from the woman. He was very red now, scratching nervously at his throat, really quite miserable. A tall man, with a lean, trim figure, an air of being both gracious and rather commandeering, he seemed confused, apologetic, repeating again and again that the woman's daughter had sought them out—said there was an emergency—they had only wanted to help—but if nothing was wrong, if nothing was wrong then—

"People are always sorry after they insult you," the woman said.

But she did not let them escape: she stood with her arms folded tightly below her breasts, swaying, smiling at them. She invited them to stay for a drink. Or coffee. It was the least she could do, she said, under the circumstances. Her daughter had dragged them in on a false alarm. The bitch: lying little bitch. But the girl couldn't help it. She was slow, slow in the head. *Mentally retarded....* The girl had backed away; she stood by the kitchen door sniffing. Oddly, she did not protest. The woman insisted they stay for a drink. She even gestured toward Arlene, one woman to another: Arlene caught sight of the chipped polish, peachy-pink.

Wesley explained that they must leave.

"A drink, huh? Maybe a drink? To thank you for your kindness?...He left some Scotch around the house, I bet I could locate it fast if I tried...." She smiled at them all the while, her expression both sullen and sly. Arlene had not noticed before how thick the woman's neck was—the tendons unnaturally defined, tough. Muscular. If it came to a fight, to wrestling together.... If that woman flung her arms wide again and went after one of them.... If she stopped her babble and went abruptly still, her gaze fixed on one of them, perhaps on Arlene, what would happen? Arlene stared at her. She could not have defended herself. The woman was mad: this was madness. She was mad. Arlene stood in the presence of madness. Never, never had she known what it was before: now she stood in its presence, utterly helpless. Her lover was helpless, mumbling about the time...trying to explain that they must leave.... The woman with the hair that looked dyed, it was so red, simply smiled at them, teasing them, backing them to the door. Her hair: the little sausage-curls, worm-like curls. Arlene would remember them. She would remember the power of the mad: their power of self, their cruelty. Whining relentless voices. Tightly folded arms. The muscular tendons of the neck, the bitter mock-delighted smile....

Finally they managed to escape. The girl went with them, crouched in the back seat of the car. Her mother stood on the porch, watching. She smiled.

Arlene stared at her: she expected the woman to shout or wave or to make some gesture. *Come back again soon! Come visit again soon!*

"Your mother seems very disturbed," Wesley said. "Where's your father?"

The girl snickered.

"You can let me off here," she said.

"Where? Here?...Wouldn't you like me to drive you to town?" Wesley asked. "To, to see someone?...There's a mental health clinic at the hospital, isn't there? Isn't there, Arlene?... Maybe you could...."

"Here, this is great," the girl said. "I got a girl friend lives here."

"But.... Where's your father?"

"Look, stop the car. I don't have to answer your goddam questions," the girl said.

Wesley braked to a stop. The girl got out. Before slamming the door, she told them: "...saw you guys lots of times parked over there... school-bus goes right by...." Her voice was intimate and nudging and sullen, as if the two of them had somehow betrayed her.

They watched her walk away: up a cinder driveway to a small one-storey house, not much more than a shanty. On both sides of this house were fields of broken corn-stalks. The girl did not glance back. Her orange jacket was the only color in that landscape, now shifting into twilight: it glowed, gleamed, a vulgar merry color.

Wesley took the Old River Road. He and Arlene were both silent. Arlene pressed her fingertips against her eyes, realizing suddenly that she was exhausted—she had ventured too far, had risked too much. It was hopeless. They passed the radio tower, on the left. Neither spoke.... *Coward,* Arlene wanted to whisper, *damned coward... all of you....* But she could not accuse him, not now. She said nothing. How exhausted she was, how many years she had known him!... and never, never would he leave his wife, never would he dare to leave her or to alter anything, anything at all, knowing what might leap into the visible world, should the tyranny of the invisible world be challenged. She could not accuse him. It was not death she feared—not death, really, that anyone feared—but the maelstrom of what was not known, could not be controlled, should the rites of ordinary life be violated. She knew her lover was as drained as she, and more humiliated: it was he, after all, who was married.

DOUBLE TRAGEDY STRIKES
TENNESSEE HILL FAMILY

—*Earl pushed the* newsclipping away, violently. Something was knocked over and spilled on the table. The clipping had been Scotch-taped on a piece of cardboard the size of an ordinary sheet of tablet paper and he pushed it away from him as soon as he saw the headline.

He sat for a while, his mouth working in silence. His body had gone cold. He listened in terror for the sound of someone crying—himself crying—but could hear nothing. *I don't have to read that clipping,* he thought.

Earl Wild had come downstairs on an ordinary weekday morning—Thursday morning, a harmless day—and when he looked over the swinging doors of the coffee shop he saw that it was too crowded, so he went across the lobby and into the bar. He sometimes came in here to be alone for breakfast; the "cocktail lounge" was shabby and comfortable in the light of eleven o'clock on a Thursday morning. He liked it. He sat in the first booth, on a seat of black leather that was slightly scratched and gave in beneath his weight, always in the same places. He had had a good night's sleep and he was hungry.

Sonny had peered in to make sure it was him, and Earl said, "Breakfast," in a flat, twangy radio voice, which was his idea of mocking the voice of a popular local radio announcer. Sonny nodded and disappeared.

He was a dim-skinned man of no special age, part Indian and part Negro, either moronic or carefully acting that part. Earl had had theories about Sonny when he had first come to live in the hotel a few years ago, but after the first week he had stopped noticing Sonny.

Sonny returned with a cup of black coffee and the morning paper and two letters for Earl. "Thanks, Sonny," Earl said, not looking at him but at the front page of the paper. But there wasn't much news—he'd heard the big story a few minutes before on the radio, a grand jury's indictment of some highway commission men over in Missouri. He wasn't interested in that. He looked at the smaller envelope, which he knew to be a bill; he had noticed the little oval window right away. *God damn it,* he thought. There was his own name behind that oval of transparent paper, no mistake about it: Earl Wild, The Cattleman's Hotel, 667 Main Street, Kansas City, Kansas. The bill was from Butler's Department Store and it was for $89.98. Earl made a contemplative, cynical *tsking* sound, as if he believed someone was watching him, but really he was not angry. He laid the bill carefully out on the table so that it would be the first thing Violet would see.

Like a clever machine his mind registered for him the last figure in his savings deposit book—$9200. That wasn't bad. And the figure in the checking account book was $455, which wasn't bad either. He kept both books in a safe in his office; the temptation for Violet to look through his things, to study these books might be too great.

He took his first swallow of coffee, grateful for that hot, bitter taste that was the beginning of his public, external day—just as the tart taste of mouthwash was the beginning of his private, physical day—and turned his attention to the other envelope, which was fat, stuffed, held together by transparent adhesive tape. He supposed this was a fan letter or a letter from someone who wanted a job at the radio station or a chance to appear on the Earl Wild show, or maybe advice or help or an audition somewhere. Letters like this came nearly every day and Earl Wild read them with care and sympathy. He even nodded a little, as if the writer of the letter might somehow be watching him. When people stopped him on the street he always spent at least five minutes talking to them, smiling and nodding, then a brisk goodbye handshake and best wishes. *Earl Wild was so friendly to me.... Earl Wild wished me good luck and he really meant it....* He always answered letters right away, poking out words on the old typewriter in the radio station office; his replies usually began, *I am very happy and honored to be in possession of your recent letter.* And he was very happy, and honored. He remembered how many years it had taken him to become Earl Wild.

This letter was addressed to "Earl Wild," with quotation marks around the name, c/o Radio Station WKKW, Kansas City, Kansas; the handwriting was slanted and crabbed, the quotation marks fussy. Earl wondered why those quotation marks, as if Earl Wild wasn't his real name—which it wasn't, but who would know that? There was no return address. He held the fat envelope up to the light and tried to make out the postmark. It was faint and smudged. He could read only "U.S. Postal" clearly. Then he studied the handwriting again and saw that it was familiar: that was his mother's handwriting.

He dropped the envelope.

Another swallow of coffee, very hot. It burned his throat all the way down, but he hardly noticed. He stared at the envelope, the handwriting, asking himself why he hadn't recognized it before. His mind seemed to be playing a joke on him. When he peered at the postmark again he could make the word *Tenn.* Tennessee. This was a letter from his mother.

Very slowly, he opened the envelope and watched himself open it, his hands not trembling. It was stuffed with a number of items—most of them snapshots, warped and curled, and a large piece of cardboard, folded awkwardly in half, with a newsclipping taped on it, and a piece of stiff pink paper. Somehow all this slipped out of the envelope and through his fingers. Earl sat for a few careful seconds, studying these things. He felt that he was in terrible danger.

"Here y'are, Mr. Wild," Sonny said primly. He brought in the first part of Earl's breakfast, which was the same every morning—a small glass of scarlet fruit juice, corn flakes with sugar already sprinkled on them, back in the kitchen, and lots of milk. Earl looked at the food and felt a thrill of satisfaction—how normal this day would be, after all—and then a deeper, more profound thrill of nausea.

"Mr. Wild, something wrong?"

"No. Put it down. Thanks."

Earl waited for him to leave. He was aware this morning of Sonny's dark, muddy, bumpy face, the way his lips were pursed tightly together as if to declare that he minded his own business, he had no comment to make on anything. Even his breathing was tight and restrained, self-conscious. Earl watched him to see if he was looking at the things spread out on the table, but he seemed to see nothing.

When Sonny left Earl reached out mechanically for the glass of juice and drained it, without tasting it. His eyes were leaping everywhere, looking for a word, a phrase, looking for his own name. But there was no accompanying letter, not even a note. He looked under the sheet of pink paper and saw a newspaper photograph, loose, and another one, also loose, but he did not allow himself to focus on what was in the pictures.

. . . a curling snapshot, people at a picnic table. . . .

. . . the back of another snapshot of the same size, dated June 1954. . . .

. . . a dim underdeveloped snapshot, his mother's face peering out of it. . . .

. . . two rows of people crowded together, one man very tall, Earl's father. . . .

. . . an upside-down newspaper clipping, a tangled

picture, the wheels of a car or a truck and a man's legs, a man's leather jacket. . . .

Earl watched his fingers unfold the piece of cardboard.

DOUBLE TRAGEDY STRIKES
TENNESSEE HILL FAMILY

He knocked it away. Some of the snapshots were pushed across the table, and the bowl of cornflakes was overturned. Earl's mouth worked silently. He was afraid he would make a sound, that people out in the lobby would come to the doorway to look. After a few minutes he took out a handkerchief and unfolded it carefully and tried to soak up the milk. The corn flakes were soggy and clung to the table, like small sucking things, bloodsuckers or snails, things under rocks in creekbeds; Earl felt the panic of nausea, wiping them up. *No. I'm not going to be sick,* he thought.

When Sonny came back the mess was just about gone. "Had an accident," Earl said. Sonny set down his tray and wiped the table with his apron, then went out again and returned with a big green sponge from the kitchen. The sponge was already stained. Sonny cleaned everything up and wiped the snapshots and papers, his lips pursed tightly together. He then served Earl the next part of his breakfast, a plate of three fried eggs and a half dozen sausages, and a plate with several pieces of toast on it. "I'll bring you some more coffee right away, Mr. Wild," he said.

Earl began eating the eggs, chewing fast. He wanted to get this food down fast before something happened to him. He picked up the sausages in his fingers, one by one, and dipped them into the ketchup on his plate. As he ate his eyes wandered helplessly around the things on the table, which were now in a new arrangement. Sonny had placed the snapshots with their faces up, though not necessarily turned so that Earl would have to see them right side up. He had made sure that nothing was touching, so the things could dry. This time Earl saw something he had not noticed before, a page ripped out of a pulp magazine. It looked familiar. He hesitated before picking it up. But if it was in a magazine it could not be about his family; it could not be dangerous.

THE GREENSBORO BOYS BIG SUCCESS AT KANSAS CITY. It was a large photograph of a country and western band, The Greensboro Boys, standing with Earl himself, and the man who owned WKKW, Mr. Marion Odom. Mr. Odom was a big, rangy, white-haired man, Earl's boss for many years. Earl knew the caption explained that the Greensboro Boys had had a big success at a show in Kansas City, backed by the radio station; they were pictured here being greeted and welcomed to the city by "Mr. Earl Wild and Mr. Marion Odom of WKKW." The picture had appeared in *Country & Western* maybe a year, a year and a half ago, and Earl had a copy of it somewhere in the office.

So that was how they'd found out where he was, he thought.

He finished the eggs. One more sausage to get down—he wiped up the rest of the ketchup with it, but paused with it halfway to his mouth. It was cold and greasy. He put it back on his plate. Then he saw the toast—forgot to eat it with the eggs—he touched one of the pieces with his forefinger and it was cold. He was not hungry but he thought it might be wise to eat. This was his normal breakfast. His body might be put off balance if he did not eat right. But the toast and the sausage were cold and he hated cold things.

Sonny came back with a pot of coffee.

"Thanks, Sonny," Earl said. He noticed that his voice was hoarse. He cleared his throat and said in his normal voice, "Thanks, Sonny. You can take all this away."

"Okay, Mr. Wild," Sonny said.

It was good to have the table clear of plates—all that food, the smeared egg yolk, the bright splash of ketchup. Now Earl Wild could concentrate.

His mind worked clean and unafraid as a machine. It told him what he could do next: knock all the things off the table and walk away.

Or, scoop them all up into the newspaper and throw everything out, in the big garbage bin at the rear of the hotel.

Or, to make sure he wouldn't be drawn back to retrieve them, he could burn everything, himself. Burn them in the metal wastebasket up in his room.

That would be the best method of disposal. He would burn them, watch them turn into wispy harmless ashes. The hell with them.

He glanced at his watch without really noting the time, wondering how long he had before Violet came in. But he didn't quite think this thought, it broke in two and he didn't complete it. He didn't think Violet's name, only the blurred shape of her, a presence like one might feel in a dream, but not see, and which one could hold off magically for a while.

So that was how they had found him out, he thought. "Earl Wild." The photograph showed him looking just like himself, no hiding the fact that it was him, Earl himself, grinning out into the camera. He was wearing an expensive silk shirt with his initials, E W, woven onto the pocket in a very complicated script, and the white string tie that was a trademark of his, and the same leather belt with the big silver buckle he was wearing at the moment, which cut into his stomach a little when he sat down. Earl himself.

He shivered and discovered that he was cold—the sweat on his body had turned cold. He poured himself fresh coffee. A smooth film on the surface of the cold coffee, broken, dissolved, by the hot coffee that rushed into it. He drank and was grateful for the bitter heat.

Should he look at one of the snapshots? Just one?

He picked up the one of the picnic. From the old box camera, a picture Earl had taken himself. Of course he recognized it, he had taken it himself. It had not turned out clearly—blurred by sunlight on both sides, cloudy misty columns that all but annihilated the faces of his grandmother and his brother Ronnie, but showed the rest of the family clear enough. Lots of bare arms, elbows, on the table; lots of empty and half-empty bottles. Beer bottles, Coke bottles. Paper plates. Earl stared at the snapshot and felt his eyes start to mist over.

His little brother Ronnie, four or five years old, wearing a striped T-shirt that the glare had partly annihilated; only one of his eyes was really clear—the right eye, grave and staring. It was a shock to see him that small, just a little boy. Next to him was someone in a sports shirt—that was Uncle Owen, Earl's father's brother, biting into a sandwich and not looking at the camera. His big bald head, his big nose. Probably drunk. He had died a long time ago of cancer of the throat. Earl couldn't remember the year now, though he could have remembered it if he tried. But he didn't want to remember. Someone was on the other side of him, out of sight, maybe Earl's cousin Bob, and then there was Earl's younger sister Mary Anne, holding a pop bottle up toward the camera, grinning. Ten years old, about. Her hair was anywhich-way and her blouse looked far too big for her, probably one of Nancy's handed-down blouses. Her shadowy, homely face, her boyish grin. Next to her, looking bored, was Nancy, with her long curled-under hair; about fourteen, fifteen. She'd grown up fast. That bitch. Moved to Memphis with her husband, then to Florida to the "Gold Coast," as she called it in postcards she'd sent back home. On the other side of Nancy there was a confusion of shapes, blurs, maybe the fir tree in the back yard, showing sunlight in strange slivers. Then . . . at the far end of the table . . . Earl's mother, ducked down almost out of sight, her arm out to ward the picture off, you could almost see her shaking her head, hear her saying *no, Earl don't you dare take that, you wait a minute Earl*— It was a poor picture of her, sexless and almost ugly, her hair skinned back against her head. Earl's father was standing beside her, a beer bottle in his hand. A half-smile, gone stiff and self-conscious; it would crack his face to smile normally, Earl thought. His father in those overalls, bare arms like hams, frizzy with hair. . . . Earl jerked his eyes off his father's face. On the left side of the table, Earl's aunt Evie, who was holding Earl's little brother in her lap, the baby that died the next winter; something like pneumonia. Evie looked very young. Next to her was her son Jason, Earl's cousin, and then Aunt Claudie, then Grandma, staring vacantly at the food on her plate, as if she hadn't known Earl was taking a picture. Sunken eyes, protruding ears, a flowered house dress much too big for her; that was Grandma Wheelwright, Earl's father's mother, who had lived with them . . . no, they had lived with her, it had been her house and her land. Earl stared at the old woman's face. *Jesus,* he thought suddenly, *she must be dead by now, she'd be so old. . . .*

Sonny came in again with more food, but Earl only half-noticed him. His vision was shaky with tears. Sonny said apologetically, "You want me to set this down here, Mr. Wild?" Earl nodded. He saw Sonny's long skinny dark hands setting down the grilled cheese sandwich and the bottle of Cott's, and for a second he couldn't think what you said to people; then he remembered. You said "Thank you" and that made them go away.

The cheese sandwich was open-faced, piled high with tomato and fat slices of onion and chili sauce. Earl wasn't hungry any more and he wasn't even going to try this. He pushed it aside. But the beer tasted all right; that would help. He took a few fast swallows and then pressed the cold bottle against his face.

. . . The snapshot of the picnic, those faces and tanned arms and the bottles and the glare. . . . Why did it frighten him so? Only a Fourth of July picnic. Only a snapshot. Yet he felt threatened, here, with invisible shapes that might force their way out of the snapshot and into the booth with him, crowding him, calling him by name. Their souls might leap out and surround him. . . . It was a shame, Earl thought, that the picture hadn't turned out better. It was the only record of that day, years ago. There could never be another picture of that day. He was sorry that he himself hadn't been in it, sitting in the middle of everyone, smiling a big smile for the camera. His pictures always turned out good. He had thick dark hair, like his father's; he was handsome, like his father. In spite of all the sourness and the drinking, his father had been a good-looking man. You could see that even from this blurred picture. But he had always worn those dirty overalls, and long underwear nine months of the year, with the top two or three buttons missing so that everyone had to look at his wooly chest-hair. Just like his own father, who'd died when Earl was a boy. Earl remembered the shame of driving to Knoxville with his father dressed like that. *Damn stubborn bastard,* Earl thought angrily.

His father had knocked him down in the driveway once, right in the mud. He had given Earl a crack on the head that had made his ear ring for days. *Damn bastard.* When Earl was twenty-two he took the pick-up truck out one night and deliberately crashed it into a tree on the highway, running it at fifteen miles an hour into the tree, and from there he had walked to Laurel and then hitched a ride to Knoxville and he had never looked back. That was that. The hell with all of them.

He reached out suddenly for another snapshot. He was so angry that nothing could frighten him now. This time he saw himself—skinny and shiny-faced, clutching his guitar, gaping at the camera while people walked in front of him. E W on the guitar. Yes, he remembered the guitar and he remembered himself, eighteen years old, at a jamboree in Snyder, Kentucky. His first show in an auditorium. He had been so nervous. . . . Skinny, frightened, with a glazed look about the eyes; not very good-looking, not in this picture. Earl's lips drew back into a tense, angry grin. Himself at the age of eighteen! He didn't know if he was embarrassed or if he wished, in a way, that he could be back inside that snapshot, back in Snyder, Kentucky twenty years ago. He flicked the snapshot aside.

The sheet of pink paper drew his eye. He unfolded it and recognized it at once: a page out of the album his mother and Mary Anne had kept. They had put snapshots and souvenirs and other things into the album. Mary Anne had written on this page, in dark green ink, in her laborious, perfect handwriting—that was about all she could do well, "penmanship" the only subject she could pass. Earl scanned the page—

Dear Mom,
I am writing to say hello & to let you know I am in good health & happy & doing O.K. I am eating right & people are very nice here. This Ft. Williams Texas where I am—

This was from a letter of his, Earl realized. Those were his words. Mary Anne had copied a letter of his into the book—his only letter after he had walked out that night—

This Ft. Williams Texas where I am is a nice town, the boarding house where I am staying is run by a nice lady, from Virginia herself, your age. I am real sorry about the fighting & things that got said & smashing the truck, but a rage came over me. I thought it best to keep going. Dont worry about me. Ronnie can have my guitar and other stuff. I hope you-know-who is over being so mad because I love him & am sorry, but I am not going to dwell on it. I love you & will write every week. This is a hard letter to write. All day Sunday today I have been writing it. I will be gone from this town when you get it, so no return address. Its better for me to keep going. Well I will close now & say love & God bless you to you & Grandma

& Mary Anne & Ronnie & you-know-who. I did
not mean to go into such a rage.

Love, your son
Earl

Earl's face reddened. He had never written again.
Never again. And, when he'd written that letter, he
had known he would never write again. The hell with
all of them, he'd thought happily; he was finished with
Tennessee! Sometimes he had composed letters to his
mother in his head and he had even made up two or
three songs that had to do with writing home: the best
one was "Just a Boy With a Wandering Soul," which
put tears into everyone's eyes, but no recording star
had ever picked it up. Which was rotten luck.

He examined the snapshot of his mother in the front
room of the house, a time-exposure shot he had taken
himself; it hadn't turned out quite right because his
mother had moved. Her face was blurred, tense and
benign at the same time. She sat with her hands in her
lap, very stiffly. Behind her on the wall was a picture
of some flowers, all blurred and underdeveloped. Earl
looked at her and felt his face heat up with shame.

He picked up another snapshot—his father in bed,
seen from an odd angle, the chin showing most. He
looked at it. No, it was a casket. His father was lying
in a casket; his father was dead. Earl blinked. He could
not understand. His father was much older than he
remembered, yet he was still his father, still with that
face—the strong stubborn jaw, the thick hair brushed
up from the forehead—

Earl pushed the picture away. He pressed the Cott's
bottle against his face.

Yes, he could feel her behind all this. *Her.* He could
feel her spirit, her will. With her graying, scanty hair,
her tired face, her tears that went so cheaply and never
changed anything. She had screamed for him to stop
fighting. *Don't hit him, he's out of his mind! He doesn't
know what he's doing!* But Earl couldn't stand his

father's bullying, couldn't stand being pushed around by him. She had told Earl that she didn't mind, she was used to his father, she didn't mind—Earl should let his father alone—

His mind jumped away from that body in the casket. If his father had just died recently, how old had he been...? Earl couldn't think clearly. He felt dizzy, sickened. He touched the cheese sandwich with his forefinger; it was cold. Not like food at all.

He felt suddenly their invisible shapes close to him, whispering at him. Earl! Earl!

No, he had not loved them. He had hated them. He had hated the house and the farm. The farm work. The animals. The pastures and the fields and the hazy mountains he'd had to look at all his life, dragging his eye out to them. He had hated *her* wistful frightened face, her homely face, her hair skinned back meekly against her skull, that tired, perplexed look she would give him, a half-smile that said *I don't mind being insulted, I can laugh at it, why can't you laugh at it too?* He had hated the giant horse-flies that hung around all winter, unkillable, and every tree and bend on the road to church, and school in Laurel where he had been kept back a year, and the red dust of the road in summer, the blazing sky, the blue line of the watershed.... *Love & God bless you to you & Grandma & Mary Anne & Ronnie & you-know-who....* Well, that was all a lie because he had hated them and hated having to love them and it would drive him mad to go back....

"What's wrong?"

Violet was leaning over him, staring right into his face.

"You look sick or something. Are you still mad? Can I sit down?"

Earl didn't move over. He looked up at her uncomprehendingly.

"Suit yourself, I'll sit over here," she said. "What's all this? What's this on the floor?" She picked up two more snapshots, a news clipping, the bill from Butler's. She glanced at the bill. "Are you mad about this, Earl? This was for my coat. I told you about it, the leopard-skin coat. Didn't I tell you about it? If you're mad please say so and don't play games. . . ."

Earl looked distractedly at her. Her words did not make sense.

Violet sat down and flicked her long streaked blond hair back. She was twenty-eight years old, with a broad sunny complacent face, her lips fashioned into a perpetual pout, in the style of a French movie star. She was very pretty and knew it. "What's all this stuff? Some mail?"

"Some things from home," Earl said.

"*Home?* Your home? You never told me you had a home," Violet said. "You mean a wife, or what?"

"Not a wife. No."

She scratched nervously at her throat. "You aren't lying to me, are you? I can take the truth. I don't have any illusions." Before Earl could stop her she picked up a handful of snapshots and leafed through them. "Who are all these people, your family? Who is *this?*" She showed him a snapshot he hadn't seen yet, one of Nancy and Mary Anne standing on the concrete abutment by the creek.

"My sisters."

"That one is very pretty, you sure she's your sister. . . .?" She squinted at it. Earl was very nervous. He didn't want her to say anything about his family. He was afraid he would grab her and do something terrible if she said the wrong words. She held up the picture of Earl at the jamboree. "This is nice. You were just a kid then, huh? Can I keep this? I'd like to keep this for myself. It would mean a lot to me."

Earl nodded vaguely.

"You got all this in the mail, just now? Who's it from? Did you read it all?"

Earl felt sick, disoriented. He had made a terrible mistake. He thought: *You made a terrible mistake.* But

266

he did not understand what the mistake was.

"Yes, I read through it. But I don't want to talk about it. I don't want to look at it and I don't want to talk about it," he said. He was leaning forward against the edge of the table to keep himself still. "So put those pictures down."

"Why, because you don't want me to see your wife? Is that it?"

"I don't have any wife."

"You look strange. You're lying to me."

"Put all those things down."

Violet held the snapshots and stared insolently at him *and he would go crazy if she told him something he did not want to know.* "Why, because there's some secret here? Something you don't want me to know back in Tennessee?"

Earl tried to hide his agitation. He knew he had made some terrible mistake but he could not think clearly enough to figure it out. "I don't want to talk about it," he said. He saw Violet's eyes drop to the pictures in her hand and he wanted suddenly to reach across the table and seize her, before she could see anything more.

"What's this, something from a newspaper? It looks like a picture of a wreck. What is this? What's *this?*" She held up the piece of cardboard with the clipping taped on it. Earl stared at her face and saw her eyes narrow, scanning the story and then scanning it again, her lips parted, her face blunt and open. And then the confused blinking of her eyes, the stricken dumb expression. . . . She looked at Earl. She said, in a whisper, "This is your family? Wheelwright?"

Earl could not speak. His mouth worked, silently, a terrible silence rising like rage in him. He drew breath but could not speak.

Violet laid everything carefully down. He saw the pity in her face, she was like an actress on television showing immediate sorrow, sympathy. If she said anything—if she told him— For a while she sat in silence,

267

meeting and then not meeting his gaze, looking around for something safe. Finally she picked up the bill from Butler's again. "*This* would have to come today," she said flatly. Earl did not reply; again he drew breath, but could not force himself to speak. "I'm sorry about this morning," Violet said carelessly, as if that were the reason for Earl's silence. They had had an argument. Earl had discovered her pouring the Listerine down the sink, because she didn't like its taste and wanted to buy something else, a sweeter-tasting brand that Earl hated, and they couldn't buy the new mouthwash until the old mouthwash was used up. Violet had yelled at him for walking in the bathroom like that, and he had yelled that the door was wide open, and she had smashed the Listerine bottle in the sink, and he had slapped her. So she'd run out into the bedroom and snatched a dress up from somewhere and Earl had helped her put it on by yanking it down over her head, and she'd tried to kick him, so he had walked her fast to the door and shoved her out into the hotel corridor, with the dress still partly over her head, and slammed the door. When he had opened it a few minutes later the corridor was empty.

Dizzily he remembered that, *Earl Wild and a woman, yelling at one another,* but he could not believe it. He could not believe that that had happened. The letter from his mother had been waiting for him downstairs, it had been waiting for hours, for him. Sonny had handed it to him along with the other letter, as if it were ordinary mail. It had been waiting for him and he hadn't known about it. Now this woman was talking to him and he had to pay attention to her words, because there was a danger in her voice, even in her face. She was saying something about food. "I ate breakfast alone at the Empire. I'm still hungry." She began to pick nervously at the grilled cheese sandwich. She pulled off strips of cheese that were like gum. She picked up some slivers of onion that dangled down from her fingers. In the booth with them were invisible shapes, groping at Earl's face, his chest, his hands. They were whispering at him. Hushed, sibilant, angry or pretending anger, affectionate anger. He could not make out their words. They were mixed up with a woman's voice. He had to listen to her cautiously, waiting, and yet he could not hear her clearly because of the sudden din in his ears. "... go up before noon the maid won't have done the room, and it's a mess ... but maybe you should lie down ... or...." She chewed the strips of cheese like gum. She licked her fingers nervously. "I could hold you, you know, we could lie down, honey, till you felt better again, and ... the room might be fixed up by now, I don't know ... it's Thursday so the sheets will be changed.... Honey? What do you want to do?"

Why didn't she write me a letter? Earl thought. *Doesn't she wish me well? Doesn't she love me?* He wiped his nose with the edge of his hand.

"Honey ...?"

He could not struggle with these shapes because they were invisible, they did not really touch him, not his body. They breathed upon him, coldly. They taunted him. They were nothing he could seize the way he could seize Violet. So he sat suspended, waiting as if on the edge of a precipice, waiting to see what he would do. He stared at the face of the woman across from him, her eyes that had fixed themselves so strangely on his. He stared at her mouth, waiting.

"Honey? What do you want to do?" she asked helplessly.

The
Stone
House

Twenty miles north of the city of Derby, in the rich plain that dipped to the shore of one of the great lakes, there lived for generations a family named Thomas. They had always grown peaches, there had always been a shallow creek meandering through their property, the great old stone house had always looked high and gaunt and weathered, but in the last fifty years changes had taken place—first electricity was installed, then the old lightning rods were taken down, then the long front lawn that eased gradually up to to the house had begun to disappear, eaten up by a road that had turned from two lanes of gravel into three lanes of blacktop into a four-lane highway. From the road the house seemed to be peering coldly through its thicket of evergreens and oaks at the busy highway, perplexed at the great trailer trucks and Greyhound buses with sleek tinted windows and young people on motorcycles, bound for the beach. When one approached the house, however, driving up the gravel lane, the house took on a domestic, almost humiliated look—the high narrow windows stained at their bottoms as if with tears, the cellar built too high above the ground so that it looked as if it were heaving the house up over it. Immediately behind the house was a garden of roses and lilac bushes, a woman's garden, at the center of which a goldfish pond lay still and cool in any weather, flagstones dusty around it and lily pads grown complacently over it as if to hide from the viewer the fact that there were no longer any goldfish. There were white wrought-iron benches in the garden, one encircling an oak tree, and they had the air of festivity suddenly paralyzed, as if something had happened and all the guests had run off to look. Behind the garden the lane turned slowly, curving around the house to dip back down to the highway, and across the lane was another, larger lawn, mostly grass, edged with great flowering shrubs and evergreens. Then the farm itself began: the barns, now used for storage, the empty stable with its brilliant haze of bees and flies, and the acres and acres of peach trees. As far as the eye could see the orchard reached out and back, the trees of a height, pruned and neat, their leaves a mild frosted green even in the bright static sunshine of summer. In late summer after a good spring the odor of ripening and then rotting fruit would materialize out of the sweet air itself, and anonymous buses from the city, rusted and sullen-looking, would struggle up the lane to let out migrant workers in stained clothes and straw hats, strangers who picked fruit in season, people who were never recognizable from one year to the next.

One evening at the beginning of the harvest the Thomas family was sitting in the front room after a late dinner. The odor of peaches in the air was mildly intoxicating; through their voices they could hear the sound of insects throwing themselves against screens, blindly and routinely, and the sound reassured them though they could not have said why. It was Saturday night and the pastor of their church, Father West, was there as usual, and the Thomas's married daughter, Hilda, and her husband and two boys, and the Thomas's two sons, unmarried, who still lived with their parents in the big house—Charley, who was thirty-one, and Kenneth, who was twenty-four. "It was no good, that lying in bed like that," Father West was saying. He was a plump middle-aged man with an actor's handsome complacent face; his dark garb became him, made him dramatic and stern even while eating. Mrs.

Thomas, who sat as usual beside him, smiled at these familiar words; Mr. Thomas, who sat in the corner beside the old floor-model radio, his legs crossed fragilely beneath a quilt in spite of the warm weather, listened with eyes lowered as if he were too modest to acknowledge these words about him. "Up and around. Exercise," the priest said. "And now that you're home you can get some good food." "That's what I tell him," Mrs. Thomas said. "He says he couldn't eat it most of the time there, at the hospital. It's no wonder he lost so much weight." "No wonder at all," the priest said severely.

They heard the sound of the boys playing outside, running and crashing through a bush alongside the house. "Hey, what are you two doing?" Hilda cried. There was silence; then the boys' footsteps pounding away around the house. "They're all right, they never hurt anything," Mrs. Thomas said. "They're just boys." She had a lean, pale face, still an attractive woman though a little nervous and, about her mouth, grimly forceful and prodding so that her younger son, Ken could feel his own mouth turn rigid when she tried to smile. The little knobs of bone at her wrists protruded gently from beneath her white sleeves. She had thin eyebrows, arched as if in continual polite amazement, and dark, shadowed eyes that seemed in no way related to the rest of her face: ironic, sombre, impatient. Ken recognized those eyes in his own face and was grateful. In his corner, sitting hesitantly as if poised on the brink of sleep, Ken's father sat with his small empty eyes, always a pale blue but lately a bluish-gray that looked burned of all substance, eyes that saw nothing.

They talked about one of Ken's cousins, who had had her sixth child in six years, and yet her husband had had to buy a new car. They talked of the firehouse that had caught fire the week before, a few miles away; Father West had seen the fire. They talked of a tractor accident the son of one of their neighbors had had, luckily nothing serious. "Say, do you remember that night, down the road—" Hilda began. "Hilda, please," Mrs. Thomas said. She made a gesture with her hand that flicked Hilda's voice off, without haste. "What night? What was that?" Charley said. He sat in his easy chair with his big feet outspread, his shoes still dusty. "Come on, Charley," Ken said, making a face. He rapped at his brother's arm playfully with his fist; he always hated it when Charley upset their mother. "You mean that accident, the motorcycle and the truck?" Charley said. He was smoking a cigar and pointed at Hilda with it. "Christ, what a mess! A kid and a girl with long hair, I remember that. She had white slacks on. We didn't have any telephone then, so Ma was right, why go and get involved?" He smoked his cigar and stared across the room as if contemplating the past. Father West began to speak and he interrupted: "How old was I then? About twelve? God, I remember that—we couldn't go out and look, had to look out the window—That was a long time ago." "I was nine, I guess," Hilda said meaninglessly. Her husband, a shy little man who worked in a Derby insurance company, touched her arm as if she had said something charming: Ken saw that.

The boys came in. They were big for their ages, with flushed damp faces and dirty bare feet. "I know what you two would like," Ken's mother said. The boys grinned; they avoided Hilda's eye, as she motioned them to stand back off the Oriental rug. Mrs. Thomas went out to the kitchen and the boys followed. "Big healthy boys," Father West said. Ken had heard him say this many times; he had the feeling that the priest did not particularly like the boys, any more than he did. The screen door swung shut and the boys ran out again. Mrs. Thomas returned with a plate of peach tarts. "Now please do have some," she said. "We didn't have much of a dinner at all." She passed the plate around. Ken took one; Charley took one. Hilda shook her head reluctantly. Her husband and Father West took one each. "Richard, will you have one?" Mrs.

Thomas said. Her husband's hand raised itself, then his arm, but he seemed at the last instant to change his mind; he shook his head. Ken's mother sighed and returned to her seat. They ate the tarts hungrily. Ken had always liked tarts except he thought they were too small; there was no point in making things so small. "Here, have another," his mother said. He reached out and took one, shrugging his shoulders. His mother glanced at him and smiled slightly. "Nothing ever lasts around here," she said to Father West. "It's always been that way. A pie for dinner and it's all gone before bedtime." "Growing boys," Father West said vaguely, as if he had been thinking of something else.

Drawn to admiration of Ken's mother, they talked of the new drive-in theatre two miles down the highway, and of how miraculous it had been that she had refused to sell that land until the time she did. But it was just an accident, she said, rejecting their praise, she had had too much to think of when the first offers were made, and when this one came along she had been able to think clearly for the first time in years, so she had accepted it. "It was Richard's idea," she said. Ken knew this was untrue, but like the others he looked politely over at his father. "Richard said we might as well sell it, wasn't doing us any good. Just a lot of taxes." Hilda covered a yawn with her generous big-boned hand; her fingernails were painted pink. "In ten years the taxes were raised four times," Mr. Thomas said. His voice seemed to be coming from a distance, as if he were imprisoned somewhere far inside his body and calling for help. "Taxes build a country up," Charley said loudly. "Every citizen should want to pay taxes to build the country up." It was an old argument, and Ken felt the same hopeful apprehension Charley probably felt, that their father would reply; but he did not. He seemed to be puzzling over Charley's words as if he did not quite understand them. After a moment Hilda yawned again. She noticed them looking at her and giggled in embarrassment. "Guess I'm thinking of tomorrow," she said. "Up at seven again." "Are you going down to the beach?" said Mrs. Thomas. "Yes, sure, they can't get enough of it." "They swim like fish," her husband said.

"Now there's just this one left," Ken's mother said brightly, picking up the plate. She brought it over to Ken's father, who watched it approach him as if he did not quite recognize it. "Richard, please try it, I know you'll like it—you always have. Would you like me to put some cream on it?" But no, no, he had to shake his head; he looked as disappointed as everyone else. "Richard? Not even with some cream?" They watched him, their own jaws slowing respectfully. "You just won't eat. You won't try," Ken's mother said, and as she spoke she turned back to the others, helpless and impatient. Ken stared at her. He did not quite know whether to admire or to fear the strength in that thin nervous body, and he had the peculiar idea that she would preside over his death too, charming and prodding and filling the house daily with the healthy rich odor of food, tempting him back to life, wrestling with him, grappling and panting to drag him along a little further before she had to surrender him finally to the wet black mud Ken always thought of as signalling death—an image taken from the creek out behind the barn, where thick mud formed in spring that they had always thought, as children, to be quicksand. "He won't try to eat," Ken's mother said, staring down at the single tart as if it had betrayed her.

She sat. For a while there was silence, then the conversation began again. It was late, the evening was nearly over. Ken felt an instant of regret. When meals ended, when church services ended, when bedroom doors closed upstairs, he felt this same unaccountable surge of regret, of melancholy, as if he himself were responsible for these curious failures. . . . Behind his mother, on the wall, hung an old picture in an ornate frame, a scene of early or late winter, snow hugging the black earth in clumps, trees protruding skeletal and black against the reddened, rouged sky. Ken felt that something was settled, irremediable: his mother sitting there, the old picture behind her, his family about him quietly, even Father West's familiar face, seemed to attach this scene to something eternal, fix it firmly, beyond his own capacity to change it. He could not change it. When at college he had thought of home and had always thought of this room, not his own of his family in here, the fireplace blazing in winter, of Hilda as a child, a teenager, a young woman, changing from one creature to another without any consciousness at all, bringing to this house a husband and children as if these were gifts offered to the old house itself; of Charley, who grew older, fatter, without changing; of their mother, who never changed and who did not even seem to grow older; of their father, whose present sickness seemed no more than an admission of some meek failure he had hid for years from them; and of that picture on the wall, cut out of an old magazine and gaudily framed by Ken's grandmother, now dead, with its blazing pink and melodramatic, deathly black that had vexed him at night for months before he had understood that the picture had no meaning in itself but gained its meaning from that position on the wall, above the old gray sofa with its lace doilies and above their mother's habitual seat, framing them, nailing them irreparably in their places. Ken wondered if anyone else had thought of this, and his heart swelled with something very like joy.

He drove Father West home, as usual. Once out of the house the priest was always quieter, older. "Your mother is a brave woman," the priest said, when Ken had stopped before the rectory. At the house a light burned, dappled with insects. The housekeeper awaited him; why didn't he leave? Ken waited. Was there something he should say, was something expected of him? He looked out at the headlights, at the road, at nothing. These moments had always frightened and annoyed him, coming as they did without warning—that farewell with one of his professors at school, that clumsy goodbye at graduation with a girl he had known for two years and had thought of comfortably and fondly but with no real emotion. The priest had opened the door but still did not get out. Yes, yes, Ken wanted to say; my mother is brave; but why do you act as if my father's dying were anything strange, anything evil? Were not all their lives related and therefore all their deaths related? Yet, looking at the priest's bemused face, Ken suddenly wondered. Was there a secret he didn't know? What was there they were supposed to reach out and touch, become united over? The moment passed. Father West got out. "Thank you," he said. "Yes, good night, Father," said Ken. "We'll be seeing you tomorrow." The priest stood with his hand on the door handle. "Ken," he said, squatting suddenly, "you should know that your mother appreciates what you've done, even if she doesn't say so. She might never say so. You and Charley both." He looked embarrassed and vaguely outlandish, bent at the knees, frowning over at Ken. Ken smiled irritably. "Yes," he said. The priest closed the door and walked off.

Ken drove away, waiting for some kind of revelation to come to him. He had always been told that his mind was precocious, shrewd; at school he had been able to understand and to criticize, adroitly, any of the historians he had studied. And the philosophers: he had exulted in their obscurities, their delirious speculations upon the recesses and corners of their own brilliant minds, but always he had kept them back from himself, their instruments of destruction far from the secret, most sacred part of himself, which he had never questioned. If he had come across Father West's remarks in a book perhaps he could have understood; but here, now, it did not make sense. He did not understand.

From the breakfast table he could see the workers getting off the bus, down the lane. He was eating pancakes with syrup on them. Consumed by his hunger, he ate deftly, almost with art, while his mother watched him, sitting at the table. Her long, blue-veined hands were encircled about a cup of coffee. "How long do you think you'll be at the library?" she said. "A couple of hours," said Ken. Comfortably he thought of the university library, its cool silent rooms, the shelves and shelves of books awaiting him. "There's just a little more mix, let me make it up," his mother said, rising. He thought of refusing but said nothing. Down the lane the bus had emptied and the workers had straggled off. Ken saw Charley and Pete, one of their hired men, walking together back to the orchard. "How's Pa this morning?" he said, picking up his glass of milk. His mother sighed without turning. The pancake batter hissed in the pan like a more impatient, exasperated kind of sigh. "The same," she said. "How'd he sleep last night?" said Ken. A group of children crossed the lane and were approaching the lawn. Ken stared. They came no closer than the edge of the lawn, where they stood and looked silently at the banks of flowers and shrubs. "The same, a little restless," she said. Ken sipped at his milk cautiously, watching the children. After a moment they turned and ran back to where a woman stood, calling to them. He could hear her harsh voice across the distance and his mouth began to curl in an expression of distaste. "If only he wouldn't keep asking about why he doesn't gain any weight," his mother said. Ken had heard this before and did not know what to say.

Suddenly two girls appeared from the orchard. Something about their clothing—it was bright and assaulting—worried his eye. They wore shorts and their long tanned legs seemed to be carrying them boldly down the lane and toward the house, as if they were being called by name. "He keeps wanting to weigh himself, and I can't stop him," Ken's mother said. "But sometimes I think he knows the truth. Sometimes he says things. . . ." One of the girls stopped; the other tugged at her shoulder. They seemed to be arguing.

"What does he say?" Ken said. His mother turned to look at him as if something in his voice had attracted her attention. "He says things. I don't want to go into it now." The girls turned, looking toward the house. They began walking again, slowly at first and then quickly. It seemed to Ken, sitting with the glass held rigid in his hand, impossible that these people should really be coming right up to the house, that they would not instead turn out the lane to the highway or turn off somewhere or simply disappear; but they did not stop. He put down his glass of milk. "Is there something wrong?" his mother said. "No, nothing," said Ken. He heard her click off the stove. "Here," she said, "it's just a little pancake. And what about lunch, you'll be sure to have a good lunch in Derby, won't you?" Ken picked up his fork automatically. He felt vaguely nauseous. The pancake was a perfect circle, touched delicately with rings of brown, a sight so familiar to him as to confuse his brain. He did not know what it was.

When he glanced up the girls were coming down the path. "I'll take care of it," he said grimly. "Some of them coming." He got up; he felt his face go hard. "What is it?" said his mother. "Nothing, some kids from back in the orchard. I'll take care of it," Ken said. "But what do they want with us?" his mother said. Ken avoided her frightened eyes. "I'll take care of it," he said. "You stay in here."

He went out on the back porch. The porch was screened, and the girls' young faces seemed to drift to him in jerking angry movements through the dusty screening. "What do you want?" he said. He opened the screen door and leaned casually in the doorway.

"She hurt herself back there," the bigger girl said. They were older than he had thought: sixteen or seventeen. "Fell down from a ladder." The other girl was holding her arm queerly, and now Ken saw that it was bleeding. He felt his mother suddenly behind him, straining around to see. "It's all right, I just want to go home," the girl said. She was staring down at her feet as if overcome with shame. The other girl, fat-faced and shrewd, was looking right at Ken as if he were to blame. "Could of broke her arm back there, and then what?" she said. Ken, watching the bleeding girl, felt his throat go dry. He stared at her arm. It was tanned and freckled, and out of a series of harsh white peelings of skin blood was eking in tight little dots. "Do you want—want me to—" Ken began. He had begun to tremble. "I don't want nothing, I want to go home," the girl cried. The fat girl pulled angrily at her shoulder, trying to make her look up. "I can get the bus, for God's sake," the girl said. "You go on back to work. Leave me alone." Ken waited for her to glance up, but she did not. "Do you want some water or something?" he said. "A bandage?" "No," said the girl. She pulled away from the fat girl. Her long brown hair fell about her face untidily and she shook it back. In the sunshine her face was a high, healthy color, her lips a little too red, her teeth slightly bared as if she were in pain. Ken felt a surge of nausea at the sight of the blood on her arm, beginning to move now in tiny rivulets. "Let me get you a bandage," he said faintly. He turned to his mother, who was going back into the house. Had he said the wrong thing? He stared at his mother's back but could not imagine her expression; what did she want him to do? The girl was backing away. "Go on back to work, for Christ's sake," she said. "I'm getting the bus. I'll see you tomorrow, okay?" "How do you know when the next bus comes?" the fat girl shouted. The other girl glanced at her, sullenly, and then up at Ken who stood still on the top step. "Oh, go to hell," the girl said. She turned and walked away. They watched her small determined shoulders, arched beneath her yellow blouse, as she followed the flagstone path impudently through Ken's mother's garden and around the house and out of sight. "She skinned it pretty bad," the girl said to Ken. "She hit some branches going down. One of those Mexican bastards jiggled the ladder, trying to be funny." Ken, staring after the girl, did not answer. "You guys ought to do something about that," the girl said threateningly. "Yes, well," he said weakly, "we'll have to ... they'll have to be ... better supervision...." He allowed the screen door to close before him.

Inside he found his mother scraping the pancake off his plate and into the sink. "She didn't want a bandage or anything," he said. He watched his mother's tense back. His legs urged him somewhere, at first he did not know where; then he realized he wanted to go into the front room to look out the window. Deliberately he sat down. "Why did you take that away?" he said. "I wasn't finished." "It was cold," his mother said. She switched on the garbage disposer. When she turned to him a moment later her face was relaxed. "When are you going to Derby?" she said. "In a while, I guess," said Ken. He looked at the kitchen floor, at the complex aqua and black design of the linoleum. "It's getting hot again," his mother said. "We should close up the house and put on the air conditioner." "Should I do that?" Ken said. He wondered at his eagerness. He was still shaky, his glasses slid down his perspiring nose, and he could not take his gaze off that floor, as if to abandon it were to lose himself. "I'd appreciate that very much," his mother said. "Your father gets so uncomfortable...." She followed him from room to room as he shut windows. At the front of the house he was able to see the girl down by the road, a bright flash of yellow through the evergreen thicket. He turned his eyes away without effort.

Some time later he left the house, driving around the lane, and the girl was gone. Yet he did not think he had heard a bus stop; he had perhaps been listening for one. He waited for traffic to pass and swung out onto the road, and then he saw some distance ahead the girl walking along the shoulder of the road, by the ditch. He stared at her yellow blouse. It seemed to swell up to him, rush back toward him, too quickly. Perhaps she would not see him as he drove by. She had not looked at him, really. She had not noticed him. Cars passed her one by one and she did not glance around. Beyond her a field stretched wild with trees and untended bushes, and it was at this she looked. Ken saw, as he passed her, that she was holding her arm against her blouse and that the blouse was stained with blood.

He stopped the car. In the rear view mirror he saw her pause, watching him. He leaned over to open the door. "I'll give you a ride," he called back. His glasses had slipped down again on his nose. The girl approached him, not hurrying, and her look was of a queer heavy sadness, as if the two of them were involved in an inexplicable sin and were doomed together. "Where do you live?" Ken said.

"Outside Derby. Four miles."

She shut the door angrily. As if he were looking at a child or an animal, a creature absolved of consciousness, Ken found himself staring at her rudely. She had long, thick brown hair, falling well past her shoulders, a rather small oval face within this heavy hair, eyes sullen with humiliation. Her lips were parted and he could see her white little teeth, pressed damply against her skin. He could smell about her an odor of something sweet yet at the same time stale, intimate. "I said outside Derby," she said.

He drove on. Beside him, she let her arm fall idly onto her lap. Ken kept glancing over at it. He felt oddly cold, tense. He could see a rivulet of blood trailing off onto her leg, the thick competent flesh of her thigh, and wanted to warn her of it. "Look, I'm sorry," he said, as if he wanted to thrust her away from him with words, "I should have offered to drive you home before. I don't know why I didn't. I'm sorry."

"Sure," she said.

"If anyone gives you trouble back there—I mean, if you come again—"

"Sure I'm coming. I need the money."

"Did you work here last year?"

"No." She opened the window on her side and leaned

her face to it. "We just moved here a few months ago. Ma and me. Look, mister, do you have a cigarette?"

"I don't smoke."

She sighed heavily. Her legs stretched, her little feet pushing against the floor. He glanced at her arm and saw the blood now smeared thinly onto her leg. Fascinated, he felt the car drifting; he looked back to the road and straightened the wheel. The girl began to hum. Then she stopped. He looked to see her profile hard against the fleeting countryside, her jaw set as if she did not trust herself.

"Are you all right?" he said.

"I guess I'm scared."

"Is your mother home now?"

"She works."

"I don't think—it doesn't look too bad— Where it's bleeding there, I mean—"

"No, that's okay. He just scared me, knocking the ladder like he did. If I was higher up.... But I got to come back the money's so good. You people really pay well. I started out picking strawberries over east of Derby, some big farm there, and they paid real low. Got a whole lot of kids and old people working, that would work for nothing."

He felt pleased. "We like to pay a fair wage."

"So I got to come back. It's just you got such a big place and so many people there. A lot of bastards, some of those kids. You wouldn't know." She looked around. "How come you don't have a radio in this car?"

"I didn't want one."

"Oh, is this your car? Your own car?"

"Yes."

"What do you do, work somewhere? You work in Derby?"

"No."

"What do you do, then?"

Ken watched the road. "I have my own work," he said coldly.

"What kind?"

"With books."

"Books? What kind, then?"

"You wouldn't be interested."

"Do you go to college or something?"

"I did."

"Did you finish?"

"Yes."

"Oh, you did?" He felt her looking at him. "I knew a guy once that said he was going to college. He quit, though, and went in the navy. Boy, was he smart . . . he was pretty smart."

"Really?" Ken said. He was surprised at the resentment in his voice. He began driving faster. He waited for her to tell him to slow down, thinking as each crossroads approached that this would be it. She did not notice his nervous glances. She had smooth, rather muscular legs, hard-looking and curiously shiny. He watched the round bone at her ankle, a little smeared with dirt, and waited for it to shift inside her skin. The sight of it seemed familiar but he could not say why. "How does your arm feel?" he said.

"Okay," he said. "Say, mister, you can let me off here. This road coming up. We live just a ways down it."

"I'll drive you down."

"No, it's okay."

"I'll be glad to."

"I can walk."

Ken grinned suddenly and turned onto the road. He felt his face go hard, really rigid, as if it had become paralyzed. "I'll drive you down," he said.

She sat forward nervously. They passed a few houses, weathered frame houses without cellars. In their bare front yards children played. At one driveway, in the ditch beside it, a number of small boys were squatting; Ken saw them throw something. A shower of pebbles hit the car. "Those little bastards," the girl muttered. Ken did not want to look at her. "There, there it is," she said, defeated. She was pointing toward a trailer on the left side of the road. Ken flinched at the sight, the trailer was so small and rusted and shabby, with its geranium plants in a bright yellow window box and its colored concrete blocks used as steps. He turned into the rutted driveway. "Well, thanks a lot," she said. She looked sadly at the trailer as if she too were seeing it for the first time. "Those bumps on the back, there, we had an accident once," she said apologetically. Ken looked at the dents. The trailer had been painted a dark blue, but the paint had dried unevenly, and now the vehicle sat heavily and bluntly in the sunshine, the land absolutely bare on all sides: no trees, nothing. "It's hot as hell in there, I suppose," the girl said.

Ken could not look away from the trailer. He felt reckless, guilty, as if he had seen too much. "You won't make any money today," he said. The girl waited. "How much do you make usually?"

"Oh, eight dollars."

He took out his billfold and handed her a ten dollar bill. She took it from him rather gravely. "Do you have a bandage or something inside? Something you can put on that?"

"Sure."

"You should wash it first."

"Yeah, sure."

She opened the door. When she did not get out at once Ken glanced around at her apprehensively. "I don't mean to be picking fruit all my life," she said. Her tone had become suddenly belligerent and helpless. "I got some prospects."

"That's good."

"I can sing a little. That's what people tell me. I sung the other week with a band around here, some guys I got in with. It was at one of those little taverns where they have dancing on the weekends."

"That's nice," Ken said slowly.

"I know I wouldn't ever be famous or anything," she said. Ken knew she envisioned herself as famous. "I'm not beautiful or anything," she said. She touched her throat disparagingly and Ken looked and saw that she was indeed beautiful, in a queer soiled way. "My voice isn't so hot—I need practice—" she said, huskily, as if she were reciting the words of a song. Ken prodded at the design on his steering wheel and saw in surprise that the grooves had started to fill in with dirt. "But a man that was there that night told me—he told me—" And she broke off, breathless. Her bloody arm had brushed forgotten against her blouse and Ken had the sudden stifling impulse to lean over to her and seize her arm and press his lips and tongue against it. He squeezed the steering wheel. "I'd like to go to Derby pretty soon, myself. Is that where you're going? I'd like to go to," she said, pausing without any real hesitation, "to the zoo sometime. I always wanted to go to a place like that...." She was easing out of the car, as if reluctantly. Ken looked away, at the absurd geraniums in the window box. The girl was silent for a moment, then she said, "Look mister, do you want to come in and have a soft drink or something?" "No," said Ken. "No."

Two days later he took her to the zoo. Linda wore a white skirt that came to the tops of her knees, a dazzling white, and a red sleeveless blouse that clung to her small shoulders. In his car he left the books he told his mother he was returning to the library. The zoo was a small one, rather shabby, and Ken took the vulgar odor of food and the impact of the sunshine as a personal punishment, something just and therefore desired. Beside him the girl walked quickly, her attention already claimed by refreshment stands, signs of lions saying "keep off the grass," picnickers on park benches. Ken was dismayed by the heat. He walked along beside her without noticing their direction. His hands felt loose and awkward; he did not know what to do with them and watched other men, noting what they did with their hands. "This way, let's go this way,"

Linda said. A sign directed them to the African animals. Ken watched the back of the girl's head as she hurried along without waiting to see if he followed. He looked surreptitiously at his watch: eleven o'clock.

A small crowd of children stood before the lions' island of rock and feeble, burnt-out moss. Across the indefinite space that separated them from the spectators' railing the lions stared sleepily, without interest. Ken made a face, of boredom or impatience, he did not know which. "They look like people. A man I knew once," Linda said. Her voice startled him. He turned to see that she was really excited, really charmed. Her youth shone in her cheeks and eyes, a dazzling young strength that seemed to fuse, in Ken's mind, with the controlled muscular strength of the animals. At the railing the children were tossing twigs and stones at the lions. Ken frowned. Something was wrong, something might happen.... He did not like disorder. But the lions did not notice, the children lost interest and moved away. Ken pushed his glasses back up on his nose. Left alone with the girl before the animals, leaning perfunctorily against the chipped green railing, he noted that the sun had been obscured by a filmy cloud, dissipated so that light seemed to glare at them from all sides, imprisoning them. The girl noticed nothing; she watched the lions. Ken could not think what he was doing here or who this girl was. He glanced around, cautiously, as if he suspected someone was watching him.

They walked on. "Tell me," said Linda, "if you have any brothers or sisters."

"One brother and one sister."

"That's nice. I don't have any. Just my mother and me, living out there." She flicked her hair back out of her face. "My father took off. He took the car one day and took off, she never saw him again. She had to buy another car and everything."

"Your father left you?"

"Yeah."

Her condition suddenly repulsed him; he did not like helplessness. But when she turned he saw that she was smiling as before, her face taking in everything, absorbing everything she saw, as if nothing before this minute really mattered. "Just a bastard," she said.

They walked on slowly, along a dirt path. It was at this moment, Ken realized after, and perhaps he half realized it at the time, that everything changed irreparably. He said, "My own father is sick."

"Oh, how sick? I mean, is it bad?"

"He's dying."

"Dying," she said. Something seemed to strike her eye, for she stopped on the walk, staring. Ken could not follow her gaze. His heart had begun to pound. Why did she stand like that, her chin uplifted as if she were striking a pose, posing for a picture? "Dying," she whispered.

She turned to him helplessly. Ken saw something in her face that made him want to lean forward and peer into her eyes, pry and pierce into her simple little brain. Yet in that instant he felt her triumph, he felt her strength, and he understood for the first time the impact of that word: he thought of his father, lying sleepless in bed, his body frail and mysterious, and he felt the truth of what this girl meant by her voice, her very look. "Yes. Dying. For a year now," Ken said. He tried not to let his mouth jerk into a grin. Something twitched beside his lip instead and he touched it with his fingers as if it were an insect. "They haven't told him yet."

"You haven't told him?" said Linda.

They began to walk again, hurriedly. He could not see her face. "But why haven't you told him," she said.

"My mother doesn't want him to know. It's better that way—he wouldn't want to know, he wouldn't want us to tell him—"

He was about to stammer.

"But why haven't you?" she said. She looked about helplessly. "That makes me feel funny. I'm sorry. I feel funny. Look at those birds over there, standing on one leg . . . why are they on one leg? The other legs are up against their stomachs. . . . Look, you should tell him, I mean you guys should tell him. I mean, nobody can live that way. . . . What if he had some special things he wanted to do, and nobody ever told him he was dying, and then at the end when it was too late. . . ."

They leaned against the railing and looked across the deep ditch to the antelopes and the strange, outlandish birds. The animals and birds seemed paralyzed, asleep in a profound dreamless sleep. Nothing moved. The trees showed, near the ground, limbs that were barren of leaves, yet the leafed limbs above these did not move, nothing moved. Ken stared into the hypnotized world beyond the ditch and felt some of its dreary enchantment touch himself. "I don't know," he said.

The girl edged away, her hand outstretched behind her on the railing. Ken followed. "Those animals there," she said, pointing at the antelopes, "none of them changed ever since they were first born. They think the same things now that they did then."

"Yes, that's true," Ken said stupidly. He stared at the antelopes, who stared back at him, and for an instant he could imagine the images he and this strange girl gave to them—a blurring of color, confused faces without souls. The girl kicked at debris around a refuse container. "Why don't they make this clean," she said. He saw her hand jerk to her eyes suddenly; she had turned from him. But in another second she turned back, her shoulders arching coquettishly. "Did you ever go to the zoo much?"

"No, I guess not."

"You like to bowl? Or dance?"

"Not really."

"Do you like to go to the movies or anything?"

"No. Well, sometimes."

"I like movies. I seen some more than once—one I saw ten times. But I shouldn't be telling you that."

"Why not?"

"You'll think I'm stupid or something. I don't know much. I had to quit school, that's one reason. But there were some things I liked to read—when I was in school—"

"What were they?"

"Oh, some things. Books." She turned to a building at their left as if it had just materialized before her. Charmed, pleased, she touched Ken's arm with a gesture he knew was not quite spontaneous. "Let's go there. That's where the snakes are."

"Do you like snakes?"

"I don't mind them. They're okay." she said. "I like anything, just about—things that are real."

"But what, what isn't real?" Ken said. He bent to hear her answer but she seemed not to be listening. Inside the building it was cool and dark. Clusters of people stood about, many of them children, hushed and grave as if vaguely offended. A small child was crying. Linda went right up to one of the glass cages and put her hands out against the glass. Ken, following her, could see faintly beyond her shoulder a limp, dark creature, something moving, now shifting out of sight behind the girl's body as if she had called it to her. "It isn't ugly," she whispered. Ken looked around then and saw it. The snake seemed to fasten itself to his shocked vision, damp and vicious, rippling, muscular and arrogant, a creature out of his secret nightmares. He felt his cheek twitch violently. He closed his eyes. "But it isn't ugly," Linda said, as if she sensed Ken's reaction. "It can't help how it is.... Look at its eyes; it has eyelashes." She spoke seriously. Yet she was not ridiculous. "All it can see of us are some shapes and colors," she said, "it doesn't know anything. It wouldn't hurt us, it says on the sign...."

Some boys ran past, jostling Ken. He stepped forward out of their way and brought his arm around as if to protect the girl, touching her shoulders. He was surprised at her warmth. "Look over there, those look

291

like dragons. Lizards," she said. They approached the cage. Ken felt the flicking of their tongues like proddings of his own flesh; the lizards seemed to be peering at him with amusement, recognizing him. "Think of all the animals we would never know about," Linda said, fascinated, "but would be living just the same. Keeping on and on, for centuries. Don't you want to know about all of them? About everything?"

Ken did not understand her. "Yes," he said slowly.

"And don't you want to—you know—go somewhere, to drive somewhere along a road you've never been on?"

"Yes."

"And leave one time and go into another—one year into another, and never look back. All the different people who meet you wouldn't know who you used to be, then. You could start out again—everything new—"

"Yes," said Ken.

"And things that aren't real— People that don't tell the truth—" She hesitated, not quite embarrassed, but simply waiting for the right words or the right gesture. At that moment a woman came into the building, pushing a child's cart down the incline. In the cart sat a child of about ten, a girl, whose body was somehow deformed. She wore yellow hair ribbons and her peevish face had a strange forced gaiety beneath them. Linda had to step back as the woman passed with her hard, righteous face. She watched the woman pass, and then with a queer sidelong glance told Ken what he had been waiting to hear: this was real, this was true and ugly, who had the strength or the blindness to deny it?

They left the building. Ken felt exhausted, as if this girl—this simple, ignorant peasant—had leaned forward on tip-toe suddenly to peer into his brain. He felt he hated her. She went ahead and sat on a bench, daintily, and crossed her ankles; she smiled at him. He could see, beneath her eyes, slight shadows, indentations, that gave her a fragile look. In his brain a torrent of words was falling, a torrent of things he had read or had heard, odors of food, of the sickroom at home, images of his parents' faces. But these fell aimlessly through his mind to be dissipated like the brilliant sunshine that shone from all angles and pierced itself on this girl's damp forehead, on the smooth curve of her bare arm, the mottled wood of the bench, and the wastepaper container beside it stuffed with junk and beset by flies and bees. These things were real. Nothing else was real, perhaps. The most casual movement of that girl's arm jerked out of his memory the cool musty years of his life in the stone house, among those people who seemed to him to be made of stone also, cast into forms so many years ago . . . as he too had been cast into a form, forced into a role.

He must have become pale. The girl watched him familiarly, as if he were one of her possessions—his angular, nervous face, his bony nose, his stern intelligent mouth unable to keep its shape—and made a slight gesture as if to comfort him. He understood then that she was older than he. He would never be as old as this girl. "Is he dying of cancer?" she said gently. Ken nodded. He felt his mouth grow bitter, as if she had enticed a truth from him he did not want to surrender. "If I were dying," the girl said dreamily, "I would want to know about it. I would want to think about it every minute." She was serious, even downcast. After a minute she got up and he followed her along the path. The park was becoming noisy. Families sat crowded at tables upon which waxed paper blew angrily; music from portable radios clashed. A small boy stood facing the path, crying, his face pale and outraged and hopeless. "I want to do something, something," the girl said suddenly. She looked up at the great oaks tilting in the wind, tilting and recovering, their leaves swirling in a violent invisible wind that tortured and caressed them. Behind her an older boy approached the crying child and grabbed his arm, swinging him around. Ken winced and looked away.

The girl stared up toward the sky. "That man the other week said I could maybe—maybe get somewhere—Oh, I don't believe him really, but it's something to think about—and he wasn't after me, he was with a real sharp girl, it wasn't that— He didn't need to say it."

Ken swallowed. "What did you sing? What song?"

"Do you want to hear it?" she said, turning. "I'll sing it to you when we go back. That's so nice of you, to want to hear it—"

"Yes, I want to hear it."

Ahead of them, in the distance, giraffes were moving languidly. Ken stared at them, for a moment forgetting where he was. He touched the girl's shoulder with his damp, urgent hand, as if directing her; she seemed not to notice. With their long necks and small heads the giraffes were proudly indifferent, like sleepwalkers calmed with the knowledge that no end to their sleep would ever come. Their elongated, distorted spots looked as if they had been drawn and painted carefully, by hand, by art. Ken and the girl watched them. They would have been standing, just so, Ken thought bitterly, and walking with their strange loping stride, legs and neck in fragile rhythm, had Ken and this girl never seen them, had no one ever seen them, had they existed at the very dawn of their world. Flickers of color, sounds, smells assaulted their brains but did not damage them. "Those are beautiful animals," Linda said. The animals gazed upon her. Her soft voice was dissipated into the hot sunlight. Ken ducked his head to see something scurrying by their feet—a crumpled napkin blown along.

An hour later they came to a refreshment stand and Ken bought the girl an ice cream cone. He had no appetite; he felt slightly sick. The hot windy sunshine seemed to be blowing back again and again to him the smells of animals and the opaque, contemptuous ovals of their eyes. He watched the girl eating the ice cream, her tongue caressing it. She ate with enthusiasm. Her face seemed to turn in upon itself, upon the very act of eating. He understood suddenly that he was waiting, and it was this waiting that exhausted him. At every step the girl's body asserted its health, its joy, while he felt his own body sink down, damp and heavy, an unfamiliar body he could hardly maneuver. "You said something before," Ken said, "about going somewhere—along a road— Do you travel a lot? You and your mother?"

"Sure," she said. She licked at the pink ice cream. "That's what I like most, different places. Change around."

"Don't you get lonely?"

For some reason she glanced down at her bandaged arm. Two neat bandages, just slightly soiled, very dainty and much smaller than Ken would have supposed them. "I guess not. I'm not afraid of anything. I want to do things and see things. I have this idea— don't laugh—that something is waiting for me, that it's getting ready for me, and I have to find it. It's so big, I mean the world, all the cities and things, and has so many promises—" As if embarrassed by this last word she paused, chewing on the cone. "Oh, hell. I don't know what I mean."

"But it makes sense—I think—" She waited, but he could not go on. He did not know what she meant. He had never thought of the world that way, or thought of it at all.

"I guess I want to go back," Ken said. The girl's eyes closed to slits, but then she began to smile. "We can come back here some other time," Ken said. "Next week." "Sure," said Linda. "But I don't like to miss work so much."

They drove back to the trailer. "It's hard for me to get around, with only that one car," she said. "I got to get the bus down at the corner." "You should buy your own car," Ken said. The girl laughed. "With what? What I make?" Ken felt his face burn. "Look," she said, "do you want to come in? Or maybe I should see what it's like first and fix it up. I left it in a mess this morning." "All right," Ken said. He turned off the ignition. She went up the concrete blocks to the door and unlocked it. Ken waited for her to glance over her shoulder at him, but she did not. She went inside; he got slowly out of the car. Behind him was the driveway, ridged with hardened channels of mud, and a gleaming new mailbox, silver and black, and the narrow road, and beyond that a scrubby woods with posted signs. "Okay, come in," the girl called. She looked grave; her hair had been brushed, her eyes were somehow calmer, more clear. The inside of the trailer was incredibly small, cluttered, vivid with anonymous inexplicable colors, fragments of clothes half out of sight, dish towels hanging to dry, a row of empty soft drink bottles with their colorful labels still intact. The odor of musty clothes, of food and nail polish and heat, saddened Ken. A divan covered with a gaudy pink bedspread took up most of the room. Linda closed the door behind him. He was stooping, already his shoulders ached. "Sit down here. It's okay. No, it won't fall over or anything, it just tilts." He sat on the divan. She sat on a stool across from him and stretched out her legs. "Are you thirsty or anything? I guess I'm pretty thirsty," she said. She turned on the radio. Ken flinched at the noise. She went to one end of the trailer; he heard her open and close something. "I guess this is sort of loud," she said, turning down the radio. It was a small red plastic radio with white dials that appeared to be luminous. She sat on the stool again and drank from a soft drink bottle, some dark, fizzing drink. "Sure you don't want any?" she said. Ken shook his head. "So how do you like our house? Our home? Would you like to live here?" Ken scratched his neck in shame. "God, if you knew how tired I am of this, how I can't wait till—till something happens— One of these days I'm going, ready or not. That's the utter truth. —Sure you don't want any? Here," she said. She offered him the bottle. Ken reached out dizzily to take it, his fingers touching its chill damp glass, but then he shook his head and drew back. "Okay," she said. "Thought I'd ask. Oh, I want to sing you that song. You really want to hear it? I'll turn this down—" She straightened and arched her back. Suddenly she became shy. "Look, I'll feel bad if you laugh or anything. I know I'm not much good—I need practice and maybe lessons." She cleared her throat and sang, slowly at first, in a very throaty self-conscious voice, "Once I was happy; now I am blue. Now I spend night-times just longing for you. You'll never know—" Her voice trailed off. She was embarrassed, apologetically, yet obviously pleased with herself. "Go on," Ken said eagerly. "Please go on." "No, I can't," she said. "But you sang it already—in front of lots of people," he said. "But just to one person, that makes it different. I don't know," she said. She turned the radio up again jerkily. A man announced something—a bargain price for razor blades. The girl seemed not to listen. She drank the soft drink, contemplating Ken over the hard rim of the bottle. Her feet were bare now and Ken watched her toes curling and uncurling on the cheap red and black woven rug. Several tiny bites, insect bites, were scattered across the tops of her feet. Her toenails had been painted a bright red. This red seemed to him immensely hot and overpowering, and no matter where he looked her toenails flashed in the corner of his eye, the bottom of his eye. He crossed his legs nervously and felt the sofa shift beneath him.

Linda finished the drink and put the bottle down. She came over to him. Ken felt her palm flatten itself against his chest as if she were feeling for his heart, checking his heart. "Why don't you make love to me," she said. "Then you'll feel better." She flicked her hair out of her face. She was gentle and her fingers, unbuttoning the top buttons of his shirt, seemed to him transfixed and dreamy. She might have just come to him across a space, an indefinite space of time, crossed over from another country and with its slow sleepy contentment still about her. Ken was bathed in perspiration. He felt heat rush at him, rush out of him.

"I don't— It wouldn't be—" he said hopelessly. "What?" she said. She bent to peer at him. "Don't you want to?" "I've never made love to anyone before—" he said. Something in her face seemed to tense suddenly, as if she were about to smile; but she did not. "I never did either," she said, and pressed her face against the side of his head so he could see nothing. Ken waited for everything to disintegrate or to explode—the movement of time itself, the announcer's voice so rhythmically and banally in its channels, the dirty cluttered inside of the trailer—but the girl only straightened and caught his wrist and looked at his watch, her eyes slitting sweetly, and said, "It's just two o'clock."

Ken heard the radio announcer say that it was two-thirty, then three. He buried his face in her hair as if trying to get away from that radio, the music that began again now, a woman singing a song like the one Linda had sung before—perhaps it was the same song—Linda lay smiling vaguely. He wondered if she was listening to the song. In his anguish he wanted to knock the radio onto the floor, but he did not dare do anything, did not even dare to turn it off. She smoothed his hair back off his forehead. "I'm sorry if I hurt you," he said. His head was pounding. Her passivity, her strange calmness seemed to drain him of all his control, so that even his brain could not keep itself clear but was beset by a jumble of memories and visions that went back no further than the zoo, as if something had happened to him there. He found himself rubbing his face, his eyes, against her bandaged arm, and drawing his teeth hungrily against the adhesive. Her skin was damp and faintly salty. He wanted to tear the bandage off with his teeth and suck at the wound itself. "I don't want to hurt you—I didn't mean to," he said. "No, it's all right," she said. She was remote, her smile remote, as if she were with him yet at the same time mysteriously elsewhere, hiding. The song ended. The announcer's handsome voice returned to list the top songs of the day. Titles were recited for several minutes. "We can leave here, I'll leave home," Ken said. Her forehead showed a sudden delicate network of tiny wrinkles, as if she were listening to something beyond his voice. "I can get a job. You won't have to work, you can live in a nice place. You ought to have a nice place...." Linda took her hair in her hands and coiled it, twisting it around her head. "So warm," she whispered. "We can have an air conditioner there," Ken said, "And anything else—I'll take you back with me to my mother—" "But why?" Linda said. "If we get married—" said Ken. "Married," said Linda. She wiped her forehead with the pink bedspread. She wiped her throat and the back of her neck, beneath the heavy hair. "It's too warm, let's sit up. Let me up," she said. "Are you all right?" said Ken. "Yes, honey, I'm all right," she said softly. Embarrassed, she began scratching at her foot, at the reddened insect bites. Ken stared down at the inflamed flesh. Before his squinting eyes it seemed to turn into a rash, an infection, a kind of festering, loathsome disease; then he blinked and saw only irritated mosquito bites again.

She put on a pink cotton robe. "What a mess this is—what am I going to do," she said, pulling at the bedspread. She held one corner up and stared at it wildly; her eyes grew damp. She let it fall. "Guess I'll fix my hair," she said. She went to the end of the trailer. Ken put on his glasses but did not think he could see much better. His eyes ached. He pressed his palms against his face. The girl, perched upon her toes before a mirror, lifted her hair slowly away from her neck. Ken hid his face in his hands, then, supposing she might see him in the mirror, he straightened and began to dress. His body seemed to him heavy and unreal, a clumsy damp mass of flesh he controlled but could not understand, as he seemed to veer along with his body, always, in his dreams. He moved very slowly. Even his hands had turned cunning and unfamiliar. Groping for one of his shoes he picked up something and brought it out from under the sofa—a black sock, crusted with dirt. His fingers might have betrayed him deliberately. Yet so profound was his inertia, as if he were enchanted, that it took him a moment before he stooped and put the sock back under the sofa. On the radio the announcer returned, enlivened, with an advertisement about chewing gum. In great rhythmic gulps his voice hypnotized Ken.

Linda returned, with another bottle of soda pop. "This is the last one we got, do you want any?" she said. He shook his head, no. She sat on the stool and stretched out her legs. Her lips were damp from the soft drink. "Well, another day I missed working at your place," she said. She had piled her hair on top of her head, had washed her face, so that she looked childishly serene, pert and self-confident. She smiled at him over the rim of the bottle. The glass clicked familiarly against her teeth. Ken, his head pounding, watched her smile and was paralyzed by it. "Look, I believe in utter truth," she said. "I don't believe in anything not real. Anything not real is just a lot of—" She must have seen him wince at what he supposed would be her vulgarity, since she stopped suddenly. With one foot she reached out and under the sofa, awkwardly, and brought out the sock with her curled toes. She let it fall between them. "Is that yours?" she said. Ken saw her glance at his feet. He did not answer. "Whose is it, then?" she said. "Look, did you wear three socks today?" She smiled at him with her chin lifted. "Did you?" "No," said Ken. "You must have," she said. "No," said Ken. He tried to hide the twitch in his cheek so she would not see. She leaned back against the wall and watched him. His eyes fell feverishly upon her careless arm, upon the bandage, and he understood for the first time in his life the satisfaction that violence would bring: the beatific gratification one might gladly sacrifice one's life for, discarding it angrily, without thought. The girl lowered the bottle from her mouth. "Another day I missed work," she said. "I guess I can't miss much more." Ken stirred. His hand, awakened by something he himself did not yet grasp, reached for his wallet. "How much do you make?" he said. "Oh, fifteen dollars or so," she said. She watched him select a bill. "Here," he said. She accepted it with an abrupt, rather shy nod of her head. "On a good day once I made thirty dollars," she said at once. Ken sat with his shoulders hunched. "You never made thirty dollars," he said hoarsely. "Yes, thirty or thirty-five, I can't remember," she said. "Picking fruit?" he said. "Yes, peaches up in a tree," she said. "Not picking fruit," Ken said. He was staring at her feet. He could not look up at her face. "I said yes, picking fruit," she said. She put out her hand to him. Her hand was so sure of itself, her graceful little fingers so still, so firm, not trembling like his, that he handed her a ten-dollar bill almost without thinking. "Fifty dollars," she said. Jerkily he reached for another bill. Sweat stung his eyes so that he could not see what it was; he handed it to her. "Sixty dollars," she said. His fingers moved but he forced them to stop. He stared at the floor.

After a moment the girl said, "Look, you're rich. You have everything. I saw that goddam goldfish pond there in the garden! What does it matter to you sixty dollars or a hundred? Two hundred? Or if you gave your car away? What does anything matter to you?" She spoke mockingly, coaxingly. "It isn't my fault you picked up that goddam sock of his, all that crap he lets lay around here like a pig, that I thought I had stuffed back in the cupboard," she said. "It isn't my fault you take everything so seriously." "No," said Ken. His mind tried to go back force itself back, to the feeling he had had for this girl in the park—the realization he had had that beside her his usual life seemed no more than a dream, a lie. It had seemed to him then that her soft confident body defined the rich limitations of what was real, just as it had seemed to him that this trailer, with its junk and sweetish-sour smell, would be a place of violent initiation, and not just another warmer, more confused, more bitterly deceptive place of imprisonment like his family's stone house.

He went home. With his books in his arms he blundered through the empty kitchen and to the stairs. Upstairs, at his room, he heard his mother calling him from somewhere. He pretended not to hear and went inside. The room had been cooled but was glaring with light shot through the pulled shade. It was too bright for his sore eyes. He put the books down on his desk and sat before them; he hid his face in his hands and waited for tears to sting his eyes, but he could not cry, nothing would happen. His eyes throbbed with pain but there was no release, nothing happened. His mother stood at the foot of the stairs, calling, "Ken? Ken?" and only then did something click in his brain, releasing him to his grief, not for himself but for his mother. He heard her voice rise to him like the voices of the dead, rising from the suffocating earth to those above who would not listen, angrily would not listen, who had better things to do.

Hell

I had been here before: there, weeds pushing up through the cracks in the sidewalk, there peeling paint on the side of the house. Marks in the clapboards that look like scratches, the beginnings of scrawls, almost like hieroglyphics.

There, the overturned ceramic pot, dried mud spilled out onto the cement floor of the terrace ... blue petunias had been in that pot, at one time, hardy healthy flowers bought at a greenhouse out along the highway, one dozen to a box, very cheap. Blue, white, and red petunias. I knew where they had been planted, exactly which color had gone where, but the memory was too trivial to bother with. So I walked up the three steps to the back door and took hold of the handle—slightly rusted, the handle of the screen door—and opened it and peered into the kitchen.

"Are you inside? Hiding inside?" I called.

No reply, as I had expected.

I took out my keys and unlocked the door. Inside, I was struck by the untidiness of the kitchen—plates stacked on the table, thick with dust, dotted with the bodies of dried insects. The refrigerator door was open. The refrigerator was empty, the shelves empty, but everything inside looked sticky, gummy. I remembered this. I went to close the refrigerator door but hesitated: why alter anything?

The real estate agent who had listed the house no

longer brought anyone to look at it; I knew this; I knew it would never be sold. It had been vacant for several years. I knew all this. I went to the front room to check the furniture beneath the dusty sheets—exactly the same—the familiar sight of a pillow with an intricate brocade covering pleased me. Then I went upstairs. As always, the mattress in the big front bedroom was bare; just as I had left it.

"Are you here? Where are you?" I called.

No one answered, so I didn't bother opening the closet door. It was a long closet, the width of the room, used for storage as well as clothing. Instead I went into the smaller bedroom, which had a high, wide window that looked out into the distance, the hill of pines, the hazy horizon. There was a brick window-box outside this window, and weeds now grew in it, but not energetically; many were only husks and dried stalks. Up here, red and white petunias had been alternated, a pleasant pattern.

"Then you must be downstairs . . . ?" I called.

I was in no hurry, so I opened the closet door to this room and noted the usual piles of towels, linen, blankets, the dangling cord of an electric blanket. The dial turned to HOT. On the bureau top—made of glass—were an expensive hairbrush with a few of my own black hairs still caught in the bristles, and a tarnished key-chain with several keys on it. They would unlock parts of the house never kept locked: the pantry, the linen closet on the landing, the bathroom door.

I picked the key-chain up, for no reason. Then I put it back down again, arranging carefully each key in its place, in the outlines made by dust.

When I went downstairs a woman was walking just ahead of me, into the kitchen. She glanced over her shoulder and said, startled, "I didn't know you were upstairs. . . ."

She went into the kitchen, to the old-fashioned sink. She said, conversationally, "My watch stopped again. . . . Is it really six o'clock? Is it that late?"

I glanced at my watch: it was twenty minutes after six.

"If you heard the church bells, it must be after six," I said.

"Yes, that's true."

"It's true."

"Yes, but I forget.... I'm like my watch, I seem to forget."

"Yes, that's true."

I was smiling at her, so she turned to accept the smile. She lifted her face. Her smile opened, mirroring mine, but less certain than mine.

"My watch needs repairing—"

"Your watch needs repairing—"

We both spoke together, and we both stopped. She laughed nervously. She was wearing her brown dress, used now for work around the house and in the garden: the stitching around one of the large pockets had begun to work loose. The pocket was shaped like a hand. Her legs were bare, not yet tanned, and her sandals were the color and texture of rope.

"I love to stare at you." I said.

"Why are you staring at me?" she said, a moment too late.

We paused.

She brushed her hair back nervously from her face. It had gone limp, perhaps with the humidity. She was still a young woman, but strain showed in her face; her smile was not convincing. She said cautiously, "Why are you staring at me?"

"I love to stare at you," I said.

"But why, why?" she whispered.

Her face seemed to wither, to age brutally. And yet she still smiled, as if she were trying to be pretty but could not remember how that went.

I had been here before: the service station at the corner, where our unpaved road meets Highway 6. The station appears to be permanently "under new management." The sign—which I painted myself—is still there, always there, propped up forgotten in a corner of a window. *Under New Management.* Years pass and have passed. What is new remains new. It becomes simply *new.*

I drove up to the second gas pump, the High Octane gasoline. Because I knew exactly what was inside the untidy office I didn't bother to look in—a cluttered desk, a filing cabinet, greasy rags, old issues of *Field and Stream, True, True Detective Files,* dust on the floor, some of it solidified into sizable spheres, like tumbleweed, even a few ragged, dried leaves from last autumn. The interiors of small rural service stations come to resemble one another, as the years pass.

I tapped the horn gently.

Where was he?

I waited a while and then tapped the horn again. This time he appeared, hurrying; he must have been in the pit, repairing an automobile.

"I'm sorry, I was in the pit—" he said.

"Your face is dirty," I said.

He stared at me, as if not remembering. Then he quickly wiped at his forehead with the back of his hand; he watched my expression, so that he knew when the smear of grease was gone.

He went to fill the gas tank as usual. I waited patiently. I noticed again the clumsy snake-like movements of the hose. Behind the glass of the pump the numbers clicked around, showing the number of gallons, the price. Yes, yes. But after a while I noticed something wrong—the numbers had stopped, the flow of gasoline had stopped. I got out of the car and saw him back there, the nozzle of the hose sunk into the opening of the gas tank, his head bowed, his chin nearly on his chest, as if he were asleep or paralyzed but not fallen to the ground.

"What's wrong? Why are you doing that?" I called.

No reply.

"Why, why? Why are you experimenting like this?" I called.

He knew I was watching him but he refused to look at me.

Let me go, he wanted to cry.

But he did not cry *Let me go.* He stood there, like that, and my eyes shamed his into looking at me, finally. My eyes shamed his. My eyes. His. My. My eyes. My eyes shamed his. And then he looked at me, finally, and I said, "You don't want to do that."

He came to life. He filled up the gas tank.

The amount of my purchase was, as always, $2.65.

I had been here before: darkness, airlessness, warmth, heat, the body of a woman whose face I had never seen. "No, don't, no, let me stop, no, let me go, no, no," she whispered. She was nearly inaudible with the strain, the exertion, but inside her head was a low-pitched scream I could hear very well. I knew that scream. "No, I'm afraid, I, I don't want to, I can't, I don't, please let me, let me go, let, let me, please. . . ." But I knew her. I knew her thoughts, her thinking in panicked wordless screams, pleas, prayers, I knew it all. But no. No. I would not be outwitted. No, I was close behind her, I urged her relentlessly forward, forward, she was not going to escape me. She wanted to bruise herself, to scrape herself raw: to end all sensation. With other men that always worked. But no. I held her still, very still, I knew exactly how to hold her thighs to keep them still. She flinched from me. But no. No pain. Pain was her way out: she knew instinctively how to go for it. But I was prepared. I interpreted freely the sounds inside her head, took them out of her head, and put in their place these visions:

a streak of pale soundless lightning
a spray of white-glowing dots

a whipping weightless cloud of moths
dot-sized bees suddenly swelling and stinging

"No, no, no, no, no," she begs, but the word is now a pulsation, a fist-like opening and closing, no, it is my word now, no, *no*.
No.

Our hands performed a handshake.

We met in an unlikely place—a vacant lot beside the grocery store, across which a muddy path leads, rutted with the marks of bicycle tires. It was a Saturday morning, just before noon, and people in town probably noticed us or half-noticed us—two men in suits, city men, obviously men from the city. They saw us shake hands. They saw the separate hands perform a handshake.

It pleased me to see his hair brushed back neatly from his forehead, his jaw firm as my own, his lips as finely shaped and firm as my own. He had grown an inch or more that summer—now he was taller than I was, which pleased me. I was pleased. I cannot be displeased.

His smile was uneven, higher on the left than on the right.

". . . anything wrong?" I asked.

Our hands in their grasping did not come apart.

One of us had a strong grip. Strong. Strong grasping fingers. One of us, pulling just a little, could feel the immediate strength of the other, not apparent to observers.

His smile wavered.

A breeze whipped down to us from the north, smelling of the cold indifferent placidity of the lakes. Involuntarily, we breathed in this air: he shuddered, I filled my lungs. At that moment something almost happened on the street behind him: a truck loaded with raw lumber, bound for Saratoga, missed by inches the rear fender of an automobile making a clumsy left turn. The

308

truck driver sounded his horn. The other driver, whose car was an old battered Chevrolet with its chrome stripped off, accelerated and sped away. A few loose pebbles struck the grill of the truck.

A meaningless event.

But my son wanted to take advantage of it—he stared, he craned his neck to look. But. But it was a distraction that would not work. Our hands didn't release one another so easily. There were fingers to contend with, eight fingers and two linked thumbs. Intelligent bones beneath the commonplace flesh. Joints, knuckles, muscles, tendons, all. My son looked back at me, his smile straining to match mine.

"Will you—?"

"Why?"

That simple word *Why,* which I whispered because I had no need to shout, seemed to calm him.

He was baffled, but under control. Always, he stands like this under his own control, his nervous nerve-shattered dominion of himself. And then, after a pause, he bares his face to me, the face of an angel from the city, complexion drained, child-like, wintry. His hand was colder than my own. I could have warmed it. I could have warmed it very well. But he tugged backward, the slightest tug, backward . . . on a measuring scale it would be registered as no more than an ounce, no more.

Then it happened—he struck me with his other hand.

His fist—the side of my face.

He shouted. Shouted at me. I fell down heavily, I felt the surprise of mud and weeds beneath my unprotected hands. Dazed, I felt the thin trickle of blood making its way from the corner of my left eye down my cheek to my jaw and to my throat, I felt it, I saw it, I negotiated its quick bright pencil-thin passage.

"Murderer! Murderer!" he shouted.

He backed away from me, terrified. But why is he terrified? I see it each time, this terror, and in pity of him I sound that word inside his throat, the syllables of that word *Murderer!* Almost—almost—I could invent for him a courage that would allow him to leap forward, to seize me, to seize my throat with his hands, to have done with all of this— Almost—

But

But he had to back away, he had to stumble in panic and back away, while people stared. His face was contorted, as always, like the face of a lesser angel, sighting the first rocks and flames and smelling the singed flesh of hell, which is always so much more terrible than anyone can imagine for himself. . . . Always he must perform his clumsy act, stumbling in the mud and backing away, away, terrified of his father's bleeding face and its serenity.

"Murderer!" we cry.

The Dreaming Woman

I think I am waking. It is almost morning—rain splashes against the window pane. Now I am soaring to a cold, worn daylight, as if rising through water. My sleep is murmurous, like the sleep of great cold-blooded fish with no nerves to them and no pain. Now I am awake hot-eyed in a strange blue channel of water, a northerly sea, waiting for love.

I am in my grandmother's house. The alarm must have rung. I am up, getting dressed, I hurry across to the bathroom already dressed, not wanting to meet my grandmother in the hall. Morning, seven-thirty. A spring morning. Everything is slow, laborious, questioning. My face in the mirror is a slow, dazed face, not yet awake. What is the purpose of my sleeping, my waking? Is it possible that...? In a few hours, at noon...? I am in my early twenties and sunk in love, violent and dazed.

My grandmother is saying something. I think we are in the kitchen. *Another cup of coffee? No? Nothing more?* She smiles at me. She is pleading with me, behind that smile, pleading with me not to leave. There is some love between us. I am aware of this love, drawing me to her, fixing and burdening me. My grandmother lives alone. My grandfather died eight months ago. She lives alone but her eyes jolt with the expectancy of seeing something in the air—hearing a noise, a terrible surprise—seeing a doorknob turn slowly.

Have another cup of coffee, please. . . . So I have another cup. She is a gentle woman with a will still strong, even a little cunning. I have always loved her. Now her eyes roll around in her head in a sad parody of terror, cartoon terror. *Once I was young like you, I wasn't always like this,* she told me once, in a kind of anger. She has lived through awful times, this ordinary woman. All times are awful for her now because my grandfather is dead. They had lived together for forty-three years, forty-three years, it is not possible to survive such a marriage. Were they always in love? Maybe not but they were together. Together. Forty-three years.

She isn't crazy but look at the locks on the windows! My poor father had to come over and equip the windows with locks. More than one to each window. The front and back doors can be bolted in three or four fanciful ways, to keep out intruders. Outside, in the unbusy street, a residential street, there are invisible robbers and murderers shifting their weight from foot to foot, impatient, waiting to break in this house. Once I leave they will know my grandmother is alone and helpless. The mailman must know. Everyone must know. Won't I have more coffee? Won't I stay and have lunch? She will make macaroni and cheese for me, one of my legendary favorite dishes. . . .

There are even little bells on the windows, please don't laugh. In the middle of each ghastly night she wakes, her heart pounding, convinced that someone . . . someone is already in the house. Didn't a bell tinkle? With so many bells it is inevitable that one will tinkle, no night is safe, no sleep can be deep enough. She reads the newspaper and notes the many stories of breaking and entering. Stories with sly racial hints to them: *The intruder could not be identified,* said the victim, *except by his color.* My cousin stays here off and on but this week she is out of town, exhausted. My father stays here sometimes, overnight. He is a large, silent man, exasperated by life and without sympathy

312

for anyone except his mother. He does not particularly like her any more but he understands her. My mother says *It's all in her head, it'll go away,* but eight months have passed and the terror seems worse.

Another cup of coffee? Please?

I hear myself telling her to call Ma around ten. Call Aunt Rose. Use the telephone, don't sit in the back bedroom worrying, don't think about *him*. Forty-three years come and go, what pain to have a man torn out of your body like that, but time comes and goes and is used up.... I hear myself speaking quickly and brightly, a favorite granddaughter. Though I am in my twenties and a woman I speak in the voice of a twelve-year-old, very wise. My grandmother listens sincerely. She has a sad, portentous, rather shrewd face, once a handsome woman but now haggard with worry. She is crazy, says my mother. Not crazy, says my father.

I float out of the house. Morning, rain. Freedom. I tie my scarf around my head. Oh, how my body yearns and aches in its daze, and how slowly a terror rises in me.... Out on the sidewalk I glance back and there is my grandmother, doomed, looking out the living room window at me. She waves, sadly. I wave back brightly. Nothing to worry about!—what is there to worry about in this world?

The bus moves with competent jerks. Morning traffic, a shrill note to the air. I am bathed in a sweat of sudden fear and excitement. Is it possible that...? A good girl, a granddaughter. Better to stay in that house with its bells and bolts...? No, my legs ache to get me off the bus and on my way, toward my own fate. Time stops. I daydream in my seat, a woman of moderate height, slender, alert, tense, with light brown hair worn loose down to my shoulders. People glance at me, wondering. They wonder if I am sleeping with my eyes open. I am in a daze, awake in a daze. There is something anonymous about me. Anyone could claim me. Look, a girl in love, a girl besieged and doomed in love, haven't we all been in love? She is fearful also, the palms of her hands begin to itch, violently she thinks *I've got to get free of him!* with a feeling of self-revulsion. She has been ashamed of her body off and on for years. A body is something you must live in. This body is as good as any other but why must there be a body, why? Oh, the shame of young girls, their passion and humiliation! Time stopped in this girl's life when she saw a certain film in sixth grade, a heart-stopping film, a film that seemed to surprise none of the other girls. Time stopped, gave a lurch, and moved on . . . now that she is older and uses this body easily, still an old sickness sometimes returns to her. Up and down the length of her there is a sudden heavy dread.

What have you decided? I don't want to hurt you.

I am in someone's room, the rain is still falling, everything inside me is falling in a perpetual haze. This man draws me downward, my soul yearns downward. At the very center of our embrace there is a strange vacuum, like the proverbial eye of a hurricane, a stillness. I feel nothing. I am waiting to feel something. I hear myself speaking to him, he speaks to me, the affectionate urgency of our speech blends in with the rain. A murmurous speech. He touches my shoulder in a comradely gesture, reassuring. But we are not comrades. We look away from each other, we turn to stare at each other. Time is dazzling and ringing about me, ready to crack open, the way time in a dream becomes liquid, having weight, the element in which we live and can only be free of in dreams. Anything can happen. Then the wave of sickish terror begins, my terror, as he encircles my body with his arms, standing close again, a little behind me, an accidental embrace that seems to swell in my brain until I can see the two of us yearning backward, our eyes aching with the strain of living through this moment. We are caught just off-balance, swaying. He seems to come upon me from a height, a magical distance. I am in love. My body is in love. I clutch at the back of his head, at his hair, as if to save myself. He kisses me. A strange warm darkness opens in me, everything opens. I move my hands across his back. We are speaking to each other. A paralysis begins in us, welding us together. I can feel sweat breaking out on his body. Like rain pounding softly against the earth he moves upon me with his mouth and his hands, coming out of the sky, and everything becomes transparent. The walls of the room fall away. There is nothing to stop this falling and nothing to register it. . . . It seems to me that he comes from the sky, his weight lowered upon me from the sky, and we freeze together in a pose that is not our own.

I am in love. My body is in love.

. . . Now I am fixing my dress. A torn fingernail snags on the material. We are speaking, speaking melodiously. We are both standing now, a few feet apart. Melodious, gentle. Our souls are at peace.

. . . The lights scatter. It is another day now: midsummer. It is late in the summer. Something vibrates invisibly, machinery in the distance of the summer. Great power in the distance. My blood rushes when I see him, my lover; my eyes don't quite take him in. A tension is between us. It is fixed, vibrating, intolerable. Why can't I hear what he is saying? He is in love with me . . . and I am in love with him. . . . But I can't quite hear what he is saying. If we could stay together all night, if we could speak to each other less brightly, less shrilly, if he weren't married. . . . *If. If.* My body seems to be rocking in a high, mad wind, my eyes ache with the effort of keeping this man, this stranger, in focus. Mid-summer. Late summer. There is an unpleasant silent din to the air, like the din of remote machinery. *Let's go out,* he says. *For God's sake let's get out of this room and talk.*

I thought that falling in love would be like a film, a movie, with music behind it. Everything musical, melodious. I thought my face would be transformed to something bright and splendid, blinding. But instead the very air is heavy. There is a demand to it, this tension. My strained smile has become permanent. . . . I don't want to hear, *I want to hear,* about his wife and their past together, the past I can never undo, I don't want to hear about his life, which is private, permanent, secret in him, I want to be free of him, *I want to love him, I want to hear his every thought.* . . . I want to pronounce sentence and stop everything, I want to lie forever in his arms as if the two of us were drowned lovers, safe and rotting in a bank of seaweed. Nonsense, we are talking nonsense. The radio is on. Nonsense from the radio.

I am wearing that yellow dress . . . it was new then. I felt a certain way in that dress, nervous and sharp. The slope of the collar gave me an alert, clever look. Behind that look there is nothing, only dazzling sound, shrillness. Everything in me has flowed outward and into him. My body is illuminated by a peculiar light when he looks at me, loving me. In the car he talks, talks. I hear myself replying. What are we to do with our lives, what is anyone to do, where is the danger, what danger, there is nothing serious in life, nothing to worry about!—no, everything is serious, deadly.

Traffic lights. Traffic. Something breaks in me. I begin to cry. He reaches out to take my hand and holds it on the car seat, against the car seat, which is warm from the sun. I can feel its warmth and the warmth of his hand. This is so simple, let us drive forever in all directions, holding hands. . . . *What are you thinking about?* he says. I am not thinking of burglars, rapists, murderers, twelve-year-old boys with tools to jimmy open windows and bright hot eyes that take in all secrets, no, I am not thinking of a body's blood, a body's swampy reveries, nothing. My skirt flutters in the air from an opened vent. It flutters helplessly about my knees. In the silence love seems to be shouting at me, it is the word *love* wearing me down, a terror. You must go through with it. In a few years it will be over. *In a few minutes it will be over,* said the doctor who was putting stitches in a deep cut on my foot, *just hold on.*

And now the long skid begins.

The car rocks as if in a sudden gust of wind. Something is wrong. We are on the highway, the speedometer flutters around seventy, all the winds of the earth are screaming in our windows and through that half-opened vent. Here comes the truth! Here it is, everything real! My lover grips the steering wheel, pumps at the brakes. Here comes the long skid. . . . Something has broken in the car, something has broken down, and I feel a buckling as if my own spine were coming undone. The sky flashes blue. Another car, seeing us, lurches comically off the road and into a ditch and we are past it, rushing past it in our long squealing skid. Everything takes a long time. Seconds pass slowly, dripping slowly, very thick. The brakes are squealing and the sound comes to us from outside, through the windows, a terrible sound. That sound will not be forgotten. My lover cries out *Hold still! Hang on!* but I don't really hear those words now; I hear them later. Years later I hear them and think of what ordinary words they were. The car swerves sideways along the scorching pavement and comes to a final terrible stop, a crash. Not a crash. Broken windows but no broken bodies. The sky has stopped. The screeching of the brakes has stopped. My face is bleeding. Outside, stumbling in the high grass, I put my hands to my face and the blood drips amazed through my fingers, not to be stopped. He comes to me to embrace me. *Get away, no, get away!* I hear myself screaming at him. I begin to scream. My blood won't stop this plunging, it is warm and urgent, like something dripping on me from the sky. My transparent skin has lost its strength and blood has burst through! I turn away from him, I turn away again and again, my body is wracked now with angry sobs. A terrible fury rises in me. I won't look at him, I won't let him look at me. There is too much shame here. Yes, I am alive, yes, yes, I am turning from him, I am not thinking of him or of his arms or of anything except blood—blood—a river of blood and the disgusting smell that comes with it. Don't touch me, don't hurt

me again, your touch is painful, on fire—I am screaming this toward him, or toward someone. Don't touch
me! Every touch is lacerating! My flesh is ripped open
and it will have to be sewn up again, the blood mopped
up, reabsorbed, scrubbed away. Some drops have fallen
on the weeds by the side of the road, brown dusty weeds
with no names, great heads of weed flowers bent over,
bowed, broken with all this heat and noise.... Get
away, leave me alone. Let me stand here alone by a
ditch and bleed away all the filth of my life.

The yellow dress is ruined. Tiny scars on my forehead. I can see them today if I look. I think the scars
are shameful but my husband has never noticed them,
nor has anyone else. I look at them often, lifting my
hair away, staring. I am thirty-seven years old. I am
in another city, married, I live near a river and I watch
boats sail upon the river, on its blue, rough water,
soundlessly. Everything moves on that river soundlessly. I sit here alone and dream out the window, very
safe, warm in the sunlight and safe in my house, married, alone, not in love, impregnable.

JOYCE CAROL OATES
National Book Award Winner

"Few contemporary writers can match the credibility and experiential power of Oates at her best."
—*New York Times Book Review*

SON OF THE MORNING   CB 24073 $2.75

THEM   CB 23944 $2.50

8010

MASTER NOVELISTS